John Ashton

The History of Gambling in England

John Ashton

The History of Gambling in England

ISBN/EAN: 9783337326654

Printed in Europe, USA, Canada, Australia, Japan

Cover: Foto ©Andreas Hilbeck / pixelio.de

More available books at **www.hansebooks.com**

THE HISTORY
OF GAMBLING
IN ENGLAND

BY

JOHN ASHTON

AUTHOR OF "SOCIAL LIFE IN THE REIGN OF QUEEN ANNE"
"A HISTORY OF ENGLISH LOTTERIES," ETC.

CONTENTS

CONTENTS

CHAPTER V

CHAPTER VI

CHAPTER VII

CHAPTER VIII

CHAPTER IX

CHAPTER X

CHAPTER XI

CONTENTS vii

CONTENTS

CHAPTER XIX

CHAPTER XX

CHAPTER XXI

CHAPTER XXII

INTRODUCTORY

GAMING is derived from the Saxon word *Gamen*, meaning *joy, pleasure, sports*, or *gaming*—and is so interpreted by Bailey, in his Dictionary of 1736 ; whilst Johnson gives Gamble—*to play extravagantly for money*, and this distinction is to be borne in mind in the perusal of this book ; although the older term was in use until the invention of the later—as we see in Cotton's *Compleat Gamester* (1674), in which he gives the following excellent definition of the word :—" *Gaming* is an enchanting *witchery*, gotten between *Idleness* and *Avarice* : an itching disease, that makes some scratch the head, whilst others, as if they were bitten by a *Tarantula*, are laughing themselves to death ; or, lastly, it is a paralytical distemper, which, seizing the arm, the man cannot chuse but shake his elbow. It hath this ill property above all other Vices, that it renders a man incapable of prosecuting any serious action, and makes him always unsatisfied with his own condition ; he is either lifted up to the top of mad joy with success, or plung'd to the bottom of despair by misfortune, always in extreams, always in a storm ; this minute the Gamester's countenance is so serene and calm, that one would think nothing could disturb it, and the next minute, so stormy and tempestuous that it threatens destruction to itself and others ; and, as he is transported with joy when he wins, so, losing, is he tost upon the billows of a high swelling passion, till he hath lost sight, both of sense and reason."

Gambling, as distinguished from *Gaming*, or playing, I take to mean an indulgence in those games, or exercises, in which *chance* assumes a more important character ; and my object is to draw attention to the fact, that the *money motive* increases, as chance predominates over skill. It is taken up as a quicker road to wealth than by pursuing honest industry, and everyone engaged in it, be it dabbling on the Stock Exchange, Betting on Horse Racing, or otherwise, hopes to win, for it is clear that if he knew he should lose, no fool would embark in it. The direct appropriation of other people's property to one's own use, is, undoubtedly, the more simple, but it has the disadvantage of being both vulgar and dangerous ; so we either appropriate our neighbour's goods, or he does ours, by gambling with him, for it is certain that if one gains, the other loses. The winner is not reverenced, and the loser is not pitied. But it is a disease that is most contagious, and if a man is known to have made a lucky *coup*, say, on the Stock Exchange, hundreds rush in to follow his example, as they would were a successful gold field discovered—the warning of those that perish by the way is unheeded.

Of the universality of gambling there is no doubt, and it seems to be inherent in human nature. We can understand its being introduced from one nation to another—but, unless it developed naturally, how can we account for aboriginals, like the natives of New England, who had never had intercourse with foreign folk, but whom Governor Winslow [1] describes as being advanced gamblers. " It happened that two of their men fell out, as they were in game (for they use gaming as much as anywhere ; and will play away all, even the skin from their backs ; yea, and for their wives' skins also, although they may be many miles distant from them, as myself have seen), and, growing to great heat, the one killed the other." [2]

[1] *Good News from New England. . . . Written by* E. W. *Lon.* 1624.
[2] See Longfellow's *Hiawatha*, for Indian gambling.

The antiquity of gambling is incontestable, and can be authentically proved, both by Egyptian paintings, and by finding the materials in tombs of undoubted genuineness; and it is even attributed to the gods themselves, as we read in Plutarch's Ἰσιδος και Ὀσιριδος. "Now the story of Isis and Osiris, its most insignificant and superfluous parts omitted, is thus briefly narrated:—Rhea, they say, having accompanied with Saturn by stealth, was discovered by the Sun, who, hereupon, denounced a curse upon her, *that she should not be delivered in any month or year.* Mercury, however, being likewise in love with the same goddess, in recompense for the favours which he had received from her, *plays at tables* with the Moon, and wins from her the seventieth part of each of her illuminations; these several parts, making, in the whole, five new days, he afterwards joined together, and added to the three hundred and sixty, of which the year formerly consisted: which days are even yet called by the Egyptians, the *Epact*, or *Superadded*, and observed by them as the birth days of their Gods."

But to descend from the sublimity of mythology to prosaic fact, we know that the Egyptians played at the game of *Tau*, or Game of Robbers, afterwards the *Ludus Latrunculorum* of the Romans, at that of *Hab em hau*, or *The Game of the Bowl*, and at *Senat*, or *Draughts*. Of this latter game we have ocular demonstration in the upper Egyptian gallery of the British Museum, where, in a case containing the throne, &c., of Queen Hatasu (B.C. 1600) are her draught board, and twenty pieces, ten of light-coloured wood, nine of dark wood, and one of ivory—all having a lion's head. These were all, probably, games of skill; but in the same case is an ivory Astragal, the earliest known form of dice, which could have been of no use except for gambling. The Astragal, which is familiarly known to us as a "knuckle bone," or "huckle bone," is still used by anatomists, as the name of a bone in the hind leg of cloven footed animals which articulates with the tibia, and helps to form the ankle joint. The bones used in gambling were, generally, those of sheep ; but the Astragals of the antelope were much prized on account of their superior elegance.   They also had regular dice, numbered like ours, which have been found at Thebes and elsewhere ; and, although there are none in our national museum, there are some in that of Berlin ; but these are not considered to be of great antiquity.   The Egyptians also played at the game of *Atep*, which is exactly like the favourite Italian game of Mora, or guessing at the number of fingers extended.   Over a picture of two Egyptians playing at this gambling game is written, "Let it be said" : or, as we might say, "Guess," or "How Many?"   Sometimes they played the game back to back, and then a third person had to act as referee.

The Chinese and Indian games of skill, such as Chess, are of great antiquity ; but, perhaps, the oldest game is that of *Enclosing*, called *Wei-ki* in Chinese, and *Go* in Japanese. It is said to have been invented by the Emperor Yao, 2300 B.C., but the earliest record of the game is in 300 B.C.   It is a game like *Krieg spiel*, a game of war.   There are not only typical representatives of the various arms, but the armies themselves, some 200 men on each side ; they form encampments, and furnish them with defences ; and they slay, not merely a single man, as in other games, but, frequently, hosts of men.   There is no record of its being a gambling game, but the modern Chinese is an inveterate gambler.

As far as we know, the ancient Jews did not gamble except by drawing, or casting lots ; and as we find no word against it in the inspired writings, and, as even one of the apostles was chosen by lot (Acts i. 26), it must be assumed that this form of gambling meets with the Divine approval.   We are not told how the lots were *drawn* ; but the *casting* of lots pre-supposes the use of dice, and this seems to have been practised from very early times, for we find in Lev. xvi. 8, that "Aaron shall cast lots upon the two goats ; one lot for the Lord, and the other lot for the scape goat." And the promised land was expressly and divinely ordained to be divided by an appeal to chance. Num. xxvi. 52 and 55, 56, "And the Lord spake unto Moses, saying. . . . Notwithstanding the land shall be divided by lot: according to the names of the tribes of their fathers they shall inherit. According to the lot shall the possession thereof be divided between many and few." The reader can find very many more references to the use of the "lot" in any Concordance of the Bible. But in their later days, as at the present time, the Jews did gamble, as Disney[1] tells us when writing on Gaming amongst the Jews.

"Though they had no written law for it, Gamesters were *excluded from the Magistracy*, incapable of being chosen into the greater or lesser Sanhedrim ; nor could they be admitted as *Witnesses* in any Court of Justice, till they were perfectly reformed. Some of their reasons for excluding such from the Magistracy were, that their gaming gave sufficient presumption of their *Avarice*, and, besides, was an employment *no way conducing to the public good*: a covetous man, and one who is not wise and public spirited, being very unfit for offices of so much trust and power, as well as dignity. The presumption of *Avarice* was the cause, also (and a very good one), of not admitting *the evidence* of such a man. And that other notion they had, that the gain arising from play was a *sort of Rapine*, is as just a ground for the *Infamy* which stained his character, and subjected him to these incapacities.

"This last consideration, that money won by gaming was looked upon as got by *Theft*, makes it reasonable to conclude that such money was to be *restored*, and that the winning gamester was *punished* as for *Theft* : which was not, by their law, a capital crime ; but answered for, in smaller cases (and, probably, in this, among the rest), by *double Restitution* : Exod. xxii. 9.

[1] *A View of Ancient Laws against Immorality and Profaneness.* By John Disney. Camb. 1729.

"But the partiality of that people is evident, in extending the notion of Theft, only to *Gaming amongst themselves* ; *i.e.*, native Jews and proselytes of righteousness ; for, if a Jew played, and won of a Gentile, it was no Theft in him : but it was forbidden to him on another account, as Gaming is an application of mind entirely useless to human society. For, say the Talmudists, 'Tho' he that games with a Gentile does not offend against the prohibition of Theft, he violates that *de rebus inanibus non incumbendo* : it does not become a man, at any time of his life, to make anything his business which does not relate to the study of wisdom or the public good.' Now, as this was only a prohibition of their doctors, perhaps the law, or usage in such cases might take place, that the offender was to be scourged."

Among the Greeks and Romans the first gambling implement was the ἀστραγαλος, or (Lat.) *Talus*, before spoken of. In the course of time the sides were numbered, and, afterwards, they were made of ivory, onyx, &c., specimens of which may be seen in the Etruscan Saloon of the British Museum, Case N. In the Terra Cotta room is a charming group of two girls playing with Astragals, and in the Third Vase room, on Stand I., is a vase, or drinking vessel, in the shape of an Astragal (E. 804). Subsequently the Tessera, or cubical die, similar to that now used, came into vogue (samples of which may be seen in Case N. in the Etruscan Saloon), and they were made of ivory, bone, porcelain, and stone. Loaded dice have been found in Pompeii. They also had other games among the Romans, such as *Par et Impar* (odd or even), in which almonds, beans, or anything else, were held in the hand, and guessed at—and the modern Italian game of Mora was also in vogue.

But gambling was looked down upon in Rome, and the term *aleator*, or gambler, was one of reproach—and many were the edicts against it : utterly useless, of course, but it was allowed during the Saturnalia. Money lost at play could not be legally recovered by the winner, and money paid by the loser might by him be recovered from the person who had won and received the same.

The excavations at Pompeii and other places in modern times have revealed things not known in writings ; and, treating of the subject of gambling, we are much indebted to Sig. Rodolfo Lanciani, Professor of Archæology in the University of Rome. Among other things, he tells us how, in the spring of 1876, during the construction of the Via Volturno, near the Prætorian Camp, a Roman tavern was discovered, containing besides many hundred amphoræ, the " sign " of the establishment engraved on a marble slab.

ABEMVS	INCENA
PVLLVM	PISCEM
PERNAM	PAONEM

BENA TORES

The meaning of this sign is double : it tells the customers that a good supper was always ready within, and that the gaming tables were always open to gamblers. The sign, in fact, is a *tabula lusoria* in itself, as shown by the characteristic arrangement of the thirty-six letters in three lines, and six groups of six letters each. Orthography has been freely sacrificed to this arrangement (*abemus* standing for *habemus*, *cena* for *cenam*). The last word of the fourth line shows that the men who patronised the establishment were the *Venatores immunes*, a special troop of Prætorians, into whose custody the *vivarium* of wild beasts and the *amphitheatrum castrense* were given.

He also tells us that so intense was the love of the Roman for games of hazard, that wherever he had excavated the pavement of a portico, of a basilica, of a bath, or any flat surface accessible to the public, he always found gaming tables engraved or scratched on the marble or stone slabs for the amusement of idle men, always ready to cheat each other out of their money.

The evidence of this fact is to be found in the Forum, in the Basilica Julia, in the corridors of the Coliseum, on the steps of the temple of Venus at Rome, in the square of the front of the portico of the Twelve Gods, and even in the House of the Vestals, after its secularisation in 393. Gaming tables are especially abundant in barracks, such as those of the seventh battalion of *vigiles*, near by St Critogono, and of the police at Ostia and Porto, and of the Roman encampment near Guise, in the Department of the Aisne. Sometimes when the camp was moved from place to place, or else from Italy to the frontiers of the empire, the men would not hesitate to carry the heavy tables with their luggage. Two, of pure Roman make, have been discovered at Rusicade, in Numidia, and at Ain-Kebira, in Mauritania. Naturally enough they could not be wanting in the Prætorian camp and in the taverns patronised by its turbulent garrison, where the time was spent in revelling and gambling, and in riots ending in fights and bloodshed. To these scenes of violence the wording of the tables often refers ; such as

LEVATE	LVDERE
NESCIS	DALVSO
RILOCV	RECEDE

"Get up! You know nothing about the game ; make room for better players !" Two paintings were discovered, in Nov. 1876, in a tavern at Pompeii, in one of which are seen two players seated on stools opposite each other, and holding on their knees the gaming table, upon which are arranged, in various lines, several *latrunculi*[1] of various colours, yellow, black and white. The man on the left shakes a yellow dice box, and exclaims, "*Exsi*" (I am out). The other points to the dice, and says, "*Non tria, duas est*" (Not three points, but two). In the next picture the same individuals have sprung to their feet, and show fight. The younger says, "Not two, but three ; I have the game !" Whereupon, the other man, after flinging at him the grossest insult, repeats his assertion, "Ego fui." The altercation ends with the appearance of the tavern-

---

[1] Pieces used in playing the *ludus latrunculorum*, before alluded to.

keeper, who pushes both men into the street, and exclaims, "Itis foris rix satis" (Go out of my shop if you want to fight).

During Sig. Lanciani's lifetime, a hundred, or more, tables have been found in Rome, and they belong to six different games of hazard ; in some of them the mere chance of dice-throwing was coupled with a certain amount of skill in moving the men. Their outline is always the same : there are three horizontal lines at an equal distance, each line containing twelve signs—thirty-six in all. The signs vary in almost every table ; there are circles, squares, vertical bars, leaves, letters, monograms, crosses, crescents and im-modest symbols : the majority of these tables (sixty-five) contain words arranged so as to make a full sentence with the thirty-six letters. These sentences speak of the fortune, and good, or bad, luck of the game, of the skill and pluck of the players, of the favour, or hostility, of bystanders and betting men. Sometimes they invite you to try the seduction of gambling, sometimes they warn of the risks incurred.

Children were initiated into the seductions of gambling by playing "nuts," a pastime cherished also by elder people. In the spring of 1878 a life-size statuette of a boy playing at nuts was discovered in the cemetery of the Agro Verano, near St Lorenzo fuori le mura. The statuette, cut in Pentelic marble, represents the young gambler leaning forward, as if he had thrown, or was about to throw, the nut ; and his countenance shows anxiety and uncertainty as to the success of his trial.

The game could be played in several ways. One, still popular among Italian boys, was to make a pyramidal "castle" with four nuts, three at the base and one on the top, and then to try and knock it down with the fifth nut thrown from a certain distance. Another way was to design a triangle on the floor with chalk, subdividing it into several compartments by means of lines parallel to the base ; the winnings were regulated according to the compartment in which the nut fell and remained. Italian boys are still very fond of this game, which they call *Campana*, because the figure drawn on the floor is in the shape of a bell: it is played with coppers. There was a third game at nuts, in which the players placed their stakes in a vase with a large opening. The one who succeeded first in throwing his missile inside the jar would gain its contents.

They also tossed "head or tail," betting on which side a piece of money, thrown up in the air, would come down. The Greeks used for this game a shell, black on one side, white on the other, and called it "Night or day." The Romans used a copper "*as*" with the head of Janus on one side, and the prow of a galley on the other, and they called their game *Capita aut navim* (head or ship).

Mahomet discountenanced gambling, as we find in the Koran (Sale's translation, Lon. 1734), p. 25. "They will ask thee concerning wine and lots. Answer: In both there is great sin, and also some things of use unto men; but their sinfulness is greater than their use." Sale has explanatory footnotes. He says "Lots. The original word, *al Meiser*, properly signifies a particular game performed with arrows, and much in use with the pagan Arabs. But by Lots we are here to understand all games whatsoever, which are subject to chance or hazard, as dice, cards, &c." And, again, on p. 94. "O true believers, surely wine, and lots, and images, and divining arrows are an abomination of the work of Satan; therefore avoid them, that ye may prosper."

À propos of this denunciation of gambling in the Koran, is the following highly interesting letter of Emmanuel Deutsch, in the *Athenæum* of Sep. 28, 1867 :—

"It may interest the writer of the note on κυβεια (Eph. iv. 14), (the only word for 'gambling' used in the Bible) in your recent 'Weekly Gossip,' to learn that this word was in very common use among Paul's kith and kin for 'cube,' 'dice,' 'dicery,' and occurs frequently in the Talmud and Midrash. As Aristotle couples a dice player (κυβευτης) with a 'bath robber' (λωποδυτης), and with a 'thief' (ληστης—a word no less frequently used in the Talmud); so the Mishnah declares unfit either as judge or witness 'a κυβεια-player, a usurer, a pigeon-flyer (betting man), a vender of illegal (seventh year) produce, and a slave.' A mitigating clause—proposed by one of the weightiest legal authorities, to the effect that the gambler and his kin should only be disqualified 'if they have but that one profession'—is distinctly negatived by the majority, and the rule remains absolute. The classical word for the gambler, or dice player, appears aramaized in the same sources into something like *kubiustis*, as the following curious instances may show. When the Angel, after having wrestled with Jacob all night, asks him to let him go, 'for the dawn hath risen,' Jacob is made to reply to him, 'Art thou a thief, or a *kubiustis*, that thou art afraid of the day?' To which the Angel replies, 'No, I am not ; but it is my turn to-day, and for the first time, to sing the Angelic Hymn of Praise in Heaven: let me go.'"

In another Talmudical passage, an early Biblical critic is discussing certain arithmetical difficulties in the Pentateuch. Thus, he finds the number of the Levites (in Numbers) to differ, when summed up from the single items, from that given in the total.. Worse than that, he finds that all the gold and silver contributed to the sanctuary is not accounted for; and, clinching his argument, he cries, " Is then your Master, Moses, a thief or a *kubiustis* ? " The critic is then informed of a certain difference between " sacred " and other coins, and he further gets a lesson in the matter of Levites and First-born, which silences him. Again, the Talmud decides that if a man have bought a slave who turns out to be a thief or a *kubiustis*—which has been erroneously explained to mean a " man-stealer "—he has no redress. He must keep him, as he bought him, or send him away, for he bought him with all his vices.

No wonder dice-playing was tantamount to a crime in those declining days. There was, notwithstanding the severe laws against it, hardly a more common and more ruinous pastime—a pastime in which Cicero himself, who places a gambler on a par with an adulterer, did not disdain to indulge in his old days, claiming it as a privilege of " Age." Augustus was a passionate dice-player. Nero played the points—for they also played it by points—at 400,000 sesterces. Caligula, after a long spell of ill-luck, in which he had lost all his money, rushed into the streets, had two innocent Roman knights seized, and ordered their goods to be confiscated. Whereupon he returned to his game, remarking that this had been the luckiest throw he had had for a long time. Claudius had his carriages arranged for dicing convenience, and wrote a work on the subject. Nor was it all fair play with those ancients. Aristotle already knows of a way by which the dice can be made to fall as the player wishes them ; and even the cunningly constructed, turret-shaped dice cup did not prevent occasional " mendings " of luck. The Berlin Museum contains one " charged " die, and another with a double four. The great affection for this game is seen, among other things, by the common proverbs taken from it, and the no less than sixty-four names given to the different throws, taken from kings, heroes, gods, hetairæ, animals, and the rest. But the word was also used in a mathematical sense. In a cosmogonical discussion of the Midrash, the earth is likened to a " cubus."

The use of dice in England is of great antiquity, dating from the advent of the Saxons and the Danes and Romans ; indeed, all the northern nations were passionately addicted to gambling. Tacitus (*de Moribus Germ.*) tells us that the ancient Germans would not only hazard all their wealth, but even stake their liberty upon the throw of the dice ; " and he who loses submits to servitude, though younger and stronger than his antagonist, and patiently permits himself to be bound, and sold in the market ; and this *madness* they dignify by the name of *honour*."

In early English times we get occasional glimpses of gambling with dice. Ordericus Vitalis (1075-1143) tells us that " the clergymen and bishops are fond of dice-playing "—and John of Salisbury (1110-1182) calls it " the damnable art of dice-playing." In 1190 a curious edict was promulgated, which shows how generally gambling prevailed even among the lower classes at that period. This edict was established for the regulation of the Christian army under the command of Richard the First of England and Philip of France during the Crusade. It prohibits any person in the army, beneath the degree of knight, from playing at any sort of game for money : knights and clergymen might play for money, but none of them were permitted to lose more than twenty shillings in one whole day and night, under a penalty of one hundred shillings, to be paid to the archbishops in the army. The two monarchs had the privilege of playing for what they pleased, but their attendants were restricted to the sum of twenty shillings, and, if they exceeded, they were to be whipped naked through the army for three days. The decrees established by the Council held at Worcester in the twenty-fourth year of Henry III. prohibited the clergy from playing at *dice* or *chess*, but neither the one nor the other of these games are mentioned in the succeeding statutes before the twelfth year of Richard II., when *diceing* is particularised and expressly forbidden.

The letter books of the Corporation of the City of London, during the thirteenth and fourteenth centuries, give us several examples of diceing. " 4 Ed. II., A.D. 1311. Elmer de Multone was attached, for that he was indicted in the Ward of Chepe for being a common night walker ; and, in the day, is wont to entice strangers and persons unknown, to a tavern, and there deceive them by using false dice. And, also, for that he was indicted in Tower Ward, for being a bruiser and night walker, against the peace ; as, also, for being a common *rorere*.[1]   And, also, for that he was indicted in the Ward of Crepelgate for playing at dice, and for that he is wont to entice men into a tavern, and to make them play at dice there against their will. He appeared, and, being asked

---

[1] Riotous person.

how he would acquit himself thereof, he said that he was not guilty, and put himself upon the country as to the same. And the jury came, by Adam Trugge and others, on the panel ; and they said, upon their oath, that he is guilty of all the trespasses aforesaid. Therefore he was committed to prison," &c.

The next is from a Proclamation made for the safe keeping of the City. 8 Ed., III. A.D. 1334. " Also, we do forbid, on the same pain of imprisonment, that any man shall go about, at this Feast of Christmas, with companions disguised with false faces,[1] or in any other manner, to the houses of the good folks of the City, for playing at dice there ; but let each one keep himself quiet and at his ease within his own house."

" 50 Ed. III., A.D. 1376. Nicholas Prestone, tailor, and John Outlawe, were attached to make answer to John atte Hille, and William, his brother, in a plea of deceit and falsehood ; for that the same John Outlawe, at divers times between the Feast of Our Lord's Nativity, in the 49th year, &c., and the First Sunday in Lent, then next ensuing, came to the said John atte Hille and William, and asked if they wished to gain some money at tables or at chequers, commonly called '*quek*' ; to which they said ' Yes' ; whereupon the same John Outlawe said they must follow him, and he would show them the place, and a man there, from whom they could easily win ; and further said that he would be partner with them, to win or to lose.

" And they followed him to the house of the said Nicholas in Friday Street, and there they found the said Nicholas with a pair of tables, on the outside of which was painted a chequer board, that is called a '*quek*.' And the said Nicholas asked them if they would play at tables for money ; whereupon the said complainants, knowing of no deceit, or ill-intent, being urged and encouraged thereto by the same John Outlawe, played with him at tables and lost a sum of money, owing to false dice.

[1] Masks.

" And the said John then left them to play alone ; and, after that, they still continued to lose. The said tables were then turned, and the complainants played with the defendant Nicholas at '*quek*' until they had lost at the games of tables and *quek* 39s. 2d. After which the complainants, wondering at their continued losing, examined the board at which they had been playing and found it to be false and deceptive ; seeing that in three quarters of the board all the black points were so depressed that all the white points in the same quarters were higher than the black points in the same ; and, on the fourth quarter of the board, all the white points were so depressed that all the black points in that quarter were higher than the white. They inspected and examined also the dice with which they had first played at tables, and found them to be false and defective. And, because they would play no longer, the said Nicholas and John Outlawe stripped John atte Hille of of a cloak, 16 shillings in value, which they still retained."

They were found guilty and sentenced to return the money lost and the cloak, or its value, and " Afterwards, on the prosecution of Ralph Strode, Common Serjeant of the said City, by another jury, they were found guilty of the fraud and deception so imputed to them. Therefore it was awarded that they should have the punishment of the pillory, to stand thereon for one hour in the day, and that the said false chequer board should be burnt beneath them, the Sheriff causing the reason for their punishment to be pro-claimed. And, after that, they were to be taken back to the Prison of Newgate, there to remain until the Mayor and Aldermen should give orders for their release."

And so dicing went on, unimpaired in popularity, in spite of legal fulminations, until Elizabeth's time, when we pro-bably hear more of it, owing to the greater dissemination of literature in that reign. In 1551 there was a famous murder, in which Mr Arden of Feversham was killed whilst playing a game of tables with one Mosbie, the paramour of his wife, who had made Mosbie a present of a pair of *silver dice* to reconcile a disagreement that had subsisted between them.   Shakespeare mentions dice and dicing thirteen times in seven plays, and in Jonson, and the early dramatists, there are many allusions to this species of gambling.

In the British Museum is a little MS. book[1] called "New Passages and Jests," which were collected by Sir Nicholas L'Estrange of Hunstanton, Bart., who died in 1669, and in one of the anecdotes we get an insight into cheating at dice.   "Sir William Herbert, playing at dice with another gentleman, there arose some questions about a cast.   Sir William's antagonist declared it was a four and a five ; he as positively insisted that it was a five and a six : the other then swore with a bitter imprecation that it was as he said.   Sir William then replied, 'Thou art a perjured knave ; for, give me a sixpence, and if there be a four upon the dice, I will return you a thousand pounds' ; at which the other was presently abashed, for, indeed, the dice were false, and of a *high cut*, without a four."

Charles Cotton, in his *Compleat Gamester*, gives us a vivid account of dicing, as it then was, at an ordinary, after dark.

"The day being shut in, you may properly compare this place to those Countries which lye far in the North, where it is as clear at midnight as at noonday. . . .   This is the time (when ravenous beasts usually seek their prey) when in comes shoals of *Huffs, Hectors, Setters, Gilts, Pads, Biters, Divers, Lifters, Filers, Budgies, Droppers, Crossbyters,* &c., and these may all pass under the general and common appellation of *Rooks*. . . .   Some of these *Rooks* will be very importunate to borrow money of you without any intention to pay you ; or to go with you seven to twelve, half a crown, or more, whereby, without a very great chance (ten to one, or more), he is sure to win.   If you are sensible hereof, and refuse his proposition, they will take it so ill, that, if you have not an especiall care, they will pick your pocket, nim your gold or silver buttons off your Cloak or Coat, or, it may be, draw your silver-hilted sword out of your belt,

---

[1] Harl. MSS., 6395.

without discovery, especially if you are eager upon your Cast, which is done thus : the silver buttons are strung, or run upon Cats guts fastned at the upper and nether ends ; now, by ripping both ends very ingeniously, give it the gentle pull, and so rub off with the buttons ; and, if your Cloak be loose, 'tis ten to one they have it.

" But that which will provoke (in my opinion) any man's rage to a just satisfaction, is their throwing many times at a good Sum with a *dry fist* ; (as they call it) that is, if they nick you, 'tis theirs ; if they lose, they owe you so much, with many other quillets : some I have known so abominably impudent, that they would snatch up the Stakes, and, thereupon, instantly draw, saying, if you will have your money, you must fight for it ; for he is a Gentleman, and will not want : however, if you will be patient, he will pay you another time ; if you are so tame as to take this, go no more to the Ordinary ; for then the whole Gang will be ever and anon watching an opportunity to make a *Mouth* of you in the like nature. If you nick them, 'tis odds, if they wait not your coming out at night and beat you : I could produce you an hundred examples of this kind, but they will rarely adventure on the attempt, unless they are backt with some *Bully-Huffs* and *Bully-Rocks*, with others, whose fortunes are as desperate as their own. We need no other testimony to confirm the danger of associating with these Anthropophagi, or Man-Eaters, than Lincolns Inn Fields, whilst *Speering's* Ordinary was kept in Bell Yard, and that you do not want a pair of Witnesses for the proof thereof, take in, also, Covent Garden.

" Neither is it the House itself to be exempted ; every night, almost, some one or other, who, either heated with Wine, or made cholerick with the loss of his Money, raises a quarrel, swords are drawn, box and candlesticks thrown at one another's heads. Tables overthrown, and all the House in such a Garboyl, that it is the perfect type of Hell. Happy is the man now that can make the frame of a Table or Chimney corner his Sanctuary ; and, if any are so fortunate as to get to the Stair head, they will rather hazard the breaking of their own necks, than have their souls pushed out of their bodies in the dark by they know not whom.

"I once observed one of the *Desperadoes* of the Town, (being half drunk) to press a Gentleman very much to lend him a crown: the Gentleman refus'd him several times, yet, still, the Borrower persisted; and, holding his head too near the *Caster's* elbow, it chanced to hit his nose: the other, thinking it to be affront enough to be denied the loan of Money, without this slight touch of the nose, drew, and, stepping back, (unawares to the Gentleman) made a full pass at him, intending to have run him through the body; but his drunkenness misguided his hand, so that he ran him only through the arm: this put the house into so great a confusion and fright, that some fled, thinking the Gentleman slain. This wicked Miscreant thought not this sufficient; but, tripping up his heels, pinn'd him, as he thought to the floor: and after this, takes the Gentleman's silver sword, leaving his in the wound, and, with a *Grand Jury* of *Dammees*, bid all stand off, if they lov'd their lives, and, so, went clear off with sword and liberty, but was, notwithstanding, (the Gentleman recovering) compel'd to make what satisfaction he was capable of making, beside a long imprisonment; and was not long abroad, before he was apprehended for Burglary committed, condemned, and justly executed.

"But, to proceed on as to play: late at night, when the company grows thin, and your eyes dim with watching, false Dice are frequently put upon the ignorant, or they are otherwise cheated by *Topping, Slurring, Stabbing,* &c., and, if you be not vigilant and careful, the box-keeper shall score you up double, or treble Boxes; and, though you have lost your money, dun you as severely for it, as if it were the justest debt in the world.

"The more subtile and genteeler sort of *Rooks*, you shall not distinguish, by their outward demeanour, from persons of condition; these will sit by, a whole evening, and observe who wins ; if the winner be *bubbleable*, they will insinuate themselves into his company, by applauding his success, advising him to leave off while he is well : and, lastly, by civilly inviting him to drink a glass of wine, where, having well warm'd themselves to make him more than half drunk, they wheadle him in to play : to which, if he con-descend, he shall quickly have no money left him in his pocket, unless, perchance, a Crown the Rooking winner lent him, in courtesie, to bear his charges homewards.

"This they do by false Dice, as *High Fullams*, 4. 5. 6. *Low Fullams*, 1. 2. 3. By *Bristle* Dice, which are fitted for their purpose by sticking a Hog's bristle, so in the corners, or otherwise in the Dice, that they shall run high, or low, as they please. This bristle must be strong and short, by which means, the bristle bending, it will not lie on that side, but will be tript over ; and this is the newest way of making a high, or low *Fullam*. The old ways are by drilling them, and loading them with quicksilver ; but that cheat may be easily discovered by their weight, or holding two corners between your forefinger and thumb ; if, holding them so, gently between your fingers, they turn, you may conclude them false : or, you may try their falsehood otherwise, by breaking, or splitting them. Others have made them by filing and rounding ; but all these ways fall short of the Art of those who make them ; some whereof are so admirably skilful in making a Bale of Dice to run what you would have them, that your Gamesters think they can never give enough for their purchase, if they prove right. They are sold in many places about the Town ; price current, (by the help of a friend) eight shillings ; whereas an ordinary Bale is sold for sixpence : for my part, I shall tell you plainly, I would have those Bales of false Dice to be sold at the price of the ears of such destructive knaves that made them.

"Another way the Rook hath to cheat, is first by *Palm-ing*, that is, he puts one Dye into the Box, and keeps the other in the hollow of his little finger ; which, noting what is uppermost when he takes him up, the same shall be when he throws the other Dye, which runs doubtfully, any cast. Observe this—that the bottom and top of all Dice are *Seven*, so that if it be four above, it must be a 3 at bottom ; so 5 and 2, 6 and 1.　Secondly, by *Topping*, and that is when they take up both Dice, and seem to put them in the Box ; and, shaking the Box, you would think them both there, by reason of the rattling occasioned with the screwing of the Box; whereas, one of them is at the top of the box, between his two forefingers, or secur'd by thrusting a forefinger into the Box.　Thirdly, by *Slurring* : that is, by taking up your Dice as you will have them advantageously lie in your hand, placing the one a top the other, not caring if the uppermost run a Millstone, (as they used to say) if the undermost run without turning, and, therefore, a smooth table is altogether requisite for this purpose : on a rugged rough board, it is a hard matter to be done, whereas, on a smooth table (the best are rub'd over with Bee's Wax to fill up all chinks and crevices) it is usual for some to slur a Dye two yards, or more, without turning.　Fourthly—by *Knapping* : that is, when you strike a Dye dead, that it shall not stir.　This is best done within the Tables ; where, note, there is no securing but of one Dye, although there are some, who boast of securing both.　I have seen some so dexterous at Knapping, that they have done it through the handle of a quart-pot, or, over a Candle and Candlestick : but that which I most admired, was throwing the same, less than Ames Ace, with two Dice, upon a Groat held in the left hand, on the one side of the handle, a foot distance, and the Dice thrown with the right hand on the other.

"Lastly—by *Stabbing*—that is, having a Smooth Box, and small in the bottom, you drop in both your Dice in such manner as you would have them sticking therein, by reason of its narrowness, the Dice lying upon one another ; so that, turning up the Box, the Dice never tumble ; if a smooth Box, if true, but little ; by which means you have bottoms according to the tops you put in ; for example—if you put in your Dice so that two fives or two fours lie a top, you have, in the bottom, turned up two twos, or two treys ; so, if Six and Ace a top, a Six and an Ace at bottom."

At this time were played several games requiring tables and dice, such as *Irish; Back-gammon; Tick-tack; Doublets; Sice-Ace* and *Catch-Dolt;* whilst the games requiring no special tables were *In and In ; Passage* and *Hazard*, which latter was the game most usually played, and of which Cotton remarks " Certainly, Hazard is the most bewitching game that is played on the Dice ; for when a man begins to play, he knows not when to leave off ; and, having once accustomed himself to play at Hazard, he hardly, ever after, minds anything else."

Ned Ward [1] (1663-1714), of course, mentions gamblers and gambling, but his experiences are of low Coffee Houses and Alsatia : and, presumably most of the Gambling Houses were of that type, for Thomas Brown [2] (1663-1704) speaks of them as follows. " In some places they call Gaming Houses *Academies* ; but I know not why they should inherit that honourable name, since there is nothing to be learn'd there, unless it be *Sleight of Hand*, which is sometimes at the Expence of all our Money, to get that of other Men's by Fraud and Cunning. The Persons that meet are generally Men of an *Infamous* character, and are in various Shapes, Habits, and Employments. Sometimes they are Squires of the *Pad*, and now and then borrow a little Money upon the *King's High Way*, to recruit their losses at the *Gaming House* ; and, when a Hue and Cry is out to apprehend them, they are as safe in one of these Houses as a *Priest* at the *Altar*, and practise the old trade of *Cross-biting Cullies*, assisting the frail *Square Die* with high and low *Fullams*, and other napping tricks, in comparison of whom the common Bulkers and Pickpockets, are a very honest society. How unaccountable is this way to *Beggary*, that when a man has but a little money, or knows not where in the world to compass any more, unless by hazarding his neck for't, will

[1] The London Spy.
[2] The Works of Mr Thomas Brown, edit. 1705.

try an experiment to leave himself none at all : or, he that
has money of his own should play the fool, and try whether
it shall not be another man's.   Was ever anything so non-
sensically pleasant ?

"One idle day I ventured into one of these *Gaming
Houses*, where I found an *Oglio of Rakes* of several Humours
and Conditions met together.   Some of them had never a
Penny left them to bless their Heads with.   One that had
play'd away even his Shirt and Cravat, and all his Clothes
but his Breeches, stood shivering in a Corner of the Room,
and another comforting him, and saying, *Damme* Jack,
whoever thought to see thee in a State of Innocency : cheer
up, Nakedness is the best Receipt in the World against a
Fever ; and then fell a Ranting as if Hell had broke loose
that very Moment. . . . I told my friend, instead of
Academies these places should be called *Cheating Houses* :
Whereupon a Bully of the *Blade* came strutting up to my
very Nose, in such a Fury, that I would willingly have given
half the Teeth in my Head for a Composition, crying out,
Split my Wind Pipe, Sir, you are a Fool, and don't understand *Trap*, the whole World's a Cheat."

In the reigns of Charles II., James II., William III.,
and Queen Anne were many notorious gamblers, such as
Count Konigsmarck, St Evremont, Beau Fielding, Col.
Macartney, who was Lord Mohun's second in his celebrated
duel with the Duke of Hamilton, and the Marquis de
Guiscard, who stabbed Harley, Earl of Oxford.   There is a
little book by Theophilus Lucas,[1] which gives a more or less
accurate life of notorious gamblers of those days ; amongst
them there is a notice of Col. Panton, of whom Lucas says :
"There was no Game but what he was an absolute Artist at,
either upon the Square, or foul Play : as at *English Ruff
and Honours, Whist, French Ruff, Gleek, L'Ombre, Lanterloo,*

---

[1] "Memoirs of the Lives, Intrigues, and Comical Adventures of the most
Famous Gamesters and Celebrated Sharpers in the Reigns of Charles II., James
II., William III., and Queen Anne," by Theophilus Lucas, Esq. London,
1714. 8vo.

Bankafalet, Beast, Basset, Brag, Piquet: he was very dextrous also at *Verquere, Tick-tack, Grand Trick-track, Irish* and *Back-Gammon;* which are all Games play'd within Tables; and he was not Ignorant of *Inn and Inn, Passage* and *Draughts,* which are Games play'd without the Tables. Moreover, he had great skill at *Billiards* and *Chess;* but, above all, his chief game was at *Hazard,* at which he got the most Money; for, in one Night, at this Play, he won as many thousand pounds as purchased him an Estate of above £1500 *per Annum,* insomuch as he built a whole Street near *Leicester-fields,* which, after his own name, he called *Panton Street.* After this good Fortune, he had such an Aversion against all manner of Games, that he would never handle Cards nor Dice again, but liv'd very handsomely on his Winnings to his dying Day, which was in the year 1681."

Perhaps the most amusing of Lucas's *Lives* is that of Richard Bourchier—about whom I extract the following anecdotes. " Fortune not favouring Mr *Bourchier* always alike, he was reduced to such a very low Ebb, that, before he was Four-and-twenty, he was obliged to be a Footman to the Right Honourable the Earl of *Mulgrave,* now Duke of *Buckingham;* in this Nobleman's Service he wore a Livery above a year and a half, when, by his genteel Carriage and Mien, marrying one Mrs *Elizabeth* Gossinn, a Lace Woman's Grand Daughter, in *Exeter Change* in the *Strand,* with whom he had about 150 Pounds; it being then the solemn Festival of *Christmas,* in the Twelve Days whereof, great Raffling was then wont to be kept in the *Temple,* he carried his Wife's Portion thither to improve it, but was so unsuccessful as to lose every Farthing. This ill Luck made Mr *Bourchier* Stark Mad; but, borrowing 20 Pounds of a Friend, he went to the *Temple* again, but had first bought a Twopenny Cord to hang himself, in case he lost that too : but the Dice turning on his side, and having won his own Money back again, and as much more to it, of one particular Gentleman who was now fretting and fuming in as bad manner as *Bourchier* was before, he very courteously pull'd the cord out of his pocket, and giving it to the Loser, said, *Having now, Sir, no occasion for this Implement myself, it is at your Service with all my Heart :* Which bantering expression made the Gentleman look very sour upon the Winner, who carried off his booty whilst he was well."

He grew prosperous, and got into high society, as bookmakers and others now do at Horse Races ; for we find that "being at the *Groom Porter's*, he flung one Main with the Earl of *Mulgrave* for £500, which he won ; and his Honour, looking wistly at him, quoth he : *I believe I should know you. Yes,* (replied the winner), *your Lordship must have some knowledge of me, for my Name is* Dick Bourchier, *who was once your Footman.* Whereupon, his Lordship, supposing that he was not in a Capacity of paying 500 pounds in case he had lost, cry'd out, *A Bite, A Bite.* But the *Groom Porter* assuring his Honour that Mr *Bourchier* was able to have paid 1000 pounds, provided his Lordship had won such a sum, he paid him what he plaid for, without any farther Scruple."

But he was not content to gamble with mere Earls, he flew at higher game. "By the favour of some of his own Nation, he was soon admitted to the presence of *Lewis le grand*, as a Gamster : he not only won 15,000 Pistoles of the King, but the Nobility also tasted of the same Fortune ; for he won 10,000 Pistoles of the Duke of *Orleans* ; almost as much of the Duke *D'Espernon*, besides many of his jewels, and a prodigious large piece of Ambergreese, valued at 20,000 crowns, as being the greatest piece that ever was seen in *Europe*, and which was afterwards laid up by the Republick of *Venice* in their treasury, to whom it was sold for a great Rarity . . . Once, Mr *Bourchier* going over to *Flanders*, with a great Train of Servants, set off in such a fine Equipage, that they drew the Eyes of all upon them wherever they went, to admire the Splendor and Gaiety of their Master, whom they took for no less than a Nobleman of the first Rank. In this Pomp, making his Tour at King

William's Tent, he happened into Play with that great Monarch, and won of him above £2500. The Duke of *Bavaria* being also there, he then took up the cudgels, and losing £15,000, the Loss put him into a great Chafe, and doubting some foul Play was put upon him, because Luck went so much against him, quoth Mr *Bourchier—Sir, if you have any suspicion of any sinister trick put upon your Highness, if you please, I'll give you a Chance for all your Money at once, tossing up at Cross and Pile,*[1] *and you shall have the advantage of throwing up the Guinea yourself.* The Elector admir'd at his bold Challenge, which, nevertheless, accepting, he tost up for £15,000, and lost the Money upon Reputation, with which *Bourchier* was very well satisfied, as not doubting in the least ; and so, taking his leave of the King and those Noblemen that were with him, he departed. Then the Elector of *Bavaria*, enquiring of his Majesty, who that Person was, that could run the Hazard of playing for so much Money at a Time, he told him it was a subject of his in *England*, that though he had no real estate of his own, yet was he able to play with any Sovereign Prince in *Germany*. Shortly after, *Bourchier* returning into England, he bought a most rich Coach and curious Sett of six Horses to it, which cost him above £3000, for a present to the Elector of *Bavaria*, who had not yet paid him anything of the £30,000 which he had won of him. Notice hereof being sent to his Highness, the generous action incited him to send over his Gentleman of Horse, into *England*, to take care of this present, which he received kindly at *Bourchier's* Hands, to whom he return'd Bills of Exchange also, drawn upon several eminent merchants in *London*, for paying what money he had lost with him at play."

Bourchier became very rich by gambling, and purchased an estate near Pershore in Worcestershire, where he was buried—but he died in London in 1702, aged 45.

Lucas tells a story about gamblers, which, although it has no reference to England, is too good to leave out.

[1] The same as our Heads and Tails.

" But, for a farther unquestionable Testimony of the Mischiefs that often arise from Gaming, this is a very remarkable, but dreadful Passage, which I am now going to recite. Near *Bellizona*, in *Switzerland*, Three Men were playing at Dice on the *Sabbath Day* ; and one of 'em, call'd *Ulrick Schrœteus*, having lost his Money, and, at last, expecting a good Cast, broke out into a most blasphemous Speech, threatening, *That, if Fortune deceiv'd him then, he would thrust his Dagger into the very body of God, as far as he could.* The cast miscarrying, the Villain drew his Dagger, and threw it against Heaven with all his Strength ; when, behold, the Dagger vanish'd, and several Drops of Blood fell upon the table in the midst of them: and the Devil immediately came and carry'd away the blasphemous Wretch, with such a Noise and Stink, that the whole City was amaz'd at it. The others, half distracted with Fear, strove to wipe out the Drops of Blood that were upon the Table, but the more they rubb'd 'em, the more plainly they appear'd. The Rumour hereof flying to the City, multitudes of People flock'd to the Place, where they found the Gamesters washing the Board ; whom they bound in Chains, and carried towards the Prison ; but, as they were upon the way, one of 'em was suddenly struck dead, with such a Number of Lice crawling out of him, as was wonderful and loathsome to behold : And the Third was immediately put to Death by the Citizens, to avert the Divine Indignation and Vengence, which seem'd to hang over their heads. The Table was preserv'd in the Place, and kept as a Monument of the Judgments of God on Blasphemers and Sabbath-breakers ; and to show the mischiefs and inconveniences that often attend Gaming."

Loaded Dice continued to be used—for on 18th April 1740 were committed to Newgate, on the oaths of seven gentlemen of distinction, Thomas Lyell, Lawrence Sydney, and John Roberts, for cheating and defrauding with false and loaded dice, those particular gentlemen, at the Masquerade, to the value of about £400, and other gentlemen not present at the examination of about £4000 more ; and out of about nine pairs of dice which were cut asunder, only one single dice was found unloaded. For this, Lyell and Sidney stood in the Pillory, near the Opera House, on 2nd June 1742, two years after the offence was committed.

And two days afterwards, a cause was tried in the Court of King's Bench, on an indictment against a gentleman for winning the sum of £500 at hazard about seven years before ; and, after a long trial, the jury found him guilty, the penalty being £2500.

To show the prevalence of dicing, it may be mentioned that when the floors of the Middle Temple Hall were taken up somewhere about 1764, among other things were found nearly one hundred pairs of dice which had fallen through the chinks of the flooring. They were about one-third smaller than those now in use. And Malcolm [1] says : " However unpleasant the yells of barrow women with their commodities are at present, no other mischief arises from them than the obstruction of the ways. It was far otherwise before 1716 when they generally carried Dice with them, and children were enticed to throw for fruit and nuts, or, indeed, any persons of a more advanced age. However, in the year just mentioned, the Lord Mayor issued an order to apprehend all retailers so offending, which speedily put an end to street gaming ; though I am sorry to observe that some miscreants now (1808) carry little wheels marked with numbers, which, being turned, govern the chance by the figure a hand in the centre points to when stopped." When I was young the itinerent vendors of sweets had a " dolly," which was a rude representation of a man, hollowed spirally ; a marble was dropped in at its head, and coming out at its toes, spun round a board until it finally subsided into one of the numerous numbered hollows it contained. When that was made illegal, a numbered teetotum was used, and now childhood is beguiled with the promise of a threepenny piece, or other prize, to be found in packets of sweets.

[1] Anecdotes of the " Manners and Customs of London during the 18th Century," by J. P. Malcolm. Lon. 1808. 4to.

CHAPTER I

BEFORE going into the history, &c., of playing cards, it may be as well to note the serious application that was made of them by some persons : and first, we will glance at the two sermons of Latimer's on cards, which he delivered in St Edward's Church, Cambridge, on the Sunday before Christmas Day 1529. In these sermons he used the card playing of the season for illustrations of spiritual truth. By having recourse to a series of similes, drawn from the rules of Primero and Trump, he illustrated his subject in a manner that for some weeks after caused his pithy sentences to be recalled at well nigh every social gathering ; and his Card Sermons became the talk both of Town and University. The novelty of his method of treatment made it a complete success ; and it was felt throughout the University that his shafts had told with more than ordinary effect. But, of course, these sermons being preached in pre-Reformation days, were considered somewhat heretical, and Buckenham, the Prior of the Dominicans at Cambridge, tried to answer Latimer in the same view. As Latimer derived his illustrations from Cards, so did Buckenham from Dice, and he instructed his hearers how they might confound Lutheranism by throwing quatre and cinque : the quatre being the " four doctors " of the Church, and the cinque being five passages from the New Testament selected by the preacher.

Says Latimer in the first of these sermons : " Now then, what is Christ's rule ? Christ's rule consisteth in many things, as in the Commandments, and the Works of Mercy and so forth. And for because I cannot declare Christ's rule unto you at one time, as it ought to be done, I will apply myself according to your custom at this time of Christmas. I will, as I said, declare unto you Christ's rule, but that shall be in Christ's Cards. And, whereas you are wont to celebrate Christmas by playing at Cards, I intend, by God's grace to deal unto you Christ's Cards, wherein you shall perceive Christ's rule. The game that we will play at shall be called The Triumph, which, if it be well played at, he that dealeth shall win ; the players shall likewise win ; and the standers and lookers on shall do the same ; insomuch that no man that is willing to play at this Triumph with these Cards, but they shall be all winners, and no losers."

Next, is a curious little Black Letter tract, by James Balmford published in 1593.[1] It is a dialogue between a Professor and a Preacher.

"*Professor.* Sir, howsoever I am perswaded by that which I reade in the common places of *Peter Martyr, par. 2, pag.* 525, *b.* that Dice condemned both by the Civill lawes and by the Fathers) are therefore unlawfull, because they depend upon chance; yet not satisfied with that which he writeth of Table playing, *pag.* 516, *b.* I would crave your opinion concerning playing at Tables and Cards.

Preacher. Saving the judgement of so excellent a Divine, so Farre as I can learne out of God's word, Cardes and Tables seeme to mee no more lawfull, (though less offensive) than Dice. For Table playing is no whit the more lawfull, because *Plato* compares the life of man thereunto, than a theefe is the more justifiable, because Christ compareth his second coming to burglarie in the night (Mat. xxiv. 43, 44). Againe, if Dice be wholly evill, because they wholly depend upon chance, then Tables and Cardes must needes be somewhat evill, because they somewhat depend upon chance. Therefore, consider well this reason, which condemneth the one as well as the other : Lots are not to be used in sport ; but games

---

[1] A Short and Plaine Dialogue concerning the unlawfulnes of playing at Cards, or Tables, or any other Game consisting in Chance.

consisting in chance, as Dice, Cardes, Tables, are Lots ; therefore not to be used in sport.

Professor. For my better instruction, prove that Lots are not to be used in sport.

Preacher. Consider with regard these three things : First, that we reade not in the Scriptures that Lots were used, but only in serious matters, both by the Jewes and Gentiles. Secondly, that a Lot, in the nature thereof doth as necessarily suppose the special providence and determining presence of God, as an oth in the nature thereof doth suppose the testifying presence of God. Yea, so that, as in an oth, so in a lot, prayer is expressed, or to bee understoode (1 Sam. xiv. 41). Thirdly, that the proper end of a Lot, as of an oth (Heb. vi. 16) is to end a controversie : and, therefore, for your better instruction, examine these reasons. Whatsoever directly, or of itselfe, or in a speciall manner, tendeth to the advancing of the name of God, is to be used religiously, and not to be used in sport, as we are not to pray or sweare in sport : but the use of Lots, directly of itselfe, and in a speciall manner, tendeth to the advancing of the name of God, in attributing to His speciall Providence in the whole and immediate disposing of the Lot, and expecting the event (Pro. xvi. 33 ; Acts i. 24, 26). Therefore the use of Lots is not to be in sport. Againe, we are not to tempte the Almightie by a vaine desire of manifestation of his power and speciall providence (Psal. lxxviii. 18, 19 ; Esa. vii. 12 ; Matth. iv. 6, 7). But, by using Lots in sport, we tempt the Almighty, vainly desiring the manifestation of his speciall providence in his immediate disposing. Lastly, whatsoever God hath sanctified to a proper end, is not to be perverted to a worse (Matth. xxi. 12, 13). But God hath sanctified Lots to a proper end, namely to end controversies (Num. xxvi. 55 ; Pro. xviii. 18), therefore man is not to pervert them to a worse, namely to play, and, by playing, to get away another man's money, which, without controversie, is his owne. For the common saying is, *Sine lucro friget lusus*, no gaining, cold gaming.

Professor. God hath sanctified Psalmes to the praise of his name, and bread and wine to represent the bodie and bloud of our crucified Saviour, which be holie ends ; and the children of God may sing Psalmes to make themselves merie in the Lord, and feede upon bread and wine, not only from necessitie, but to cheere themselves ; why, then, may not God's children recreate themselves by lotterie, notwithstanding God hath sanctified the same to end a controversie ?

Preacher. Because we finde not in the Scriptures any dispensation for recreation by lotterie, as we do for godlie mirth by singing (Jam. v. 13), and for religious and sober cheering ourselves by eating and drinking (Deut. viii. 9, 10). And, therefore, (it being withall considered that the ends you speake of, be not proper, though holy) it followeth, that God who only disposeth the Lot touching the event, and is, therefore, a principall actor, is not to bee set on worke by lotterie in any case, but when hee dispenseth with us, or gives us leave so to doe. But dispensation for recreation by lotterie cannot be shewed.

Professor. Lots may be used for profit in a matter of right (Num. xxvi. 55), why not, for pleasure ?

Preacher. Then othes may be used for pleasure, for they may for profit, in a matter of truth (Exod. xxii. 8, 11). But, indeede, lots, (as othes) are not to be used for profit or pleasure, but only to end a controversie.

Professor. The wit is exercised by Tables and Cards, therefore they be no lots.

Preacher. Yet Lotterie is used by casting Dice, and by shufling and cutting, before the wit is exercised. But how doth this follow ? Because Cards and Tables bee not naked Lots, consisting only in chance (as Dice) they are, therefore, no lots at all. Although (being used without cogging, or packing) they consist principally in chance, from whence they are to receive denomination. In which respect, a Lot is called in Latin, *Sors*, that is, chance or hazard. And *Lyra* upon Pro. xvi. saith, To use Lots, is, by a variable event of some sensible thing, to determine some doubtfull or uncertaine matter, as to draw cuts, or to cast Dice. But, whether you will call Cards and Tables, Lots, or no, you play with chance, or use Lotterie. Then, consider whether exercise of wit doth sanctifie playing with lotterie, or playing with lotterie make such exercising of wit a sinne (Hag. ii. 13, 14). For as calling God to witness by vaine swearing, is a sinne, (2 Cor. i. 13) so making God an umpire, by playing with lotterie, must needs be a sinne ; yea, such a sin as maketh the offender (in some respects) more blame worthie. For there bee moe occasions of swearing than of lotterie. Secondly, vaine othes most commonly slip out unawares, whereas lots cannot be used but with deliberation. Thirdly, swearing is to satisfie other, whereas this kind of lotterie is altogether to fulfil our own lusts. Therefore, take heede, that you be not guiltie of perverting the ordinance of the Lord, of taking the name of God in vaine, and of tempting the Almightie, by a gamesome putting off things to hazard, and making play of lotterie, except you thinke that God hath no government in vaine actions, or hath dispensed with such lewd games.

Professor. In shooting, there is a chance, by a sudden blast, yet shooting is no lotterie.

Preacher. It is true ; for chance commeth by accident, and not of the nature of the game, to be used.

Professor. Lots are secret, and the whole disposing of them is of God (Pro. xvi. 33); but it is otherwise in tables and Cards.

Preacher. Lots are cast into the lap by man, and that openly, lest conveiance should be suspected ; but the disposing of the chance is secret, that it may be chance indeed, and wholly of God, who directeth all things (Prov. xvi. 13, 9, 33). So in Tables, man by faire casting Dice truly made, and in Cards, by shuffling and cutting, doth openly dispose the Dice and Cards so, as whereby a variable event may follow ; but it is only and immediately of God that the Dice bee so cast, and the Cards so shuffled and cut, as that this or that game followeth, except there be cogging and packing.   So that, in faire play, man's wit is not exercised in disposing the chance, but in making the best of it, being past.

Professor. The end of our play is recreation, and not to make God an umpire; but recreation (no doubt) is lawfull.

Preacher. It may be the souldiers had no such end when they cast lots for Christ his coate (Mat. xxvii. 25), but this should be your end when you use lotterie, as the end of an oth should be, to call God to witnesse.   Therefore, as swearing, so lotterie, without due respect, is sinne.   Againe, howsoever recreation be your pretended end, yet, remember that wee must not doe evill that good may come of it (Rom. iii. 8).   And that therefore we are to recreate ourselves by lawfull recreations.   Then see how Cardes and Tables be lawfull.

Professor. If they be not abused by swearing or brawling, playing for too long time, or too much money.

Preacher. Though I am perswaded that it is not lawfull to play for any money, considering that thankes cannot be given in faith for that which is so gotten (Deut. xxiii. 18, Esa. lxi. 8) Gamesters worke not with their hands the thing that is good, to be free from stealing (Ephe. iv. 28), and the loser hath not answerable benefit for his money so lost (Gen. xxix. 15) contrary to that equitie which Aristotle, by the light of nature hath taught long since; yet I grant, if Cards and Tables, so used as you speak, be lesse sinfull, but how they bee lawfull I see not yet.

Professor. Good men, and well learned, use them.

Preacher. We must live by precept, not by examples, except they be undoubtedly good.   Therefore, examine whether they bee good and well learned in doing so, or no. For every man may erre (Ro. iii. 4).

Professor. It is not good to be too just, or too wise (Eccl. vii. 18).

Preacher. It is not good to be too wise, or too foolish, in despising the word of God (Prov. i. 22) and not regarding the weaknesse of other (Rom. xiv. 21). Let us therefore beware that we love not pleasure more than godlinesse (2 Tim. iii. 4)."

The following broadside, which was bought in the streets, about 1850, is a copy of one which appeared in the newspapers about the year 1744, when it was entitled "Cards Spiritualized." The name of the soldier is there stated to be one Richard Middleton, who attended divine service, at a church in Glasgow, with the rest of the regiment.

"THE PERPETUAL ALMANACK, or SOLDIER'S PRAYER BOOK.

giving an Account of Richard Lane, a Private belonging to the 47th Regiment of Foot, who was taken before the Mayor of the Town for Playing at Cards during Divine Service.

The Sergeant commanded the Soldiers at Church, and when the Parson had read the prayers, he took his text. Those who had a Bible, took it out, but the Soldier had neither Bible nor Common Prayer Book, but, pulling out a Pack of Cards he spread them before him. He, first, looked at one card, and then at another: the Sergeant of the Company saw him, and said, 'Richard, put up the Cards, this is not the place for them.' 'Never mind that,' said Richard. When the service was over, the Constable took Richard prisoner, and brought him before the Mayor. 'Well,' says the Mayor, 'what have you brought that Soldier here for?' 'For playing Cards in church.' 'Well, Soldier, what have you to say for yourself?' 'Much, I hope, Sir.' 'Very good; if not, I will punish you more than ever man was punished.' 'I have been,' said the Soldier, 'about six weeks on the march. I have had but little to subsist on. I have neither Bible, nor Prayer Book— I have nothing but a Pack of Cards, and I hope to satisfy your Worship of the purity of my intentions.' 'Very good,' said the Mayor. Then, spreading the cards before the Mayor, he began with the Ace.

'When I see the Ace, it reminds me that there is only one God.

When I see the Deuce, it reminds me of the Father and the Son.

When I see the Tray, it reminds me of Father, Son and Holy Ghost.

When I see the Four, it reminds me of the four Evangelists that preached, viz., Matthew, Mark, Luke and John.

When I see the Five, it reminds me of the Five Wise Virgins that trimmed their lamps. There were ten, but five were wise, and five foolish, who were shut out.

When I see the Six, it reminds me that in Six days the Lord made Heaven and Earth.

When I see the Seven, it reminds me that on the seventh day God rested from the works which he had made, and hallowed it.

When I see the Eight, it reminds me of the eight righteous persons that were saved when God drowned the world, viz., Noah and his wife, his three sons and their wives.

When I see the Nine, it reminds me of the nine lepers that were cleansed by our Saviour. There were ten, but nine never returned God thanks.

When I see the Ten, it reminds me of the Ten Commandments, which God handed down to Moses, on a table of stone.

When I see the King, it reminds me of the Great King of Heaven, which is God Almighty.

When I see the Queen, it reminds me of the Queen of Sheba, who went to hear the wisdom of Solomon; for she was as wise a woman as he was a man. She brought with her fifty boys and fifty girls, all dressed in boy's apparel for King Solomon to tell which were boys, and which were girls. King Solomon sent for water for them to wash themselves; the girls washed to the elbows, and the boys only to the wrist, so King Solomon told by that.'

'Well,' said the Mayor, 'you have given a description of all the Cards in the pack, except one.' 'Which is that?' said the Soldier. 'The Knave,' said the Mayor. 'I will give your honour a description of that, too, if you will not be angry.' 'I will not,' said the Mayor, 'if you will not term me to be the Knave.' 'Well,' said the Soldier, 'the greatest knave I know, is the constable that brought me here.' 'I do not know,' said the Mayor, 'whether he is the greatest knave, but I know he is the greatest fool.'

'When I count how many spots there are in a pack of cards, I find 365, as many days as there are in a year.[1]

When I count the number of cards in a pack, I find there are 52, as many weeks as there are in a year.

When I count the tricks at Cards, I find 13, as many months as there are in a year. So you see, Sir, the Pack of Cards serves for a Bible, Almanack, and Common Prayer Book to me.'

The Mayor called for some bread and beef for the Soldier, gave him some money, and told him to go about his business, saying that he was the cleverest man he ever heard in his life."

The origin of Playing Cards is involved in mystery, although the Chinese claim to have invented them, saying that the Tien-Tsze, pae, or dotted cards, now in use, were invented in the reign of Leun-ho, A.D. 1120, for the amusement of his wives; and that they were in common use in the reign of Kaow-Tsung, who ascended the throne A.D. 1131. The generally received opinion is that they are of Oriental extraction, and that they were brought into Europe by the gipsies, and were first used in Spain. How, or when they were introduced into England, is not known. In Anstis's *History of the Order of the Garter*, vol. i., p. 307, is to be found the earliest mention of Cards, if, indeed, the Four Kings there mentioned are connected with Cards. The date would be 1278.

"This Enquiry touching the Title of Kings, calls to

---

[1] I fail to see how this is made out.—J. A.

remembrance the Plays forbidden the Clergy, denominated *Ludos de Rege et Regina*, which might be *Cards, Chesse*, or the Game since used even to this Age at *Christmas*, called *Questions and Commands*, and also that Edward I. plaid *ad quatuor Reges* (Wardrobe Rolls, 6 Ed. 1, *Waltero Storton ad opus Regis ad ludendum ad Quatuor Reges* viii. s. v. d.) which the Collector guesses might be the Game of Cards, wherein are Kings of the four Suits; for he conceives this Play of some Antiquity, because the term *Knave*, representing a Youth, is given to the next Card in Consequence to the King and Queen, and is as it were the Son of them, for, in this Sense this Word, Knave, was heretofore used; thus *Chaucer* saith, That *Alla*, King of *Northumberland* begot a Knave Child."

The Hon. Daines Barrington, in a paper read by him to the Society of Antiquaries, Feb. 23, 1786, after quoting Anstis, went on to say that "Edward the First (when Prince of Wales) served nearly five years in Syria, and, therefore, whilst military operations were suspended, must, naturally, have wished for some sedentary amusements. Now the Asiatics scarcely ever change their customs; and, as they play at Cards (though, in many respects, different from ours), it is not improbable that Edward might have been taught the game, *ad quatuor reges*, whilst he continued so long in this part of the globe.

" If, however, this article in the Wardrobe account is not allowed to allude to *playing cards*, the next writer who mentions the more early introduction of them is P. Menestrier, who, from such another article in the Privy purse expences of the Kings of France, says they were provided for Charles VI. by his limner, after that King was deprived of his senses in 1392. The entry is the following : ' Donné a Jacquemin Gringonneur, Peintre, pour *trois jeux* de Cartes, a or et a diverses couleurs, de plusieurs devises, pour porter vers le dit Seigneur Roi pour son abatement, cinquante six sols Parisis.' "

Still supposing the game of " Four Kings " to have been

a game at cards, it seems strange that Chaucer, who was born fifty years afterwards, should not have made some mention of Cards as a pastime, for, in his *Franklin's Tale*, he only mentions that " They dancen ; and they play at ches and tables."   The first authentic date we have of playing Cards in England, shows that they had long been in use in 1463, and were manufactured here, for, by an Act of Parliament (3 Edward IV. cap. 4), the *importation* of playing cards was forbidden.

We get an early notice of cards *temp* Richard III. in the Paston letters[1] from Margery Paston to John Paston, 24 Dec. 1484.

" To my ryght worschipful husband John Paston.

Ryght worschipful husbond, I recomaund me onto you. Plese it you to wete that I sent your eldest sunne to my Lady Morlee to have Knolage wat sports wer husyd in her hows in Kyrstemesse next folloyng after the decysse of my lord, her husbond ; and sche seyd that ther wer non dysgysyngs, ner harpyng, ner syngyn, ner non lowd dysports, but playing at the tabyllys and schesse and cards. Sweche dysports sche gave her folkys leve to play and non odyr."

Royalty was occasionally given to gambling, and we find among the private disbursements of Edward the Second such entries as :

" Item. paid to the King himself, to play at cross and pile, by the hands of Richard de Meremoth, the receiver of the Treasury, Twelve pence.

Item. paid there to Henry, the King's barber, for money which he lent to the King, to play at cross and pile, Five shillings.

Item. paid there to Peres Barnard, usher of the King's chamber, money which he lent to the King, and which he lost at cross and pile, to Monsieur Robert Wattewylle, Eight pence.

---

[1] Edit. 1875 (Gairdner), vol. iii., p. 314.

Item. paid to the King himself, to play at cross and pile, by Peres Barnard, two shillings, which the said Peres won of him."

Also Royalty was fond of playing at cards, which, indeed, were popular from the highest to the lowest ; and we find that James IV. of Scotland surprised his future bride, Margaret, sister to Henry VIII., when he paid her his first visit, playing at cards.[1] " The Kynge came privily to the said castell (of Newbattle) and entred within the chammer with a small company, where he founde the quene playing at the cardes." And in the Privy purse expenses of Elizabeth of York, queen to Henry VII., we find, under date of 1502 : " Item. to the Quenes grace upon the Feest of St Stephen for hure disporte at cardes this Christmas C.s. (100 shillings)." Whilst to show their popularity in this reign, it was enacted in 1494 (11 Hen. VII. c. 2), that no artificer labourer, or servant, shall play at any unlawful game (cards included) but in Christmas.

Shakespeare makes Henry VIII. play at Cards, for in his play of that name (Act v. sc. i.) there occurs, " And left him at Primero with the Duke of Suffolk "; whilst, in the *Merry Wives of Windsor* (Act iv. sc. 5), Falstaff says, " I never prosper'd since I forswore myself at Primero." Stow tells us how, in Elizabeth's time, " from All Hallows eve to the following Candlemas day, there was, among other sports, playing at Cards for counters, nails, and points, in every house, more for pastime than for gain." When Mary was Princess, in her Privy Purse expenses there are numerous entries of money given her wherewith to play at cards.

---

[1] Leland's *Collectanea*, vol. iii., Appendix, p. 284.

CHAPTER II

LEGISLATION about Cards was thought necessary in Henry
VIII.'s time, for we see in 33 Hen. VIII., cap. 9, sec. xvi. :
" Be it also enacted by the authority aforesaid. That no
manner of artificer, or craftsman of any handicraft or occupation, husbandman, apprentice, labourer, servant at hus-
bandry, journeyman, or servant of artificer, mariners, fisher-
men, watermen, or any serving man, shall from the said
feast of the Nativity of *St John Baptist*, play at the tables,
tennis, dice, cards, bowls, clash, coyting, logating, or any
unlawful game, out of *Christmas*, under the pain of xx s. to
be forfeit for every time," &c.—an edict which was somewhat modified by sec. xxii., which provided " In what cases
servants may play at dice, cards, tables, bowls, or tennis."

This interference with the amusements of the people did
not lead to good results, as Holinshed tells us (1526) : " In
the moneth of Maie was a proclamation made against all
unlawfull games, according to the statute made in this
behalfe, and commissions awarded to every shire for the
execution of the same ; so that, in all places, tables, dice,
cards, and bouls were taken and burnt. Wherfore the
people murmured against the cardinall, saieing : that he
grudged at everie man's plesure, saving his owne. But this
proclamation small time indured. For, when yong men
were forbidden bouls and such other games, some fell to
drinking, some to feretting of other men's conies, some to
stealing of deere in parks and other unthriftinesse."

With the exception of the grumbles of the Elizabethan puritans, such as Stubbes and others, we hear very little of card playing. Taylor, the "Water Poet," in his *Wit and Mirth* gives a little story anent it, and mentions a game now forgotten. " An unhappy boy that kept his father's sheepe in the country, did use to carry a paire[1] of Cards in his pocket, and, meeting with boyes as good as himselfe, would fall to cards at the Cambrian game of whip-her-ginny, or English One and Thirty ; at which sport, hee would some dayes lose a sheepe or two : for which, if his father corrected him, hee (in revenge), would drive the sheepe home at night over a narrow bridge, where some of them falling besides the bridge, were drowned in the swift brooke. The old man, being wearied with his ungracious dealing, complained to a Justice, thinking to affright him from doing any more the like. In briefe, before the Justice the youth was brought, where, (using small reverence and lesse manners), the Justice said to him : Sirrah, you are a notable villaine, you play at Cards, and lose your father's sheepe at One and Thirty. The Boy replied that it was a lye. A lye, quoth the Justice, you saucy knave, dost thou give me the lye ? No, qd the boy, I gave thee not the lye, but you told me the lye, for I never lost sheepe at One and Thirty ; for, when my game was one and thirty, I alwayes woune. Indeed, said the Justice, thou saist true, but I have another accusation against thee, which is, that you drive your father's sheepe over a narrow bridge where some of them are oftentimes drowned. That's a lye, too, quoth the boy, for those that go over the bridge are well enough, it is only those that fall beside which are drowned : Whereto the Justice said to the boy's father, Old man, why hast thou brought in two false accusations against thy soune, for he never lost sheepe at one and thirty, nor were there any drowned that went over the bridge."

In *Taylor's Motto* the same author names many other games at cards which were then in vogue :—

<hr>

[1] Pack.

> " The Prodigall's estate, like to a flux,
> The Mercer, Draper, and the Silk-man sucks;
> The Taylor, Millainer, Dogs, Drabs and Dice,
> They trip, or Passage, or the Most at thrice ;
> At Irish, Tick tacke, Doublets, Draughts, or Chesse
> He flings his money free with carelessnesse :
> At Novum, Mumchance, mischance (chuse ye which),
> At One and Thirty, or at Poore and Rich,
> Ruffe, Flam, Trump, Noddy, Whisk, Hole, Sant, New Cut,
> Unto the keeping of foure Knaves, he'l put
> His whole estate at Loadum, or at Gleeke,
> At Tickle me quickly, he's a merry Greeke,
> At Primefisto, Post and Payre, Primero,
> Maw, Whip-her-ginny, he's a lib'rall Hero :
> At My sow pigg'd ; and (Reader, never doubt ye,
> He's skill'd in all games except), Looke about ye.
> Bowles, Shove groate, Tennis, no game comes amiss,
> His purse a purse for anybody is."

Naturally, under the Puritans, card playing was anathema, and we hear nothing about it, if we except the political satire by Henry Nevile, which was published in 1659, the year after Cromwell's death. It is entitled " Shuffling, Cutting, and Dealing in a Game at Picquet : Being acted from the Year 1653 to 1658 by O. P. [Oliver, Protector] and others, with great applause. *Tempora mutantur et nos.*" It is well worth reading, but it is too long for reproduction here.

But, as soon as the King enjoyed his own again, dicing and card playing were rampant, as Pepys tells us. "7 *Feb.* 1661. Among others Mr Creed and Captain Ferrers tell me the stories of my Lord Duke of Buckingham's and my Lord's falling out at Havre de Grace, at Cards ; they two and my Lord St Albans playing. The Duke did, to my Lord's dishonour, often say that he did, in his conscience, know the contrary to what he then said, about the difference at Cards ; and so did take up the money that he should have lost to my Lord, which, my Lord resenting, said nothing then, but that he doubted not but there were ways enough to get his money of him. So they parted that night ; and my Lord sent Sir R. Stayner, the next morning, to the Duke, to know whether he did remember what he said last night, and whether he would owne it with his sword and a second ; which he said he would, and so both sides agreed. But my Lord St Albans, and the Queen, and Ambassador Montagu did waylay them at their lodgings till the difference was made up, to my Lord's honour ; who hath got great reputation thereby."

"17 *Feb.* 1667. This evening, going to the Queene's side,[1] to see the ladies, I did find the Queene, the Duchesse of York, and another or two, at cards, with a room full of great ladies and men, which I was amazed at to see on a Sunday, having not believed it ; but, contrarily, flatly denied the same, a little while since, to my cousin Roger Pepys."

"1 *Jan.* 1668. By and by I met with Mr Brisband ; and having it in my mind this Christmas to do what I never can remember that I did, go to see the gaming at the Groome-Porter's, I, having, in my coming from the playhouse, stepped into the two Temple halls, and there saw the dirty prentices and idle people playing, wherein I was mistaken in thinking to have seen gentlemen of quality playing there, as I think it was when I was a little child, that one of my father's servants, John Bassum, I think, carried me in his arms thither, where, after staying an hour, they began to play at about eight at night ; where, to see how differently one man took his losing from another, one cursing and swearing, and another only muttering and grumbling to himself, a third without any apparent discontent at all : to see how the dice will run good luck in one hand for half an hour together, and on another have no good luck at all : to see how easily here, where they play nothing but guinnys, a £100 is won or lost : to see two or three gentlemen come in there drunk, and, putting their stock of gold together, one 22 pieces, the second 4, and the third 5 pieces ; and these two play one with another, and forget how much each of them brought, but he that brought the 22 thinks that he brought no more than the rest : to

---

[1] Her Majesty's apartments at Whitehall Palace.

see the different humours of gamesters to change their luck, when it is bad, to shift their places, to alter their manner of throwing, and that with great industry, as if there was anything in it : to see how some old gamesters, that have no money now to spend as formerly, do come and sit and look on, and, among others, Sir Lewes Dives,[1] who was here, and hath been a great gamester in his time : to hear their cursing and damning to no purpose, as one man being to throw a seven, if he could ; and, failing to do it after a great many throws, cried he would be damned if ever he flung seven more while he lived, his despair of throwing it being so great, while others did it, as their luck served, almost every throw : to see how persons of the best quality do here sit down, and play with people of any, though meaner ; and to see how people in ordinary clothes shall come hither and play away 100, or 2, or 300 guinnys, without any kind of difficulty ; and, lastly, to see the formality of the groome-porter, who is their judge of all disputes in play, and all quarrels that may arise therein, and how his under officers are there to observe true play at each table and to give new dice, is a consideration I never could have thought had been in the world had I not seen it. And mighty glad I am that I did see it, and, it may be, will find another evening before Christmas be over, to see it again, when I may stay later, for their heat of play begins not till about eleven or twelve o'clock ; which did give me another pretty observation of a man that did win mighty fast when I was there. I think he won £100 at single pieces in a little time. While all the rest envied him his good fortune, he cursed it, saying, it come so early upon me, for this fortune, two hours hence, would be worth something to me, but then I shall have no such luck. This kind of prophane, mad entertainment they give themselves. And so, I, having enough for once, refusing to venture, though Brisband pressed me hard, and tempted me with saying that no man was ever known to lose the

[1] Of Bromham, Bedfordshire.

first time, the devil being too cunning to discourage a gamester, and he offered, also, to lend me 10 pieces to venture ; but I did refuse, and so went away."

We get a good account of the Gaming-house of this period in "The Nicker Nicked ; or, the Cheats of Gaming Discovered" (1669), but as it closely resembles Cotton's account of an Ordinary, I only give a portion of it.

"If what has been said, will not make you detest this abominable kind of life ; will the almost certain loss of your money do it ? I will undertake to demonstrate that it is ten to one you shall be a loser at the year's end, with constant play upon the square. If, then, twenty persons bring two hundred pounds a piece, which makes four thousand pounds, and resolve to play, for example, three or four hours a day for a year ; I will wager the box shall have fifteen hundred pounds of the money, and that eighteen out of the twenty persons shall be losers.

"I have seen (in a lower instance) three persons sit down at Twelvepenny In and In, and each draw forty shillings a piece ; and, in little more than two hours, the box has had three pounds of the money ; and all the three gamesters have been losers, and laughed at for their indiscretion.

"At an Ordinary, you shall scarce have a night pass without a quarrel, and you must either tamely put up with an affront, or else be engaged in a duel next morning, upon some trifling insignificant occasion, pretended to be a point of honour.

"Most gamesters begin at small game ; and, by degrees, if their money, or estates, hold out, they rise to great sums ; some have played, first of all, their money, then their rings, coach and horses, even their wearing clothes and perukes ; and then, such a farm ; and, at last, perhaps, a lordship. You may read, in our histories,[1] how Sir Miles Partridge played at Dice with King Henry the Eighth for Jesus Bells, so called, which were the greatest in England, and hung in a tower of St Paul's Church ; and won them ; whereby he

[1] Strype's Stow's Survey, ed. 1720, Book iii., p. 148.

brought them to ring in his pocket; but the ropes, afterwards, catched about his neck, for, in Edward the Sixth's days, he was hanged for some criminal offences.[1]

"Consider how many people have been ruined by play. Sir Arthur Smithouse is yet fresh in memory: he had a fair estate, which in a few years he so lost at play that he died in great want and penury. Since that Mr Ba———, who was a Clerk in the Six Clerks Office, and well cliented, fell to play, and won, by extraordinary fortune, two thousand pieces in ready gold: was not content with that; played on; lost all he had won, and almost all his own estate; sold his place in the office; and, at last marched off to a foreign plantation to begin a new world with the sweat of his brow. For that is commonly the destiny of a decayed gamester, either to go to some foreign plantation, or to be preferred to the dignity of a box-keeper.

"It is not denied, but most gamesters have, at one time or other, a considerable run of winning, but, (such is the infatuation of play) I could never hear of a man that gave over, a winner, (I mean to give over so as never to play again;) I am sure it is a *rara avis*: for if you once 'break bulk,' as they phrase it, you are in again for all. Sir Humphrey Foster had lost the greatest part of his estate, and then (playing, it is said, for a dead horse,) did, by happy fortune, recover it again, then gave over, and wisely too.

"If a man has a competent estate of his own, and plays whether himself or another man shall have it, it is extreme folly; if his estate be small, then to hazard the loss even of that and reduce himself to absolute beggary is direct madness. Besides, it has been generally observed, that the loss of one hundred pounds shall do you more prejudice in disquieting your mind than the gain of two hundred pounds shall do you good, were you sure to keep it."

The "Groom Porter" has been more than once mentioned in these pages. He was formerly an officer of the Lord Steward's department of the Royal Household. When the

---

[1] For complicity with the Duke of Somerset.

office was first appointed is unknown, but Henry Fitzalan, Earl of Arundel, Lord Chamberlain to Henry VIII. from 1526 to 1530, compiled a book containing the duties of the officers, in which is set forth " the roome and service belonging to a groome porter to do." His business was to see the King's lodgings furnished with tables, chairs, stools, firing, rushes for strewing the floors, to provide cards, dice, &c., and to decide disputes arising at dice, cards, bowling, &c. The Groom Porter's is referred to as a place of excessive play in the seventeenth year of the reign of Henry VIII. (1526), when it was directed that the privy chamber shall be " kept honestly," and that it " be not used by frequent and intemperate play, as the Groom Porter's house."

Play at Court was lawful, and encouraged, from Christmas to Epiphany, and this was the Groom Porter's legitimate time. When the King felt disposed, and it was his pleasure to play, it was the etiquette and custom to announce to the company, that " His Majesty was out "; on which intimation all Court ceremony and restraint were set aside, and the sport commenced ; and when the Royal Gamester had either lost, or won, to his heart's content, notice of the Royal pleasure to discontinue the game was, with like formality, announced by intimation that " His Majesty was at home," whereupon play forthwith ceased, and the etiquette and ceremony of the palace was resumed.

The fact of the Christmas gambling is noted in Jonson's *Alchemist*—

> " He will win you,
> By irresistible luck, within this fortnight
> Enough to buy a barony. This will set him
> Upmost at the Groom Porter's all the Christmas."

We saw that Pepys visited the Groom Porter's at Christmas, so also did Evelyn.

" 6 *Jan.* 1662. This evening, according to custom, his Majesty opened the revels of that night, by throwing the dice himself in the privy chamber, where was a table set on purpose, and lost his £100. (The year before he won

£1500.)   The ladies, also, played very deep.   I came away
when the Duke of Ormond had won about £1000, and left
them still at passage, cards, &c.   At other tables, both there
and at the Groom Porter's, observing the wicked folly and
monstrous excess of passion amongst some losers : sorry am
I that such a wretched custom as play to that excess should
be countenanced in a Court, which ought to be an example
of virtue to the rest of the kingdom."

"8 *Jan.* 1668.   I saw deep and prodigious gaming at
the Groom Porters, vast heaps of gold squandered away in a
vain and profuse manner.   This I looked on as a horrid vice,
and unsuitable to a Christian Court."

In the reign of James II. the Groom Porter's was still an
institution, and so it was in William III.'s time, for we read
in *The Flying Post*, No. 573, Jan. 10-13, 1699.   "Friday
last, being Twelf-day, the King, according to custom, plaid
at the Groom Porter's ; where, we hear, Esqre. Frampton [1] was
the greatest gainer."

In Queen Anne's time he was still in evidence, as we find
in the *London Gazette*, December 6-10, 1705.   " Whereas Her
Majesty, by her Letters Patent to Thomas Archer, Esqre., con-
stituting him Her Groom Porter, hath given full power to
him and such Deputies as he shall appoint to supervise,
regulate and authorize (by and under the Rules, Conditions,
and Restrictions by the Law prescribed,) all manner of Gaming
within this Kingdom.   And, whereas, several of Her Majesty's
Subjects, keeping Plays or Games in their Houses, have
been lately abused, and had Moneys extorted from them
by several ill disposed Persons, contrary to Law.   These
are, therefore, to give Notice, That no Person whatsoever,
not producing his Authority from the said Groom Porter,
under Seal of his Office, hath any Power to act anything
under the said Patent.   And, to the end that all such Persons
offending as aforesaid, may be proceeded against according
to Law, it is hereby desired, that Notice be given of all such

---

[1] Probably Tregonwell Frampton, Keeper of the King's running horses at Newmarket, a position he held under William III., Anne, and George I. and II.

Abuses to the said Groom Porter, or his Deputies, at his Office, at Mr Stephenson's, a Scrivener's House, over against Old Man's Coffee House, near Whitehall."

We get a glimpse of the Groom Porters of this reign in Mrs Centlivre's play of *The Busy Body* :

" *Sir Geo. Airy.* Oh, I honour Men of the Sword ; and I presume this Gentleman is lately come from Spain or Portugal —by his Scars.

" *Marplot.* No, really, Sir George, mine sprung from civil Fury : Happening last night into the Groom porter's—I had a strong inclination to go ten Guineas with a sort of a—sort of a—kind of a Milk Sop, as I thought : a Pox of the Dice, he flung out, and my Pockets being empty, as Charles knows they sometimes are, he prov'd a Surly North Briton, and broke my face for my deficiency."

Both George I. and George the Second played at the Groom Porter's at Christmas. In the first number of the *Gentleman's Magazine*, we read how George II. and his Queen spent their Epiphany. "Wednesday, Jan. 5, 1731. This being Twelfth Day . . . their Majesties, the Prince of Wales, and the three eldest Princesses, preceded by the Heralds, &c., went to the Chapel Royal, and heard divine Service. The King and Prince made the Offerings at the Altar, of Gold, Frankincense and Myrrh, according to Custom. At night, their Majesties &c. play'd at *Hazard*, for the benefit of the Groom Porter, and 'twas said the King won 600 Guineas, and the Queen 360, Princess Amelia 20, Princess Caroline 10, the Earl of Portmore and the Duke of Grafton, several thousands." And we have a similar record in *the Grub Street Journal* under date of 7 Jan., 1736. The Office of Groom Porter was abolished during the reign of George III. probably in 1772, for in the *Annual Register* for that year, under date 6 Jan., it says : "Their Majesties not being accustomed to play at Hazard, ordered a handsome gratuity to the Groom Porter ; and orders were given, that, for the future, there be no card playing amongst the servants."

Card playing was justifiable, and legal, at Christmas.

An ordinance for governing the household of the Duke of Clarence, in the reign of Edward IV., forbade all games at dice, cards, or other hazard for money *except during the twelve days at Christmas*. And, again, in the reign of Henry VII., an Act was passed against unlawful games, which expressly forbids artificers, labourers, servants, or apprentices to play at any such, *except at Christmas* : and, at some of the Colleges, Cards are introduced into the Combination Rooms, during the twelve days of Christmas, but never appear there during the remainder of the year.

Kirchmayer[1] gives a curious custom of gambling in church on Christmas day :

> " Then comes the day wherein the Lorde
>   did bring his birth to passe ;
> Whereas at midnight up they rise,
>   and every man to Masse.
> The time so holy counted is,
>   that divers earnestly
> Do think the waters all to wine
>   are changed sodainly ;
> In that same house that Christ himselfe
>   was borne, and came to light,
> And unto water streight againe
>   transformde and altred quight.
> There are beside that mindfully
>   the money still do watch
> That first to aultar commes, which then
>   they privily do snatch.
> The priestes, least others should it have,
>   take oft the same away,
> Whereby they thinke, throughout the yeare
>   to have good luck in play,
> And not to lose : then straight at game
>   till day-light they do strive,
> To make some pleasant proofe how well
>   their hallowed pence will thrive.
> Three Masses every priest doth sing
>   upon that solemne day,
> With offerings unto every one,
>   that so the more may play."

[1] The Popish Kingdome, or, Reigne of Antichrist, written in Latin Verse by Thomas Naogeorgus, and Englished by Barnabe Googe, 1570.

CHAPTER III

BUT to return to the Chronology of Gambling. From the Restoration of Charles II. to the time of Anne, gambling was common ; but in the reign of this latter monarch, it either reached a much higher pitch, or else, in that Augustan Age of Literature, we hear more about it. Any way, we only know what we read about it. In the epilogue to Mrs Centlivre's play of *the Gamester*, published in 1705, the audience is thus addressed :

> "You Roaring Boys, who know the Midnight Cares
> Of Rattling Tatts,[1] ye Sons of Hopes and Fears ;
> Who Labour hard to bring your Ruin on,
> And diligently toil to be undone ;
> You're Fortune's sporting Footballs at the best,
> Few are his Joys, and small the Gamester's Rest :
> Suppose then, Fortune only rules the Dice,
> And on the Square you Play ; yet, who that's Wise
> Wou'd to the Credit of a Faithless Main
> Trust his good Dad's hard-gotten hoarded Gain?
> But, then, such Vultures round a Table wait,
> And, hovering, watch the Bubble's sickly State ;
> The young fond Gambler, covetous of more,
> Like *Esop's* Dog, loses his certain Store.
> Then the Spung squeez'd by all, grows dry,—And, now,
> Compleatly Wretched, turns a Sharper too ;
> These Fools, for want of Bubbles, too, play Fair,
> And lose to one another on the Square.
>
> .   .   .   .
>
> This Itch for Play, has, likewise, fatal been,
> And more than *Cupid*, drawn the Ladies in,

---

[1] Cant term for false Dice.

> A Thousand Guineas for *Basset* prevails,
> A Bait when Cash runs low, that seldom fails ;
> And, when the Fair One can't the Debt defray,
> In Sterling Coin, does Sterling Beauty pay."

Ward, in a Satire called *Adam and Eve stript of their furbelows*, published in 1705, has an Article on the Gambling lady of the period, entitled, *Bad Luck to him that has her; Or, The Gaming Lady*, of which the following is a portion :

"When an unfortunate Night has happen'd to empty her Cabinet . . . her Jewels are carry'd privately into *Lumbard Street*, and Fortune is to be tempted the next Night with another Sum borrow'd of my Lady's Goldsmith at the Extortion of a Pawnbroker ; and, if that fails, then she sells off her Wardrobe, to the great Grief of her Maids ; stretches her Credit amongst those she deals with, pawns her Honour to her Intimates, or makes her Waiting-Woman dive into the Bottom of her Trunk, and lug out her green Net Purse, full of old *Jacobus's*, which she has got in her Time by her Servitude, in Hopes to recover her Losses by a Turn of Fortune, that she may conceal her bad Luck from the Knowledge of her Husband : But she is generally such a Bubble to some Smock fac'd Gamester, who can win her Money first, carry off the Loser in a Hackney Coach, and kiss her into a good humour before he parts with her, that she is generally driven to the last Extremity, and then forc'd to confess all to her forgiving Spouse, who, either thro' his fond Affection, natural Generosity, or Danger of Scandal, supplies her with Money to redeem her Moveables, buy her new Apparel, and to pay her Debts upon Honour, that her Ladyship may be *in Statu quo ;* in which Condition she never long continues, but repeats the same Game over and over, to the End of the Chapter : For she is so strangely infatuated with the Itch of Card Playing, that she makes the Devil's Books her very *Practice of Piety* ; and, were she at her Parish Church, in the Height of her Devotion, should any Body, in the Interim, but stand at the Church Door, and hold up the *Knave of Clubs*, she would take it to be a Challenge at *Lanctre Loo*; and, starting from her Prayers, would follow her beloved *Pam*, as a deluded Traveller does an *Ignis fatuus*."

No. 120 of *the Guardian* (July 29, 1713), by Steele, is devoted to female Gambling as it was in the time of Queen Anne, and the following is a portion of it:

"Their *Passions* suffer no less by this Practice than their Understandings and Imaginations. What Hope and Fear, Joy and Anger, Sorrow and Discontent break out all at once in a fair Assembly upon So noble an Occasion as that of turning up a Card? Who can consider without a Secret Indignation that all those Affections of the Mind which should be consecrated to their Children, Husbands and Parents, are thus vilely prostituted and thrown away upon a Hand at Loo. For my own part, I cannot but be grieved when I see a fine Woman fretting and bleeding inwardly from such trivial Motives; when I behold the Face of an Angel agitated and discomposed by the Heart of a Fury.

"Our Minds are of such a Make, that they, naturally, give themselves up to every Diversion to which they are much accustomed, and we always find that Play, when followed with Assiduity, engrosses the whole Woman, She quickly grows uneasie in her own Family, takes but little Pleasure in all the domestick, innocent, Endearments of Life, and grows more fond of *Pamm* than of her Husband. My friend *Theophrastus*, the best of Husbands and of Fathers, has often complained to me, with Tears in his Eyes, of the late Hours he is forced to keep, if he would enjoy his Wife's Conversation. When she returns to me with Joy in her Face, it does not arise, says he, from the Sight of her Husband, but from the good Luck she has had at Cards. On the contrary, says he, if she has been a Loser, I am doubly a Sufferer by it. She comes home out of humour, is angry with every Body, displeased with all I can do, or say, and, in Reality, for no other Reason but because she has been throwing away my Estate. What charming Bedfellows and Companions for Life, are Men likely to meet with, that chuse their Wives out of such Women of Vogue and Fashion? What a Race of Worthies, what Patriots, what Heroes, must we expect from Mothers of this Make?

" I come, in the next Place, to consider all the ill Consequences which Gaming has on the *Bodies* of our Female Adventurers. It is so ordered that almost everything which corrupts the Soul, decays the Body. The Beauties of the Face and Mind are generally destroyed by the same means. This Consideration should have a particular Weight with the Female World, who were designed to please the Eye, and attract the Regards of the other half of the Species. Now, there is nothing that wears out a fine Face like the Vigils of the Card Table, and those cutting Passions which naturally attend them. Hollow Eyes, haggard Looks, and pale Complexions, are the natural Indications of a Female Gamester. Her Morning Sleeps are not able to repair her Midnight Watchings. I have known a Woman carried off half dead from *Bassette*, and have, many a time grieved to see a Person of Quality gliding by me, in her Chair, at two a Clock in the Morning, and looking like a Spectre amidst a flare of Flambeaux. In short, I never knew a thorough paced Female Gamester hold her Beauty two Winters together.

" But there is still another Case in which the Body is more endangered than in the former. All Play Debts must be paid in Specie, or by an Equivalent. The Man who plays beyond his Income, pawns his Estate ; the Woman must find out something else to Mortgage when her Pin Money is gone. The Husband has his Lands to dispose of, the Wife, her Person."

Almost all writers of the time note and deplore the gambling propensity of Ladies : and Pope, in his *Rape of the Lock* (Canto III.), gives us a picture of a gambling lady, and a graphic description of the game of *Ombre*, which was played in the afternoon :—

" Meanwhile declining from the Noon of Day,
The Sun obliquely shoots his burning Ray ;
The hungry Judges soon the Sentence sign,
And Wretches hang, that Jury-men may Dine ;
The Merchant from th' *Exchange* returns in Peace,
And the long Labours of the *Toilette* cease—
    Belinda now, whom Thirst of Fame invites,
Burns to encounter two adventrous Knights,
At *Ombre* singly to decide their Doom ;
And swells her Breast with Conquests yet to come.
Strait the three Bands prepare in Arms to join,
Each Band the number of the Sacred Nine.
Soon as she spreads her Hand, th' Aerial Guard
Descend, and sit on each important Card :
First, *Ariel* perch'd upon a *Matadore*,
Then each, according to the Rank they bore ;
For *Sylphs*, yet mindful of their ancient Race,
Are, as when Women, wondrous fond of Place.
    Behold, four *Kings* in Majesty rever'd,
With hoary Whiskers and a forky Beard ;
And four fair *Queens* whose hands sustain a Flow'r,
Th' expressive Emblem of their softer Pow'r ;
Four *Knaves* in Garbs succinct, a trusty Band,
Caps on their heads, and Halberds in their hand ;
And Particolour'd Troops, a shining Train,
Draw forth to Combat on the Velvet Plain.
    The skilful Nymph reviews her Force with Care,
Let Spades be Trumps, she said, and Trumps they were.
Now move to War her Sable *Matadores*,
In Show, like Leaders of the swarthy *Moors*.
Spadillo first, unconquerable Lord !
Led off two captive Trumps, and swept the Board.
As many more *Manillio* forc'd to yield,
And march'd a Victor from the verdant Field.
Him *Basto* follow'd, but his Fate, more hard,
Gain'd but one Trump and one Plebeian Card.
With his broad Sabre, next, a Chief in Years,
The hoary Majesty of *Spades* appears ;
Puts forth one manly Leg, to sight reveal'd ;
The rest, his many-colour'd Robe conceal'd.
The Rebel-*Knave*, that dares his Prince engage,
Proves the just Victim of his Royal Rage.
Ev'n mighty *Pam*, that Kings and Queens o'erthrew,
And mow'd down Armies in the Fights of *Loo*,
Sad Chance of War ! now, destitute of Aid,

> Falls undistinguish'd by the Victor Spade !
>   Thus far, both Armies to *Belinda* yield ;
> Now, to the *Baron* Fate inclines the Field.
> His warlike *Amazon* her Host invades,
> Th' Imperial Consort of the Crown of *Spades*.
> The *Club's* black Tyrant first her Victim dy'd,
> Spite of his haughty Mien, and barb'rous Pride :
> What boots the Regal Circle on his Head,
> His Giant Limbs in State unwieldy spread ?
> That, long behind, he trails his pompous Robe,
> And, of all Monarchs, only grasps the Globe."
>   The *Baron*, now his *Diamonds* pours apace ;
> Th' embroider'd *King* who shows but half his Face,
> And his refulgent *Queen*, with Pow'rs combin'd,
> Of broken Troops an easie Conquest find.
> *Clubs, Diamonds, Hearts*, in wild Disorder seen,
> With Throngs promiscuous strow the level Green.
> Thus, when dispers'd, a routed Army runs,
> Of *Asia's* Troops, and *Africk's* Sable Sons ;
> With like Confusion different Nations fly,
> In various Habits, and of various Dye,
> The pierc'd Battalions dis-united fall
> In Heaps on Heaps ; one Fate o'erwhelms them all.
>   The *Knave* of *Diamonds* now exerts his Arts,
> And wins (oh, shameful Chance !) the *Queen* of *Hearts*.
> At this, the Blood the Virgin's Cheek forsook,
> A livid Paleness spreads o'er all her Look ;
> She sees, and trembles at th' approaching Ill,
> Just in the Jaws of Ruin, and *Codille*.
> And now, (as oft in some distemper'd State)
> On one nice *Trick* depends the gen'ral Fate,
> An *Ace* of *Hearts* steps forth ; The *King*, unseen,
> Lurk'd in her Hand, and mourn'd his captive *Queen*.
> He springs to Vengeance with an eager Pace,
> And falls like Thunder on the prostrate *Ace*.
> The Nymph exulting, fills with Shouts the Sky,
> The Walls, the Woods, and long Canals reply."

Things did not improve in the next reign, for Malcolm tells us, that gaming was dreadfully prevalent in 1718, which might be demonstrated by the effect of one night's search by the Leet Jury of Westminster, who presented no less than thirty-five houses to the Justices for prosecution. And in the reign of George II. we have numerous notices of gambling : and the first number of the *Gentleman's Magazine* in 1731 gives for the information of its readers the following list of officers established in the most notorious gaming houses :—

" 1. A *Commissioner*, always a Proprietor, who looks in of a Night, and the Week's Accompt is audited by him, and two others of the Proprietors.—2. A *Director*, who superintends the Room.—3. An *Operator*, who deals the Cards at a cheating Game, called *Faro*.—4. Two *Crowpees*,[1] who watch the Cards, and gather the Money for the Bank.—5. Two *Puffs*, who have Money given them to decoy others to play. —6. A *Clerk*, who is a Check upon the Puffs, to see that they sink none of the Money that is given them to play with.—7. A *Squib*, is a Puff of a lower Rank, who serves at half Salary, while he is learning to deal.—8. A *Flasher*, to swear how often the Bank has been stript.—9. A *Dunner*, who goes about to recover Money lost at Play.—10. A *Waiter*, to fill out Wine, snuff Candles, and attend in the Gaming Room.—11. An *Attorney*, a *Newgate* Solicitor.— 12. A *Captain*, who is to fight a Gentleman that is peevish at losing his money.—13. An *Usher*, who lights Gentlemen up and down Stairs, and gives the Word to the Porter.— 14. A *Porter*, who is, generally, a Soldier of the Foot Guards. —15. An *Orderly Man*, who walks up and down the outside of the Door, to give Notice to the Porter, and alarm the House, at the Approach of the Constables.—16. A *Runner*, who is to get Intelligence of the Justices meeting. — 17. *Linkboys, Coachmen, Chairmen, Drawers, or others*, who bring the first Intelligence of the Justices Meetings, or, of the Constables being out, at Half a Guinea Reward. —18. *Common Bail Affidavit Men, Ruffians, Bravoes, Assassins*, cum multis aliis."

We have read before (p. 49) of the King's gambling at the Groom Porter's on 5 Jan. 1731, but, to show the fairness and equality of the law, I will give the very next paragraph : " At Night (5 Jan.) Mr *Sharpless*, High Constable of *Holborn* Division, with several of his petty Constables,

---

[1] Croupiers.

searched a notorious Gaming House behind *Gray's Inn Walks*, by Vertue of a Warrant from the Right Hon. Lord *Delawar*, and eleven other of his Majesty's Justices of the Peace for the County of *Middlesex*; but the Gamesters, having previous Notice, they all fled, except the Master of the House, who was apprehended, and bound in a Recognizance of £200 penalty, pursuant to the old Statute of 33 Hen. VIII."

The *Grub Street Journal* of 28 Dec. 1733, gives a practical hint how to utilise Gambling: "Dear *Bavy*.—As Gaming is becoming fashionable, and the Increase of the Poor a general Complaint, I propose to have a Poor's Box fix'd up in some convenient Place in every House, which may contain all Money that shall be won at Cards, or any other Games; and that a proper Person be appointed in every Parish to keep the Key, and to collect Weekly from each House what has been dropt into the Box, in order to distribute it among the poor, every *Sunday*. A Friend of mine, being obliged to play pretty high in a Family, where he visited, had, generally, Luck on his Side. In some time, the Master of the Family became extreamly embarrass'd in the World. My Friend, being acquainted with it, and touch'd with so moving a Circumstance, went home, and, opening a Drawer where he had deposited the Winnings brought from his House, repaid him; thereby, he retrieved his Credit, and whereby the whole Family was saved from Ruin.—Yours &c., JEREMY HINT."

Another letter in the same Journal, 2 Sept. 1736, shows how the canker of gambling was surely eating into the very heart of the nation. It is *à propos* of private Gaming Houses. "I beg leave, through your Means, to make a few Remarks upon the great Encrease of a Vice, which, if not timely prevented, will end in the Ruin of the young and unwary of both Sexes; I mean, Play in private Houses, and more particularly that artful and cheating *Game* of *Quadrille*. It is the constant business of the *Puffs* who belong to the Gaming Societies, to make a general Acquaintance, and, by a Volubility of Tongue, to commend Company and Conversation : to advise young People, or those who have but lately come to Town, to improve themselves in the *Beau Monde*. The young and unwary, thro' their Inexperience, greedily swallow this Advice, and deliver themselves up to the Conduct of these Harpies who swarm in every Corner, where Visiting is in Fashion : by whom they are introduced into these polite Families, and taught to lose their Money and Reputation in a genteel Manner. These Societies consist mostly of two or three insignificant old Maids, the same number of gay Widows ; a batter'd old Beau or two, who, in King William's time, were the Pink of the Mode : The Master of the House, some decay'd Person of a good Family, made use of merely as a Cypher to carry on the Business, by having the Honour to be marry'd to the Lady, who, to oblige her Friends and People of good Fashion only, suffers her House to be made use of for these Purposes. In these places it is that young Ladies of moderate Fortunes are drawn in, to the infallible Ruin of their Reputations ; and when, by false Cards, Slipping, Signs, and Crimp, they are stript of their last Guinea, their wretched companions will not know them. Any one acquainted with the West End of the Town cannot but have observed all this with Regret, if they have Honour and Compassion in them. Nor need I mention the West End only. I believe all Points of the Compass are infected, and it were to be wished a Remedy could be found out to prevent it."

An attempt to remedy this state of things was made, in 1739, by passing "an Act for the more efficient preventing of excessive and deceitful gaming" (12 Geo. II. c. 28), which provided that the Person that keeps a house, or other place, to game in, forfeits £200, half to the prosecutor, and half to the poor of the parish, except at Bath, where the half goes to poor in the Hospital. Lotteries, Sales, Shares in Houses to be determined by Lottery, Raffle, &c., are under this Act, the Lands, Houses, &c. forfeited. All persons gaming in the places aforesaid, or adventurers in Lotteries, on conviction forfeit £50. The games forbidden are Ace of Hearts, Faro, Basset and Hazard, except in Royal Palaces. Justices of Peace refusing to act and convict on this Act forfeit £10.

But this Act did not go far enough, and it was amended by the 18 Geo. II. c. 34. The Journals of the House of Lords have a curious story to tell about this Act.

"*Dies Lunæ*, 29 *Aprilis* 1745. The House (according to Order) was adjourned during Pleasure, and put into Committee upon the Bill intituled 'An Act to amend, explain, and make more effectual, the Laws in being, to prevent excessive and deceitful Gaming: and to restrain and prevent the excessive Increase of Horse Races.'

After some time the House was resumed.

And the Earl of Warwick reported from the said Committee that they had gone through the Bill, and made some Amendments thereto; which he would be ready to report, when the House will please to receive the same.

Ordered. That the Report be received to-morrow.

The House being informed 'That Mr Burdus, Chairman of the Quarter Sessions for the City and Liberty of Westminster, Sir Thomas de Veil, and Mr Lane, Chairman of the Quarter Sessions for the County of Middlesex, were at the door.'

They were called in, and, at the Bar, severally gave an account that claims of privilege of Peerage were made, and insisted on, by the Ladies Mordington and Casselis, in order to intimidate the peace officers from doing their duty in suppressing the public gaming houses kept by the said Ladies.

And the said Burdus thereupon delivered in an instrument in writing, under the hand of the said Lady Mordington, containing the claim she made of privilege for her officers and servants employed by her in the said gaming house.

And then they were directed to withdraw.

And the said Instrument was read, as follows:—

' I, Dame Mary, Baroness of Mordington, do hold a house in the Great Piazza, Covent Garden, for and as an Assembly, where all persons of credit are at liberty to frequent and play at such diversions as are used at other Assemblys. And I have hired Joseph Dewberry, William Horsely, Ham Cropper, and George Sanders, as my servants, or managers, (under me) thereof. I have given them orders to direct the management of the other inferior servants, (namely) John Bright, Richard Davis, John Hill, John Vandenvoren, as box-keepers. Gilbert Richardson, housekeeper, John Chaplain, regulator, William Stanley and Henry Huggins, servants that wait on the Company at the said Assembly, William Penny and Joseph Penny, as porters thereof. And all the above mentioned persons I claim as my domestick servants, and demand all those privileges that belong to me, as a Peeress of Great Britain, appertaining to my said Assembly. M. MORDINGTON. Dated 8 Jan. 1745.'

Resolved and declared that no Person is entitled to Privilege of Peerage against any prosecution, or proceeding, for keeping any public or common gaming house, or any house, room, or place for playing at any game, or games prohibited by any law now in force."

These ladies had already been presented by the Grand Jury for the County of Middlesex on 10 May 1744, together with the proprietors of the avenues leading to and from the several Playhouses in Covent Garden and Drury Lane, the proprietors of Sadler's Wells, and the proprietors of New Wells in Goodman's Fields, The London Spaw, Clerkenwell, and Halden's New Theatre, in May Fair.

One of the most curious anecdotes of gambling, about this date, is the following[1] :—" 1735. Oct. A child of James and Elizabeth Leesh of Chester le street, was played for at cards, at the sign of the Salmon, one game, four

---

[1] Local Records, &c., of Remarkable events. Compiled by John Sykes. Newcastle, 1824, p. 79.

shillings against the child, by Henry and John Trotter, Robert Thomson and Thomas Ellison, which was won by the latter, and delivered to them accordingly."

The law was occasionally put in motion, as we find. "*Gent. Mag.*, Oct. 31, 1750.   About 9 o'clock at night, a party of soldiers and constables, with proper warrants, enter'd a notorious gaming house, behind the *Hoop* tavern in the *Strand*, and seiz'd 36 gamblers, and carry'd them to the vestry room at *St Martin's*, where the justices were sitting for that purpose; 21 of them, next morning, for want of bail, were committed to the *Gatehouse*, and the others bound in a recognizance of £80, to answer at the next Sessions ; the fine gaming tables, which cost £200, were chopt to pieces, and a great part burnt."

"Feb. 1, 1751.   Justice *Fielding* having received information of a rendezvous of gamesters in the *Strand*, procured a strong party of guards, who seized 45 at the table, which they broke to pieces, and carry'd the gamesters before the justice, who committed 39 of them to the *Gatehouse* and admitted the other 6 to bail.   There were three tables broken to pieces, which cost near £60 apiece ; under each of them were observed two iron rollers, and two private springs, which those who were in the secret could touch, and stop the turning whenever they had any youngsters to deal with, and, so, cheated them of their money."

"Ap. 17, 1751.   *Thomas Lediard*, Esq., attended by a constable and a party of guards, went this night to the Long Room, in James St., Westminster, where there was a Masquerade, in order to suppress the notorious practice of gaming, for which such assemblies are calculated.   The whole was conducted without opposition, or mischief. Seventeen were committed to the gatehouse, some were discharged, and others gave sufficient bail, never to play at any unlawful game, or resort to any gaming house.   Numbers escaped over the Park wall, and other places, notwithstanding the vigilance of the magistrate and his assistants. The gaming tables were broke to pieces."

We have many instances of the industry and vigilance of the London magistrates, especially Fielding, who, in 1756, wrote a warning to the public,[1] entitled "The artifices and stratagems of the profligate and wicked part of the inhabitants of this great metropolis, in order to defraud and impose upon the weak and unwary, being multiplied to an incredible degree, *Mr Fielding* has taken the pains to lay before the public a detail of such of them as have fallen under his own immediate observation as a Magistrate: in the recital of which he has mark'd the progress of deceit from the lowest pickpocket to the most accomplish'd gambler. That none may be in ignorance of the snares that are continually laid for them, this history of Gambling is inserted." And in *Ferdinand Count Fathom*, by Smollett, Fielding's contemporary and brother novelist, we have a full description of a professional gambler's life.

[1] *Gent.'s Mag.*, V. xxvi. 564.

CHAPTER IV

NOR was it only in London that this gambling fever existed : it equally polluted the quieter resorts of men, and at fashionable watering places, like Bath, it was rampant, as Oliver Goldsmith writes in his life of Beau Nash, of whom he tells several anecdotes connected with play. " When he first figured at *Bath*, there were few laws against this destructive amusement. The gaming table was the constant resource of despair and indigence, and the frequent ruin of opulent fortunes. Wherever people of fashion came, needy adventurers were generally found in waiting. With such Bath swarmed, and, among this class, Mr Nash was certainly to be numbered in the beginning ; only, with this difference, that he wanted the corrupt heart, too commonly attending a life of expedients ; for he was generous, humane, and honourable, even though, by profession, a gambler.

A thousand instances might be given of his integrity, even in this infamous profession, where his generosity often impelled him to act in contradiction to his interest. Wherever he found a novice in the hands of a sharper, he generally forewarned him of the danger ; whenever he found any inclined to play, yet ignorant of the game, he would offer his services, and play for them. I remember an instance to this effect, though too nearly concerned in the affair to publish the gentleman's name of whom it is related.

In the year 1725, there came to Bath a giddy youth, who had just resigned his fellowship at Oxford. He brought his whole fortune with him there ; it was but a trifle, however, he was resolved to venture it all. Good fortune seemed kinder than could be expected. Without the smallest skill in play, he won a sum sufficient to make any unambitious man happy. His desire of gain increasing with his gains, in the October following he was *at all*, and added four thousand pounds to his former capital. Mr Nash, one night, after losing a considerable sum to this undeserving son of fortune, invited him to supper. Sir, cried this honest, though veteran gamester, perhaps you may imagine I have invited you, in order to have my revenge at home ; but, sir, I scorn such an inhospitable action. I desired the favour of your company to give you some advice, which, you will pardon me, sir, you seem to stand in need of. You are now high in spirits, and drawn away by a torrent of success. But, there will come a time, when you will repent having left the calm of a college life for the turbulent profession of a gamester. Ill runs will come, as certain as day and night succeed each other. Be therefore advised ; remain content with your present gains ; for, be persuaded that, had you the Bank of England, with your present ignorance of gaming, it would vanish like a fairy dream. You are a stranger to me ; but, to convince you of the part I take in your welfare, I'll give you fifty guineas, to forfeit twenty, every time you lose two hundred at one sitting. The young gentleman refused his offer, and was at last undone !

" The late Duke of B. being chagrined at losing a considerable sum, pressed Mr Nash to tie him up for the future from playing deep. Accordingly, the beau gave his grace an hundred guineas, to forfeit ten thousand, whenever he lost a sum, to the same amount, at play at one sitting. The duke loved play to distraction ; and, soon after, at hazard, lost eight thousand guineas, and was going to throw for three thousand more, when Nash, catching hold of the dice box, entreated his grace to reflect upon the penalty if he lost. The duke, for that time, desisted ; but so strong was the furor of play upon him that, soon after losing a considerable sum at Newmarket, he was contented to pay the penalty.

" When the late Earl of T——d was a youth, he was passionately fond of play, and never better pleased than with having Mr Nash for his antagonist. Nash saw, with concern, his lordship's foible, and undertook to cure him, though by a very disagreeable remedy. Conscious of his own superior skill, he determined to engage him in single play for a very considerable sum. His lordship, in proportion as he lost his game, lost his temper, too ; and, as he approached the gulph, seemed still more eager for ruin. He lost his estate ; some writings were put into the winner's possession : his very equipage deposited as a last stake, and he lost that also. But, when our generous gamester had found his lordship sufficiently punished for his temerity, he returned all, only stipulating that he should be paid five thousand pounds whenever he should think proper to make the demand. However, he never made any such demand during his lordship's life ; but, some time after his decease, Mr Nash's affairs being in the wane, he demanded the money of his lordship's heirs, who honourably paid it without any hesitation."

There is a sad story told of a lady gambler at Bath, which must have occurred about this time, say 1750 or thereabouts. Miss Frances Braddock, daughter of a distinguished officer, Maj.-Gen. Braddock, was the admiration of the circle in which she moved. Her person was elegant, her face beautiful, and her mind accomplished. Unhappily for her, she spent a season at Bath, where she was courted by the fashionables there present, for her taste was admirable and her wit brilliant. Her father, at his death, bequeathed twelve thousand pounds between her and her sister (a large amount in those days), besides a considerable sum to her brother, Maj.-Gen. Braddock, who was, in the American War, surrounded by Indians, and mortally wounded, dying 13th July 1755. Four years after her father's death, her sister died, by which her fortune was doubled —but, alas ! in the course of one short month, she lost the whole ; gambled away at cards,

It soon became known that she was penniless, and her sensitive spirit being unable to brook the real and fictitious condolences, she robed herself in maiden white, and, tying a gold and silver girdle together, she hanged herself therewith, dying at the early age of twenty-three years.

Gossiping Horace Walpole gives us many anecdotes of gambling in his time, scattered among his letters to Sir Horace Mann, &c. In one of them (Dec. 26, 1748), he tells a story of Sir William Burdett, of whom he says ; " in short, to give you his character at once, there is a wager entered in the bet book at White's (a MS. of which I may, one day or other, give you an account), that the first baronet that will be hanged, is this Sir William Burdett."

The Baronet casually met Lord Castledurrow (afterwards Viscount Ashbrook), and Captain (afterwards Lord) Rodney, " a young seaman, who has made a fortune by very gallant behaviour during the war," and he asked them to dinner.

" When they came, he presented them to a lady, dressed foreign, as a princess of the house of Brandenburg : she had a toad eater, and there was another man, who gave himself for a count. After dinner, Sir William looked at his watch, and said ' J—s ! it is not so late as I thought, by an hour ; Princess, will your Highness say how we shall divert ourselves till it is time to go to the play ! ' Oh ! ' said she, ' for my part, you know I abominate everything but Pharaoh.' ' I am very sorry, Madam,' replied he, very gravely, ' but I don't know whom your Highness will get to tally to you ; you know I am ruined by dealing.' ' Oh ! ' says she, ' the Count will deal to us.' ' I would, with all my soul,' said the Count,' but I protest I have no money about me.' She insisted : at last the Count said, ' Since your Highness commands us peremptorily, I believe Sir William has four or five hundred pounds of mine, that I am to pay away in the city to-morrow ; if he will be so good as to step to his bureau for that sum, I will make a bank of it.' Mr Rodney owns he was a little astonished at seeing the Count shuffle with the faces of the cards upwards; but, concluding that Sir William Burdett, at whose house he was, was a relation, or particular friend of Lord Castledurrow, he was unwilling to affront my lord.   In short, my lord and he lost about a hundred and fifty apiece, and it was settled that they should meet for payment, the next morning, at Ranelagh.   In the meantime, Lord C. had the curiosity to inquire a little into the character of his new friend, the Baronet; and being *au fait*, he went up to him at Ranelagh, and apostrophised him; 'Sir William, here is the sum I think I lost last night; since that, I have heard that you are a professed pickpocket, and, therefore, desire to have no farther acquaintance with you.' Sir William bowed, took the money and no notice; but, as they were going away, he followed Lord Castledurrow, and said, 'Good God! my lord, my equipage is not come; will you be so good as to set me down at Buckingham Gate?' and, without waiting for an answer, whipped into the chariot, and came to town with him.   If you don't admire the coolness of this impudence, I shall wonder."

"10 *Jan.* 1750. To make up for my long silence, and to make up a long letter, I will string another story, which I have just heard, to this.   General Wade was at a low gaming house, and had a very fine snuff-box, which, on a sudden, he missed.   Everybody denied having taken it: he insisted on searching the company.   He did: there remained only one man, who had stood behind him, but refused to be searched, unless the General would go into another room, alone, with him.   There the man told him, that he was born a gentleman, was reduced, and lived by what little bets he could pick up there, and by fragments which the waiters sometimes gave him.   'At this moment I have half a fowl in my pocket; I was afraid of being exposed; here it is!   Now, Sir, you may search me.'   Wade was so struck, that he gave the man a hundred pounds; and, immediately, the genius of generosity, whose province is almost a sinecure, was very glad of the opportunity of making him find his own snuff-box, or another very like it, in his own pocket again."

" 19 *Dec.* 1750. Poor Lord Lempster is more Cerberus [1] than ever ; (you remember his *bon mot* that proved such a blunder ;) he has lost twelve thousand pounds at hazard, to an ensign of the guards."

" 23 *Feb.* 1755. The great event is the catastrophe of Sir John Bland, who has *flirted* away his whole fortune at hazard. He, t'other night, exceeded what was lost by the late Duke of Bedford, having, at one period of the night, (though he recovered the greatest part of it) lost two and thirty thousand pounds. The citizens put on their double channeled pumps, and trudge to St James's Street, in expectation of seeing judgments executed on White's— angels with flaming swords, and devils flying away with dice boxes, like the prints in Sadeler's Hermits.[2] Sir John lost this immense sum to a Captain Scott,[3] who, at present, has nothing but a few debts and his commission."

" 20 *Ap.* 1756. I shall send you, soon, the fruits of my last party to Strawberry ; Dick Edgecumbe, George Selwyn, and Williams were with me ; we composed a coat of arms for the two clubs at White's, which is actually engraving from a very pretty painting of Edgecumbe,[4] whom Mr Chute, as Strawberry King at Arms, has appointed our chief herald painter ; here is the blazon :—

Vert (for card table), between three parolis proper, on a chevron table (for hazard table), two rouleaus in saltire, between two dice proper ; in a canton, sable, a white ball (for election), argent.

Supporters, An old Knave of *Clubs* on the dexter, a

---

[1] When he was on his travels, and ran much in debt, his parents paid his debts ; some more came out afterwards ; he wrote to his mother, that he could only compare himself to Cerberus, who, when one head was cut off, had another spring up in its room.

[2] Cannot be found in Solitudo, sive Vitæ Patrum Eremicolarum, &c. Johann & Raphael Sadeler. 1594.

[3] Afterwards General Scott.

[4] This painting was bought at the Strawberry Hill Sale, by Arthur's Club House, for twenty-two shillings.

young Knave on the sinister side; both accoutred proper.

Crest, Issuing out of an earl's coronet (Lord Darlington) an arm shaking a dice box, all proper.

Motto (alluding to the crest), *Cogit amor nummi.* The arms encircled by a claret bottle ticket, by way of Order."

" 14 *May* 1761. Jemmy Lumley, last week, had a party of whist at his own house; the combatants, Lucy Southwell, that curtseys like a bear, Mrs Prijeau, and a Mrs Mackenzie. They played from six in the evening till twelve the next day; Jemmy never winning one rubber, and rising a loser of two thousand pounds. How it happened, I know not, nor why his suspicions arrived so late, but he fancied himself cheated, and refused to pay. However, *the bear* had no share in his evil surmises: on the contrary, a day or two afterwards, he promised a dinner at Hampstead to Lucy and her virtuous sister. As he went to the rendezvous, his chaise was stopped by somebody, who advised him not to proceed. Yet, no whit daunted, he advanced. In the garden, he found the gentle conqueress, Mrs Mackenzie, who accosted him in the most friendly manner. After a few compliments, she asked him if he did not intend to pay her. 'No, indeed I shan't, I shan't; your servant, your servant.' 'Shan't you,' said the fair virago; and, taking a horsewhip from beneath her hoop, she fell upon him with as much vehemence as the Empress Queen would upon the King of Prussia, if she could catch him alone in the garden at Hampstead. Jemmy cried out Murder; his servants rushed in, rescued him from the jaws of the lioness, and carried him off in his chaise to town. The Southwells, who were already arrived, and descended, on the noise of the fray, finding nobody to pay for the dinner, and fearing they must, set out for London without it."

" 3 *Dec.* 1761. If you are acquainted with my Lady Barrymore, pray tell her that, in less than two hours, t'other night, the Duke of Cumberland lost four hundred and fifty pounds at Loo; Miss Pelham won three hundred, and I, the rest. However, in general, Loo is extremely gone to decay : I am to play at Princess Emily's to-morrow, for the first time this winter; and it is with difficulty that she has made a party."

" 2 *Feb*. 1770. The gaming at Almack's, which has taken the *pas* of White's, is worthy of the decline of our Empire, or Commonwealth, which you please. The young men of the age lose five, ten, fifteen thousands pounds in an evening there. Lord Stavordale, not one and twenty, lost eleven thousand there, last Tuesday, but recovered it by one great hand at hazard : he swore a great oath,—' Now, if I had been playing *deep*, I might have won millions.' His cousin, Charles Fox, shines equally there, and in the House of Commons."

" 18 *Aug*. 1776. To-day I have heard the shocking news of Mr Damer's death, who shot himself yesterday, at three o'clock in the morning, at a tavern in Covent Garden. My first alarm was for Mr Conway; not knowing what effect such a horrid surprise would have on him, scarce re-covered from an attack himself; happily, it proves his nerves were not affected, for I have had a very calm letter from him on the occasion. Mr Charles Fox, with infinite good nature, met Mrs Damer coming to town, and stopped her to prepare her for the dismal event. It is almost impossible to refrain from bursting into common-place reflections on this occasion; but, can the walls of Almack's help moralizing, when £5000 a year, in present, and £22,000 in reversion, are not sufficient for happiness, and cannot check a pistol !"

" 19 *Jan*. 1777. Lord Dillon told me this morning that Lord Besborough and he, playing at quinze t'other night with Miss Pelham, and, happening to laugh, she flew in a passion and said, ' It was terrible to play with *boys* !' And our two ages together, said Lord Dillon, make up above a hundred and forty."

" 6 *Feb*. 1780. Within this week there has been a cast at hazard at the Cocoa Tree, the difference of which amounted to a hundred and four score thousand pounds.

Mr O'Birne, an Irish gamester, had won one hundred thousand pounds of a young Mr Harvey, of Chigwell, just started from a midshipman [1] into an estate, by his elder brother's death.   O'Birne said, 'You never can pay me.'   'I can,' said the youth ; my estate will sell for the debt.'   'No,' said O., 'I will win ten thousand—you shall throw for the odd ninety.'   They did, and Harvey won."

"29 *Jan.* 1791. Pray delight in the following story : Caroline Vernon, *fille d'honneur*, lost, t'other night, two hundred pounds at faro, and bade Martindale mark it up. He said he would rather have a draft on her banker.   'Oh ! willingly'; and she gave him one.   Next morning, he hurried to Drummond's, lest all her money should be drawn out.   'Sir,' said the clerk, 'would you receive the contents immediately?'   'Assuredly.'   'Why, sir, have you read the note?'   Martindale took it ; it was, 'Pay the bearer two hundred blows, well applied.'   The nymph tells the story herself ; and, yet, I think, the clerk had the more humour of the two."

There can be no doubt but that in the last half of the eighteenth century, gambling for large sums was very rife. We have evidence of it on all hands.

"*Ann. Reg.*, 8 *Feb.* 1766. We are informed that a lady, at the West end of the town, lost, one night, at a sitting, 3000 guineas at Loo."

Par parenthèse, the same volume has (p. 191) the following horrible story : "*A circumstantial and authentic account of the miserable case of Richard Parsons, as transmitted in a letter from William Dallaway, Esq., High Sheriff of Gloucestershire, to his friend in London.*

"On the 20th of February last, Richard Parsons, and three more men met at a private house at Chalford, in order to play at cards, about six o'clock in the evening.   They played at loo till about eleven or twelve that night, when they changed their game to whist : after a few deals, a dispute

---

[1] Afterwards Admiral Sir Eliab Harvey, Knt., G.C.B., who fought at Trafalgar.

arose about the state of the game. Parsons affirmed, with oaths, that they were six, which the others denied, upon which he wished 'that he might never enter the kingdom of heaven, that his flesh might rot upon his bones, if they were not six in the game.' These wishes were several times repeated, both then and afterwards. Upon this, the candle was put out by one James Young, a stander by, who says he was shocked with the oaths and expressions he heard ; and that he put out the candle with a design to put an end to the game.

"Presently, upon this, they adjourned to another house, and there began a fresh game, when Parsons and his partner had great success. Then they played at loo again till four in the morning. During this second playing, Parson complained to one Rolles, his partner, of a bad pain in his leg, which, from that time, increased. There was an appearance of a swelling, and, afterwards, the colour changing to that of a mortified state. On the following Sunday, he rode to Minchin Hampton, to get the advice of Mr Pegler, the surgeon in that town, who attended him from the Thursday after February 27. Notwithstanding all the applications that were made, the mortification increased, and showed itself in different parts of the body. On Monday, March 3, at the request of some of his female relations, the clergyman of Bisley attended him, and administered the sacrament, without any knowledge of what had happened before, and which he continued a stranger to, till he saw the account in the *Gloucester Journal*. Parsons appeared to be extremely ignorant of religion, having been accustomed to swear, to drink (though he was not in liquor when he uttered the above execrable wish), to game, and to profane the Sabbath, though he was only in his nineteenth year. After he had received the Sacrament, he appeared to have some sense of the ordinance ; for he said, 'Now I must never sin again ; he hoped God would forgive him, having been wicked not above six years, and that, whatsoever should happen, he would not play at cards again.'

" After this, he was in great agony, chiefly delirious, spoke of his companions by name, and seemed as if his imagination was engaged at cards. He started, had distracted looks and gestures, and, in a dreadful fit of shaking and trembling, died on Tuesday morning, the 4th of March last : and was buried the next day at the parish church of Bisley. His eyes were open when he died, and could not be closed by the common methods ; so that they remained open when he was put into the coffin. From this circumstance arose a report, that he *wished his eyes might never close* ; but this was a mistake ; for, from the most creditable witnesses, I am fully convinced that no such wish was uttered ; and the fact is, that he did close his eyes after he was taken with the mortification, and either dozed or slept several times.

" When the body came to be laid out, it appeared all over discoloured, or spotted ; and it might be said, in the most literal sense, that his flesh rotted on his bones before he died."

But this is a digression. Among the deaths recorded in the *Gents' Magazine* for 1776, is " Ap. 30. William G——, Esq.: who, having been left £18,000, a few months before, by his father, lost it all by gaming, in less than a month ; in the Rules of the King's Bench."

" *Oct.* 25, 1777. At the Sessions for the County of Norfolk, a tradesman of Norwich, for cheating at cards, was fined £20, and sentenced to suffer six months' imprisonment in the castle, without bail or main prize ; and, in case the said fine was not paid at the expiration of the term, then to stand on the pillory, one hour, with his ears nailed to the same."

The gamblers of those days were giants in their way, there were George Selwyn, Lord Carlisle, Stephen Fox, who, on one occasion was fleeced most unmercifully at a West-end gambling house. He went into it with £13,000, and left without a farthing. His younger brother, Charles James, was a notorious gambler, and, if the following anecdote is true, not over honourable. He ranked among the admirers of Mrs Crewe. A gentleman lost a considerable sum to this lady at play, and, being obliged to leave town suddenly, gave Mr Fox the money to pay her, begging him to apologise to the lady for his not having paid the debt of honour in person. Fox, unfortunately, lost every shilling of it before morning. Mrs Crewe often met the supposed debtor afterwards, and, surprised that he never noticed the circumstance, at length, delicately hinted the matter to him. "Bless me," said he, "I paid the money to Mr Fox three months ago." "Oh! did you, Sir?" said Mrs Crewe, good-naturedly, "then probably he paid me, and I forgot it."

Steinmetz[1] (vol. i., p. 323) says : "Fox's best friends are said to have been half-ruined in annuities given by them as securities for him to the Jews. £500,000 a year of such annuities of Fox and his 'society' were advertised to be sold at one time. Walpole wondered what Fox would do when he had sold the estates of his friends. Walpole further notes that, in the debate on the Thirty-nine Articles, Feb. 6, 1772, Fox did not shine; nor could it be wondered at. He had sat up playing at hazard, at Almack's, from Tuesday evening, the 4th, till five in the afternoon of Wednesday, the 5th. An hour before, he had recovered £12,000 that he had lost ; and by dinner, which was at five o'clock, he had ended, losing £11,000! On the Thursday, he spoke in the above debate ; went to dinner at half-past eleven, at night ; from thence to White's, where he drank till seven the next morning ; thence to Almack's, where he won £6000 ; and, between three and four in the afternoon, he set out for Newmarket. His brother Stephen lost £11,000 two nights after, and Charles £10,000 more on the 13th, so that in three nights the two brothers—the eldest not *twenty-five* years of age—lost £32,000!"

<hr>

[1] "The Gaming Table, &c.," by A. Steinmetz. Lon. 1870.

CHAPTER V

WE have previously read how ladies of position kept
gambling houses, and pleaded their privilege to do so;
they, however, had to bow to the law. In the latter part
of the eighteenth century many ladies opened their houses,
the best known, probably, being Lady Buckinghamshire and
Lady Archer. The former is said to have slept with a
blunderbuss and a pair of pistols by her bedside, to protect
her Faro bank; and the latter was notorious for her " make
up," as we may see by the two following notices in the
Morning Post.

"*Jan.* 5, 1789. The Lady Archer, whose death was announced in this paper of Saturday, is not the celebrated
character whose *cosmetic powers* have long been held in
public estimation."

"*Jan.* 8, 1789. It is said that the dealers in *Carmine
and dead white*, as well as the *perfumers* in general, have it
in contemplation to present an Address to Lady Archer, in
gratitude for her not having DIED according to a late
alarming report."

We get portraits of these two ladies in a satirical print by
Gillray (31st March 1792), which is entitled " Modern Hospitality, or a Friendly Party in High Life," where they are
shewn keeping a Faro bank; and as these fair ones were
then somewhat *passées*, the picture has the following :—" To
those earthly Divinities who charmed twenty years ago, this
Honourable method of banishing mortifying reflections is

dedicated.   O, Woman! Woman! everlasting is your power over us, for in youth you charm away our hearts, and, in your after years, you charm away our purses!" The players are easily recognised. Lady Archer, who sits on the extreme left, has won largely ; rouleaux of gold and bank notes are before her, and, on her right hand, are two heaps of loose gold : and the painted old gambler smiles as she shows her cards, saying, "The Knave wins all !" Her next-door neighbour, the Prince of Wales, who has staked and lost his last piece, lifts his hands and eyes in astonishment at the luck.   Lady Buckinghamshire has doubled her stake, playing on two cards, and is, evidently, annoyed at her loss, while poor, black-muzzled Fox laments the loss of his last three pieces.

Gillray portrayed these two ladies on several occasions. There are two pictures of St James's and St Giles's, and in "Dividing the Spoil, St James's, 1796," we see Lady Archer and Lady Buckinghamshire quarrelling over gold, bank notes, a sword, and an order.   One other lady, probably Lady Mount Edgecumbe, is scrutinising a bill, whilst a fourth, with a pile of gold and notes before her, looks on smilingly.

Another print (16th May 1796) is called " Faro's Daughters, or the Kenyonian Blow Up to Gamblers."   Here we see Lady Archer and Mrs Concannon placed together in the pillory, where they are mutually upbraiding each other.   The *motif* for this picture was a speech of Lord Kenyon's, who, at a trial to recover £15, won at gaming on Sunday, at a public-house, commented very severely on the hold the vice of gaming had on all classes of society, from the highest to the lowest.   The former, he said, set the example to the latter, and, he added, " They think they are too great for the law ; I wish they could be punished "—and then continued, " If any prosecutions of this kind are fairly brought before me, and the parties are justly convicted, whatever be their rank or station in the country, though they be the first ladies in the land, they shall certainly exhibit themselves in the pillory."

They were getting somewhat too notorious. In spite of Lady Buckinghamshire's precautions of blunderbuss and pistols, her croupier, Martindale, announced, on 30th Jan. 1797, that the box containing the cash of the Faro bank had unaccountably disappeared. All eyes were turned towards her ladyship. Mrs Concannon said she once lost a gold snuff-box from the table when she went to speak to Lord C. Another lady said she lost her purse there the previous winter, and a story was told that a certain lady had taken *by mistake* a cloak which did not belong to her at a rout given by the late Countess of Guildford. Unfortunately, a discovery was made, and when the servant knocked at the door to demand it, some very valuable lace with which it was trimmed had been taken off. Some surmised that the lady who stole the cloak might also have stolen the Faro bank.

Townsend and his meddlesome police would poke their noses into the business, and, although they did not recover the Faro bank, something did come out of their interference, as we read in the *Times* of 13th March 1797. "PUBLIC OFFICE, MARLBOROUGH STREET. — FARO BANKS. — On Saturday came on to be heard informations against Lady Buckinghamshire, Lady Elizabeth Luttrell, Mrs Sturt, and Mr Concannon, for having, on the night of the 30th of last January, played at *Faro*, at Lady Buckinghamshire's house, in St James's Square, and Mr Martindale was charged with being the proprietor of the table.

"The evidence went to prove that the defendants had gaming parties at their different houses in rotation ; and, that when they met at Lady B.'s, the witnesses used to wait upon them in the gambling room, and that they played at *E. O., Rouge et Noir*, &c., from about eleven or twelve till three or four o'clock in the morning. After hearing counsel the Magistrates convicted *Henry Martindale* in the penalty of £200, and *each of the ladies* in £50. The information against Mr Concannon was quashed, on account of his being summoned by a wrong Christian name."

Gillray improved this occasion, giving us " Discipline à la Kenyon," and drew Lady Buckinghamshire tied to the tail of a cart, on which is a placard, " FARO'S DAUGHTERS BEWARE " : the Lord Chief Justice is depicted as administering a sound flogging both with birch and cat-o'-nine-tails to the delinquent lady, whilst Lady Luttrell and Mrs Sturt stand in the pillory guarded by a stalwart constable.

These ladies do not seem to have survived the century, for the *Morning Post* of Jan. 12, 1800, says : " Society has reason to rejoice in the complete downfall of the Faro Dames, who were so long the disgrace of human nature. Their *die* is cast, and their *odd tricks* avail no longer.   The *game* is up, and very few of them have *cut* with *honours.*" Mrs Concannon still kept on, but not in London, as is seen by the following paragraph. *Morning Herald*, 18th Dec. 1802 : " The visitors to Mrs Concannon's *petits soupers* at *Paris*, are not attracted by *billets* previously circulated, but by *cards*, afterwards *dealt out* in an elegant and scientific manner ; not to mince the matter, they are the rendezvous of *deep play* : and the only questionable point about the matter is, whether the *Irish* or the *French* will prove victors at the close of so desperate a winter's campaign."

The following extracts from *The Times* tell us much about the fashionable professional lady gamblers :—

" *Feb.* 5, 1793.   Mrs Sturt's house in St James Square was opened yesterday evening, for the first time this season, for public play.   The visitors were numerous."

" *Feb.* 6, 1793.   Some of the *Faro ladies* have opened their play-houses, and announced the *Road to Ruin* until further notice.   The *Gamesters* was publicly rehearsed in St James Square on Monday night."

" *Feb.* 10, 1793.   The profits of FARO are become so considerably reduced that most of the Banks now lose almost every evening, after defraying the expenses of the house, which are very considerable.   Those *public spirited* Ladies who give such frequent routs, do so at a certain gain : for the sum of TWENTY-FIVE guineas is regularly advanced by the bank holders towards the night's expenses. The *punters* at Mrs HOBART'S and Mrs STURT'S Faro banks have dropped off considerably ; and those who continue are got so *knowing* that heavy complaints are made that they bring no grist to the mill. There have not been above eight punters at Mrs STURT'S bank any night this season. The *pigeons* are all flown, and the punters are nothing better than hawks."

"14 *Mar.* 1793. The BANKING *Ladies* in St James Square do not see themselves much obliged to the *Abbé de St Farre*, and his brother, for introducing so many noble Emigrants to their houses. These people come with their crown pieces and half guineas, and absolutely form a circle round the Faro tables, to the total exclusion of our English Lords and Ladies, who can scarcely get one *punt* during the whole evening."

"2 *May* 1793. A *Banking* Lady, in St James Square, is about to commence a prosecution, because it is said, that there was much *filching* at her FARO table. The house was quite in an uproar, on Tuesday night, in consequence of a paragraph that appeared in a Morning Paper of the preceding day. The Lady *vows* she will call in the aid of an *Attorney* to *support her reputation* : and observes, that the *credit* of her house will suffer, if such reports are permitted to go unpunished. The *Faro Ladies* are, in the sporting phrase, almost *done up*. Jewels, trinkets, watches, laces, &c., are often at the pawnbrokers, and scarcely anything is left to raise money upon except their *pads*.[1] If justice is to be *hoodwinked*, and *gambling* and *sharking* permitted, why not make it an article of revenue, as in foreign countries, and lay a heavy tax on it."

"2 *Apr.* 1794. Lord HAMPDEN'S *Faro Bank* is broken up for the present season. Lady Buckinghamshire, Mrs Sturt and Mrs Concannon alternately divide the *Beau monde* at their respective houses. Instead of having two different hot suppers at *one* and *three* in the morning, the *Faro*

---

[1] Ladies then wore their hair very high-combed over pads of horse hair.

Banks will now scarcely afford bread and cheese and porter.

"One of the Faro Banks in St James Square lost £7000 last year by bad debts. A young son of Levi is a considerable debtor to one of them ; but not finding it convenient to pay what is not recoverable by law, he no longer appears in those fashionable circles."

"4 *Ap.* 1794. It is impossible to conceive a more complete system of fraud and dishonour than is practised every night at the *Faro banks*. Though every table has four croupiers, yet the Bank holders find that double that number are necessary to watch all the little tricks and artifices of some of the *fashionable punters*. But Mrs G—— beats all her associates in the art of doubling, or cocking a card."

"25 *June* 1794. The Faro Banks being no longer a profitable game, certain Ladies in St James Square have substituted another instead of it, called *Roulet* : but it is, in fact, only the old game of E.O. under a different title."

"30 *Dec.* 1795. It is to the credit of the rising generation of females, that they have unanimously quitted those infamous meetings, called Private Pharoes, where some of their shameless Mammas, and the faded reputations of the present age, still expose their vices, and cheat the boys who have not been long enough in the army to wear out their first cockades."

"17 *Dec.* 1794. It is said to be the intention of some of the leading circles in the fashionable world, to abolish the tax of *Card money*,[1] as an imposition upon hospitality. This would prove the return of good sense, inasmuch as it tends to substantiate the truth—that when one person invites another to partake of the conviviality of his house, he should not lay an impost upon him, even more exorbitant than that which he would pay, were he to attend a Tavern Club.

---

[1] The guests paid a small sum each into a pool (generally the snuffer tray) for every new pack of cards used, and this was popularly supposed to be a perquisite of the servants.

When a friend is invited, it is an insult to friendship, to make him pay for his entertainment."

"22 *March* 1796. The *tabbies* at Bath are in a state of insurrection, in consequence of an example set by Lady Elcho, who neither visits, nor receives Company that *pay for* Cards : the laudable reformation is adopted so generally, that many of the *Dowagers*, who have so long fed upon *Card money*, are turning their thoughts to some more creditable means of earning their livelihood."

"24 *March* 1796. We hope the Ladies in London, who stand upon a nice point of honour, will follow the example of the Bath Ladies, and exclude the odious, and pitiful, custom of taking card money at their houses.   It is a meanness, which no persons who pretend to the honour of keeping good company, ought to allow.   We are afraid that many a party is formed, rather to derive benefit from the card tables, than for the sake of hospitality."

This custom died hard, for I find in the *Morning Herald*, 15th Dec. 1802 : " In a pleasant village near the Metropolis, noted for its constant ' tea and turn-out ' parties, the extortion of *Card Money* had, lately, risen to such a pitch, that it was no unusual thing for the *Lady* of the House, upon the breaking up of a table, to immediately examine the sub. cargo of the candlestick, and, previous to the departure of her guests, proclaim aloud the lamentable defalcation of a pitiful shilling, which they might, perchance, have forgot to *contribute*.   We are happy to find that some of the most respectable people in the place have resolved to discountenance and abolish this *shabby genteel* custom, which has too long prevailed ; a shameful degradation of everything like English hospitality."

" *Times*, 2 *Nov.* 1797. At some of our first Boarding Schools, the fair pupils are now taught to play whist and casino.   Amongst their *winning* ways, this may not be the least agreeable to Papa and Mamma.

" It is calculated that a clever child, by its Cards, and its novels, may pay for its own education.

"At a boarding school in the neighbourhood of Moor-fields, the mistress complains that she is unable to teach her scholars either Whist, or Pharo."

"22 *Dec.* 1797. So completely has gambling got the better of dancing, that at a private Ball, last week, a gentle-man asking a young lady, from Bath, to dance the next two dances, she very ingenuously replied, 'Yes, if you will play two rubbers at Casino.'"

Enough has been written to give us a good insight into female gambling. I will now continue with that of the men, and first let us have a description of a gaming house from the *Times* of 14th Feb. 1793.

"The number of new gaming houses, established at the West-end of the town, is, indeed, a mattter of very serious evil : but they are not likely to decrease while examples of the same nature are held forth in the higher circles of life. It is needless to point out any one of these houses in par-ticular : it is sufficient for us to expose the tricks that are practised at many of them to swindle the unsuspecting young men of fortune, who are entrapped into these whirl-pools of destruction. The first thing necessary is, to give the guests a good dinner and plenty of wine, which most of these houses do, gratis. When they are sufficiently intoxi-cated, and having lost all the money about them, their acceptance is obtained to Bills of Exchange to a consider-able amount, which are frequently paid, to avoid the dis-agreeable circumstance of a public exposition in a Court of Justice, which is always threatened, though the gamesters well know that no such measure durst be adopted by them.

"Should any reluctance, or hesitation, be shewn by the injured party, to accept these Bills, he is shewn into a long room, with a target at the end of it, and several pistols lying about, where he is given to understand that these sharpers practice a considerable time of the day in shooting at a mark, and have arrived at such perfection in this exercise, that they can shoot a pistol ball, within an inch of the mark, from the common distance taken by duellists. A hint is then dropped, that further hesitation will render the use of the pistols necessary, and will again be the case, should he ever divulge what he has seen, and heard.

" If further particulars, or proofs, are wanting, they may be known, on application to certain *Military characters*, who have already made some noise in the world."

Nor was it only public play—gambling was universal. Michael Kelly, the vocalist, does not seem to think it anything very extraordinary, when he tells the following story :—" While at Margate, Mr and Mrs Crouch, and myself, were staying at the Hotel, kept by a man whose manners were as free and easy as any I have ever met with. He was proverbial for his *nonchalance*, and a perfect master of the art of making out a bill. One day, Johnstone dined with us, and we drank our usual quantum of wine. In the course of the evening, our bashful host, who, amongst other good qualities, was a notorious gambler, forced upon us some Pink Champagne, which he wished us to give our opinions of. My friend Jack Johnstone, who never was an enemy to the juice of the grape, took such copious draughts of the sparkling beverage, that his eyes began to twinkle, and his speech became somewhat of the thickest : my honest host, on perceiving this, thinking, I suppose, to amuse him, entered our room with a backgammon table and dice, and asked Johnstone if he would like to play a game. Johnstone, at that time, was considered fond of play, of which circumstance mine host was perfectly aware. Mrs Crouch and I earnestly entreated Jack to go to bed, but we could not prevail upon him to do so ; he whispered me, saying, ' You shall see how I will serve the fellow for his impudence,' and to it they went. The end of the business was, that before they parted, Johnstone won nearly two hundred pounds, and I retired to bed, delighted to see the biter bit."

Of another Kelly, or rather O'Kelly (the Colonel who was owner of the famous race horse, Eclipse), Harcourt [1] tells some

---

[1] " The Gaming Calendar," by Seymour Harcourt : Lon. 1820.

stories, and, indeed the book is a mine of anecdotes, some of which I reproduce :—

"Dennis O'Kelly was much attached to Ascot, where his horses occupied him by day, and the hazard table by night.

"Here it was, that repeatedly turning over a QUIRE OF BANK NOTES, a gentleman asked him 'what he was in want of?' when he replied, 'he was looking for *a little one.*' The enquirer said 'he could accommodate him, and desired to know for what sum?' When he answered 'A FIFTY, or something of *that sort*, just to set the *Caster.*' At this time it was supposed he had seven or eight thousand pounds in notes in his hand, but no one for less than a *hundred*. He always threw with great success; and, when he held the box, was seldom known to refuse throwing for *any sum* that the company chose to set him ; and, when ' out,' was always as liberal in *setting the Caster*, and preventing stagnation of *trade at the table*, which, from the great property always about him, it was his good fortune very often to deprive of the last *floating guinea*, when the *box*, of course, became *dormant* for want of a single adventurer.

"It was his usual custom to carry a great number of *bank notes* in his waistcoat pocket, twisted up together with the greatest indifference. When, in his attendance upon a hazard table at Windsor, during the races, being a *standing better*, and every chair full, a person's hand was observed, by those on the opposite side of the table, just in the act of drawing two notes out of his pocket. The alarm was given, and the hand, from the person behind, was *instantaneously* withdrawn, and the notes left more than half out of the pocket. The company became clamorous for the offender being taken before a magistrate, and many attempted to secure him for the purpose ; the Captain very *philosophically* seizing him by the collar, kicked him down stairs, and exultingly exclaimed, ' 'twas a *sufficient punishment* to be deprived of the pleasure of keeping company with *jontlemon.*'

"A bet for a large sum was once proposed to Col. O'Kelly,

at a race, and accepted.　The proposer asked the Colonel where lay his estates to answer for the amount if he lost? ' My estates! by *Jasus*,' cried O'Kelly.　'Oh, if that's what you *mane*, I've a map of them here.'　Then, opening his pocket book, he exhibited bank notes to ten times the sum in question, and, ultimately, added the enquirer's contribution to them."

"*An advertisement copied from the Courier, 5 Mar.* 1794. As Faro is the most fashionable circular game in the *haut ton*, in exclusion of melancholy Whist, and to prevent a company being cantoned into separate parties, a gentleman, of unexceptionable character, will, on invitation, do himself the honour to attend the rout of any lady, nobleman, or gentleman, with a Faro Bank and Fund, adequate to the style of play, from 500 to 2000 guineas.　Address G. A. by letter, to be left at Mr Harding's, Piccadilly, nearly opposite Bond Street.—*N.B.* This advertisement will not appear again."

" On *Sunday* night, towards the end of December 1795. Gen. Tarleton lost £800 at Mrs Concannon's ; Mr Hankey, £300.　The Prince was to have been there, but sent a late excuse.　Mr Boone of the Guards ; Mr Derby, son of the late Admiral, and Mr Dashwood, frequently rise winners or losers of £5000 nightly.　Lord Cholmondeley, Thompson & Co. were Faro Bankers at Brookes's, till which there was no Faro Bank of *male* celebrity, except at the Cocoa Tree."

" Henry Weston, who was hanged for forgery, was nephew to the late Admiral Sir Hugh Palliser.

" Having an unlimited control of the whole large property of his employer, Mr Cowan, during his absence from town he was tempted, first to gamble in the funds, where, being unfortunate, he went next to a Gaming House in Pall Mall, and lost a very large sum, and, at length, gamed away nearly all his master's property.　This, he hoped to patch up by forgery of Gen. Tonyn's name, by which he obtained from the Bank of England above £10,000.　Even this only lasted two nights ; and, procuring a woman to personate the

General's sister, he obtained another large supply, and went off. He was soon taken, and cut his throat on his return ; but not effectually. He was convicted at the Old Bailey on the 18th March 1796, and suffered on the 6th July, aged only twenty-three years.

" He sent Lord Kenyon a list of a number of professional gamblers, and, among them, was a person of very high rank. Weston, at different times, lost above £46,000 at play ; and, at a house in Pall Mall, where he lost a considerable part of it, three young officers also lost no less than £35,000.

" It was stated, some time since, in the Court of King's Bench, that the dinners given by gambling houses in and about Oxendon Street, amounted to £15,000 per annum ! "

" The following facts were disclosed on a motion in the Court of King's Bench, 24 Nov. 1797. Joseph Atkinson and Mary, his wife, had, for many years, kept a Gaming House, No. 15, under the Piazza, Covent Garden. They, daily, gave magnificent play dinners ; cards of invitation for which were sent to the clerks of merchants, bankers and brokers in the city. Atkinson used to say he liked citizens, whom he called *flats*, better than any one else, for, when they had dined, they played freely ; and, after they had lost all their money, they had credit to borrow more. When he had *cleaned them out*, when *the Pigeons were completely plucked*, they were sent to some of their solvent friends. After dinner, play was introduced, and, till dinner time the next day, the different games at cards, dice and E.O. were continually going on.

" Theophilus Bellasis had long been an infamous character, well known at Bow Street, where he had been charged with breaking into the counting-house of Sir James Sanderson, Bart. Bellasis was sometimes clerk, and sometimes client, to John Shepherd, an attorney of that Court ; and at other times, Shepherd was the prosecutor of those who kept Gaming Houses, and Bellasis attorney. Sir William Addington was so well aware that these two men commenced prosecutions solely for the purpose of *hush money* that he refused to act.   Atkinson at one time gave them £100, at another £80 ; and, in this way, they had amassed an immense sum, and undertook, for a specific amount, to defend keepers of Gaming Houses against all prosecutions !

" Mr Garrow, on a former occasion, charged Atkinson with using *dispatches*, that is, *loaded dice*, which in, five minutes, would dispatch £500 out of the pocket of any young man when intoxicated with champagne."

"*Jan.* 26, 1798. A notice came on in the King's Bench, Cornet William Moore, 3rd Dragoon Guards, *v.* Captain Hankey.   The former had won off the latter, at play, £14,000, for which Hankey had given his bond ; but a Court of Inquiry having declared that Moore had cheated him out of it, he made his application to set aside the bond."

It will be remembered that in that famous prosecution, in 1797, of Lady Buckinghamshire and her friends, their manager, Henry Martindale, was fined £200.   Next year he was bankrupt, and we read that " The debts proved under Mr Martindale's commission amounted to £328,000, besides Debts of Honour, which were struck off to the amount of £150,000.

" His failure is said to be owing to misplaced confidence in a subordinate, who robbed him of thousands.   The first suspicion was occasioned by his purchasing an estate of £500 a year, but other purchases followed to a considerable extent, and it was soon discovered that the Faro Bank had been robbed, sometimes of two thousand guineas a week !

" On the 14th of April 1798, other arrears to a large amount were submitted to and rejected by the Commissioners, who declared a first dividend of one shilling and fivepence in the pound."

" The Right Honourable Charles James Fox had an old gambling debt to pay to Sir John Lade.   Finding himself in cash after a lucky run at Faro, he sent a complimentary card to the knight, desiring to discharge the claim.   Sir

John no sooner saw the money than he called for pen and ink, and began to figure. 'What now,' cried Fox. 'Only calculating the interest,' replied the other. 'Are you so,' coolly rejoined Charles, and pocketed the cash. 'I thought it was a debt of honour. As you seem to consider it a trading debt, and as I make it an invariable rule to pay my Jew creditors last, you must wait a little longer for your money.'"

Before leaving the eighteenth century, let us hear what Col. Hanger[1] (4th Lord Coleraine) says of private gambling in his time, and undoubtedly he mixed in the very highest society. "If a gentleman in these days has but a few guineas in his purse, and will walk directly up to the Faro table, he will be the most welcome guest in the house; it is not necessary for him to speak, or even bow, to a single lady in the room, unless some unfortunate woman at the gaming-table ask him politely for the loan of a few guineas; then his answer need be but short—'No, Dolly, no; can't'; for this ever will be received as wit, though the unfortunate lady's bosom may be heaving, not from the tenderer passions, but with grief and despair at having lost the last farthing.

"When I first came into the world (1751?) there was no such thing as a Faro table admitted into the house of a woman of fashion; in those days they had too much pride to receive tribute[2] from the proprietor of such a machine. In former times there was no such thing as gaming at a private house, although there was more deep play at the clubs at that time than ever was before, or has been since. It is lamentable to see lovely woman destroying her health and beauty at six o'clock in the morning at a gaming-table. Can any woman expect to give to her husband a vigorous and healthy offspring, whose mind, night after night, is thus distracted, and whose body is relaxed by anxiety and the fatigue of late hours? It is impossible."

---

[1] Life, Adventures, and Opinions of Col. George Hanger, written by himself. London, 1801.

[2] In some houses in this age the lady of the house is paid fifty guineas each night by the proprietor of the Faro table.—G. H.

CHAPTER VI

HANGER speaks of gambling at the clubs, but in his time there were very few of them, and the oldest of all was "White's" in St James Street. Originally a Chocolate House, established in 1698, it was the rendezvous for the Tories in London. It was destroyed by fire on 28th April, 1733, a fact which is immortalised by Hogarth in his sixth picture of the *Rake's Progress*. The earliest record of it, as a Club, that remains, is a book of rules and list of members of the old Club at White's, dated 30th October 1736. In 1755 it removed to the east side of St James Street to No. 38, and there it still remains. In 1797, according to the rules of the Club, " Every Member who plays at Chess, Draughts, or Backgammon, do pay One Shilling each time of playing by daylight, and half-a-crown each by candlelight." We have had many references to the gambling that took place at White's, and when betting is discussed, the Club's famous betting-book will be duly noticed. It is now one of the most aristocratic clubs in London.

The Cocoa Tree Club, which was, probably, made into a Club before 1746, and was somewhat lower down St James Street than White's, was the Whig Club, but it does not seem to have been so much used for gambling as its elder *confrère*.

Almack's Club was essentially for gambling, and was founded in 1764 by twenty-seven noblemen and gentlemen. Among its original rules are the following :—

" 21. No gaming in the eating room, except tossing up for reckonings, on penalty of paying the whole bill of the members present.

" 40. That every person playing at the new guinea table do keep fifty guineas before him.

" 41. That every person playing at the twenty guinea table do not keep less than twenty guineas before him."

Here is an extract from the Club books which shows the style of play. " Mr Thynne having won only 12,000 guineas during the last two months, retired in disgust. March 21, 1772."

The Club subsequently became Goosetree's, and after him was taken by a wine merchant and money lender named Brookes, and Brookes's it is to this day, at 60 St James Street, to which locality it moved from Pall Mall in October 1778.

These, with Arthur's, were all the clubs for the nobility and gentry, until the Regency, when clubs multiplied. There were any amount of gambling houses, but they were public—but, of course, a club was strictly confined to its members.

So gambling went on merrily among all classes, as we may see by the following notices from the *Morning Post* :

" 5 *July* 1797. Is Mr Ogden (now called the Newmarket Oracle), the same person who, five-and-twenty years since, was an annual pedestrian to Ascot, covered with dust, amusing himself with *pricking in the belt, hustling in the hat*, &c., amongst the lowest class of rustics, at the inferior booths of the fair ?

" Is D—k—y B———w, who has now his snug farm, the same person who, some years since, *drove post chaise* for T———y of Bagshot, could neither read nor write, and was introduced to *the family* only by his pre-eminence at cribbage ?

" Is Mr Twycross (with his phaeton), the same person who, some years since, became a bankrupt in Tavistock Street, immediately commenced the Man of Fashion at Bath, kept running horses, &c., *secundum artem* ?

" Is Mr Phillips (who has now his town and country house, in the most fashionable style,) the same who was, originally, a linen draper and bankrupt at Salisbury, and who made his first *family entré* in the metropolis, by his superiority at *Billiards* (with Capt. Wallace, Orrell, &c.) at Cropley's in Bow Street ?

"Was poor carbuncled P———e (so many years the favourite decoy duck of *the family*) the very barber of Oxford who, in the midst of the operation upon a gentleman's face, laid down his razor, swearing that he would never shave another man so long as he lived, and immediately became the hero of the Card Table, *the bones*, *the box*, and the *cock-pit*? "

" 5 *April* 1805. The sum lately lost at play by a lady of high rank is variously stated. Some say it does not amount to more than £200,000, while others assert that it is little short of £700,000.   Her Lord is very unhappy on the occasion, and is still undecided with respect to the best mode to be adopted in the unfortunate predicament."

" 30 *June* 1806. The Marquis of H———d is said to have been so successful at play, this season, as to have cleared £60,000.   The Earl of B———e has won upwards of £50,000, clear of all deductions.   A Right Reverend is stated to be amongst those who are *minus* on this occasion."

" 8 *July* 1806.   A certain Noble Marquis, who has been very fortunate, this season, in his gaming speculations, had a run of ill-luck last week.   At one sitting his Lordship was *minus* no less a sum than *thirteen thousand pounds* ! "

" 15 *July* 1806.   The noble Marquis, who has been so great a gainer this season, at *hazard*, never plays with any-one, from a PRINCE, to a *Commoner*, without having the stakes *first* laid on the table.   His lordship was always considered as a *sure card*, but, now, his fame is established, from the circumstance of his having cleared £35,000, after deducting all his losses for the last six months."

" *Morning Herald*, 16 *June* 1804.   A noble Lord, lately high in office, and who manifests a strong inclination to be re-instated in his political power, lost, at the UNION, a night or two back, 4000 guineas before twelve o'clock ; but, continuing to play, his luck took a turn, and he rose a winner of a 1000 before five the next morning."

I have, also, two newspaper cuttings, but know not whence they came. " *Mar.* 28, 1811. The brother of a Noble Marquis is said to have lately won, at *hazard*, upwards of £30,000, all in one night ! " " *April* 3, 1811. A young gentleman of family and fortune lost £7000, on Sunday Morning, at a gaming house in the neighbourhood of Pall Mall."

This brings us to the time when, owing to the mental affliction of George III., the Prince of Wales became Regent, and during his reign, both as Regent and King, gambling throve ; and I propose to quote somewhat from Captain Gronow, whose chatty Reminiscences are about the best of those times. But before doing so I must tell the following anecdote which relates to that General Scott whom Gronow mentions.

Lord C—— had a most unfortunate propensity to gamble ; and, in one night, he lost £33,000 to General Scott. Mortified at his ill-fortune he paid the money and wished to keep the circumstance secret ; it was, however, whispered about. His lordship, to divert his chagrin, went, a few nights afterwards, to a Masquerade at Carlisle House, Soho, and he found all the company running after three Irish young ladies of the name of G——e, in the character of the three witches in *Macbeth*. These ladies were so well acquainted with everything that was going on in the great world that they kept the room in a continual roar of laughter by the brilliancy of their wit, and the happiness of its application to some people of rank who were present. They knew Lord C—— and they knew of his loss, though he did not know them. He walked up to them, and, in a solemn tone of voice, thus addressed them :—

> " Ye black and midnight hags,—what do ye do ?
> Live ye ? or are ye aught that man may question ?
> Quickly unclasp to me the book of fate,
> And tell if good, or ill, my steps await."

> *First Witch.* "All hail, C——e ! all hail to thee !
> Once annual lord of thousands thirty-three !"
> *Second Witch.* "All hail, C——e ! all hail to thee !
> All hail ! though poor thou soon shalt be !"
> *Hecate.* " C——e, all hail ! thy evil star
> Sheds baleful influence—Oh, beware !
> Beware that Thane !   Beware that Scott !
> Or, poverty shall be thy lot !
> He'll drain thy youth as dry as hay—
> Hither, Sisters, haste away !"

At the concluding words, whirling a watchman's rattle, which she held in her hand, the dome echoed with the sound ; the astonished peer shrunk into himself with terror —retired—vowed never to lose more than a hundred pounds at a sitting ; abided by the determination, and retrieved his fortune.

[1] " The politics of White's Club were, then, decidedly Tory.   It was here that play was carried on to an extent which made many ravages in large fortunes, the traces of which have not disappeared at the present day.   General Scott, the father-in-law of George Canning and the Duke of Portland, was known to have won, at White's, £200,000 ; thanks to his notorious sobriety and knowledge of the game of whist.   The General possessed a great advantage over his companions by avoiding those indulgences at the table, which used to muddle other men's brains.   He confined himself to dining off something like a boiled chicken, with toast and water ; by such a regimen he came to the whist table with a clear head, and possessing, as he did, a remarkable memory, with great coolness and judgment, he was able, honestly, to win the enormous sum of £200,000.

" At Brooke's, for nearly half a century, the play was of a more gambling character than at White's.   Faro and Macao were indulged in to an extent which enabled a man to win, or to lose, a considerable fortune in one night.   It was here that Charles James Fox, Selwyn, Lord Carlisle, Lord Robert Spencer, General Fitzpatrick, and other great Whigs, won,

[1] Reminiscences, 1st Ser.

and lost, hundreds of thousands ; frequently remaining at the table for many hours without rising.

" On one occasion, Lord Robert Spencer contrived to lose the last shilling of his considerable fortune, given to him by his brother, the Duke of Marlborough : General Fitzpatrick, being much in the same condition, they agreed to raise a sum of money, in order that they might keep a Faro bank. The members of the club made no objection, and, ere long, they carried out their design. As is generally the case, the bank was a winner, and Lord Robert bagged, as his share of the profits, £100,000. He retired, strange to say, from the fœtid atmosphere of play, with the money in his pocket, and never again gambled. George Harley Drummond, of the famous banking house, Charing Cross, only played once, in his whole life, at White's Club, at whist, on which occasion he lost £20,000 to Brummell. This event caused him to retire from the banking house, of which he was a partner.

" Lord Carlisle was one of the most remarkable victims amongst the players at Brooke's, and Charles Fox, his friend, was not more fortunate, being, subsequently, always in pecuniary difficulties. Many a time, after a long night of hard play, the loser found himself at the Israelitish establishment of Howard and Gibbs, then the fashionable and patronized money-lenders. These gentlemen never failed to make hard terms with the borrower, although ample security was, invariably, demanded.

" The Guard's Club was established for the three regiments of Foot Guards, and was conducted upon a military system. Billiards and low whist were the only games indulged in. The dinner was, perhaps, better than at most clubs, and considerably cheaper. Arthur's and Graham's were less aristocratic than those I have mentioned ; it was, at the latter, that a most painful circumstance took place. A nobleman, of the highest position and influence in society, was detected in cheating at cards, and, after a trial, which did not terminate in his favour, he died of a broken heart.

" Upon one occasion, some gentlemen, of both White's and Brooke's, had the honour to dine with the Prince Regent, and, during the conversation, the Prince inquired what sort of dinners they got at their clubs ; upon which, Sir Thomas Stepney, one of the guests, observed that their dinners were always the same, ' the eternal joints, or beef-steaks, the boiled fowl with oyster sauce, and an apple tart —this is what we have, sir, and very monotonous fare it is.' The Prince, without further remark, rang the bell for his cook, Wattier, and, in the presence of those who dined at the Royal table, asked him whether he would take a house and organize a dinner club. Wattier assented, and named Madison, the Prince's page, manager, and Labourie, from the Royal kitchen, as the cook. The club flourished only a few years, owing to the high play that was carried on there. The Duke of York patronized it, and was a member. The dinners were exquisite ; the best Parisian cooks could not beat Labourie. The favourite game played there was Macao. Upon one occasion Jack Bouverie, brother of Lady Heytesbury, was losing large sums, and became very irri-table ; Raikes, with bad taste, laughed at Bouverie, and attempted to amuse us with some of his stale jokes ; upon which Bouverie threw his play bowl, with the few counters it contained, at Raikes' head : unfortunately, it struck him, and made the City dandy angry, but no serious results followed this open insult."

Captain Gronow gives a personal story of his own gambling. After Napoleon's escape from Elba, he had the offer of an appointment on the staff of General Picton, but his funds were somewhat low. " So I set about thinking how I should manage to get my outfit, in order to appear at Brussels in a manner worthy of the *aide-de-camp* of the great general. As my funds were at a low ebb, I went to Cox and Greenwood's, those staunch friends of the hard up soldier. Sailors may talk of the ' little cherub that sits up aloft,' but commend me for liberality, kindness, and generosity to my old friends in Craig's Court. I there obtained £200, which I took with me to a gambling house in St James' Square, where I managed, by some wonderful accident, to win £600 ; and, having thus obtained the sinews of war, I made numerous purchases, amongst others, two first-rate horses at Tattersall's for a high figure."

He gives several instances of the English love for gambling, as exemplified at Paris, after its occupation by the Allies.

" Fox, the secretary of the embassy, was an excellent man, but odd, indolent, and careless in the extreme ; he was seldom seen in the daytime, unless it was either at the embassy, in a state of *negligée*, or in bed. At night, he used to go to the Salon des Etrangers ; and, if he possessed a Napoleon, it was sure to be thrown away at hazard, or *rouge et noir*. On one occasion, however, fortune favoured him in a most extraordinary manner. The late Henry Baring having recommended him to take the dice box, Fox replied, ' I will do so for the last time, for all my money is thrown away upon this infernal table.' Fox staked all he had in his pockets ; he threw in *eleven* times, breaking the bank, and taking home for his share 60,000 francs. After this, several days passed without any tidings being heard of him ; but, upon calling at the embassy to get my passport *viséd*, I went into his room, and saw it filled with Cashmere shawls, silk, Chantilly veils, bonnets, gloves, shoes, and other articles of ladies' dress. On my asking the purpose of all this millinery, Fox replied, ' Why, my dear Gronow, it was the only means to prevent those rascals at the Salon winning back my money.'

" The play which took place in these saloons was, frequently, of the most reckless character ; large fortunes were often lost, the losers disappearing, never more to be heard of. Amongst the English *habitués* were the Hon. George T——, the late Henry Baring, Lord Thanet, Tom Sowerby, Cuthbert, Mr Steer, Henry Broadwood, and Bob Arnold.

" The late Henry Baring was more fortunate at hazard than

his countrymen, but his love of gambling was the cause of his being excluded from the banking establishment.   Col. Sowerby, of the Guards, was one of the most inveterate players in Paris : and, as is frequently the case with a fair player, a considerable loser.   But, perhaps, the most incurable gamester amongst the English, was Lord Thanet, whose income was not less than £50,000 a year, every farthing of which he lost at play.   Cuthbert dissipated the whole of his fortune in the like manner.   In fact, I do not remember any instance where those who spent their time in this den did not lose all they possessed. . . .

"Amongst others who visited the Salon des Etrangers were Sir Francis Vincent, Gooch, Green, Ball Hughes, and many others whose names I no longer remember.   As at Crockford's, a magnificent supper was provided every night, for all who thought proper to avail themselves of it.   The games principally played were *rouge et noir* and hazard ; the former producing an immense profit ; for, not only were the whole of the expenses of this costly establishment defrayed by the winnings of the bank, but a very large sum was paid annually to the municipality of Paris.   I recollect a young Irishman, Mr Gough, losing a large fortune at this *tapis vert*.   After returning home about two A.M. he sat down and wrote a letter, giving reasons why he was about to commit suicide : these, it is needless to say, were simply his gambling reverses. A pistol shot through the brain terminated his existence. Sir Francis Vincent—a man of old family and considerable fortune—was another victim of this French hell, who contrived to get rid of his magnificent property, and then disappeared from society."

"Soon after Lord Granville's appointment [as British Ambassador] a strange occurrence took place at one of the public gambling houses.   A colonel, on half-pay, in the British service, having lost every farthing he possessed, determined to destroy himself, together with all who were instrumental to his ruin.   Accordingly, he placed a canister full of fulminating powder under the table, and set it on fire :

it blew up, but, fortunately, no one was hurt. The police arrested the colonel, and placed him in prison ; he was, however, through the humane interposition of our ambassador, sent out of France as a madman."

The Duke of Wellington [1] had, in his early career, lost a considerable sum of money at play, and had been on the point of selling his commission in Dublin, with the view of relieving himself from some debts of honour which he had incurred.

"At a dinner party at Mr Greenwood's, of that excellent firm, Cox & Greenwood, I met Sir Harry Calvert, then Adjutant-General, who accompanied the Duke of York, as one of his staff, in his disastrous campaign in Holland ; and he told us the following anecdote :—Lord Camden, the Viceroy, had been applied to by Lord Mornington, the brother of Captain Wesley (so the name was then spelt), for a Commissionership of Customs, or anything else in the gift of the Lord Lieutenant of Ireland, as it was the intention of the Captain to sell his commission to pay his debts. Lord Camden, in an interview with Captain Wesley, inquired whether he left the army in disgust, or what motive induced him to relinquish a service in which he was well qualified to distinguish himself. Captain Wesley explained everything that had occurred, upon which the Lord Lieutenant expressed a wish to be of service to him. 'What can I do for you ? Point out any plan by which you can be extricated from your present difficulties.' The answer was, 'I have no alternative but to sell my commission ; for I am poor, and unable to pay off my debts of honour.' 'Remain in the army,' said Lord Camden, 'and I will assist you in paying off your liabilities.' 'I should like to study my profession at Angers,' replied the young soldier, 'for the French are the great masters of the art of war.' Lord Camden assented to the proposition, supplied him with the means of living in France, and paid his debts. . . .

"The lesson the Duke of Wellington had learnt at the

[1] Reminiscences, 3rd Ser.

gambling table, as a young man, was deeply impressed upon him ; he, afterwards, never touched a card ; and so firmly did he set his face against gambling, that, in Paris, none of his staff, from Lord Fitzroy Somerset down to Freemantle, was ever to be seen either at Frascati's, or the Salon des Etrangers."

Ball Hughes was a dandy of the Regency, and from his fortune he was nick-named "the golden Ball "; of him Gronow says : " His fortune had dwindled down to a fourth of its original amount, for he was, perhaps, the greatest gambler of his day. His love of play was such, that, at one period of his life, he would rather play at pitch and toss than be without his favourite excitement. He told me that, at one time, he had lost considerable sums at battledore and shuttlecock. On one occasion, immediately after dinner, he and the eccentric Lord Petersham commenced playing with these toys, and continued hard at work during the whole of the night ; next morning, he was found by his valet lying on the ground fast asleep, but ready for any other species of speculation."

Of another dandy, Scrope Davies, he says : " As was the case with many of the foremost men of that day, the greater number of his hours were passed at the gambling table, where, for a length of time, he was eminently successful ; for he was a first-rate calculator. He seldom played against individuals ; he preferred going to the regular establishments. But, on one occasion, he had, by a remarkable run of good luck, completely ruined a young man, who had just reached his majority, and come into the possession of a considerable fortune. The poor youth sank down upon a sofa, in abject misery, when he reflected that he was a beggar ; for he was on the point of marriage. Scrope Davies, touched by his despair, entered into conversation with him, and ended by giving him back the whole of his losses, upon a solemn promise that he would never play again. The only thing that Scrope retained of his winnings was one of the little carriages of that day, called a *dormeuse* from its being fitted up with a bed, for he said, ' When I travel in it, I shall sleep the better for having acted rightly.' The youth kept his promise ; but when his benefactor wanted money, he forgot that he owed all he possessed to Scrope's generosity, and refused to assist him.

" For a long time Scrope Davies was a lucky player ; but the time arrived when Fortune deserted her old favourite ; and, shortly after the Dandy dynasty was overthrown, he found himself unable to mingle with the rich, the giddy, and the gay. With the wreck of his fortune, and, indeed, with little to live upon beyond the amount of his own Cambridge fellowship, he sought repose in Paris, and there, indulging in literary leisure, bade the world farewell."

" Raggett,[1] the well known club proprietor of White's, and the Roxburgh club in St James's Square, was a notable character in his way. He began life as a poor man, and died extremely rich. It was his custom to wait upon the members of these clubs whenever play was going on. Upon one occasion, at the Roxburgh, the following gentlemen, Hervey Combe, Tippoo Smith, Ward (the member for London), and Sir John Malcolm, played for high stakes at whist ; they sat during that night, viz., Monday, the following day and night, and only separated on Wednesday morning at eleven o'clock ; indeed, the party only broke up then, owing to Hervey Combe being obliged to attend the funeral of one of his partners who was buried on that day. Hervey Combe, on looking over his card, found that he was a winner of thirty thousand pounds from Sir John Malcolm, and he jocularly said, ' Well, Sir John, you shall have your revenge whenever you like.' Sir John replied, ' Thank you ; another sitting of the kind will oblige me to return again to India.' Hervey Combe, on settling with Raggett, pulled out of his pocket, a handful of counters, which amounted to several hundred pounds, over and above the thirty thousand he had won of the baronet, and he gave them to Raggett, saying, ' I give them to you for sitting so

[1] Reminiscences, 4th Ser

long with us, and providing us with all required.'   Raggett
was overjoyed, and, in mentioning what had occurred to one
of his friends, a few days afterwards, he added, ' I make it a
rule never to allow any of my servants to be present when
gentlemen play at my clubs, for it is my invariable custom
to sweep the carpet after the gambling is over, and I,
generally, find on the floor a few counters, which pays me
for the trouble of sitting up.   By this means I have made a
decent fortune.' "

CHAPTER VII

THE *Annual Register* about this time supplies us with several gambling anecdotes, the following being almost incredible :—1*5th April* 1812.—"On Wednesday evening an extraordinary investigation took place at Bow Street. Croker, the officer, was passing along the Hampstead road, when he observed, at a short distance before him, two men on a wall, and, directly after, saw the tallest of them, a stout man, about six feet high, hanging by his neck, from a lamp post attached to the wall, being that instant tied up and turned off by the short man. This unexpected and extraordinary sight astonished the officer ; he made up to the spot with all speed ; and, just after he arrived there, the tall man, who had been hanged, fell to the ground, the handkerchief, with which he had been suspended, having given way. Croker produced his staff, said he was an officer, and demanded to know of the other man the cause of such conduct. In the meantime, the man who had been hanged recovered, got up, and, on Croker's interfering, gave him a violent blow on the nose, which nearly knocked him backwards. The short man was endeavouring to make off; however, the officer procured assistance, and both were brought to the office, when the account they gave was that they worked on canals. They had been together on Wednesday afternoon, tossed up for money, and afterwards for their clothes ; the tall man, who was hanged, won the other's jacket, trousers, and shoes ; they then tossed up which should hang the other, and the short one won the toss. They got upon the wall, the one to submit, and the other to hang him on the lamp iron. They both agreed in this statement. The tall one, who had been hanged, said, if he had won the toss, he would have hanged the other. He said he then felt the effects of his hanging in his neck, and his eyes were so much swelled that he saw double. The magistrates expressed their horror and disgust, and ordered the man who had been hanged to find bail for the violent and unjustifiable assault on the officer, and the short one for hanging the other. Not having bail, they were committed to Bridewell for trial."

7th Feb. 1816.—"Yesterday, a gentleman, the head in a firm of a first-rate concern in the City, put a period to his existence by blowing out his brains. He had gone to the masquerade at the Argyll Rooms a few nights since, and accompanied a female home in a coach with two men, friends of the woman. When they got to her residence, the two men proposed to the gentleman to play for a dozen of champagne to treat the lady with, which the gentleman declined. They, however, after a great deal of persuasion, prevailed on him to play for small sums, and, according to the usual tricks of gamblers, allowed him to win at first, till they began to play for double, when, there is no doubt, the fellows produced loaded dice, and the gentleman lost to the amount of £1800, which brought him to his reflection and senses. He then invented an excuse for not paying that sum, by saying he was under an agreement with his partner not to draw for a larger amount than £300 for his private account, and gave them a draft for that amount, promising the remainder at a future day. This promise, however, he did not attend to, not feeling himself bound by such a villainous transaction. But the robbers found out who he was, and his residence, and had the audacity to go yesterday morning, armed with bludgeons, and attack him publicly on his own premises, in the presence of those employed there, demanding payment of their nefarious debt of *honour*, and threatening him, if he did not pay, that he should fight. This exposure had such an effect upon his feelings, that he made an excuse to retire, when he destroyed himself by blowing out his brains with a pistol. This rash act is additionally to be lamented, as it prevents the bringing to condign punishment the plundering villains who were the cause of it, there being no evidence to convict them."

"*Horse Guards*, 18*th Nov.* 1816.—At a general Court-martial held at Cambray, in France, on the 23rd September 1816, and continued by adjournments to the 26th of the same month, Lieutenant the Honourable Augustus Stanhope, of the 12th regiment of Light Dragoons, was arraigned on the undermentioned charge, viz. :—

" For behaving in a scandalous, infamous manner, such as is unbecoming the character of an officer and a gentleman, in conspiring, with a certain other person, to draw in and seduce Lord Beauchamp to game and play with them, for the purposes of gain and advantage ; and that, in pursuance of such conspiracy, he, Lieutenant Stanhope (having engaged Lord Beauchamp to come to his quarters in Paris, on Sunday, the 17th day of March 1816, upon an invitation to dine with him), did, in company and concert of such other person, draw in, seduce, and prevail upon Lord Beauchamp to play with them at a certain game of chance with cards, for very high stakes, whereby, on an account kept by them, Lieut. Stanhope, and the said other person, or one of them, of the losses and gains in the course of the play, he, Lieut. Stanhope, claimed to have won from Lord Beauchamp the sum of £8000 and upwards, and the said other person claimed to have won off Lord Beauchamp the further sum of £7000 and upwards.

" That, in further pursuance of the said concert and conspiracy, he, Lord Beauchamp, at the same time and place, was required by Lieut. Stanhope to write and sign two promissory notes, or engagements, to pay at the expiration of three years the said several sums of money so claimed to have been won off him, Lord Beauchamp, by Lieut. Stanhope and the said other person respectively.

" That he, Lord Beauchamp, was, at that time, about sixteen

years of age, ignorant of, and unused to play, and affected by the wine he had been prevailed upon to take by the parties."

Lieut. Stanhope was found guilty and dismissed from the army.

The *Annual Register* also gives numerous cases of duels arising from gambling, but they are, comparatively, uninteresting, and are all of the same type, paltry quarrels over the gaming-table.

We have a metrical description of gambling about this time supposed to have been written by a gambler who had to retire to France, and I here give a portion of it.[1]

> " Ah me ! what sad pangs ev'ry fibre now feels,
> When I view the success of my exquisite *deals*,
> My *cutting* and *shuffling*, perform'd with such ease :
> (And their talent is rare who can *cut* when they please).
> Ev'ry bet at Macao was decidedly mine ;
> For, faithful to me, was the snug winning Nine ;
> And the dice-box, alike, against Squire or Lord,
> Brought whatever I pleased on the fortunate board.
> Yet exil'd, in spite of success, to this land ;
> I have made of my gains but a very *bad hand*,
> For here, gallant Greeks ! my sad fortune deplore,
> No *pigeon* takes wing to the Gallican shore ;
> And the nation, composed of sly slippery elves,
> Admits of no *plucking*, except by themselves ;
> Whilst Bourbon the pious, to vermin-like rats,
> Grants Licences special, for *doing the flats.*
> Ye haunts of St James's ! ye Cyprian fair !
> How sweet your amusements ! how *winning* your air !
> Long, long have I served you, and valued you well,
> From the Regent's proud palace, to Bennet Street *hell*,
> Where nobles and simples alike take their swing,
> With th' intention of being *at all in the ring.*
> Their eyes are attracted with rouleaus of gold,
> Or with thousands in paper, so neat in the fold :
> Impatient they view them, and seize them elate,
> And, when pocketing most, they most swallow the bait.
> There's N—g—nt's proud lord, who, to angle for pelf,
> Will soon find the secret of diddling himself ;

---

[1] The Greeks—a poem, by Ἕλλην. Lon. 1817. 8vo.

There's H—rb—rt, who, lately, as knowing ones tell,
Won a tight seven hundred at house in Pall Mall ;
Captain D—v—s, who, now, is a chick of the game,
But, although in *high feather*, the odds will soon tame ;
And the Marquis of Bl—ndf—rd, who *touch'd 'em up rare*,
For a thousand in Bennet Street (all on the square),
Where a service of plate gives a *shine* to the job,
The whole made of crowns from young gentlemen's fob.
There's Ll—yd and C—in—ck, who'd a martinette be ;
For none *drills* a guinea more ably than he—
So his adjutant told him (a pretty good wipe,
Which the Colonel accepted and put in his pipe).
There's a certain rum baronet every one knows,
Who, on Saturday nights to the *two sevens* goes ;
With J—— and Cl——, Billy W—— and two more,
So drunk that they keep merry hell in a roar ;
Long D—b—n, thin C—rt—r, a son of a gun,
Bill B——, the Doctor, that figure of fun :
They have all won a little, and now *are in force*,
But they'll find that it soon will return to its source :
The knowing ones watch them, and give them their fill,
And they'll soon be reduced to discounting their bill.

. . . .

In fine, ev'ry object of popular fame,
Old hens, youthful chickens and cocks of the game,
Though distant, I ever shall keep you in view ;
For all my enjoyments were centred in you.
To A. B.'s and Bailiff's I waft a sad tear ;
For I know they have found me a friend that was *dear* ;
And the Bill-doers, too, who have fleeced Johnny Raw,
And, lastly, the Jem'men who *follow* the law.
To the tradesmen who tick, a remembrance most kind,
I thus send, and assure them that Fortune is blind.
This truth is a sad one ; I've learn'd it too late ;
But 'twill serve those, who now may take heed from my fate :
For the purses of others, 'tis pretty well known,
I look'd too, but ne'er had an *eye* to my own ;
For which my Annuitants sternly refuse
My freedom, and, thereby have *narrowed my views.*
    Time was, when so splendid, so gay, debonair,
I've had of these vermin a brace at my chair,
The slaves of my chamber, the shades at my doors,
Subservient, and bowing obedience by scores ;
For, *soit dit en passant*, when ruin'd's a rake,
The greater's the plunder his liv'rymen make :

> Then, the produce of filching, to noble in need,
> Is lent out on annuity, mortgage, or deed :
> So, the Peer, or the Commoner going to rack,
> May sit with his Creditor stuck at his back,
> Unconscious, howe'er, of so monstrous a bore,
> The effects of a C--rp—w, a S—dl—y, or M—re,
> Who the *parties* procure, 'mongst such miscreant trash ;
> For nothing's degrading in touching the cash—
> A pound is the same, both in value and weight,
> Though it came from the basest, or first in the State.
> I grieve, whilst I think of the years which have flown,
> Of the thousands I've squandered, the pleasures I've known,
> Of the many occasions, which fortune has cast
> In my way to be rich, which I slighted as fast—
> How oft', independent I might have retired
> With enough to live happy—nay, more than required :
> But Greeks are like Cyprians, and Fate has decreed
> That they both should spend fortunes, and perish in need ;
> That their treasures, with dreams of enchantment, should pass,
> And leave them no solace, except from the—glass ;
> That, at length, youth and beauty, good luck, and foul play,
> Should all thrive a season—then vanish away."

This pamphlet, which has a companion called " The Pigeons," gives a very curious list of the most fashionable gaming houses in existence in 1817.

" Of *hells* in general, it may be said that they are *infernally* productive, since Mr T—l—r finds that the banking business is nothing compared to these money mills, and since so many fortunes have been made from them. Who would think that a man could *rise* from one of these *lower regions* to a seat in Parliament ? or that high military rank could be purchased by ' The Colour's red '—' Gentlemen, make your game ! '

Major-General R——w, M.P., thus got his high promotion and his seat in the British Senate ; for his papa was *n'importe* ; but, progressively (and in a very odd way too), he got a little money, which, placing in a hell of which he was proprietor, he soon purchased an estate, and bought his son on in the army. Many other instances, too tedious to mention, have occurred of fortune thus made.

By a house of fashionable resort being called a club-house, the proprietors are enabled to exclude *wolves in sheep's clothing*, *i.e.* spies and informers ; for, by taking a mere trifle for a subscription, you get a knowledge of the subscriber, whether a *good man and true, or not* ; and, being entered in a book—before he can *turn over a new leaf*, he may be *turned to* good account.

Where the houses are not really, or apparently, club-houses, large sums are often paid to police officers, as well as to more imposing informers, who contrive to introduce themselves.   Bob Holloway pretty well knew this, as he was, literally, in the pay of all of them, of which more may be said in time and place.   Hush money varies according to the magnitude of the concern, from £250 to £1000 per annum.

No. 77 ST JAMES'S STREET.

NICK-NAMED THE TWO SEVENS.

Firm: Messrs T. C. C. T.

Here is a *rouge et noir* table ; the best possible treatment may be depended upon, as well as great civility and great circumspection in not lending money but to well-known people.   The *firm* attends very constantly, and a certain lawyer watches most attentively the transactions of the house.   The bank won't set you above £50 ; this is the common plan ; and it gives a decided advantage to the bank, as the loser has less chance of bringing himself back than if play was unlimited, as in France.   Upon the whole, the French first-rate gaming-houses beat our hells hollow, and they are carried on upon a much more extensive, handsome, and attractive plan : but 77 has that

'Within which far surpasseth show.'—*Hamlet.*

They are scurvy about refreshments here, and very apt to grumble if a customer have a run of luck.   On the other hand, however, a Prussian Officer, not very long ago, made a devil of a row about losing a very large sum, but all in vain.

Cerberus, who waits at the door, has a particularly watchful eye and a rare nose for a police officer. Mistakes, however, have occurred.

The produce of this bank (which Paddy B—— calls the Devil's Exchequer, whence you get neither principal nor interest), furnishes carriages, town and country houses, and all the luxuries of life: and may, perhaps, one day send a Member to Parliament or a General to the field, like Mrs R——w's concern; no house can have a better chance, as no house is better situated for the purpose. We would, however, advise the dealer to be less slovenly and liable to mistake than he is. The house is now shut up.

———

Opposite this house is a hazard table, which never opens until midnight, and is attended by the ultra royalists and officers of all the regiments of guards, horse and foot, besides decided amateurs.

———

BENNET STREET, ST JAMES'S.

CORNER HOUSE—RED BAIZE DOOR—*called* A CLUB HOUSE.

Firm : Messrs Fielder, Miller and Carlos. Formerly Fielder, Roubel, Miller and Co.

This is what is called a topping house, where high rank and title resort. We mentioned in the poem the luck of a certain Duke's son there; and, of late, there has been a lucky run in favour of the frequenters of the bank—but *lauda finem.* Its crisis has arrived.

The noble Marquess, on the night that he lost the money at No. 40 which was closed against him, went full charged with the Tuscan grape, and attacked poor Fielder, *vi et pugnis*, and, at length, was necessitated to leave this house also.

Here, all things are in a very high style, served on plate, et cetera. It is supposed that the *customer's specie* is melted down to furnish this luxury, which is reversing the ordinary plan : it is, commonly, the family plate which is melted by the gamester into specie ; but here it is the current coin which is molten and shaped into salvers, waiters, &c. This is, however, all in the way of business ; for we have heard of parson's wives having silk gowns made out of burial scarves, and we know a presbyterian minister who has converted mourning rings into a splendid piece of plate. Therefore, why should not these conveyancers of property, convey a portion into their wives and mistress's pockets, or *ridicules*, and transform guineas into gold snuff boxes ; or crowns, &c., into a service of plate?

The receipts of these houses are immense : We know the wife of a proprietor of a hell, not an hundred miles from St James's Palace, who was so majestic in her deportment, and so magnificent in her attire, that she gained the name of *Proserpine.*

The neighbourhood of Bennet Street is very convenient : if a pigeon be refused admittance on the score of not being known, and receive the *stale answer*—' Sir, this house is only open to the gentlemen of the Club,' he has only to *go down* St James's Street into the Square or to Pall Mall, and he will find accommodation all the way : the descent is *easy* even to the most intoxicated dandy or guardsman, who will experience the truth of the '*facilis descensus Averni.*'

No. 10 ST JAMES'S SQUARE.

A *low* HOUSE, HUMOUROUSLY CALLED *the Pigeon hole.*

Firm : Abbot Watson, Davies, Fearlove, Leach, and Holdsworth.

This snug little *trap* is doing remarkably well. *Fama volat,* that it has netted thirty thousand within twelve months. Whether the exact sum, in so very small a time be true or not, we cannot pretend to say ; but we know that a great deal of work is done there, and it is said to have divided twenty-seven thousand in the half-year ending Midsummer 1817.

A certain little doctor is a great friend (we do not say a decoy) to the house, and, of course, a great favourite. There are many links to this chain ; and a good bill would be done there, or an I.O.U. taken from *gem'men* of respectability.

There is a *littleness* about the concern, both outside and inside ; and your topping Greeks prefer a larger scale of establishment. The firm, notwithstanding, goes on slow and sure ; and there is no saying what they may realise with time, brisk trade and good customers, although great complaints are made of emigrations to France, the Insolvent Act, the want of *honour* in the young men of the present day, and, *especially, of our disclosures of their mysteries.* The north country dialect is here spoken in perfection.

One of the firm is *Abbot*, of a religious establishment of a somewhat different kind. It is a *nunnery*, to which confessors are, of course, admitted at the usual hours, on the terms, to use a sporting phrase, of play, or pay. This Abbot is said to be worth nearly a hundred thousand pounds. 'Two strings to my bow' is his suitable motto, for he has a wife and family also.

He is more *parsimonious* than abstemious, as befits the order of which he is the worthy principal, and of which we shall furnish a ludicrous instance. He once had particular occasion for a sovereign. Now, how could he save his money ? He was extricated by a most delightful thought, and he, accordingly, sat down to play against his own firm for *one pound*. Oh ! what a slippery jade is Fortune ! Luck was against him, and he rose IN DEBT to the bank, little short of £500. His junior partners, however, most liberally (it is said) took the entire case into their serious consideration, and FORGAVE HIM THE DEBT ! What other house can produce an instance of such splendid munificence ? —Lieut. N——g, R.N., has lately extracted from the house above £2000. They would almost as soon see the devil as the lieutenant, for Fortune has never deserted him hitherto :—but, even this, like a fire to insurance offices, or a large prize in a lottery, is not without its good effects! It is, after all, baiting with sprats to catch salmon. We are happy to find that this officer has been so prudent as to retire on his good luck!

To Mr Holdsworth, quitting a neighbouring hell under more respectable circumstances, pocketing a trifle of what is so easily gained, can, he thinks, be no very great harm. However, it now became absolutely necessary that he should do business on his own account, when circumstances utterly prevented his doing it on the account of others. Papa Leach advanced the needful, and he is, as we see, one of this firm.

Perhaps Mr Watson may have some recollection, however imperfect, of Messrs Crook and Co., of York Street, Covent Garden, his old masters. We may, probably, at a future opportunity, assist the elucidation of some occurrences in that quarter. We believe that Mr Crook never speaks of him with any particular respect! It was here that Mr L——p D——s lately won nearly £5000 of Crockford, Kelly, Lavisne, &c. It is a great chance if they have not obtained their revenge ere this.

A singular escape was recently sustained here by Major A——y. He is not only a man of mettle, but of *metal*; in plain English, he has money, and was allowed partial success, *pour encourager les autres*. We only *suppose* that arrangements were made for his next appearance. All were silent and ready. The anxious moment arrived, St James's clock struck nine,—the customary signal to begin,—yet he had not arrived : therefore, it was thought advisable to commence operations. The company loudly expressed impatience and offence at waiting for anyone. The house conceded, and lo! the cards were dealt—when, to the astonishment and dismay of the company, there were *fifteen trente et un et après*, in one deal! wonderful! mysterious chance! The Major entered at this critical moment, and took out his well-stored pocket-book ; but, when he learnt what had happened, and saw his narrow escape, he coolly returned it to his pocket, saying, as he retired, ' I will never enter a house where such a *chance* has happened ! ! ' We need not be surprised at the sum which THIS firm is said to have cleared.

They affect to carry their heads high, and to despise common menaces, saying, that THEY have the countenance of the Hon. Messrs ——, sons of a high and most esteemed legal character.

MRS LEACH'S, No. 6 KING STREET, ST JAMES'S.

Is a particularly snug and quiet shop, and the name of the proprietor is singularly appropriate. This concern is suspended.

THE ELDER DAVIS, No. 10 KING STREET, ST JAMES'S.

Is but a small affair, recently opened. It gets on swimmingly.

No. 40 PALL MALL.

Firm : Messrs Roubel, Fuller and Hewetson. Formerly Roubel, Fielder, Miller and Co.

Parlez moi de cela ! a Frenchman would say directly on entering this establishment. It is more *à la Française*, and, of course, more of a gambling house than any of the others. The firm are good judges of these matters, and *do things* in very good form.

There is great variety ; and the addresses of some lovely frail ones may be had. This is an equal advantage to Greek and Pigeon—*Tros Tyrius ve.* Besides the ' sprightly dance they so dearly love,' dull Sunday don't stand in their way as in other places. Here, also, they have borrowed from the Continental manners.

This concern is a thriving one, although a prodigious hoax was practised on them the year before last, when thieves, in the characters of police officers, led on by an 'alien' disguised in the habiliments of officers of the foot guards, introduced themselves, and carried off all the cash, to the great discomfiture of the party, and to the alarm of the respectable visitors there assembled. Colonel N——g went off like a shot ; many forgot to *take their change* ; and some young bloods were thought to have taken more than their change : it was a most delicious scamper. The Argus-eyed attendants have been more vigilant ever since ; and a dark-looking man in a great-coat, or other suspicious habit, is very much watched.

We felicitate the town on this establishment : it is the most attractive to the Greeks, and the most expeditive to the pigeon who wishes to be soon *done*; for what will not women, play, and good cheer effect ? Here, if a man escape one way, he must be sure to fall another ; and, it may be observed, that the adventurous youth may tell his tale in a small compass—

'Incidit in Scyllam, cupiens vitare Charybdim.'

We hear that something of a schism exists among the proprietors of this house. It is too *good* a thing, however, to break up. While on this subject, we would ask Mr Miller, whether he and George Shade, the printer, did not bamboozle —— and —— and —— and —— out of a round sum, on the suppression of a certain pamphlet ?

The Lisle Street, Panton Street, and Covent Garden *hells* are *below* notice, compared to those foregoing ones, so near the Court, and enjoying such *deserved* celebrity.

---

71 PALL MALL.

Firm : Taylor, Phillips, Lowe and Fielder.

The ex-banker of Southwark, we apprehend, finds his connection with Mr Phillips more lucrative than that with

Sir M. B———.   Much might have been said on this establishment, but we have our reasons for not entering into details at present.   Mr Phillips has been abroad, and, consequently, gives himself the airs of a travelled man, sets up for an *homme d'esprit*, fancies himself clever, and thinks he may be MIS*taken* for a gentleman.

> 'Oh! formose puer, nimium te crede colori!'

We have not done with you.   We remember Sir John Lade.   Of Captain Lowe, we can only say, that he deserves a better fate.

SUNDAY HOUSES.

Our moral readers may start at the designation of this department; yet common sense will tell them that, as the Sunday Houses are but few, their profits must be the greater.   Don't tell me about religion, morality, decorum, etc.   Those who hear *gentlemen* express themselves in these sinks of corruption, will at once discover that they are men of the world, who can adapt their conversation to their hearers.   First under this head is

77 JERMYN STREET.

George Smith, George Pope and Co.

The scenes which nightly occur at this house, beggar all description.   It is a hazard table, where the chances are little in favour of the uninitiated player.   The first proprietor is low in stature as in breeding, a corpulent, self-sufficient, strutting, coxcombical, irreligious prig.   Mr P. is a respectable, decent, modest personage enough in his way.   He is humble, and is forced to succumb to the other, who is the monied partner.   Many tradesmen, broken, breaking, or in the *right way*, honour this house with their presence.   This house, not being large enough for its trade, the proprietors have opened another in St James's Street.

OLDFIELD, BENNET AND CO.,

27 *Bury Street.*

Mr Oldfield is not a well-proportioned man. He has red hair, and soon betrays his dunghill origin. He is a pragmatical, bloated, officious, flippant coxcomb, with the *tout-ensemble* of a waiter.

At the Sunday houses, Mr Kelly, proprietor of the public rooms at Cheltenham, which are not sufficient for him, is a steady hand, and, being a stout stentor of an Hibernian, keeps all his comrades in great awe. He, like Lord Y——, frequently plays by deputy ; but that is only for small sums. However, like the bear in the boat of Gay—

> '—— He thought there might be picking
> Even in the breast bone of a chicken.'

Bennet of Jermyn Street is tall and robust, with black hair and eyes, and a rather blue beard ; and, as for Crockford, ' Do you know me ? Excellent well ! You're a fishmonger.' "

CHAPTER VIII

À propos of Crockford, or Crockey, as he was familiarly called, his was perhaps the most celebrated gambling house in London, and deserves especial mention. It was on the site now occupied by the Devonshire Club, No. 50 St James's Street.

William Crockford was born in 1775, his father being a fishmonger in a small way of business, having a shop adjoining Temple Bar, which was pulled down in 1846. His father dying when he was young, the business was carried on, first by his mother, and afterwards by himself, but he soon took to betting and gambling, became a proficient at cards, and was more particularly skilled in the games of whist, piquet and cribbage ; he frequented the better kind of sporting houses in the neighbourhood of St James's market, where the latter game, more especially, was much played, and for large sums, by opulent tradesmen and others. He made some money at gambling, became connected with a gaming house in King Street, St James's, and then he turned his attention to horse racing ; frequenting Tattersalls as a bookmaker, and becoming the owner of race horses. He had a splendid mansion and grounds at Newmarket, where he trained his stud, and at one time owned the celebrated horse Sultan, the sire of Bay Middleton, who won the Derby in 1836. But the roguery at Newmarket was too much even for him, and he sold his racing stud, and confined himself to his London businesses. About this time he is metrically described in a little pamphlet called "Leg-

giana," which described the *Legs* who used to frequent The
Sun tavern in Jermyn Street.

> "Seated within the box, to window nearest,
> See *Crocky*, richest, cunningest, and queerest
> Of all the motley group that here assemble
> To sport their blunt, chaff, blackguard and dissemble ;
> Who live (as slang has termed it) on the mace,
> Tho' *Crocky's* heavy pull is, now, *deuce ace.*
> His wine, or grog, as may be, placed before him,
> And looking stupid as his mother bore him,
> For *Crock*, tho' skilful in his betting duty,
> Is not, 'twill be allowed, the greatest beauty ;
> Nor does his *mug* (we mean no disrespect)
> Exhibit outward sign of intellect ;
> In other words, old *Crocky's* chubby face
> Bespeaks not inward store of mental grace ;
> Besides, each night, he's drunk as any lord,
> And clips his mother English every word.
> His head, howe'er, tho' thick to chance beholders,
> Is screw'd right well upon his brawny shoulders ;
> He's quick as thought, and ripe at calculation,
> Malgrè the drink's most potent visitation.
> His pencil, list, and betting book on table,
> His wits at work, as hard as he is able,
> His odds matur'd, at scarce a moment's pains,
> Out pops the offspring of his ready brains,
> In some enormous, captivating wager,
> 'Gainst one horse winning *Derby*, *Oaks* and *Leger.*
> The bait is tak'n by some astonished wight,
> Who chuckles, thinking it a glorious bite,
> Nor takes the pains the figures o'er to run,
> And see, by calculation, that *he's done* ;
> While *Crocky* books it, cash, *for certain, won.*
> And why, forsooth, is *Crocky* to be blamed
> More than those legs who're *honourable* named,
> Whose inclination is plain sense to jockey,
> But who lack brains to *work the pull* like *Crocky*?
> Who, by the way, gives vast accommodation,
> Nor bothers any one by litigation.
> And, if a bet you'd have, you've nought to do,
> But give it *Crock*, and, with it, *sovereigns two* ;
> You'll quickly, if you win it, touch the treasure,
> For *Crock* (unlike some legs) dubs up with pleasure."

Crockford was indicted on several occasions, and by different persons, for his share in the nuisance of the public gaming-house in King Street; but his policy always led him to a settlement of the matter with the prosecutor, in preference to the risk of imprisonment and the treadmill.

On one occasion an indictment was preferred, and a true bill found against him and others, for keeping the before-mentioned house; and it was not without difficulty and delay, creative of direful alarm, that the matter could be arranged so as to prevent the parties being brought to trial.

The prosecutor was a person known as Baron d'A——, who formerly held a commission in the German Legion. This gentleman had been desperate, and, of course, unfortunate in his speculation at *rouge et noir*; and, at last, lost not only his pay, but the proceeds of the sale of his commission. Thus reduced, he became equally desperate in determination, and occasionally made demands and levied contributions from the parties who had won from him, but, compliance with such demands becoming less frequent and less willing, he resorted to the process of indictment, and made Crockford one of the objects of his attack. On the true bill being found, Crockford put in the necessary bail; between the period of which and the day appointed for trial, communication was opened with the baron, with a view to amicable settlement and non-appearance of the prosecutor on the day of trial; but in the negotiation Crockford's party relied too much on the poverty and distress of the baron, believing that the griping hand of necessity would oblige him to accept any offered sum to relieve his wants. Under such belief an inconsiderable amount was tendered, but refused. The baron had, fortunately for him, met with a shrewd adviser, who persuaded him to hold out against any overtures short of a handsome consideration; and he did so, notwithstanding the fact that a considerable advance had been made on the original sum offered to him.

The eve of trial approached, and Crockford's alarm was great. At length came the eventful day of his appearance at Clerkenwell Sessions. What was to be done? Incarceration and hard labour stared him in the face, and with them all the evil consequences connected with his absence from his newly established club.

In this dilemma he sought the advice and active service of Guy, his principal acting man in St James's Street. This man accompanied Crockford to the scene of trial, and, discovering the baron in the precinct of the Court, contrived to get into friendly conversation with him, a scheme which led to some judicious hints on the impolicy of his longer holding out against the liberal offer which he (Guy) had now the authority to make from Crockford. Fortunately for the latter the indictment was low down in the list of the day's business, and this gave opportunity to Guy to proceed more leisurely in his designs. He prevailed on the baron to accompany him to a tavern in the neighbourhood, and there, under the influence of copious draughts of wine, an arrangement was ultimately effected. The proposal, once entertained by the baron, was not left to the chance of change, nor was the baron permitted to consult with his adviser in the matter; time was precious, the cause was approaching its hearing, and at this crisis Guy called a coach, took from his pocket a tempting sum, hurried the baron into the vehicle, gave him the money, and never left him until he had seen him on board a vessel bound for a foreign country.

At the commencement of the season 1821-22, luck went against Crockford's gaming establishment, and night after night their capital decreased, so that, at last, it was with difficulty they could supply the funds requisite for the night's bank. One night, their last £5000 was scraped together, and they were all on wires; for an hour after play had commenced £3000 had flown away. Crockford could stand it no longer; he left the house, meditating whether he should hang or drown himself: but scarcely was his back turned than the run of luck changed, and, within two hours, the bank had not only recovered their night's loss, but a good round sum besides. For the remainder of the season Fortune was in their favour, and, at its close, the proprietors had netted over £200,000.

Crockford began building his new club house in St James's Street in 1827, and workmen were engaged on it day and night. A huge ice house was dug which so affected the Guard's club house, which adjoined the northern end of Crockford's premises, that one entire side of it fell with a crash, leaving the entire interior completely exposed to the public gaze. There are two *bon môts* on the subject, preserved.

> " ' What can the workmen be about ?
> Do, Crockford, let the secret out,
> Why thus our houses fall.
> Quoth he, ' Since folks are out of town,
> I find it better to pull down,
> Than have no *pull at all.*' "

> " See, passenger, at Crockford's high behest,
> *Red coats* by *black legs* ousted from their nest ;
> The arts of peace o'ermatching reckless war,
> And gallant *rouge* outdone by wily *noir.*"

The Club was opened in the latter part of 1827 with a great flourish of trumpets, and cards to view, which were eagerly sought after by the *élite*. *The Times* of 1st Jan. 1828 gives an account of the royal displeasure at this Club, which comes extremely *à propos* from the unsullied lips of George IV. "CROCKFORD'S HELL. The establishment of the Pandemonium in St James's, under the entire superintendence of the fishmonger and his unblushing patronizers, lately called forth the opinion of the highest personage in the kingdom, who expressed himself in a manner which reflected the utmost credit on his head and heart. A Nobleman of some standing at Court, in answer to a question from his royal master, denied, in the most unequivocal way, having become a subscriber to this splendid temple of vice. The monarch evinced his satisfaction at the intelligence, and, in his usual nervous style, denounced such infamous receptacles for plunder, as not only a disgrace to the country at large, but the age in which we live."

The number of members belonging to the Club was from 1000 to 1200, exclusive of the privilege, or right of entrée permitted to ambassadors and foreigners of distinction during their diplomatic sojourn, or temporary visit, to this country, and the Duke of Wellington, although he did not gamble, was one of the earliest members. The annual subscription was twenty-five pounds, and, for this, the members had the most luxurious club of its time, with wines and viands at a very low rate, although the latter were presided over by the celebrated *chef*, Ude, to whom Crockford paid a salary of £1200! The *Annual Register*, for 1834, tells a very amusing story of Ude in connection with Crockford's Club.

"On July 25 M. Eustache Ude, the celebrated French cook, appeared at Bow Street on a summons at the suit of the Marquess of Queensberry, for unlawfully disposing of certain birds called 'red game,' between the 19th of March and the 1st of August, contrary to the provisions of the Game Laws.

"Sir Roger Griesley deposed that he was a member of Crockford's Club House, and one of the managing committee of that establishment. The defendant was cook there, and, on the 19th of June, witness dined at the Club house, and saw grouse served in the room, but did not partake of it.

"*M. Ude :* Vell, my dear Sare Rojer, vat is all dis to me? Certainement you must know dat I don't know vat de devil goes up into de dining room. How de devil can I tell veder black game, or vite game, or red game go up to de dining room? Dere is plenty of game always go on in de house, but dat is nothing to me. My only business is to cook for de palates of dose who like de game.

Sir Roger Griesley : I really don't know what, in common justice, M. Ude can have to do in this matter. He is the cook of the establishment, certainly, but he only prepares what is ordered. The Committee order the things, and he provides according to that order.

"*M. Ude :* Tank you, my dear Sare Rojer. I knew you

vould get me out of de scrape vot de noble marquis has got me into dis time.

"*Charles, Marquess of Queensberry, sworn:* I was a member of the Committee at Crockford's, but am not now. I was at Crockford's on the 19th, and dined, and grouse was served at the table.

"*M. Ude:* But, my noble friend (great laughter), as I said to my friend Sare Rojer, I know noting at all about vot vent into de room. I never sawed it at all. De orders are given to me. I send my people to de butcher, and to de poulterer, and to de fishmonger, and de tings are brought, and I command dem to be cooked, and dey are cooked, and dat is all I know about it.

"*Sir F. Roe:* Whether you know it, or not, the Act of Parliament makes you liable.

"*M. Ude:* Upon my honour dat is very hard. Ven I got de summons I remonstrated vid my Lord Alvanley, and he say, 'Oh, never mind, Ude, say dey vere pigeons, instead of grouse.' 'Ah, my lord,' say I, 'I can not do better dan dem pigeons, because dat bird is so common in dis house.' (Loud Laughter).

"*Sir F. Roè,* who appeared greatly to enjoy the scene, said he must, upon the oaths of the noble marquess and Sir Roger Griesley, convict the defendant; but he should, certainly, put the lowest penalty, namely 5s.

"*M. Ude:* Vel, I shall pay de money, but it is dam hard. Ve have always game in our house, and de poor devil of a cook have to pay de penalty for it. (Great laughter)."

The following is a contemporary description of this palatial establishment.

"On entering from the street, a magnificent vestibule and staircase break upon the view; to the right and left of the hall are reading and dining rooms. The staircase is of a sinuous form, sustained in its landing by four columns of the Doric order, above which are a series of examples of the Ionic order, forming a quadrangle with apertures to the chief apartments. Above the pillars is a covered ceiling, perforated with luminous panels of stained glass, from which springs a dome of surpassing beauty : from the dome depends a lantern containing a magnificent chandelier.

" *The State Drawing Room* next attracts attention, a most noble apartment, baffling perfect description of its beauty, but decorated in the most florid style of Louis Quatorze. The room presents a series of panels containing subjects, in the style of Watteau, from the pencil of Mr Martin, a relative of the celebrated historical painter of that name : these panels are alternated with splendid mirrors. A chandelier of exquisite workmanship hangs from the centre of the ceiling, and three large tables, beautifully carved and gilded, and covered with rich blue and crimson velvet, are placed in different parts of the room. The upholstery and decorative adjuncts are imitative of the gorgeous taste of George the Fourth. Royalty can scarcely be conceived to vie with the style and consummate splendour of this magnificent chamber.

" *The lofty and capacious Dining Room*, supported by marble pillars, and furnished in the most substantial and aristocratic style of comfort, is equal to any arrangement of the kind in the most lordly mansions.

" *The Drawing Room* is allowed to be one of the most elegant apartments in the kingdom.

" *The Sanctum Sanctorum*, or *Play Room*, is comparatively small, but handsomely furnished. In the centre of the apartment stands the *all attractive Hazard Table*, innocent and unpretending enough in its form and appearance, but fatally mischievous and destructive in its conjunctive influence with box and dice. On this table, it may, with truth, be asserted that the greater portion, if not the whole of Crockford's immense wealth was achieved ; and for this piece of plain, unassuming mahogany, he had, doubtless, a more profound veneration than for the most costly piece of furniture that ever graced a palace. This bench of business is large, and of oval shape, well stuffed, and covered with fine green cloth, marked with yellow lines, denoting the

different departments of speculation.   Round these compartments are double lines, similarly marked, for the odds, or
proportions, between what is technically known as the *main*
and *chance*.   In the centre, on each side, are indented posi-
tions for the croupiers, or persons engaged at the table in
calling the main and chance, regulating the stakes, and paying and receiving money, as the events decisive of gain and
loss occur.   Over the table is suspended a three light lamp,
conveniently shaded, so as to show its full luminous power
on the cloth, and, at the same time, to protect the eyes of
the croupiers from the light's too strong effect.   At another
part of the room is fixed a writing table, or desk, where the
Pluto of the place was wont to preside, to mete out loans on
draft or other security, and to answer all demands by successful players.   Chairs of easy make, dice boxes, bowls for
holding counters representing sums from £1 to £200, with
small hand rakes used by players to draw their counters
from any inconvenient distance on the table, may be said to
complete the furniture, machinery, and implements of this
great workshop."

It is said that during the first two seasons Crockford must
have netted about £300,000, but his expenses were heavy,
the item of dice alone (at about a guinea a pair) was £2000
per annum ; three new pairs being provided for the opening
play each night, and very often as many more called for by
players, or put down by Crockford himself with a view to
change a player's luck.

Crockford was bound by his agreement with his committee to put down a bank, or capital, of £5000, nightly,
during the sitting of Parliament, and he was not permitted
to terminate the play until a stated hour, as long as any of
that £5000 remained.

He died at his mansion in Carlton House Terrace, on
25 May 1844, aged 69.   He died a very wealthy man,
although he experienced very heavy losses in sundry speculations.   A contemporary says of him :

" The entire property amassed by Mr Crockford must

have been immense, regard being had to the fact that, exclusively of a sum of money, amounting to nearly half a million sterling, bequeathed to his widow, he is confidently reported to have distributed amongst his children, about two years ago, a sum nearly equalling, if not exceeding that amount : a circumstance not at all improbable in a man of foresight, like Mr Crockford, and one which will fully account, as well for the bequest of the whole bulk of his remaining fortune to his widow, as for such bequest being absolute, and free from all condition. In estimating the wealth acquired by Mr Crockford through the medium and success of his French hazard bank (for this was the never-failing source of gain), there must be taken into account the heavy and extravagant expenditure of the establishment in St James's Street ; his own expensive, though by no means foolishly extravagant, mode of living ; the maintenance and education of a very numerous family, the advances of money from time to time, made to fit them out and further their prospects in life ; the expense of a racing stud ; a considerable outlay in suppressing various indictments preferred against him for his former proprietorship in King Street, and the heavy losses more recently sustained by other venture and speculation. It may be fairly calculated that the certain profits of the hazard table must have embraced millions ! and some idea may be formed of the extent of evil to others consequent on such an accumulation of capital extracted from their means."

Captain Gronow [1] gives us a very graphic description of this club, drawn from the life, for he was a member thereof.

"I have alluded, in my first volume, to the high play which took place at White's and Brookes's in the olden time, and at Wattier's in the days of Brummel and the dandies. Charles Fox, George Selwyn, Lord Carlisle, Fitzpatrick, Horace Walpole, the Duke of Queensberry, and others, lost whole fortunes at faro, macao and hazard ;

[1] Reminiscences, 3 Ser.

almost the only winners, indeed, of that generation were General Scott, father-in-law of Canning, the Duke of Portland, and Lord Robert Spencer ; Lord Robert, indeed, bought the beautiful estate of Woolbidding, in Sussex, with the proceeds of his gains by keeping the bank at Brookes's.

But in the reign of George IV. a new star rose upon the horizon in the person of Mr William Crockford ; and the old-fashioned game of faro, macao and lansquenet gave place to the all-devouring thirst for the game of hazard. Crockey, when still a young man, had relinquished the peaceful trade of a fishmonger for a share in a " hell," where, with his partner Gye, he managed to win, after a sitting of twenty-four hours, the enormous sum of one hundred thousand pounds from Lords Thanet and Granville, Mr Ball Hughes, and two other gentlemen whose names I do not now remember. With this capital added to his former gains, he built the well known palace in St James's Street, where a club was established, and play organised, on a scale of magnificence and liberality hitherto unknown in Europe.

One may safely say, without exaggeration, that Crockford won the whole of the ready money of the then existing generation. As is often the case at Lord's cricket ground, the great match of the gentlemen of England against the professional players was won by the latter. It was a very hollow thing, and in a very few years twelve hundred thousand pounds were swept away by the fortunate fishmonger. He did not, however, die worth more than a sixth part of this vast sum ; the difference being swallowed up in various unlucky speculations.

No one can describe the splendour and excitement of the early days of Crockey. A supper of the most exquisite kind, prepared by the famous Ude, and accompanied by the best wines in the world, together with every luxury of the season, was furnished gratis. The members of the club included all the celebrities of England, from the Duke of Wellington, to the youngest Ensign of the Guards ; and, at the gay and festive board, which was constantly replenished from midnight to early dawn, the most brilliant sallies of wit, the most agreeable conversation, the most interesting anecdotes, interspersed with grave political discussions and acute logical reasoning on every conceivable subject, proceeded from the soldiers, scholars, statesmen, poets and men of pleasure, who, when the 'house was up,' and balls and parties at an end, delighted to finish their evening with a little supper, and a good deal of hazard at old Crockey's. The tone of the club was most excellent. A most gentlemanlike feeling prevailed, and none of the rudeness, familiarity and ill breeding which disgrace some of the minor clubs of the present day, would have been tolerated for a moment.

" Though not many years have elapsed since the time of which I write, the supper table had a very different appearance from what it would present, did the club now exist. Beards were completely unknown, and the rare mustachios were only worn by officers of the Household Brigade, or hussar regiments. Stiff white neckcloths, blue coats and brass buttons, rather short waisted white waistcoats, and tremendously embroidered shirt fronts, with gorgeous studs of great value, were considered the right thing. A late deservedly popular Colonel in the Guards used to give Storr & Mortimer £25 a year, to furnish him with a new set of studs every Saturday night during the London season.

" The great foreign diplomatists, Prince Talleyrand, Count Pozzo di Borgo, General Alava, the Duke of Palmella, Prince Esterhazy, the French, Russian, Spanish, Portuguese, and Austrian ambassadors, and all persons of distinction and eminence who arrived in England, belonged to Crockford's as a matter of course ; but many rued the day when they became members of that fascinating but dangerous *coterie*. The great Duke himself, always rather a friend of the dandies, did not disdain to appear now and then at this charming club ; whilst the late Lord Raglan, Lord Anglesey, Sir Hussey Vivian, and many more of our Peninsula and

Waterloo heroes, were constant visitors. The two great novelists of the day, who have since become great statesmen, Disraeli and Bulwer Lytton, displayed at that brilliant supper-table, the one his sable, the other his auburn curls ; there Horace Twiss made proof of an appetite, and Edward Montague of a thirst, which astonished all beholders ; whilst the bitter jests of Sir Joseph Copley, Colonel Armstrong, and John Wilson Croker, and the brilliant wit of Alvanley, were the delight of all present, and their *bon mots* were the next day retailed all over England.

"In the play-room might be heard the clear ringing voice of that agreeable reprobate, Tom Duncombe, as he cheerfully called 'Seven,' and the powerful hand of the vigorous Sefton in throwing for a ten. There might be noted the scientific dribbling of a four by 'King' Allen, the tremendous backing of nines and fives by Ball Hughes and Auriol, the enormous stakes played for by Lords Lichfield and Chesterfield, George Payne, Sir St Vincent Cotton, D'Orsay, and George Anson, and, above all, the gentlemanly bearing and calm and unmoved demeanour, under losses or gains, of all the men of that generation.

"The old fishmonger himself, seated snug and sly at his desk in the corner of the room, watchful as the dragon that guarded the golden apples of the Hesperides, would only give credit to good and approved signatures. Who that ever entered that dangerous little room can ever forget the large green table, with the croupiers, Page, Darking, and Bacon, with their suave manners, sleek appearance, stiff white neck cloths, and the almost miraculous quickness and dexterity with which they swept away the money of the unfortunate punters when the fatal cry of 'Deuce ace,' 'Aces,' or 'Sixes out,' was heard in answer to the caster's bold cry of 'Seven,' or 'Nine,' or 'Five's the main.'

"*O noctes cœnæque deûm !* but the brightest medal has its reverse, and after all the wit and gaiety and excitement of the night, how disagreeable the waking up, and how very unpleasant the sight of the little card, with its numerous figures marked down on the debtor side in the fine bold hand of Mr Page. Alas, poor Crockey's! shorn of its former glory, has become a sort of refuge for the destitute, a cheap dining-house.[1] How are the mighty fallen! Irish buckeens, spring captains, 'welchers' from Newmarket, and suspicious looking foreigners, may be seen swaggering after dinner through the marble halls, and up that gorgeous staircase where once the chivalry of England loved to congregate; and those who remember Crockford's in all its glory, cast, as they pass, a look of unavailing regret at its dingy walls, with many a sigh to the memory of the pleasant days they passed there, and the gay companions and noble gentlemen who have long since gone to their last home."

One more story about Crockford's, told by Sir George Chetwynd,[2] and I have done with this subject. Speaking of Mr George Payne, he says: "Many were the stories he told of his early life, of his hunting, of the enormous sum he lost on the Leger before he came of age, of his never seeing daylight for a whole week in one winter, owing to being challenged by a friend to play a certain number of games at écarté, which resulted in their playing every night for six days till seven o'clock in the morning. Of course it was dark then at that season, and he used not to get up till 3.30 to 4 o'clock. He was fond of describing Crockford's when the conversation turned on hazard or cards, and used to speak of the lavish way in which the old fishmonger supplied his guests (or victims) with the finest hot-house peaches, grapes, and every conceivable delicacy that could be obtained for money, and all this gratis. A number of men who did not care to play at hazard, used purposely to lose a hundred or two a year at the tables, to have the pleasure of dining and supping with their friends, who all flocked to the magnificent rooms, which, at night, presented the appearance of a

---

[1] After Crockford's death the club-house was sold. It was re-decorated in 1849, and opened as "The Military, Naval, and County Service Club," but this only lasted till 1851, when it was turned into a dining-house, called the "Wellington."

[2] "Racing Reminiscences." Lon. 1891.

luxurious club. Mr Payne used to narrate that, after dinner, he would sometimes stroll round there early, and, finding hardly anyone there except Crockford at his desk, used to sit down and play a game of backgammon with him, both being fine players."

CHAPTER IX

THE West End of London literally swarmed with gambling houses, for the most part of a very different description from Crockford's, as may be seen by the two following quotations from *The Times*, Jan. 24, 1833 :—

" THE HELLS IN THE QUADRANT.

" Those seats of vice (the gaming-houses) which for some time past have existed in the Quadrant, appear to be done up, as, since Saturday, not one of them has been opened. Since the five persons have been apprehended, the visitors have been extremely scarce ; nor was their confidence restored, even by the proprietors having the chain up at the street door, coupled with a fellow's being employed at each of the hells, to patrol before the different establishments, for the purpose of giving the requisite information as to who sought admission into those dens of destruction. Although a very active search has been made for the purpose of ascertaining what has become of Daly, the clerk of the Athenæum Club-house, who left that establishment on the 8th instant, no trace had been found of him—one of the many lamentable cases of loss of character and ruin which overtake those who suffer themselves to be lured into those houses. Daly, who enjoyed the confidence of the whole of the members, was suddenly missed on the above day. On looking over his papers, a diary was found, from which it appeared that he had lost large sums of money at No. 60, and, as it has since been ascertained he was there on the previous day, it is supposed that he lost twenty-four £5 notes, at play, which belonged to his employers. Upon this discovery being made, some gentlemen of the Athenæum waited on the parish officers, to ascertain whether they could not put a stop to the gaming-houses. It was, however, found that it could not be done unless some person would come forward and identify those at play ; a relation of Daly accordingly went to the house and supplied the necessary proof. It was at this establishment, a few months since, the foreigners who had been fleeced made an attempt to rob the bank ; and, shortly after that, placards were posted on the walls in the neighbourhood of the Quadrant, cautioning persons from going into any of the hells, as drugged wine was invariably given to those who were going to play."

May 9th : "Three prisoners, out of six, answered to the indictment of keeping and maintaining a common gaming-house, and pleaded guilty. The prosecuting counsel, Mr Clarkson, said that the house in question was situate No. 4 Regent's Circus, six doors from the house which was lately prosecuted. He should have been able to prove that on February the 7th, 9th, 12th, and 14th last, the games of *rouge et noir* and *roulette* were played for sums varying from one sovereign to one shilling. He should also have proved that on some one, or on all those occasions, the defendants acted in the capacities of doorkeeper, banker, and waiter. He (Mr Clarkson) was informed by the officers of St James's parish, that, at the last Sessions there were twenty-seven houses of this description situate therein, and out of that number only two had been closed in the interval, but three new ones had been opened, so that the number had been increased rather than otherwise.

"Mr Phillips, for the defence, said that those houses had nothing to do with the present case. He would advise the parish officers to go to Crockford's, not far distant from the house in question, where they would find lords and peers of the realm at play.

"The bench sentenced two of the prisoners to three months', and one to fourteen days' imprisonment, in the House of Correction, whilst the bail of one who did not appear was estreated."

Of the hells in London in 1833, we get a very fair notion in a long article in *Fraser's Magazine* for August of that year, from which I take the following small portion :—

"On an average, during the last twenty years, about thirty hells have been regularly open in London for the accommodation of the lowest and most vile set of hazard players. The game of hazard is the principal one played at the low houses, and is, like the characters who play it, the most desperate and ruinous of all games. The wretched men who follow this play are partial to it, because it gives a chance, from a run of good luck, to become speedily possessed of all the money on the table : no man who plays hazard ever despairs of making his fortune at some time. Such is the nature of this destructive game, that I can now point out several men, whom you see daily, who were in rags and wretchedness on Monday, and, before the termination of the week, they ride in a newly-purchased Stanhope of their own, having several thousand pounds in their possession. The few instances of such successes which, unfortunately, occur, are generally well-known, and, consequently, encourage the hopes of others, who nightly attend these places, sacrificing all considerations of life to the carrying (if it only be a few shillings) their all, every twenty-four hours, to stake in this great lottery, under the delusive hope of catching Dame Fortune, at some time, in a merry mood. Thousands annually fall, in health, fame, and fortune, by this maddening infatuation, whilst not one in a thousand finds an oasis in the desert.

"The inferior houses of play are always situated in obscure courts, or other places of retirement, and, most frequently, are kept shut up during the day as well as at night, as if unoccupied, or some appearance of trade is carried on as a blind. A back room is selected for all operations, if one can be procured sufficiently capacious for the accommodation of forty or fifty persons at one time. In the centre of the room is fixed a substantial circular table, immoveable to any power of pressure against it by the company who go to play ; a circle of inlaid white holly wood is formed in the middle of the table of about four feet diameter, and a lamp is suspended immediately over this ring.   A man, designated the Groom Porter, is mounted on a stool, with a stick in his hand, having a transverse piece of wood affixed to its end, which is used by him to rake in the dice after having been thrown out of the box by the caster (the person who throws the dice).

"The avowed profits of keeping a table of this kind is the receipt of a piece for each *box hand*,—that is, when a player wins three times successively, he pays a certain sum to the table, and there is an aperture in the table made to receive these contributions.   At the minor establishments, the price of a *box hand* varies from a shilling to half-a-crown, according to the terms on which the house is known to have been originally opened.   If there is much play, these payments produce ample profits to the keeper of the house ; but their remuneration for running the risk of keeping an unlawful table of play, is plunder.

" At all these houses, as at the higher ones, there is always a set of men who are dependent on the keepers of the house, who hang about the table like sharks for prey, waiting for those who stay late, or are inebriated, and come in towards morning to play when there are but few lookers on ; unfair means are then resorted to with impunity, and all share the plunder.   About eleven o'clock, when all honest and regular persons are preparing for rest, the play commences, the adventurers being seated around the table : one takes the box and dice, putting what he is disposed to play for into the ring marked on the table ; as soon as it is covered with a like sum, or set, as it is termed, by another person, the player calls a main, and at the same moment throws the dice ; if the number called comes up, the caster wins ; but if any other main comes uppermost on the dice the thrower takes that chance for his own, and his adversary has the one he called ; the throwing then continues, during which bets are made by others on the event until it is decided. If the caster throws deuce ace, or aces, when he first calls a main, it is said to be crabbed, and he loses ; but if he throws the number named he is said to have nicked it, and thereby wins it. Also, if he should call six or eight, and throws the double sixes he wins ; or, if seven be the number called, and eleven is thrown, it is a nick, because those chances are nicks to these mains ; which regulation is necessary to the equalisation of all the chances of this game when calling a main. The odds against any number being thrown against another varies from two to one to six to five, and, consequently, keeps all the table engaged in betting. All bets are staked, and the noise occasioned by proposing and accepting wagers is most uproarious and deafening among the low players, each having one eye on the black spots marked on the dice as they land from the box, and the other on the stakes, ready to snatch it if successful. To prevent the noise being heard in the streets, shutters, closely fitted to the window frames, are affixed, which are padded and covered with green baize : there is, invariably, an inner door placed in the passage, having an aperture in it, through which all who enter the door from the street may be viewed ; this precaution answers two purposes, it deadens the sound of noisy voices at the table and prevents surprise by the officers of justice.

" The generality of the minor gambling houses are kept by prize-fighters and other desperate characters, who bully and hector the more timid out of their money by deciding that bets have been lost, when, in fact, they have been won. Bread, cheese and beer are supplied to the players, and a glass of gin is handed, when called for, gratis. To these places thieves resort, and such other loose characters as are lost to every feeling of honesty and shame : a table of this nature in full operation is a terrific sight ; all the bad passions appertaining to the vicious propensities of mankind are portrayed on the countenances of the players.

"An assembly of the most horrible demons could not exhibit a more appalling effect; recklessness and desperation overshadow every noble trait which should enlighten the countenance of a human being. Many, in their desperation, strip themselves, on the spot, of their clothes, either to stake against money or to pledge to the table keeper for a trifle to renew their play: and many instances occur of men going home half naked, having lost their all.

"They assemble in parties of from forty to fifty persons, who probably bring, on an average, each night, from one to twenty shillings to play with. As the money is lost the players depart, if they cannot borrow or beg more; and this goes on sometimes in the winter season, for fourteen to sixteen hours in succession; so that from 100 to 140 persons may be calculated to visit one gambling table in the course of a night; and it not unfrequently happens that, ultimately, all the money brought to the table gets into the hands of one or two of the most fortunate adventurers, save that which is paid to the table for box hands; whilst the losers separate only to devise plans by which a few more shillings may be procured for the next night's play. Every man so engaged is destined either to become, by success, a more finished and mischievous gambler, or to appear at the bar of the Old Bailey, where, indeed, most of them may be said to have figured already.

"The successful players, by degrees, improve their external appearance, and obtain admission into houses of higher play, where 2s. 6d. or 3s. 4d. is demanded for the box hands. At these places silver counters are used, representing the aliquot parts of a pound; these are called *pieces*, one of which is a box hand. If success attends them in the first step of advancement, they next become initiated into Crown houses, and associate with gamblers of respectable exterior; where, if they show talents, they either become confederates in forming schemes of plunder, and in aiding establishments

to carry on their concerns in defiance of the law, or fall back
to their old station of playing *chicken hazard*, as the small)
play is designated."

And so things went on for ten years longer, until the
scandal was too grievous to be borne, and a Select Committee sat in Parliament, in 1844, on the subject of gaming.
This was principally brought about by the revelations in the
case of *Smith* v. *Bond*, which was tried before Lord Abinger
and a special jury at the Middlesex Sittings after Michaelmas Term, 1842. It was a common gaming-house case
brought under the statute of Anne (9th, c. 14), which was
enacted to repress excessive gaming.

The parish of St George's, Hanover Square, swarmed with
hells, and the efforts of the parish officers had hitherto been
unable to put them down. The play at such houses was
notoriously unfair, and the keepers had thriven in proportion
to the number and wealth of the victims they had been able
to fleece. It was therefore resolved to bring an action under
this statute, which not only prohibits excessive gaming, but
enables the loser of above £10 at a sitting, to recover treble
the amount of his losses ; or, if he does not choose to take
this course himself, any informer is enabled to sue for and
obtain the penalty, one half of which is to benefit the poor
of the parish in which the offence was committed, and the
other half is to go to the person bringing the action.

In the case tried before Lord Abinger, the gaming-house
went by the name of the Minor St James's Club-house ; but
there was not the least pretence for calling it a club ; any-
body went there to play with hardly the formality of a first
introduction. The keepers did a thriving trade, at French
Hazard chiefly, and it was proved by the plaintiff, who had
been one of the coterie who kept the table, that Mr Bredell had
lost £200, Mr Fitzroy Stanhope £50, the Marquis of Conyngham £500 on each of two separate occasions, Lord Cantalupe
£400, and other noblemen and gentlemen various sums.

An ingenious plea was put in by counsel on behalf of
Bond, the keeper of the so-called club, that the sums in

question were paid by cheques, and as a cheque is not held to be a payment in law until cashed, and as the banks at which the cheques were payable were not in the parish of St George's, Hanover Square, the offence was not completed in that parish, and the plaintiff could not recover. The Chief Baron overruled the objection, and under his direction the jury returned a verdict for the plaintiff for £3508, being treble the amount actually proved to have been lost, thus teaching a very useful lesson to the keepers of gaming-houses generally. Had Lords Conyngham and Cantalupe and Mr Stanhope come forward as witnesses, and certified to their losses on the two occasions mentioned, additional penalties would have accrued to the amount of £5820.

The Act of 1822 (3 Geo. IV., c. 114) was still in force, by which a gaming-house keeper might be imprisoned with hard labour, and the Police Act of 1839 (2 and 3 Vic., c. 47, § 48) provided that "it shall be lawful for the Commissioners, by Order in Writing, to authorize the Superintendent to enter any such House, or Room, with such Constables as shall be directed by the Commissioners to accompany him, and, if necessary, to use Force for the Purpose of effecting such Entry, whether by breaking open Doors, or otherwise, and to take into Custody all Persons who shall be found therein, and to seize and destroy all Tables and Instruments of gaming found in such House, or Premises; and, also, to seize all Monies and Securities for Money found therein, and the Owner, or Keeper of the said Gaming-House, or other person having the Care and Management thereof; and, also, every Banker, Croupier, and other Person who shall act in any manner in conducting the said Gaming-House, shall be liable to a Penalty of not more than One Hundred Pounds; or, in the discretion of the Magistrate before whom he shall be convicted of the Offence, may be committed to the House of Correction, with or without hard Labour, for a Time not more than Six Calendar Months; and, upon Conviction of any such Offender, all the Monies and Securities for Monies, which shall have been seized, as aforesaid, shall be paid to the said Receiver, to be, by him, applied towards defraying the Charge of the Police of the Metropolis ; and every Person found in such Premises, without lawful Excuse, shall be liable to a Penalty of not more than Five Pounds."

But all this legislation was of no use ; the gaming-tables continued to flourish until after the Report of the Select Committee. What they were like at that time may best be learnt by the following extract from an article in *Bentley's Magazine* for June 1844, entitled " A Fashionable Gaming-house, Confessions of a Croupier."

" The —— gaming-house, —— Street, some years ago, was kept by three well-known individuals. After passing through two lobbies you entered the play-room, which formed a *coup d'œil* of no ordinary attraction. It was a large room, richly carpeted. Two rich and massive chandeliers, suspended from the ceiling, showed the dazzling gilt and colour of the empanelled walls ; from which, at alternate distances, extended elegant mirror branches with lights. The chimney piece was furnished with a plate of glass, which reached the ceiling, the sides were concealed by falling drapery of crimson and gold, and supported by two gilt full-length figures bearing lights. At the opposite end were placed two *beaufets*, furnished with costly plate, glass, etc. In the middle was fixed the hazard table, of a long oval form, having an adumbrated lamp hanging over the centre. On the right stood the *rouge et noir* and *roulette* tables, idly placed, ' to make up a show.' Not so that on the left, for, there, stood the supper table. This was laid out with viands worthy the contemplation of an epicure, on whitest damask, in costly china, and in forms delicate and *recherché*. Everything which might court the most fastidious taste was there spread in luxuriant profusion ; game, poultry, ham, tongue, not forgetting the substantial sirloin ; lobster salads, oysters, *en outre les petites misères* ; confectionery and preserves ; creams, jellies, and pine apples. Silver candelabra lighted each end of this long and well supplied table, while the middle was reserved for the display of one of still greater magnificence, said to have been designed and executed for his Royal Highness, the late Duke of ——. It was composed of a large figure of Hercules contending with the Hydra with seven heads. This gorgeous piece of plate supported seven wax lights. Iolaus (who assisted Hercules) was, also, represented, bearing the lighted brand wherewith to staunch the blood, lest another head should spring from the wound."

This is much ; but when to this is added—

'Something, still, which prompts the eternal sigh !'

ONE THOUSAND SOVEREIGNS! a shining golden heap! and TEN THOUSAND POUNDS in notes! the reader may imagine the scene which every evening met the eye. Yes ! every evening, into a silver vase, which stood on the hazard table, were emptied ten bags, each containing one hundred sovereigns !

On some evenings, there would, perhaps, be no play, and insufferably tedious would have been the hours from eleven till three but for the relief offered by some tragi-comic incident. The London season was about to open ; the Newmarket Spring Meeting had just closed, and Tattersall's, consequently, exhibited a slight gathering. The members of Crockford's, as yet, presented a meagre attendance ; the Opera Bills announced attractive novelties, and the minor theatres promised their many marvels. In fact, the busy, bustling hive of human interests was on the move. The dormant began to stir, the watchful to speculate ; the beauty to take her promenade in the yet pale sunshine ; the invalid to snatch his walk at the meridian hour ; the gambler to devise his means of expense, and the banker-hell-keeper how to frustrate them.

It was one evening, about this period, that a party entered to try the fortune of an hour. The result of the evening's play was against the bank. One of the visitors won five hundred pounds, which, for a whim, he took away in gold.

He tied the sovereigns up in a white pocket handkerchief, threw them over his shoulder, and, in that manner, walked up St James's Street. From that night, the same party continued to visit us ; and, with occasional droppers in of ex-colonels, majors, captains, etc., we, generally, made up a table. What ! enter again, after having won five hundred pounds ! 'Oh! infatuated man,' I hear the reader exclaim. Yes ! for of all things unfathomable and absorbing, there is nothing so unfathomably deep as the desires of the human heart, when stimulated by the excitement of speculation.

For some weeks the play had been constant, and, as the season advanced, the company increased, and the money began to return to the bank. Sometimes play began late, perhaps not till after one.

Among our very constant visitors was a gallant captain. He came early, and was good to lose a hundred pounds, and satisfied to win fifty. His entrance was always met by a ready welcome.

'Here comes the gallant captain ! How are you, captain ?'

' Hearty, thank ye ! ' he replied. ' I say, how was it that my cheque was not paid this morning ? '

' Not paid ! you're joking, captain ! '

' Joking ! ' replied the captain. ' No, I'll be d—d if it is a joke.'

The captain, on the previous evening, having won, had put up his counters and wished for a fifty pound note.

' Certainly,' said one of the triumvirs, looking into the box. ' A fifty, did you say, captain ? I am sorry to say I have not got a fifty. Make it a hundred, captain. You will soon do it if you put it down a little spicy.'

' No,' rejoined the captain, ' I don't want to play any more, for I must leave town early to-morrow morning.'

' Well ; but what is to be done ? ' said the manager. Then, calling to his partner, he inquired if he had a fifty pound note for Captain ——.

' No, I have not ; but I will write a cheque for him ; that will be all the same.'

Away went the captain, as light hearted as a cricket, to sleep away the few remaining hours that intervened before another day wakes us all to our divers duties. Who has not noticed the punctuality of the banker's clerks wending their way to their daily toil. Not quite so early as these, yet not much later, did the captain doff his night gear; then made his appearance at the banker's, nothing doubting. He presents 'the bit o' writin'' 'Two twenties and ten in gold.' The clerk puts forward his attenuated fingers, examines it: a pause ensues. How can it be? The date is right, and the autograph is genuine; but there is no order to pay it.

'No order to pay it?' echoed the captain, much annoyed.

Between ourselves, the private mark was wanting: which was, perhaps, a pin hole, or not a pin hole.

On the evening I have referred to, he received counters for this cheque, and was, already, deep in the game, when the *chef* made his appearance. The above *ruse* was frequently resorted to.

It is customary to lend money to parties on cheque, or otherwise, if the applicants are considered safe. One of the visitors, who was passionately addicted to play and the turf, having lost his ready money, borrowed three hundred pounds in counters, and, having lost these also, gave a cheque for the amount; but with this condition, that it should not be sent in to his banker's in the country for some few days. No sooner, however, was his back turned than an *employé* was instructed to start off very early the following morning to get the cheque cashed; the date, which was left open, being first clapped in. The cheque was paid; and two or three nights afterwards the young gentleman came for an explanation of the circumstance, and to remonstrate. The poor *employé*, as usual, was made the scapegoat, and was roundly abused for his stupidity in not understanding that he was particularly ordered not to present it till further notice.

It was the practice, also, to present post-dated cheques, which had been refused payment, and even to sue on them. Sometimes, after an evening's play, a gentleman would find himself the winner of a couple of hundred pounds, when, all but folding up the notes, and preparing to go, he would find, to his mortification, a small account against him, of, perhaps, seventy or eighty pounds. 'Eighty pounds! impossible! there must be some mistake.' Expostulation was vain. 'It is down in the book. It is perfectly correct, you may rest assured. I pledge you my honour of this.'

Sometimes it happened that a gentleman would borrow one hundred pounds, of course in counters, on a cheque or a short bill. Perhaps he might win thirty or forty pounds, in which case, the one hundred pounds in counters would be taken from him and his cheque returned, and he would be left to do his best with the small capital remaining to him, with the privilege of renewing the transaction, should he lose it. Counters, so borrowed, were not allowed to be lent to a friend.

Nevertheless, it may seem not a bad 'hedge,' technically speaking, to have the opportunity of borrowing hundred after hundred, as some people would do, till a hand came off. I have known persons to come in without a penny, and declare the Caster, in or out, ten pounds, and losing the bet, would ask for a hundred pounds, would receive it and lose it, and receive in the same way to the amount of six or seven hundred pounds, and then would declare that they would not pay one farthing unless accommodated with another hundred. I have known a man of high rank lose to the amount of fourteen hundred pounds, on account, which, under the circumstances, his lordship had more sense than to pay. But, for the bold style, I will quote a city wine merchant. Having lost his cash, he requested a hundred pounds, which he received; he then asked for another, which he also received. He demanded another! After a few words, and a reference to a friend then at the table, this, too, was given to him, and a cheque for £300

was received for the advance made. It so happened that
the third hundred was lost also. He, then, peremptorily
demanded more, and, upon being refused, he requested to
see the cheque, disputing the amount, which being handed
to him, he immediately tore it to pieces, and left the room.

.   .   .   .   .   .

It may be thought that a gentleman who has lost above
a thousand pounds in a gaming-house may have the right
of *entrée* by prescription. Nothing is more unlike the fact.
From the height of his prosperity to its declension, every
occultation in his course is noted with the nicest observation ; for instance, playing for lower stakes, a more febrile
excitement when losing, occasionally borrowing of a friend,
a cheque not punctually paid ; and, finally, a small sum
borrowed of the bank, to enable him to take up a bill under
a very pressing emergency. These are the little circumstances which lead to his ultimate exclusion. On some fine
evening during the ensuing season, he calls, thinking to be
admitted as heretofore ; but he is stopped at the first door
with the ready excuse, that 'there is nothing doing.' On
the next call, he is told 'there is no play going on.'

'No play ? So you said the last time I called ; and I
have since understood from a friend that there was play.
Let me in ; I want to see the manager.'

'He is not in, sir.'

'Oh, very well, I shall take some other opportunity of
seeing him.'

When he does see the *chef*, the latter expresses most
sincere regret at the occurrence, and makes a most specious
promise to have the interdict removed. Thus assured, who
is now to oppose his entrance ? Not the porter, surely !
Yes ; the very same person still insists that the great man
is not within ; that he knows nothing about the explanation
given, and, therefore, cannot admit him. Thus repulsed, the
applicant murmurs a threat about not paying, and thus ends
the matter."

CHAPTER X

SUCH, then, was gambling, when the Select Committee on gaming sat in 1844, and Mr (afterwards Sir) Richard Mayne, in his evidence, shows the craftiness of the gaming-house keepers, and the difficulties of the police in obtaining a conviction.   He says :—

"Superintendent Baker was the Superintendent who entered all those houses.   With the permission of the Committee, I will read his report, in which he states the difficulties he has met with : 'I beg, most respectfully, to lay before the Commissioners a few observations for their consideration, being extremely anxious that something more should be done respecting the gaming-houses, to put them down, which are the cause of so many young men's ruin, and, at the same time, show to the Commissioners the difficulties I have to contend with, before an entry can be effected ; from the reluctance of the housekeepers to make the required affidavits, from not wishing to have their names brought forward in such matters ; also, from the great difficulty in gaining an entrance to a gaming-house, from their extreme caution and watchfulness, besides the strength of their doors and fastenings, which gives them ample time to remove any implement of gaming from the premises : their vigilance is such that it is impossible to obtain an entry for the purpose of seeing play, unless treachery is used with some of the players, which is attended by danger and great expense.   On the slightest alarm, the cloths, which are thrown loose over a common table, &c., are, in one moment, removed, and secreted about the persons of the keepers, &c.; and, as the present law stands, the police are not empowered to search them at all : there are no complaints from the housekeepers respecting the gaming-houses, and, in every instance of putting them down, the police have been obliged almost to compel them to go to the police court to swear to the necessary affidavits ; such has been their reluctance.   As the present law stands, before I can enter a gaming-house with safety, I am obliged to go through the following forms : 1st, to make such inquiry as to leave no doubt that gaming is carried on in a house ; 2nd, to make a report of the circumstance to the Commissioners ; 3rd, to show the said report to the housekeepers residing in the parish and neighbourhood where the house is situated, and the offence carried on, for them to make the necessary affidavits ; 4th, to prepare affidavits for the house-keepers to sign, in the presence of the magistrates ; 5th, to make a report of the same to the Commissioners when sworn to ; 6th, to make out the Commissioners' warrant for me and the police under my command to enter ; 7th, to endeavour, if possible, to get an officer in disguise into the gaming-house to witness play being carried on, previous to my entry, which is the most difficult task to encounter, as no one is admitted unless brought there by a Bonnet or a play-man, as a pigeon or freshman, commonly known as Punters or Flats. Since my entry into No. 34 St James's Street, kept by Isaiah Smart, whose son was killed by a fall from the roof in endeavouring to escape from the police, there is no doubt the gamblers have exercised the greatest ingenuity in their power in order to entrap me into a false entry on their premises by lighting up the rooms as if play was going on ; employing persons to watch, both outside and in, to give the alarm on the appearance of any of the police passing ; so that, if I was tempted to make an entry with-out taking the precaution of having an officer inside to prove gaming, there is not the least doubt but that they would instantly catch at the opportunity of bringing an action against me for trespass, &c., and thereby effect my ruin.   I have received information that such is the case in the event of my making one false step, and which I have every reason to believe is true.'"

Crockford was examined, but the Committee got very little out of that old fox, except the fact that he had given up all active connection with the establishment in St James's Street for over four years.

Mr Mayne was recalled on the 9th May 1844, and gave evidence that, two nights previously, an entry was made into all houses, known to be gaming-houses in town, seventeen in number, with the result of a fine haul of men, money, and gaming implements.

The outcome of the Select Committees of both Houses of Parliament was the passing, on 8th August 1845, of 8-9 Vic., c. 109, " An Act to amend the Law against Games and Wagers "—and for many years afterwards professional gaming-houses in London were a tradition of the past. Now, however, they abound, thanks to the laxity of the law with regard to so-called clubs.

Here, then, ends the account of this phase of gambling, as it has been thought inexpedient to give any modern instances of play at so-called Clubs, or Card-sharping.

CHAPTER XI

BETTING, or rather, that peculiar form of wager which consists in a material pledge in corroboration of controverted
assertions, is of very ancient date, and we meet with it in one
of the early books of the Bible, see Judges xiv. where in vv.
12, 13, Samson makes a distinct bet—owns he has lost in
v. 18, and pays his bet, v. 19.

" 12. And Samson said unto them, I will now put a riddle
unto you : if ye can certainly declare it me within the seven
days of the feast, and find it out, then I will give you thirty
sheets and thirty changes of garments.

" 13. But, if ye cannot declare it me, then shall you give
me thirty sheets and thirty changes of garments. And they
said unto him, put forth thy riddle that we may hear it.

" 14. And he said unto them, out of the eater came forth
meat, and out of the strong came forth sweetness. And
they could not, in three days, expound the riddle.

" 15. And it came to pass, on the seventh day, that they
said unto Samson's wife, Entice thy husband, that he may
declare unto us the riddle, lest we burn thee and thy father's
house with fire : have ye called us to take that we have? is
it not so ?

" 16. And Samson's wife wept before him, and said, Thou
dost but hate me, and lovest me not : thou hast put forth a
riddle unto the children of my people, and hast not told it
me. And he said unto her, I have not told it my father,
nor my mother, and shall I tell it thee ?

" 16. And she wept before him the seven days, while the feast lasted ; and it came to pass, on the seventh day, that he told her, because she lay sore upon him : and she told the riddle to the children of her people.

" 18. And the men of the city said unto him, on the seventh day, before the sun went down, what is sweeter than honey ? and what is stronger than a lion ?   And he said unto them, if ye had not plowed with my heifer, ye had not found out my riddle.

" 19. And the Spirit of the Lord came upon him, and he went down to Ashkelon, and slew thirty men of them, and took their spoil, and gave changes of raiment unto them which expounded the riddle.   And his anger was kindled, and he went up to his father's house,

" 20. But Samson's wife was given to his companion, whom he had used as his friend."

Now, in this very ancient story, we find embodied as much roguery and crime as in any modern turf episode.   Samson bet without any means of paying, if he lost : he lost, and was a defaulter.   But, to pay this " debt of honour," he had recourse to wholesale murder and robbery—to satisfy men, who to his own knowledge, had (to use a modern expression) " tampered with the stable."

The early Greeks betted, as we find in Homer's *Iliad*, b. xxiii. 485-7 where Idomeneus offers a bet to the lesser Ajax to back his own opinion :

Δεῦρό νυν ἢ τρίποδος περιδώμεθον, ἠὲ λέβητος·
" Ἴστορα δ' Ἀτρείδην Ἀγαμέμνονα θείομεν ἄμφω.
Ὁππότεραι πρόσθ' Ἵπποι' ἵνα γνοίης ἀποτίνων.

>   " Now, come on !   .
> A wager stake we, of tripod, or of caldron ;
> And make we both Atreidès Agamemnon
> Judge, whether foremost are those mares : and so
> Learn shalt thou, to thy cost !"

In Homer's *Odyssey*, xxiii. 78, Eurycleia wagers her life to Penelope that Ulysses has returned : Aristophanes in his *Equites*, 791 ; *Acharnes*, 772, 1115 ; and *Nebulæ*, 644, gives examples of wagers ; and, in the eighth idyll of Theocritus, Daphins proposes a bet to Menalcas about a singing match.

Among the Romans, Virgil tells us of a wager in his third *Eclogue* of the *Bucolics*, 28-50, between Menalcas and Damœtas, which is virtually the same as that of Theocritus, and Valerius Maximus tells us how a triumph was awarded by the senate to Lutatius, the Consul, who had defeated the Carthaginian fleet. The prætor Valerius, having also been present in the action, asserted that the victory was his, and that a triumph was due to him also. The question came before the judge ; but not until Valerius had first, in support of his assertion, deposited a stake, against which Lutatius deposited another. But in classical time they seem to have known little about odds.

The word wager is an English word—and was spelt in Middle English, *Wageoure*, or *Wajour*, as in *The Babee's Book*.

> "No *waiour* non with hym thou lay,
> Ne at the dyce with hym to play."

It was in early use, for we have the *Wager of Battel*, which was a practical bet between two men as to the justice of their cause. This ordeal was in force until 1819, when it was done away with by 59 Geo. III., c. 46.

In Shakespeare's time betting was common, and the practice of giving and taking odds was well known, as we may see in *Hamlet*, Act v. s. 2, where Osrick, speaking to Hamlet, says, "The King, sir, hath wagered with him six Barbary horses ; against which he hath imponed, as I take it, six French Rapiers and poniards, with their assigns, as girdles, hangers and so." In *Cymbeline*, Act i. s. 5, we have a bet, which is so serious that it has to be recorded. Iachimo says, "I dare thereupon pawn the moiety of my estate to your ring, which, in my opinion, o'ervalues it something," and, ultimately, ten thousand crowns are laid against the ring, and Iachimo says, "I will fetch my gold, and have our two wagers recorded."

By the way, there was an epitaph on Combe, the usurer,

which has been attributed to Shakespeare, which intimates the laying of odds.

> "Ten in the hundred lies here ingraved ;
> 'Tis a hundred to ten, his soul is not sav'd."

It is recorded of Sir John Packington, called "Lusty Packington" (Queen Elizabeth called him "her Temperance"), that he entered into articles to swim against three noblemen for £3000 from Westminster Bridge to Greenwich ; but the queen, by her special command, prevented the bet being carried out.

Howell in his *Epistolæ Ho-Elianæ* says : " If one would try a petty conclusion how much smoke there is in a pound of Tobacco, the ashes will tell him : for, let a pound be exactly weighed, and the ashes kept charily and weighed afterwards, what wants of a pound weight in the ashes, cannot be denied to have been smoke which evaporated into air. I have been told that Sir Walter Rawleigh won a wager of Queen Elizabeth upon this nicety."

Men betted, but their wagers are not recorded until the eighteenth century, and one of the earliest of these is told in *Malcolm's Anecdotes of the Manners and Customs of London during the eighteenth century*. " Mrs Crackenthorpe, the Female Tatler of 1709, tells us ' that four worthy Senators lately threw their hats into a river, laid a crown each whose hat should first swim to the mill, and ran hallooing after them ; and he that won the prize, was in a greater rapture than if he had carried the most dangerous point in Parliament.' "

" There was an established Cock pit in Prescot Street, Goodman's Fields, 1712 : there the Gentlemen of the East entertained themselves, while the Nobles and others of the West were entertained by the edifying exhibition of the agility of their running footmen. His Grace of Grafton declared *his* man was unrivalled in speed ; and the Lord Cholmondeley betted him that *his* excelled even the unrivalled ; accordingly, the ground was prepared for a two mile heat, in Hyde Park ; the race was run, *and one of the parties was victor*, but *which*, my informant does not say."

"I have frequently observed, in the course of my researches, the strange methods and customs peculiar to gaming, horse racing, dice and wagers ; the latter are generally governed by whim and extreme folly. We have already noticed Noblemen running their Coaches and Footmen. In 1729, a Poulterer of Leadenhall Market betted £50, he would walk 202 times round the area of Upper Moorfields in 27 hours, and, accordingly, proceeded at the rate of five miles an hour on the *amusing pursuit*, to the infinite improvement of his business, and great edification of hundreds of spectators. Wagers are now a favourite custom with too many of the Londoners ; they very frequently, however, originate over the bottle, or the porter pot."

" To characterise the follies of the day, it will be necessary to add to the account of the *walking* man, another, of a *hopping man*, who engaged to hop 500 yards, in 50 hops, in St James's Park, which he performed in 46. This important event occurred in December 1731."

In No. 145 of the *Spectator* (16th Aug. 1711) is a letter about the prevalence of laying wagers. "Among other things which your own experience must suggest to you, it will be very obliging if you please to take notice of wagerers.

. . . . . .

" Not long ago, I was relating that I had read such a passage in Tacitus ; up starts my young gentleman, in a full company, and, pulling out his purse, offered to lay me ten guineas, to be staked, immediately, in that gentleman's hands, pointing to one smoking at another table, that I was utterly mistaken. I was dumb for want of ten guineas ; he went on unmercifully to triumph over my ignorance how to take him up, and told the whole room he had read Tacitus twenty times over, and such a remarkable incident as that, could not escape him. He has, at this time, three considerable wagers depending between him and some of his companions, who are rich enough to hold an argument with him. He has five guineas upon questions in geography, two that the Isle of Wight is a peninsula, and three guineas to one, that the world is round. We have a gentleman comes to our coffee house, who deals mightily in antique scandal; my disputant has laid him twenty pieces upon a point of history."

It was in the early part of the eighteenth century that betting was made a part of professional gambling, as we read in Smollett's *Adventures of Ferdinand, Count Fathom.* On his return to England "he perceived that gaming was now managed in such a manner, as rendered skill and dexterity of no advantage; for the spirit of play having overspread the land, like a pestilence, raged to such a degree of madness and desperation, that the unhappy people who were infected, laid aside all thoughts of amusement, economy, or caution, and risqued their fortunes upon issues equally extravagant, childish and absurd.

" The whole mystery of the art was reduced to the simple exercise of tossing up a guinea, and the lust of laying wagers, which they indulged to a surprising pitch of ridiculous intemperance. In one corner of the room might be heard a pair of lordlings running their grandmothers against each other, that is, betting sums on the longest liver; in another, the success of the wager depended upon the sex of the landlady's next child : one of the waiters happening to drop down in an apoplectic fit, a certain noble peer exclaimed, ' Dead, for a thousand pounds.' The challenge was immediately accepted; and when the master of the house sent for a surgeon to attempt the cure, the nobleman, who set the price upon the patient's head, insisted upon his being left to the efforts of nature alone, otherwise the wager should be void : nay, when the landlord harped upon the loss he should sustain by the death of a trusty servant, his lordship obviated the objection, by desiring that the fellow might be charged in the bill."

Horace Walpole in a letter to Sir H. Mann (1 Sep.

1750) tells a similar tale. "They have put in the papers a good story made on White's; a man dropped down dead at the door, was carried in; the club immediately made bets whether he was dead or not, and when they were going to bleed him, the wagerers for his death interposed, and said it would affect the fairness of the bet." But there is no such bet mentioned in White's betting book.

They even betted in the House of Commons. In the course of a debate Mr Pulteney charged Sir Robert Walpole with misquoting Horace; the prime minister replied by offering to bet that he had not done so, and the wager was accepted. The clerk of the House was called upon to decide the question, and declared Pulteney right; upon which Sir Robert threw a guinea across the House, to be picked up by his opponent, with the remark that it was the first public money he had touched for a long time.

Brookes' betting book has C. J. Fox's name frequently. In 1744 he bet Lord Northington that he would be called to the Bar within four years time. In 1755, he received one guinea from Lord Bolingbroke, upon condition of paying him a thousand pounds when the debts of the country amounted to a hundred and seventy-one millions; an event Fox lived to see come to pass.

In the *Connoisseur* of 9th May 1754 is an article on the prevalence of wagers. It says: "Tho' most of our follies are imported from France, this had its rise and progress entirely in England. In the last illness of Louis XIV. Lord Stair laid a wager on his death; and we may guess what the French thought of it, from the manner in which Voltaire mentions it, in his *Siecle de Louis XIV.* 'Le roi fut attaqué vers le milieu du mois d'Août. Le Comte de Stair, ambassadeur d'Angleterre *paria, selon le genie de sa nation*, que le roi ne passeroit pas le mois de Septembre.' 'The King,' says he, 'was taken ill about the middle of August; when Lord Stair, the Ambassador from England, *betted according to the custom of his nation*, that the king would not live beyond September.'

I am in some pain lest this custom should get among the ladies. They are, at present, very deep in cards and dice ; and while my lord is gaining abroad, her ladyship has her rout at home. I am inclined to suspect that our women of fashion will, also, learn to divert themselves with this polite practice of laying wagers. A birthday suit, the age of a beauty, who invented a particular fashion, or who were supposed to be together at the last masquerade, would, frequently give occasion for bets. This would, also, afford them a new method for the ready propagation of scandal, as the truth of several stories which are continually flitting about the town, would, naturally, be brought to the same test. Should they proceed further, to stake the lives of their acquaintances against each other, they would, doubtless, bet with the same fearless spirit, as they are known to do at *brag* ; one husband would, perhaps, be pitted against another, or a woman of the town against a maid of honour. In a word, if this once becomes fashionable among the ladies, we shall soon see the time, when an allowance for bet money will be stipulated in the marriage articles.

As the vices and follies of persons of distinction are very apt to spread, I am much afraid lest this branch of gaming should descend to the common people. Indeed, it seems already to have got among them. We have frequent accounts of tradesmen riding, walking, eating and drinking for a wager. The contested election in the City has occasioned several extraordinary bets. I know a butcher in Leadenhall Market, who laid an ox to a shin of beef on the success of Sir John Barnard against the field ; and have been told of a publican in Thames Street, who ventured a hogshead of entire beer on the candidate who serves him with beer."

Walpole tells one or two stories about betting in the course of his chatty letters. " Dec. 19, 1750. There has been a droll cause in Westminster Hall: a man laid another a wager that he produced a person who should weigh as much again as the Duke.[1]   When they had betted, they recollected not knowing how to desire the Duke to step into a scale.   They agreed to establish his weight at twenty stone, which, however, is supposed to be two more than he weighs.   One Bright,[2] was then produced, who is since dead, and who, actually, weighed forty-two stone and a half. As soon as he was dead, the person who had lost, objected that he had been weighed in his clothes, and though it was impossible that his clothes could weigh above two stone, they went to law.   There were the Duke's twenty stone bawled over a thousand times; but the righteous law decided against the man who had won!"

" 10th July 1774.   One of them has committed a murder, and intends to repeat it.   He betted £1500 that a man could live twelve hours under water; hired a desperate fellow, sunk him in a ship, by way of experiment, and both ship and man have not appeared since.   Another man and ship are to be tried for their lives, instead of Mr Blake, the assassin."

On 30 June 1765 a wager of 1000 guineas was decided between two noblemen, one of whom had constructed a machine which was to work a boat at the rate of 25 miles an hour: a canal was prepared near the banks of the Thames, on which to try it, but the tackle breaking, the bet was lost.

28 Feb. 1770.   A bet was laid by a noble earl that he would procure a man to ride to Edinburgh from London, and back, in less time than another noble earl could make a million of scores, or distinct dots, in the most expeditious manner that he could contrive.

On 12th June 1771 was tried before Lord Mansfield and a special jury, in the Court of King's Bench, a cause wherein Lord March was plaintiff, and Mr Pigot, defendant.   The action was brought to recover the sum of 500 guineas for a wager which Lord March had laid with Mr Pigot, whether

---

[1] Cumberland.
[2] Edward Bright died at Malden in Essex, 10th Nov. 1750.

Sir William Codrington or old Mr Pigot would die first. Mr Pigot happened to die suddenly from gout in his head on the morning previous to the laying of the wager, and the younger Mr Pigot thought, from this circumstance, that it was no bet. The defendant's counsel said, that if you make a bet for two horses to run, and one of them should die before the race came off, there could be no bet ; and he hoped that the jury would find for his client. After a short charge from the judge, the jury brought in a verdict for the plaintiff of 500 guineas, and full costs of suit.

On 1st July 1777 a case came before the Lord Chief-Justice Mansfield, which is one of the most extraordinary that ever was tried in a Court of Justice, respecting the sex of the Chevalier d'Eon, formerly ambassador to England from the Court of France.

The action was brought by Mr Hayes, surgeon, against one, Jacques, a broker and underwriter, for the recovery of £700, the said Jacques having, about six years previously, received premiums of fifteen guineas per cent., for every one of which he stood engaged to return *one hundred guineas*, whenever it should be proved that the Chevalier d'Eon was, actually, a woman.

Mr Buller opened the case as counsel for Mr Hayes. He stated the fairness of the transaction, and the justifiable nature of the demand, as Mr Hayes, the plaintiff, thought himself now to be in possession of that proof which would determine the sex of the Chevalier d'Eon, and, for ever, render the case indisputable.

In proof of the fact, M. de Goux, a surgeon, was the first witness called, and gave his testimony to the following effect : That he had been acquainted with the Chevalier d'Eon from the time when the Duc de Nivernois resided in England in quality of ambassador from the Court of France. That to his certain knowledge, the person called the Chevalier d'Eon was a woman.

Being closely interrogated by the counsel for the defendant, as to the mode of his acquiring such a degree of certainty relative to the sex of the party, M. de Goux gave this account of the matter : That, about five years ago, he was called in by the Chevalier d'Eon, to lend his professional aid, as she, at that time, laboured under a disorder which rendered an examination of the afflicted part absolutely necessary. That this examination led, of course, to that discovery of the sex of which M. de Goux was now enabled to give such testimony.

The second witness called on the part of the plaintiff was M. de Morande. He swore that, so long ago as the 3rd of July 1774, the Chevalier d'Eon made a free disclosure of her sex to the witness. That she had even proceeded so far as to display her bosom on the occasion. That, in consequence of this disclosure of sex, she, the Chevalier d'Eon, had exhibited the contents of her female wardrobe, which consisted of sacques, petticoats, and other habiliments calculated for feminine use. That, on the said 3rd day of July 1774, the witness paid a morning visit to the Chevalier d'Eon, and, finding her in bed, accosted her in a style of gallantry respecting her sex. That, so far from being offended with this freedom, the said Chevalier desired the witness to approach nearer to her bed, and then permitted him to have manual proof of her being, in very truth, a woman.

Mr Mansfield, on the part of the defendant, pleaded that this was one of those gambling, indecent and unnecessary cases, that ought never to be permitted to come into a Court of Justice ; that, besides the inutility and indecency of the case, the plaintiff had taken advantage of his client, being in possession of intelligence that enabled him to lay with greater certainty, although with such great odds on his side ; that the plaintiff, at the time of laying the wager, knew that the Court of France treated with the Chevalier, as a woman, to grant her a pension ; and that the French Court must have had some strong circumstances to imbibe that idea ; therefore, he hoped the jury would reprobate such wagers. The defendant's counsel did not attempt to contradict the plaintiff's evidence, by proving the masculine gender.

Lord Mansfield expressed his abhorrence of the whole transaction, and the more so, for their bringing it into a Court of Justice, when it might have been settled elsewhere ; wishing it had been in his power, in concurrence with the jury, to have made both parties lose ; but, as the law had not expressly prohibited it, and the wager was laid, the question before them was, who had won ? His Lordship remarked that the indecency of the proceeding arose more from the unnecessary questions asked, than from the case itself; that the witnesses had declared they perfectly knew the Chevalier d'Eon to be a woman ; if she is not a woman, they are certainly perjured : there was, therefore, no need of inquiring how, or by what methods they knew it, which was all the indecency.

As to the fraud suggested, of the plaintiff's knowing more than the defendant, he seemed to think there was no foundation for it. His Lordship then recited a wager entered into by two gentlemen, in his own presence, about the dimensions of the Venus de Medicis, for £100. One of the gentlemen said, " I will not deceive you ; I tell you fairly, I have been there, and measured it myself." " Well," says the other, " and do you think I should be such a fool, as to lay if I had not measured it ? . . .   I will lay for all that."

His Lordship then went on to state to the jury, that this Chevalier had publicly appeared as a man, had been employed by the Court of France, as a man, as a military man, in a civil office, and as a Minister of State here, and in Russia ; there was all the presumption against the plaintiff, and the *onus probandi* lay upon him, which might never been come at ; for it appeared, the only proposition of a discovery of sex that had been made to the Chevalier, by some gentlemen on an excursion, had been resented by d'Eon, who had instantly quitted their company on that account : it might, therefore, never have been in his power to have proved his wager, but for some accidental quarrels between d'Eon and some of her countrymen. His Lordship was, therefore, of opinion that the jury should find a verdict for the plaintiff.

The jury, without hesitation, gave a verdict for the plaintiff, £700, and 40s. Yet, when d'Eon died, in London, in 1810, *it was proved, without a shadow of a doubt, that he was a man.*

CHAPTER XII

Gluttonous Wager—Walk to Constantinople and back—Sir John Lade and Lord Cholmondeley—Other Wagers—Betting on Napoleon—Bet on a Coat—Lord Brougham—Brunel and Stephenson—Captain Barclay—Story by Mr Ross—The Earl of March's Coach—Selby's drive to Brighton—White's betting book.

A DIFFERENT kind of wager is recorded in *The World*, of 4th May 1787. "At the Wheel, at Hackington Fen, on Wednesday sen'night, a fen farmer laid a wager he could eat *two dozen* of penny mutton pies, and drink a gallon of ale in half an hour, which he performed *with ease*, in half the time, and said he had but a *scanty* supper and wished for something more ; in less than half an hour after, he ate a threepenny loaf and a pound of cheese, and still swore he was hungry. The landlord, unwilling to starve his *delicate guest*, set before him a leg of pork, which his voracious appetite gormandized with great composure. He thanked the landlord for his civility, and said, ' I hate to go to bed with an empty stomach.' "

In the *Annual Register* we read, September 1788. " A young Irish gentleman, for a very considerable wager, set out on Monday the 22nd instant, to walk to Constantinople and back again in one year. It is said that the young gentleman has £20,000 depending on the performance of this exploit. 1st June 1789, Mr Whaley arrived about this time in Dublin from his journey to the Holy Land, considerably within the limited time of twelve months. The above wager, however whimsical, is not without a precedent. Some years ago, a baronet of some fortune, in the north, laid a considerable wager that he would go to Lapland, bring home two females of that country and two reindeer in a given time.   He performed his journey, and effected his purpose in every respect.   The Lapland women lived with him for about a year, but, having a wish to go back to their own country, the baronet very generously furnished them with means and money."

In Trinity Term, 1790, was argued in the Court of King's Bench, whether all wagers, by the 14th George III., were not void, as gaming contracts, and being contrary to the policy of the law?   Lord Kenyon and Justices Ashurst and Grose were of opinion, that the law had not declared all wagers illegal, however desirable such a law might be. Wagers that led to a breach of the peace, to immorality, the injury of a third person, or that had a libellous tendency, were void ; but some wagers, between indifferent people, were, certainly legal, both by the common law, and by statute.   Mr Justice Buller differed from the rest of the Court.

Times, October 2, 1795.   "A curious circumstance occurred here (Brighton) yesterday.   Sir JOHN LADE, for a trifling wager, undertook to carry Lord CHOLMONDELEY, on *his back*, from opposite the Pavilion, twice round the Steine. Several ladies attended to be spectators of this extraordinary feat of the dwarf carrying the giant.   When his Lordship declared himself ready, Sir John desired him to *strip*. 'Strip!' exclaimed the other, 'why, surely, you promised to carry me in my clothes!'   'By no means,' replied the Baronet, I engaged to carry *you*, but not an inch of clothes. So, therefore, my Lord, make ready, and let us not *disappoint* the ladies.'   After much laughable altercation, it was, at length, decided that Sir JOHN had won his wager, the Peer declining to exhibit *in puris naturalibus*."

Times, September 11, 1797.   "A *Mr Marston*, of the Borough, has laid a bet of 2000 guineas, that he will, in the course of the ensuing week, go into one of the great wheels of the water works at London Bridge, while it is in its swiftest motion with an ebb tide, stay there five minutes, and come out again with safety, though not without accident, in a different part from that in which he went in : and, afterwards, walk one mile within an hour, on condition that the lower bucket of the wheel is two feet from the river bottom."

A wager was made, in 1806, in the Castle Yard, York, between Thomas Hodgson and Samuel Whitehead, as to which should succeed in assuming the most singular character. Umpires were selected, whose duty it was to decide upon the comparative absurdity of the costumes in which the two men appeared. On the appointed day, Hodgson came before the umpires, decorated with bank notes of various value on his coat and waistcoat, a row of five guinea notes, and a long netted purse of gold round his hat, whilst a piece of paper, bearing the words " John Bull," was attached to his back. Whitehead was dressed like a woman on one side ; one half of his face was painted, and he wore a silk stocking and a slipper on one leg. The other half of his face was blacked, to resemble a negro : on the corresponding side of his body he wore a gaudy, long-tailed, linen coat ; and his leg was cased in half a pair of leather breeches, with a boot and spur. One would fancy that Whitehead must have presented the most singular appearance, by far, but the umpires thought differently, and awarded the stakes to Hodgson.

In the early part of this century sporting men were fond of betting on the duration of the lives of celebrities. Napoleon I. was specially the subject of these wagers. It is related that, at a dinner party in 1809, Sir Mark Sykes offered to pay any one who would give him a hundred guineas down, a guinea a day, so long as Napoleon lived. The offer was taken by a clergyman present ; and, for three years, Sir Mark Skyes paid him three hundred and sixty-five guineas per annum. He, then, thought he had thrown away enough money, and disputed further payment. The recipient, who was not at all disposed to lose his comfortable annuity, brought an action, which, after lengthy litigation, was decided in favour of the baronet.

A gentleman made a bet of 1000 guineas that he would have a coat made in the course of a single day, from the first process of shearing the sheep to its completion by the tailor. The wager was decided at Newbury on the 25th of June 1811, by Mr John Coxeter of Greenham Mills, near that town. At five o'clock that morning, Sir John Throckmorton, Bart., presented two Southdown wether sheep to Mr Coxeter. Accordingly, the sheep were shorn, the wool spun, the yarn spooled, warped, loomed and wove, the cloth burred, milled, rowed, dyed, dried, sheared and pressed, and put into the hands of the tailors by four o'clock that afternoon ; and, at twenty minutes past six, the coat entirely finished, was presented by Mr Coxeter to Sir John Throckmorton, who appeared, wearing it, before an assemblage of upwards of 5000 spectators, who rent the air with their acclamations.

The religious impostor, Johanna Southcott, was the subject of at least one wager, for, concerning that, an action was brought on a bet that she would be delivered of a son, on or before 1st Nov. 1814. As she was a single woman it was held that no action could be sustained, as the wager involved the perpetration of an immorality.

I cannot give chapter and verse for the next two anecdotes, but they are generally accepted as true. The first is about Lord Brougham, who, in his college days, went one autumn to Dumfries in order to make one at the Caledonian Hunt meeting. According to the then custom, everybody dined at a *table d'hôte*, and, after dinner, betting set in. Brougham offered to bet the whole company that none of them would write down the manner in which he meant to go to the races next day. Those who accepted his challenge wrote down their conjectures and Brougham wrote down his intention of travelling in a sedan chair, a mode of conveyance no one had hit upon. To the races he went, an immense crowd seeing him safely chaired to the course. The bet was then renewed, as to the manner of his return to Dumfries, the acceptors taxing their wits to imagine the most improbable methods of travelling. Brougham had calculated upon this, and won the double event by returning in a post chaise and pair.

The other is a story of Brunel and Stephenson. They were travelling together in a railway carriage, Stephenson being wrapped in a dark plaid, on the exact disposition of the folds of which he rather plumed himself. " You are looking at my plaid," said he to Brunel ; " I'll bet you ten pounds you can-not put it on, properly, the first time." " I'll bet ten pounds against the plaid," said Brunel. " If I put it on right when we get out at the next station the plaid is mine ; if I miss I pay you ten pounds." " Done," said Stephenson. Brunel sat silent until the train stopped ; then, stepping on the plat-form, he asked for the plaid, which was slowly unwound by its owner and handed over : not to be handed back again, for Brunel wound it round his own shoulders as if he had always worn it. He had never tried it before, but, when challenged, did not like to be beaten, and, at once, set to work to study the folds of the plaid. " I got the thing pretty clear in my head before we reached the station, and when I saw him get out of it I knew I was right, so I put it on at once."

Wagers about walking and running are very numerous, still a few might be mentioned, beginning with Foster Powell, who, on 29th Nov. 1773, commenced a journey from London to York and back in six days. He walked from London to Stamford, 88 miles, on the first day ; to Doncaster, 72 miles, on the second ; to York, 37 miles, and 22 miles back to Ferrybridge on the third ; to Grantham, 65 miles, on the fourth ; to Eaton, 54 miles, on the fifth ; and the final spin of 56 miles on the sixth—making a total of 394 miles between Monday morning and Saturday night, and winning a wager of one hundred guineas.

Soon afterwards a reputed centenarian, and, admittedly, a *very* aged man, undertook to walk 10 miles on the Hammer-smith Road in 2 hours and 30 minutes, for a wager of ten guineas, and he accomplished his task in 2 hours 23 minutes.

Captain Barclay, a famous pedestrian, in the early part of

the present century, began his exploits at the early age of fifteen by walking six miles in an hour, fair toe and heel. His next feat was to walk from Ury, in Kincardineshire, to Boroughbridge, in Yorkshire, about 300 miles, in five very hot days. He hazarded the large sum of 5000 guineas, that he would walk 90 miles in 20 hours 30 minutes, and he accomplished this arduous task in 19 hours 22 minutes. But his greatest pedestrian feat was performed in July 1809, and is thus described in the *Annual Register* :

" July 13. *Captain Barclay.* This gentleman, on Wednesday, completed his arduous pedestrian undertaking to walk a thousand miles in a thousand successive hours, at the rate of a mile in each and every hour. He had until four o'clock P.M. to finish his task, but he performed his last mile in the quarter of an hour after three, with perfect ease and great spirit, amidst an immense concourse of spectators. For the last two days he appeared in higher spirits, and performed his mile with more ease, and in shorter time, than he had done for some days past. With the change of the weather he had thrown off his loose greatcoat, which he wore during the rainy period, and, on Wednesday, performed in a flannel jacket. He also put on shoes remarkably thicker than any which he had used in any previous part of his performance. When asked how he meant to act after he had finished his feat, he said he should, that night, take a good sound sleep, but that he must have himself awaked twice, or thrice, in the night to avoid the danger of a too sudden transition from almost constant exertion, to a state of long repose.

"One hundred to one, and, indeed, any odds, were offered on Wednesday morning ; but so strong was the confidence in his success that no bets could be obtained. The multitude of people who resorted to the scene of action, in the course of the concluding days, was unprecedented. Not a bed could be procured, on Tuesday night, at Newmarket, Cambridge, or any of the towns and villages in the vicinity, and every horse, and every species of vehicle was engaged.

"Captain Barclay had £16,000 depending upon his undertaking.   The aggregate of the bets is supposed to amount to £100,000."

In those days there were sportsmen like Osbaldeston and Ross, who were ready for any wager.   Let the latter tell a little story.

"A large party were assembled at Black Hall, in Kincardineshire, time, the end of July, or beginning of August. We had all been shooting snipe and flapper-ducks, in a large morass on the estate called Lumphannon.   We had been wading amongst bulrushes, up to our middles, for seven or eight hours, and had had a capital dinner.   After the ladies had gone to the drawing room, I fell asleep ; and, about nine o'clock, was awakened by the late Sir Andrew Keith Hay, who said, 'Ross, old fellow! I want you to jump up, and go as my umpire with Lord Kennedy, to Inverness.   I have made a bet of twenty-five hundred pounds a side, that I get there, on foot, before him!'   Nothing came amiss to the men of that day.   My answer was, 'All right, I'm ready'; and off we started, there and then, in morning costume, with thin shoes and silk stockings on our feet.   We went straight across the mountains, and it was a longish walk. I called to my servant to follow with my walking shoes and worsted stockings, and Lord Kennedy did the same.   They overtook us after we had gone seven or eight miles.   Fancy my disgust!   My idiot bought me, certainly, worsted stockings, but, instead of shoes, a pair of tight Wellington boots!   The sole of one boot vanished twenty-five miles from Inverness, and I had, now, to finish the walk barefooted.   We walked all night, next day, and the next night —raining in torrents all the way.   We crossed the Grampians, making a perfectly straight line, and got to Inverness at one P.M.   We never saw, or heard, anything of Sir A. L. Hay, (he went by the coach road, viâ Huntly and Elgin, thirty-six miles further than we, but a good road) who appeared at ten A.M. much cast down at finding he had been beaten."

There have been divers wagers about coaching, and also

about horses, which have nothing to do with horse racing,
and a few may be chronicled here.

On 29th August 1750, at seven in the morning, was
decided, at Newmarket, a remarkable wager for 1000
guineas, laid by Count Taaf against the Earl of March and
Lord Eglinton, who were to provide a four wheeled carriage,
with a man in it, to be drawn by four horses at a speed of
19 miles an hour; which was performed in 53 min. 27 sec.
It was rather an imposing affair. A groom, dressed in
crimson velvet, rode before to clear the way: the boy who
sat in the vehicle was dressed in a white satin jacket, black
velvet cap, and red silk stockings, whilst the four postillions
were clothed in blue satin waistcoats, buckskin breeches, with
white silk stockings, and black velvet caps. The carriage is
thus described : " The pole was small, but lapp'd with fine
wire ; the perch had a plate underneath, two cords went on
each side, from the back carriage to the fore carriage,
fastened to springs. The harness was of thin leather,
covered with silk ; the seat for the man to sit on, was of
leather straps, and covered with velvet ; the boxes of the
wheels were brass, and had tins of oil to drop slowly for an
hour : the breechings for the horses were of whale bone ; the
bars were small wood, strengthened with steel springs, as were
most parts of the carriage ; but all so light that a man could
carry the whole, with the harness ; being but 2 cwt. and a
half." Two or three other carriages had been made previously, but had been disapproved of, and several horses had
been killed in trials—costing between £600 and £700.

In April and finishing on 3rd May 1758, at Newmarket,
Miss Pond, daughter of Mr Pond, the compiler and publisher
of the *Racing Calendar*, bearing his name, laid a wager of
200 guineas that she could ride 1000 miles in a 1000 hours,
and finished her match in a little more than two-thirds of
the time. At the conclusion, the country people strewed
flowers in her path. It has been said that this feat was performed on *one horse*.

In the beginning of June 1800, a naval officer undertook,

for a wager, to ride a blind horse round Sheerness race-course without guiding the reins with his hands ; this he performed to the no small amusement of the spectators, by cutting the reins asunder, and fastening the several parts to his feet in his stirrups.

Perhaps the best known match of modern times was one made at the Ascot meeting of 1888, of £1000 to £500 that a coach could not be driven to Brighton and back in eight hours. James Selby, a professional whip, started from the White Horse Cellar, Piccadilly, punctually at 10 A.M. on July 13, and arrived at Brighton, at the Old Ship, at 1.56 P.M. The coach was turned round and the return journey instantly started ; White Horse Cellar being reached at 5.50 P.M. : thus winning the match by ten minutes. Selby died at the end of the year.

The betting book of White's Club, dates from the year 1743—the older book and all the other records of the Club having been destroyed in the fire of 1743. The following are some of the wagers therein recorded. The early ones are principally pitting lives against one another.

Feb. y 3, 1743/4. Lord Montford betts Mr Wardour twenty Guineas on each, that Mr Shephard outlives Sir Hans Sloan, the Dutchess Dowager of Marlborough, and Duke of Somerset.—Voide.

Mr J^{no} Jeffreys betts Mr Stephen Jansen Fifty Guineas, that thirteen Members of Parliament don't Die from the first of Jany 1744/5 to the first of Jany 1745/6 exclusive of what may be killed in battle.

Ld Leicester betts Lord Montfort One Hundred Guineas that Six or more Peers of the British Parliament, including Catholics, Minors, Bishops, and Sixteen Scotch Lords, shall Die between the 2 of Decem^r 1744, and the First of Decem^r 1745 inclusive.

16 *July* 1746. Mr Heath wagers Mr Fanshawe five guineas that the eldest son of the Pretender is dead, on, or before this day. To be returned if the Pretender was dead. —pd. Novr 28.

Octr 20th 1746. Mr Heath gave Col. Perry Twenty Pounds, for which Col. Perry is to pay Mr Heath one hundred pounds if ever he loses more than one hundred pounds in any four and twenty hours.

Novr ye 14, 1746. Mr Fox betts Mr John Jeffreys five guineas on Number Two against Number One in the present Lottery.

Lord Montfort wagers S^r Wm. Stanhope 20 guineas that Lady Mary Coke has a child beford Ly Kildare, and 20 guineas more that L^y Mary Coke has a child before L^y Fawkener.

January the 14th, 1747/8. Mr Fanshawe wagers Lord Dalkeith one guinea, that his peruke is better than his Lordship's, to be judged of by the majority of members the next time they both shall meet.

These are fair specimens, and, after this date, the bets begin to be political and personal, and devoid of interest.

CHAPTER XIII

BUT this style of betting is harmless compared to that curse
of the England of our time, betting upon horse racing, which
can be compared to nothing but a social cancer, eating into
the very vitals of the nation ; and it is especially a pity that
so noble an animal as the horse should be made the uncon-
scious medium of such a degrading passion as gambling—
still, the fact exists, and horse racing from its commencement
must be treated in a history of gambling in England.

Horses must have been introduced into this country at a
very early age, for, when Cæsar invaded Britain, he was
opposed by vast numbers of horsemen, and many centuries
had not elapsed before there was competition, as to speed,
among the animals. William of Malmesbury tells us that
running horses were sent from France by Stugh, the founder
of the house of Capet, as a present to King Athelstan. We
never hear of any races being run, and Fitzstephen, who was
secretary to Sir Thomas à Becket, and lived in the reign of
Henry II., scarcely describes what we should term a horse
race. Speaking of a certain Smoothfield, outside London
(Smithfield), he says :

" There, every Friday, unless it be one of the more solemn
festivals, is a noted show of well bred horses for sale. The
earls, barons and knights, who are, at the time resident in
the City, as well as most of the Citizens, flock thither, either
to look on, or buy. It is pleasant to see the nags, with their

sleek and shining coats, smoothly ambling along, raising and setting down, alternatively, as it were, their feet on either side : in one part are horses better adapted to esquires ; these, whose pace is rougher, but yet expeditious, lift up and set down, as it were, the two opposite fore and hind feet together : in another, the young blood colts not yet accustomed to the bridle. In a third, are the horses for burden, strong and stout limbed ; and, in a fourth, the more valuable chargers, of an elegant shape and noble height, with nimbly moving ears, erect necks, and plump haunches. In the movement of these, the purchasers observe, first, their easy pace, and, then, their gallop, which is when their fore feet are raised from the ground, and set down together, and the hind ones in like manner alternately. When a race is to be run by such horses as these, and, perhaps, by others, which, in like manner, according to their breed, are strong for carriage and vigorous for the course, the people raise a shout, and order the common horses to be withdrawn to another part of the field. The jockeys, who are boys expert in the management of horses, which they regulate by means of curb bridles, sometimes by threes, and sometimes by twos, according as the match is made, prepare themselves for the contest. Their chief aim is to prevent a competitor getting before them. The horses, too, after their manner, are eager for the race ; their limbs tremble, and, impatient of delay, they cannot stand still ; upon the signal being given, they stretch out their limbs, hurry over the course, and are borne along with unremitting speed. The riders, inspired with the love of praise, and the hope of victory, clap spurs to their flying horses, lashing them with their whips, and inciting them with their shouts."

In a metrical romance of the thirteenth century, " Syr Beuys of Hampton," printed by W. Copland in 1550, there is mention of a race

> " In somer in whitsontyde
> whan knightes most on horsbacke ride
> a cours let they make on a daye
> Stedes and palfraye for to assaye

> whiche horse that best may ren
> thre myles the cours was then
> who that might ryd should
> have £Ll. of redy golde."

Edward III. bought some running horses at £13, 6s. 8d. each ; and in the ninth year of his reign the King of Navarre made him a present of two running horses. Still, very little is heard of race horses until the time of Elizabeth and James I. Bishop Hall, of Exeter and Norwich, in one of his Satires, writes :

> " Dost thou prize
> Thy brute beasts' worth by their dam's qualities ?
> Say'st thou, this colt shall prove a swift-paced steed,
> Only because a jennet did him breed ?
> Or say'st thou, this same horse shall win the prize,
> Because his dam was swiftest Trunchifice,[1]
> Or Runcevall his syre ; himself a galloway ?
> While, like a tireling jade, he lags half way."

In 1599, private matches by gentlemen, who were their own riders, were very common, and, in the reign of James I., public races were established at various places, where the discipline and mode of preparing the horses for running, etc., were much the same as they are now. The most celebrated races of that time were called the " Bell Courses," the prize of the winner being a bell—hence the saying of " to bear the bell " ; and a tradition of it still remains in the couplet with which children's races are started.

> " Bell horses ! Bell horses ! what time of day ?
> One o'clock, two o'clock, three, and away ! "

Perhaps the oldest record that we have of these silver bells is those of Paisley, which date from 1620, or 1608, as on that date there is an entry in the town books showing the purchase of a silver bell. The silver bells are now run for, but there are 100 guineas attached to them. Silver

---

[1] Truncifer is a famous horse mentioned in the metrical romance of Sir Bevis of Hampton.

bells were also run for in this reign, at Gatherly, in York-shire, Croydon, Chester, and Theobalds, the King's hunting lodge.   Mr J. C. Whyte, in his *History of the British Turf*, says that in Harl. MS. 2150, fol. 235, is an account of a ceremony performed with the race for a bell at Chester, in the presence of the Mayor, at the Cross, in the Rodhi, or Roody, an open place near the City.   I have examined the MS. but cannot find the passage, so extract from his work the following :

" A silver bell, valued at about three shillings and six-pence, placed on the point of a lance, shall be given to him, who shall run the best and furthest on horseback before them on Shrove Tuesday.   These bells went by the name of St George's bells, and the younger Randel Holme tells us that, in the last year of this reign (1624) John Brereton, innkeeper, Mayor of Chester, first caused the horses entered for this race, then called St George's Race, to start from the point beyond the new Tower, and appointed them to run five times round the Roody ; and, he continues, he, who won the last course, or trayne, received the bell, of a good value, £8 or £10, and to have it for ever, which moneyes were collected of the citizens for that purpose.   By the use of the term, for ever, it would appear that the bell had been used, formerly, as a mark of temporary distinction only, by the successful horsemen, and, afterwards, returned to the Cor-poration."

On fol. 354 of this MS. we find " What ye companys gave toward S. George's Rase for the contynuance of a bell or cup."   To this there is no date, but it amounted to £36, 8s. 4d,   The 3s. 6d. silver bell was substituted for a wooden ball, which used to be raced for, as a prize, in the 31st year of King Henry VIII.

We see how simple, and for what small prizes they ran in the early days of horse racing in England—it is sad to record that betting, almost immediately, attended the popularity of the sport.   This we see in Shirley's play of *Hide Parke*, acted at Drury Lane in 1637.

"*Confused noyse of betting within, after that a shoute.*
Mistress Caroll. They are started.
   Enter Bonvile, Rider, Bonavent, Tryer, Fairefield.
Rider. Twenty pounds to fifteene.
Lord Bonvile. 'Tis done we'e.
Fairefield. Forty pounds to thirty.
Lord Bonvile. Done, done. Ile take all oddes.
Tryer. My Lord, I hold as much.
Lord Bonvile. Not so.
Tryer. Forty pounds to twenty.
Lord Bonvile. Done, done.
Mistress Bonavent. You ha lost all, my Lord, and it were a Million.
Lord Bonvile. In your imagination, who can helpe it ?
Mistress Bonavent. *Venture* hath the start and keepes it.
Lord Bonvile. Gentlemen, you have a fine time to triumph,
   'Tis not your oddes that makes you win.
     Within. Venture ! Venture !   [*Exeunt Men.*
Julietta. Shall we venture nothing o' th' horses ?
   What oddes against my Lord ?
Mistress Caroll. Silke stockings.
Julietta. To a paire of perfum'd gloves I take it.
Mistress Caroll. Done !
Mistress Bonavent. And I as much.
Julietta. Done with you both.
Mistress Caroll. Ile have 'em Spanish sent.
Julietta. The Stockings shal be Scarlet : if you choose
   Your sent, Ile choose my colour.
Mistress Caroll. 'Tis done ; if *Venture*
   Knew but my lay, it would halfe breake his necke now,
   And crying a *Jockey* hay.   [*A shoute within.*
Julietta. Is the wind in that coast ? harke the noyse.
   Is *Jockey* now ?
Mistress Caroll. 'Tis but a paire of gloves.
Julietta. Still it holds.   [*Enter my Lord.*
   How ha you sped, my Lord ?
Lord Bonvile. Won ! won ! I knew by instinct,
   The mare would put some tricke upon him.
Mistress Bonavent. Then we ha lost ; but, good my Lord, the circum-
     stance.
Lord Bonvile. Great *John* at all adventure, and grave *Jockey*
   Mounted their severall Mares, I sha' not tell
   The story out for laughing, ha ! ha ! ha !
   But this in briefe, *Jockey* was left behind,
   The pitty and the scorne of all the oddes,
   Plaid 'bout my eares like Cannon, but lesse dangerous.

> I tooke all, still ; the acclamation was
> For *Venture*, whose disdainefull Mare threw durt
> In my old *Jockey's* face, all hopes forsaking us ;
> Two hundred pieces desperate, and two thousand
> Oathes sent after them ; upon the suddaine,
> When we expected no such tricke, we saw
> My rider, that was domineering ripe,
> Vault ore his Mare into a tender slough.
> Where he was much beholding to one shoulder,
> For saving of his necke, his beast recovered,
> And he, by this time, somewhat mortified,
> Besides mortified, hath left the triumph
> To his Olympick Adversary, who shall
> Ride hither in full pompe on his *Bucephalus*,
> With his victorious bagpipe."

Newmarket, hitherto, a royal hunting place, was made into a race course in 1640, and we get a peep of what it was like in an old ballad (said to be of about this time) called " Newmarket," published by D'Urfey, in his *Pills to purge Melancholy*.

> " Let cullies that lose at a race,
>   Go venture at hazard to win,
>   Or he, that is bubbl'd at dice,
>   Recover at cocking again.
>   Let jades that are foundered, be brought ;
>   Let jockeys play crimp to make sport ;
>   Another makes racing a trade,
>   And dreams of his projects to come,
>   And many a crimp match has made
>   By bubbing[1] another man's groom."

Oliver Cromwell kept " running horses," but there is no mention of his having used them in racing : It is more probable that he bred from them. With the Restoration, horse racing was revived, and was much encouraged by Charles II. who appointed races for his own amusement at Datchet Mead, when he resided at Windsor. Newmarket, however, became the principal locality for this sport, and the round course was made in 1666. The King attended the

---

[1] Bribing.

races in person, established a house for his own accommodation, and kept and entered horses in his own name. Instead of bells, he gave a silver bowl or cup, value 100 guineas, on which prize the exploits and pedigree of the successful horse were generally engraved.

The times of James II. were too troubled for him to amuse himself with horse racing, and William III. had no leisure for the sport, although he added to the plates, and founded an academy for riding, but, under Anne, the turf was again under royal patronage.

The Queen was fond of racing, and gave £100 gold cups to be raced for; nay, more, she not only kept race horses, but ran them in her own name. Her six year old grey gelding Pepper, ran for her gold cup, at York (over Clifton and Rawcliffe Ing's), on July 28, 1712. Over the same course, and for the same stake, on Aug. 3, 1714, ran her grey horse Mustard, which in 1714 was entered to run in Whitsun Week, at Guildford, in Surrey, for the £50 plate; and, sad to tell, her brown horse Star, ran at York, for a plate value £14, and won it, on July 30, 1714, the very day on which the Queen was struck with apoplexy, expiring the next day.

She paid a visit to Newmarket, in April 1705, going to Cambridge once or twice during her stay. Narcissus Luttrell tells us: "Aprill 26, 1705. The queen has ordered her house at Newmarket to be rebuilt, and gave a thousand pounds towards paving the town; and bought a running horse of Mr Holloway, which cost a 1000 guineas, and gave it to the Prince." Prince George of Denmark shared his royal consort's love of horse racing, and gave, at least, two gold plates to be raced for, worth 100 guineas each. This seems to have been a very horsey year for the Queen, for Luttrell tells us that "the queen has appointed horse races to be at Datchet, after her return from Winchester to Windsor."

A few racing mems of this time will illustrate to what an extent the passion for the turf was carried. 1702: "They write from Newmarket, That the Lord Godolphin's and Mr Harvy's Horses ran for £3000. His Lordship won: As, also, the Earl of Argile, and the Duke of Devonshire's; the latter's Horse won, by which Mr Pheasant got a considerable sum." 1703: "The great horse race at Newmarket, run for 1000 guineas between the Lord Treasurer and the Duke of Argyle, was won by the latter." Perhaps the earliest Sporting Paper is "News from *Newmarket*, or, An Account of the Horses Match'd to Run there in *March*, *April*, and May, 1704. The Weight, Miles, Wagers and Forfeits. Printed for *John Nutt* near Stationer's Hall, price 2d." 1707: "Last Monday was a horse race at Newmarket, between Lord Granby's Grantham, and Mr Young's Blundel, for £3000—the latter won." On April 10, 1708, at Newmarket, the Duke of Bedford's bay horse (9 stone) had a match with Mr Minchall's bay colt (8½ stone) for 1000 guineas, but there is no record of which won. These were the highest stakes mentioned during the reign: they were, generally, for 200 or 300 guineas.

The first mention I can find of Epsom Races, is in this reign, and is in the *London Gazette*, April and May 26/3, 1703, when three small plates were to be run for, of £30, £10 and £5 value. On May 25, 1704, there was only one to be competed for, and that for £20. They had very early "Epsom Spring Meetings"; for, in the *Daily Courant*, Feb. 15, 1709, it says: "On Epsom Downes, in Surrey, on the first Monday after the Frost, a plate of £20 will be run for," &c. Races on these downs have been held continuously since 1730.

The most famous sporting man of his time was Tregonwell Frampton, Esq. of Moreton, Dorsetshire, "The Father of the Turf," who was keeper of her Majesty's running horses at Newmarket—a post which he had filled in the time of William III., and which he continued to hold under Georges I. and II. He is described as being "the oldest, and as they say, the cunningest jockey in England:

one day he lost 1000 guineas, the next he won 2000, and so, alternately. He made as light of throwing away £500 or £1000, at a time, as other men do of their pocket money, and was perfectly calm, cheerful and unconcerned when he lost a thousand pounds, as when he won it."

George I. is said to have been at Newmarket in 1716, 1717, and 1718, but neither he nor his successor cared for horse racing, although they still kept "running horses." George III. used to attend Ascot Races, and his uncle the "butcher," Duke of Cumberland, was a great patron of the turf, and was the breeder of the celebrated horse Eclipse. As Walpole says of him, 29th Dec. 1763: "The beginning of October, one is certain that everybody will be at Newmarket, and the Duke of Cumberland will lose, and Shafto[1] win, two or three thousand pounds." It was about this time that the betting ring started, and roguery was not uncommon, as we may see by the following:

At the Kingston Lent Assizes, 1767, a case was tried between an unnamed gentleman, as plaintiff, and Mr Wm. Courtney, defendant; the action was upon a wager of 100 guineas, which was reduced to writing, that plaintiff procured three horses that should go ninety miles in three hours, which defendant laid he did not. The plaintiff proved his case very well; but, it appearing to the court and jury that it was an unfair bet, the jury gave a verdict for the defendant. It seems that the way in which the plaintiff performed his undertaking, was by starting all the three horses together, so that they had but thirty miles apiece to run in the three hours, which, of course, was easily done.

In chronological order comes a story of a duel in which the notorious black leg, Dick England, was concerned.

"Mr Richard England was put to the Bar, at the Old Bailey (1796) charged with the 'wilful murder' of Mr Rowlls, brewer, of Kingston, in a duel at Crauford Bridge, June 18, 1784.

[1] Robert Shafto, Esq., of Whitworth, M.P. for Durham, well known on the Turf.

" Lord Derby, the first witness, gave evidence that he was present at Ascot races. When in the stand upon the race course, he heard Mr England cautioning the gentlemen present not to bet with the deceased, as he neither paid what he lost, nor what he borrowed. On which Mr Rowlls went up to him, called him rascal, or scoundrel, and offered to strike him ; when Mr England bid him stand off, or he would be obliged to knock him down ; saying, at the same time—'We have interrupted the company sufficiently here, and, if you have anything further to say to me, you know where I am to be found.' A further altercation ensued ; but his Lordship, being at the other end of the stand, did not distinctly hear it, and, then, the parties retired.

" Lord Dartrey, afterwards Lord Cremorne, and his lady, with a gentleman, were at the inn at the time when the duel was fought. They went into the garden, and endeavoured to prevent the duel ; Mr Rowlls desired his Lordship and others not to interfere ; and, on a second attempt of his Lordship to make peace, Mr Rowlls said, if they did not retire, he must, though reluctantly, call them impertinent. Mr England, at the same time, stepped forward, and took off his hat ; he said—'Gentlemen, I have been cruelly treated ; I have been injured in my honour and character ; let reparation be made, and I am ready to have done this moment.' Lady Dartrey retired. His Lordship stood in the bower of the garden until he saw Mr Rowlls fall. One, or two, witnesses were called, who proved nothing material. A paper, containing the prisoner's defence, being read, *the Earl of Derby, the Marquis of Hertford, Mr Whitbread, jun., Col. Bishopp, and other gentlemen*, were called to his character. They all spoke of him as a man of *decent, gentlemanly deportment*, who, instead of seeking quarrels, was studious to avoid them. He had been friendly to Englishmen while abroad, and had rendered some service to the military at the siege of Newport.

" Mr Justice Rooke summed up the evidence ; after which,

the jury retired for about three-quarters of an hour, when they returned a verdict of *Manslaughter*.

"The prisoner, having fled from the laws of his country for twelve years, the Court was disposed to show no lenity. He was, therefore, sentenced to pay a fine of one shilling, and be imprisoned in Newgate for twelve months."

We have a terrible instance in a man, otherwise amiable in all relations of life, of the infatuation for the Turf. Lord Foley, who died July 2, 1793, entered upon the Turf with an estate of £18,000 a year, and £100,000 ready money. He left it with a ruined constitution, an incumbered estate, and not a shilling of ready money!

Here are three paragraphs from the *Times* about this date relative to racing :

17th April 1794. "Poor *Newmarket* is completely done up! The Spring meeting boasts so few bets in the calendar of gambling, that the chance will not pay post chaise hire to the black legs. Thus falls the destructive sport of the Turf —and, as that is the case, it would do honour to his Majesty to change the *King's Plates* into rewards for the *improvement of Agriculture.*" This suggestion has been carried out in the present reign.

25th May 1795. "The Duke of Queensberry was a principal loser at Epsom Races. The noble Duke had his *vis-a-vis*, and six horses, driving about the course, with two very pretty *emigrées* in it. The Duke was in his cabriolet. The Duke of Bedford, Lords Egremont and Derby were, also, on the course. Several carriages were broken to pieces; and one Lady had her arm broken.

"There was much private business done in the *swindling way* at the last Epsom Races. One black legged fellow cleared near a thousand pounds by the old trick of an E.O. Table. Another had a *faro table*, and was on the eve of *doing business*, when he was detected with a *palmed card*: almost the whole of what may be justly styled the 'vagabond gamblers' of London were present.

"Mr Bowes, half brother of the Earl of Strathmore, was

robbed of a gold watch, and a purse containing 30 guineas, at Epsom races, on Thursday last. Many other persons shared a similar fate, both on the same evening, and Friday. Upwards of 30 carriages were robbed, coming from the races."

8th Sep. 1797. " Never, since *racing* was patronised by the *Merry Monarch*, has the Turf been so much on the decline as at this period. His Grace of Bedford is the only person who retains a considerable stud. Lord Grosvenor has disposed of nearly the whole of his, with the reserve of two, or three, capital horses, and some few brood mares."

CHAPTER XIV

THE singular contest which took place between Mrs Thornton[1] and Mr Flint in 1804 was the talk of its time. An intimacy existed between the families of Col. Thornton and Mr Flint, the two ladies being sisters. In the course of one of their rides in Thornville Park, the lady of Colonel Thornton and Mr Flint were conversing on the qualities of their respective horses ; the difference of opinion was great, and the horses were occasionally put at full speed for the purpose of ascertaining the point in question ; old Vingarillo, on whom the lady rode, distancing his antagonist every time. Which so discomforted Mr Flint, that he was induced to challenge the lady to ride on a future day. The challenge was readily accepted, and it was agreed that the race should take place on the last day of the York August meeting 1804. This curious match was announced in the following manner :—

"A match for 500 gs., and 1000 gs. bye—four miles—between Colonel Thornton's Vingarillo and Mr Flint's br. h. Thornville by Volunteer—Mrs Thornton to ride her weight against Mr Flint's."

On Sunday, August the 25th, this race took place, and the following description of it appeared in the *York Herald* :—

" Never did we witness such an assemblage of people as were drawn together on the above occasion—100,000, at

---

[1] A Miss Alicia Meynell, daughter of a respectable watchmaker of Norwich, aged 22—but not married to Col. Thornton.

least.   Nearly ten times the number appeared on Knaves-mire than did on the day when Bay Malton ran, or when Eclipse went over the course, leaving the two best horses of the day a mile and a half behind.   Indeed, expectation was raised to the highest pitch, from the novelty of the match. Thousands from every part of the surrounding country thronged to the ground.   In order to keep the course as clear as possible, several additional people were employed ; and, much to the credit of the 6th Light Dragoons, a party of them, also, were on the ground on horseback, for the pur-pose, and which, unquestionably, was the cause of many lives being saved.

"About four o'clock, Mrs Thornton appeared on the ground, full of spirit, her horse led by Colonel Thornton, and followed by two gentlemen ; afterwards appeared Mr Flint.   They started a little past four o'clock.   The lady took the lead for upwards of three miles, in most capital style : her horse, however, had much the shorter stroke of the two.   When within a mile of being home, Mr Flint pushed forward, and got the lead, which he kept.   Mrs Thornton used every exertion ; but, finding it impossible to win the race, she drew up, in a sportsmanlike style, when within about two distances.

"At the commencement of the running, bets were 5 and 6 to 4 on the lady ; in running the first three miles 7 to 4 and 2 to 1 in her favour.   Indeed, the oldest sportsman on the stand thought she must have won.   In running the last mile the odds were in favour of Mr Flint.   Never, surely, did a woman ride in better style.   It was difficult to say whether her horsemanship, her dress, or her beauty, were most admired——the *tout ensemble* was *unique*.   Her dress was a leopard-coloured body, with blue sleeves, the rest buff and blue cap.   Mr Flint rode in white.   The race was run in nine minutes and fifty-nine seconds.

"Thus ended the most interesting race ever ran upon Knavesmire.   No words could express the disappointment felt at the defeat of Mrs Thornton.   The spirit she displayed, and the good humour with which she bore her loss, greatly diminished the joy, even of the winners."

This exhibition of herself seems to have fired her ambition, for we read in the *Morning Post*, Aug. 20, 1805 :

" Mrs Thornton is to ride 9 st. against Mr Bromford, who is to ride 13 st. over the York Course, four miles ; to run the last race on Saturday in the next August meeting, for four hogsheads of Coti Roti p.p. and 2000 guineas h. ft. ; and Mrs T. bets Mr B. 700 gs. to 600 gs. p.p. ; the 2000 gs. h. ft. provided it is declared to the Stewards four days before starting, Mrs T. to have the choice of four horses.

" Mr B. to ride Allegro, sister to Allegranti.

" *N.B.*, Colonel T., or any gentleman he may name, to be permitted to follow the lady over the course, to assist her in case of any accident."

But, on the eventful 24th Aug., for some reason or other, Mr Bromford declined the race, paid forfeit, and the lady cantered over the course. Later in the day she really had a race, which is thus described in the *Annual Register* :

" Afterwards commenced a match, in which the above lady was to ride two miles against Mr Buckle, the jockey, well known at Newmarket, and other places of sport, as a rider of the first celebrity. Mrs Thornton appeared dressed for the contest in a purple cap and waistcoat, nankeen coloured skirts, purple shoes and embroidered stockings ; she was in high health and spirits, and seemed eager for the decision of the match. Mr Buckle was dressed in a blue cap, with a blue bodied jacket, and white sleeves. Mrs Thornton carried 9 st. 6 lb., Mr Buckle 13 st. 6 lbs. At half-past three they started. Mrs Thornton took the lead, which she kept for some time ; Mr Buckle then put in trial his jockeyship, and passed the lady, which he kept for only a few lengths, when Mrs Thornton, by the most excellent horsemanship, pushed forward, and came in, in a style far superior to anything of the kind we ever witnessed, gaining her race by half a neck ; and, on her winning, she was hailed with the most reiterated shouts of congratulation.

"A sad disturbance took place, in the stand, in the after-noon, in consequence of a dispute between Mr Flint (who rode against Mrs Thornton last year) and Colonel Thornton, respecting £1000. Mr Flint had posted the Colonel on Thursday, and the Colonel recriminated on Friday. This day, Mr Flint came to the stand with a new horse whip, which he applied to the Colonel's shoulders with great activity, in the presence of a crowd of ladies. All the gentlemen in the place, indignant at this gross and violent outrage, hissed and hooted him. He was arrested by order of the Lord Mayor and several magistrates, who were pre-sent, and given into custody of the City runners, until he can find bail, himself in £1000, and two sureties in £500 each. Colonel Thornton is also bound over to prosecute the party for the assault."

The sequel to this story is told in the same Magazine, 5th Feb. 1806. "In the Court of King's Bench, an application was made on behalf of Colonel Thornton, for leave to file a criminal information against Mr Flint, for challenging him to fight a duel, and horse-whipping him on the race ground at York last summer, &c. The quarrel arose out of a bet of 1500 guineas which Mr Flint claims to have won of Colonel Thornton by the race he rode against Mrs Thornton, whose bets were adopted by her husband. Whereas Colonel Thornton maintains that, of the bet alluded to, £1000 was a mere nominal thing, intended to attract company to the race, and that nothing more than 500 guineas were seriously intended by the parties. After a full hearing of the whole case, Lord Ellenborough was of opinion, that the case before the Court was one in which their Lordships ought not to interpose with its extraordinary power. On the contrary, he conceived it would be degrading its process to interfere in favour of such parties in such a cause. Colonel Thornton had chosen to appeal to the Jockey Club, and should have abided by their decision. He had, however, not found them exactly fitting his notion of justice; and, therefore, for every thing that had happened since, he must have recourse to the ordinary mode of obtaining redress, namely, by preferring a Bill of Indictment at the Sessions of the County. The other judges being of the same opinion, the rule was discharged." Flint afterwards became very poor, and was manager at a horse bazaar at York, where he met with his end, according to the Coroner's jury's verdict—"Died from taking too large a dose of prussic acid as a medicine."

We now come to a piece of rascality on the turf, which ended in a man being hanged. The first heard about it is reported in the *Annual Register*, 6th May 1811. "An occurrence has taken place at Newmarket, which is the subject of general consternation and surprise among the frequenters of the Turf. Several horses were entered for the Claret Stakes, and, as usual, were taken out in the morning for exercise. They all drank, as we understand, at one water trough. Some time after they had been watered, six of them were observed to stagger, and then to roll about in the greatest agony. One is since dead. On examining the watering trough, it was found that the water had been poisoned. The horses were the property of Mr Sitwell, Sir F. Standish, and Lord Kinnaird. Suspicion has attached upon one of the jockies."

22nd July, 1812. "Daniel Dawson was arraigned at the Cambridge Assizes, on an indictment, with numerous counts, viz., for poisoning a horse belonging to Mr Adams, of Royston, Herts, and a blood mare belonging to Mr Northey, at Newmarket, in 1809 ; and, also, for poisoning a horse belonging to Sir F. Standish, and another belonging to Lord Foley in 1811, at the same place. He was tried and convicted on the first case only.

" The principal witness was Cecil Bishop, an accomplice with the prisoner. He had been, for some time, acquainted with Dawson, and on application to him, had furnished him with corrosive sublimate to sicken horses. He went on to prove that Dawson and he had become progressively acquainted ; and, that, on the prisoner complaining that the stuff was not strong enough, he prepared him a solution of arsenic. Witness described this as not offensive in smell; the prisoner having informed him that the horses had thrown up their heads, and refused to partake of the water into which the corrosive sublimate had been infused. The prisoner complained that the stuff was not strong enough; and, on being informed that if it was made strong it would kill the horses, he replied that he did not mind that; the Newmarket frequenters were rogues, and if he (meaning witness) had a fortune to lose they would plunder him of it. The prisoner afterwards informed witness he used the stuff, which was then strong enough, as it had killed a hackney and two brood mares.

" Mrs Tillbrook, a housekeeper at Newmarket, where the prisoner lodged, proved having found a bottle of liquid concealed under Dawson's bed, previous to the horses having been poisoned; and that Dawson was out late on the Saturday and Sunday evenings previous to that event, which took place on the Monday. After Dawson had left the house, she found the bottle, which she identified as having contained the said liquid, and which a chemist proved to have contained poison. Witness also proved that Dawson had cautioned her that he had poison in the house for some dogs, lest anyone should have the curiosity to taste it. Other witnesses proved a chain of circumstances which left no doubt of the prisoner's guilt.

" Mr King, for the prisoner, took a legal objection that no criminal offence had been committed, and that the subject was a matter of trespass. He contended that the indictment must fail, as it was necessary to prove that the prisoner had malice against the owner of the horse, to impoverish him, and not against the animal. He also contended that the object of the prisoner was to injure and not to kill. The objections was overruled without reply, and the prisoner was convicted.

" The judge pronounced sentence of death on the prisoner, and informed him, in strong language, he could not expect mercy to be extended to him:" and the man was duly hanged.

Another gruesome episode of the Turf was the suicide of Mr Roger Brograve early in June 1813, owing to losses by betting. He was the brother of Sir George Brograve, and had been a captain in the 2nd Dragoons, and for some years had betted heavily. Originally, he had a competent, if not a splendid fortune, but, at the previous Newmarket meeting, he had lost heavily, and he was known to have lost £10,000 on the Derby. This he could not meet, and he shot himself. Hundreds of similar cases might be given, but this one must serve as an example. That large sums were wagered and lost and won at this time we may learn from the fact that in 1816 no less a sum than £300,000 is said to have been paid and received at Tattersall's in the betting settlement on that year's Epsom races.

Of the origin of bookmaking, Mr Dixon (The Druid) has written so well in *The Post and the Paddock*, that I cannot do better than copy him *verbatim* :

" Betting between one and the field was the fashion which Turf speculation assumed in the days of powder and periwigs, and Ogden (the only betting man who was ever admitted to the Club at Newmarket), Davies, Holland, Deavden, Kettle, Bickham, and Watts, ruled on the Turf 'Change. With Jem Bland, Jerry Cloves, Myers (an ex-butler), Richard (the Leicester Stockinger), Mat Milton, Tommy Swan of Bedale (who never took or laid but one bet on a Sunday), Highton, Holliday, Gully, Justice, Crockford, Briscoe, Crutch Robinson, Ridsdale, Frank Richardson, and Bob Steward, etc., the art of bookmaking arose, and, henceforward, what had been more of a pastime among owners, who would back their horses for a rattler when the humour took them, and not shrink from having £5000 to £6000 on a single match, degenerated into a science. All the above, with the exception of two, have passed away, like the Mastodons, never to return. Nature must have broken the mould in which she formed the crafty Robinson, as he leant on his crutch, with his back against the outer wall of the Newmarket Betting Rooms, and, with his knowing, quiet leer, and one hand in his pocket, offered to 'lay agin Plenipo.'

"The two Blands, Joe and 'Facetious Jemmy,' were equally odd hands. Epsom had fired up the latter's desire to come on to the turf, and he descended from his coachman's box at Hedley for that purpose, and sported his 'noble lord' hat, white cords, deep bass voice, and vulgar dialect, on it, for the first time, about 1812. He did not trouble it much after he had 'dropped his sugar' on Shillelah, though that *contretemps* did not completely knock him out of time. His acute rough expressions, such as '*never coomed anigh*,' and so on, as well as his long nose, and white, flabby cheeks, made him a man of mark, even before he got enough, by laying all round, to set up a mansion in Piccadilly. Joe, his brother, had, originally, been a post boy, and rose from thence to be a stable keeper in Great Wardour Street ; but, the great hit of his life was his successful farming of turnpike gates, at which he was supposed to have made about £25,000. 'Ludlow Bond' was not so coarse in his style as this *par nobile*, but ambitious and vain to the last degree. It was the knowledge of this latter quality, on the part of Ludlow's real owners, 'the Yorkshire Blacksmith & Co.,' which induced them to put him forward as the ostensible owner of the horse, as no one would back a horse which was known to be theirs. Bond liked the notoriety which this nominal ownership conferred on him, and was, no doubt, a mere puppet, without exactly knowing who pulled the strings. Discreditable as the affair was, he always gloried in it ; in fact he was so determined not to let the memory of it die out, that he christened a yearling which he bought from the Duke of Grafton, 'Ludlow Junior.' At times he appeared on the heath on a grey hack, and went by the nickname of '*Death on the Pale Horse*,' and, shortly after the Doncaster outburst, he came on in a handsome travelling carriage, with two servants in livery in the rumble.

"Mr Gully, although he did great execution at the Corner in Andover's year, may be styled a mere fancy bettor now, and, as a judge of racing and the points of a horse combined, he has scarcely a peer among his own, or the younger generation of turfites. His fame at the Corner was at its zenith a quarter of a century ago, when he was a betting partner with Ridsdale. Rumour averred that they won £35,000 on Margrave for the St Leger (1832), and £50,000 on St Giles for the Derby ; and it was in consequence of a dispute as to the Margrave winnings, that the Siamese link between them was so abruptly dissolved. Their joint books also showed a balance of £80,000 if Red Rover could only have brought Priam to grief for the Derby. There was a joke too, soon after this time, that Mr Gully and his friend Justice descended on to Cheltenham, and so completely cleaned out the local ring there, that the two did not even think it worth while stopping for the second race day. One of the lesser lights was found wandering moodily about the ring on that day, and remarked to a sympathiser that he was ' looking for the few half crowns that Gully and Justice had condescended to leave.' "

In the second quarter of this century the Turf was getting in a scandalous condition. A fair race was hardly known for the St Leger, and, in 1827, Mameluke was got rid of by a series of false starts. In 1832 was the Ludlow scandal, just alluded to. This horse was the property of a man named Beardsworth, who was such a rogue that no one would bet on or against his horse, so it was apparently purchased by Ephraim Bond, the keeper of a gambling house, called the Athenæum Club, in St James's Street. In reality it was owned by four people, Beardsworth, Bond and his brother, and a mysterious fourth party, whose name was not divulged. Ludlow was beaten by Margrave, a horse owned by Gully, the ex-prize fighter, who boldly accused Squire Osbaldistone of being the unknown fourth owner of Ludlow. The consequence was a duel, in which both combatants had very narrow escapes ; Gully especially, for his opponent's bullet went through his hat and ploughed a furrow in his hair.

In 1834 Plenipotentiary, or as it was called for brevity, Plenipo, the favourite for the St Leger, was undoubtedly "nobbled," either by his owner, Batson, or his trainer, George Paine, either of which were capable of any dishonourable conduct.

There were, afterwards, many minor Turf scandals, but they culminated in the Derby of 1844 which is known as Running Rein's Derby, which ran as a three-year-old, being in reality four years. As this fraud was the subject of an action, its story may be well told in the following synopsis of the trial.

IN THE EXCHEQUER.

July 1.

Before Mr Baron Alderson.

WOOD *v.* PEEL.

This action, which excited the most lively interest in the *Sporting World*, arose out of the late Derby race at Epsom, in which a horse belonging to the plaintiff, called Running Rein, had come in first. It was alleged, however, that this horse had not been truly described, that he was not of the age which qualified him to run for the Derby, and that he ought not, therefore, to be deemed the winner of the race. Colonel Peel, the owner of Orlando, the second horse, had claimed the stakes, on the ground that Running Rein was not the horse represented ; and Mr Wood, the owner of Running Rein, brought this action against the Colonel.

Mr Cockburn, who conducted the plaintiff's case, gave the pedigree of Running Rein, and his whole history. Among other things, Mr Cockburn mentioned that, in October 1843, Running Rein won a race at Newmarket ; that he was objected to on the score of age, but, eventually, the stewards had decided in his favour. The horse was, originally, the property of Mr Goodman ; and, Mr Cockburn said, it was because suspicion attached to some transactions of Goodman, and because certain parties had betted heavily against Running Rein, that opposition was raised against Mr Wood receiving the stakes.   He made a severe attack on Lord George Bentinck, who, he asserted, was the real party in the cause. Witnesses for the plaintiff described the horse at various periods of its career : it was of a bay colour, with black legs, and a little white on the forehead ; its heels were cracked, and in 1842 it broke the skin on one leg, which left a scar.   George Hitchcock, a breaker of colts, employed to break Running Rein in October 1842, was cross-examined to this effect :

"I know George Dockeray, the trainer.   I never said to him, 'Damn it, this colt has been broken before ; here is the mark of the pad on his back.'   I showed him the mark, but I never said those words, or any words to that effect.   I don't know why I showed him the mark.   It was not big enough for the mark of a pad, and it was not the place for the saddle to make it.   I told Lord George Bentinck the same.   The mark of the pad never wears out.   I recollect being asked, in the presence of Mr Smith, what had I there ? and I recollect answering, a four years' old.   I have not the slightest doubt of it.   Mr Smith struck me for it.   I did not say afterwards that I had forgotten all about the horse whipping, and that the marks of the pad had worn out.   I never said, either, that somebody had behaved very well to me."

At an early period of the examination of witnesses, Mr Baron Alderson expressed a wish that he and the jury should see the horse ; and Mr Cockburn said he had no objection.   On the cross-examination of William Smith, a training groom residing at Epsom, it came out that the horse had been smuggled out of the way, that it might not be seen by the defendant's agents.   The Judge, animadverting on this, and on the evident perjury of the witness, said it would be better that the horse should be seen by him and other parties.   The Solicitor-General, who appeared for the defendant, was anxious that the horse should be seen by veterinary surgeons.   To which the other side objected, maintaining that the mark of mouth, by which alone these surgeons could judge of the age of a horse, was a fallible criterion.

On the conclusion of the evidence for the plaintiff, the Solicitor-General, in addressing the jury for the defence, denounced the case as a gross and scandalous fraud on the part of the plaintiff. The case of the defendant was, that the horse was not Running Rein at all, but a colt by Gladiator, out of a dam belonging originally to Sir Charles Ibbotson ; and that it had the name Running Rein imposed upon it, being originally called Maccabeus, and having been entered for certain stakes under that designation. But his allegations were against Goodman, not against Mr Wood : the former had entered into a conspiracy with other persons to run horses above the proper age. The Gladiator colt had been entered for races, under the name of Maccabeus, before Goodman purchased him ; and to run these races while the colt was in training for the Derby, for which he was entered as Running Rein, Goodman hired an Irish horse, which he disguised as Maccabeus, though a year older than that horse. The Gladiator colt, the *soi distant* Running Rein, when he ran for the Derby in 1844, was four years old, the race being for three-year-old horses. After hearing some evidence in support of these statements, the case was adjourned till the following day.

The next day, when Mr Baron Alderson took his seat on the Bench, a conversation ensued between Mr Cockburn and the Judge, respecting the production of the horse. Mr Cockburn asserted that it had been taken away without Mr Wood's knowledge, and thus it was out of his power to produce it ; he felt it would be vain to strive against the effect which must be produced by the non-production of the horse, after the remarks of the learned judge on that point. After some more conversation, however, the case proceeded, and two witnesses for the defence were examined, whose evidence went to prove that Running Rein was, in fact, the Gladiator colt. Mr George Odell, a horse dealer at Northampton, said he could swear to that fact ; the colt had two marks on one leg.

Mr Baron Alderson remarked—" Now, if we could see the

horse, that would prove the case. Who keeps him away? It is quite childish to act in this manner."

Mr Cockburn now stated that Mr Wood was convinced that he had been deceived, and gave up the case.

Mr Baron Alderson then briefly addressed the jury with much warmth, and in a most emphatic manner; directing them to find a verdict for the defendant, observing:

"Since the opening of the case, a most atrocious fraud has been proved to have been practised; and I have seen, with great regret, gentlemen associating themselves with persons much below themselves in station. If gentlemen would associate with gentlemen, and race with gentlemen, we should have no such practises. But, if gentlemen will condescend to race with blackguards, they must expect to be cheated."

The jury found for the defendant, and the effect of their verdict was that the Derby Stakes went to Orlando, and that Crenoline should be considered the winner of the Two-Year-Old Plate at Newmarket, run the previous year.

This ought to have been sufficient roguery, one would think, for one race, but it was not. A horse named Ratan was so evidently "nobbled," that two men connected with it, Rogers and Braham, were warned off all the Jockey Club's premises.

And yet another case. A horse named Leander ran in this race, and so injured its leg that it was shot. Shortly afterwards, it was suspected that it was four instead of three years old, and on its being exhumed, *the lower jaw was missing*. The resurrectionists, however, cut off the head, and veterinary experts confirmed the previous suspicions. For this, the owners, Messrs Lichtwald, were for ever disqualified from racing. This case occupied much time before the Select Committee of the House of Lords.

The Select Committee on Gaming in the Commons in 1844 report that "Your Committee have some evidence to show that frauds are, occasionally, committed in Horse racing, and in Betting on the Turf; but they feel difficulty in suggesting any remedy for this evil, more stringent, or more likely to be effectual, than those already in existence."

The House of Lords reported in similar terms, but they added : " The Committee have inquired into certain transactions which have, lately, been brought before the Courts of Law, arising from the fraudulent practices of Individuals substituting other horses for those named in stakes which are limited to horses of a certain age, and thus obtaining the advantages arising from running, at even weights, Three-year-olds against Two-year-olds, and Four-year-olds against Three-year-olds.   The success, however, which has attended the prosecutions instituted for the Recovery of the Stakes thus unjustly won, and the rules which the Committee are led to believe will be, hereafter, strictly attended to, as to the examination, by competent persons, of all horses which may be objected to, render it unnecessary for them to make any further comment upon this part of their inquiry."

But the Commons Committee reported on another subject, the Gaming-houses in race towns, and the Gaming-booths on the courses.

" The suppression of Gaming-houses in race towns, and in other places out of the Metropolitan Police District, is to be effected under the common law, and under the enactment of Statutes different from the Metropolitan Police Act.   Much laxity and neglect have, hitherto, prevailed in this respect ; and your Committee think that the attention of Magistrates might, usefully, be directed to this matter.   But, if it should be found that the powers given by the existing law are insufficient, your Committee would recommend that additional powers should be conferred.

" Your Committee have found that it is the practice on some race courses to let out ground for the erection of Gaming-booths, during the races, in order that the high rents paid by the keepers of these booths may be added to the fund from whence prizes to be run for are to be given ; and some of the witnesses examined have stated that certain race meetings, which they have named, could not be kept up, if this practice were to be discontinued."

CHAPTER XV

THIS system of gambling on race courses began the previous century.   In Canto I. of *The Gambler's, A Poem*, Lon. 1777, we read :

> "But, chief, we see a bricking, sharping sort,
>   *Span farthing, Hustle Cap*, their joy and sport ;
> The sport of infancy ! 'till riper age
> Mature the man, and call him to the stage.
> In each shoot forth the dawning seeds of vice,
> The growing Jockey, or the man of Dice.
> Some prick the Belt, self tutor'd, young in sin,
> Anxious to take their wond'ring fellows in.
> Here, a surrounding groupe of little Squires,
> As chink the brazen belts, Chuck farthing fires :
> While *Sçavoir-vivres* early signs betray
> Of bold adventures, and the rage of play.
> These, haply shall some future bard engage,
> The hopeful *Kelly's*[1] of the rising age.
> But, when maturer years confirm the sin,
> And opening minds suck the dear poison in,
> Adieu, *Span farthing! Hustle Cap*, farewell !
> With nobler passions, nobler views, they swell :
> Dice, tennis, Cards, inferior sports succeed,
> And the gay triumph of the High bred Steed."

Complaints of racecourse gambling began early in the present century.   In the *Gentleman's Magazine* for 1801 (p. 327) we read : "Mr Urban—As the quarter sessions will take place in most parts of England in the course of the

---

[1] Capt. Kelly, owner of Eclipse.

present month, I wish, through the medium of your extensively circulated Magazine, to submit to the serious consideration of the County Magistrates, the absolute necessity for adopting some vigorous measures, in order to check the career of those infamous swindlers, who are in the constant habit of attending our fairs and races with E.O. tables, &c.   It is an alarming fact that there is scarcely a fair, or a race, of the least celebrity, which is not infested with these villains, many of whom clear £500 annually by plundering the unsuspecting rustics, who attend such places, of their property."

Goldsmith, in his life of Beau Nash, tells us that E.O. was first set up at Tunbridge, in the reign of George I., and was introduced into Bath by Nash: and, as the game was a very popular one, I give the following description of it, as found in Rice's *History of the British Turf* :

" The E.O. table was circular in form, and, though made in various sizes, was, commonly, four feet in diameter.   The outside edge formed the counter, or *depôt*, on which the stakes were placed, and was marked all round with the letters E.O. from which the game took its name.   The interior of the table consisted of a stationary gallery, in which the ball rolled, and an independent round table, moving on an axis, by means of handles.   The ball was started in one direction, and this rotary table turned in the other.   This part was divided into forty compartments of equal size, twenty of which were marked E. and twenty O. The principle was pretty much as that of roulette without a zero ; but the ingenuity of the proprietors appears, at an early date in the history of these tables, to have supplied this defect.   At first the game was played on the same terms as hazard then was, viz., whoever won, or threw in three times successively, paid, when gold was played for, half a guinea to the proprietors of the table.   This, however, as might have been expected, was too simple and unsophisticated a method of procedure to last.   The game was too fair ; but, as it was very popular, it must be made profitable to the man of business, who could not be expected to travel from race meeting to race meeting all over the country, for half guineas in cases of exceptional luck. Accordingly, he became obliged to take all bets offered either for E. or for O., and made two of his forty spaces into 'bar holes.' The name sufficiently explains the utility of the device to the keeper of the table. If the ball fell into either of these 'bar holes,' he won all the bets on the opposite letter, and did not pay to that on which it fell. Unfair tables, having the compartments of one letter larger than another, abounded ; but there seems to have been little necessity to cheat at the game, as, with a proportion of two in forty, or five per cent., in his favour, the keeper should have reaped a heavy harvest of profit from his venture. The gentlemen who had played the game at the time when the occasional half guinea was thought enough to remunerate the proprietor, could hardly have liked the innovation, regarding the five per cent. 'pull' against them as 'a circumstance which, in the long run, would infallibly exhaust the *Exchequer*' much more than the breeches pockets of the young squires.

The booths at Ascot Heath, and the taverns in Windsor, were, at race time, great haunts for the keepers of the E.O. tables, some of whom were respectable men in their calling, and might be trusted to give twenty, or even more, shillings for a guinea ; but the majority, gambling for twopenny pieces and sixpences, were little, if anything, better than the thimble-rig and prick-the-garter gentry of that, or the three-card practitioners of our own, time. Ascot, indeed, was, then, a race meeting of the first importance, and the week was a fair of the most attractive character to the Berkshire landlords and their tenantry. The Oatlands Stakes was transferred to Newmarket from Ascot, after a memorable race, when a hundred thousand pounds changed hands ; and we read that the Turf was a barren and dreary prospect—for the losers. 'Horses are daily thrown out of training, jockeys are going into mourning, grooms are becoming E.O. merchants, and strappers are going on the highway.'"

In the *Quarterly Review* for 1834, a description is given of gambling at races, as it then was. "Doncaster, Epsom, Ascot, Warwick, and most of our numerous race grounds and race towns are scenes of destructive and universal gambling among the lower orders, which our absurdly lax police never attempt to suppress; and yet, without the slightest approach to an improperly harsh interference with the pleasures of the people, the roulette and E.O. tables which plunder the peasantry at these places, for the benefit of travelling sharpers (certainly equally respectable with some bipeds of prey who drive coroneted cabs near St James's), might be put down by any watchful magistrate."

The Commons Select Committee on Gaming in 1844 tells us a great deal about the gambling at Doncaster, during race meetings. A Mr Richard Baxter was the witness, and he said:

"The extent to which gambling has been carried on, both upon the course, and in the town of Doncaster, has varied at different periods. Twenty years ago, in 1824, was my first acquaintance with the matter: I went, as a stranger, to live in Doncaster, and I found that there were 40 or 50 houses, and men stationed at the doors, and passing up and down the streets, not only, by word, inviting the passers by to go into those houses, but putting into their hands cards (one of which I have here)—

To Noblemen and Gentlemen.

ROULETTE.

Bank.　£1000.

At Mason's (the Tailor), Scott Lane.

—explanatory of the game that was going on there, and, without any secrecy, or reserve, stating the name of the party at whose house the game was carried on.

" Being a stranger in the town, I went into almost all the houses, and found them playing, in some with dice, and in some with balls, at the different games, the names of all of which I do not know : but gambling was going on to this extent, and no check to it, whatever, was put by the local authorities. At the same time, upon the race course, the thimble men were in hundreds, with their tables, as well as by the roadsides on every approach to Doncaster, playing, and cheating the people out of their money, as fast as they could induce them to play. As I was a stranger in the place, I did not think it becoming in me, at that time, to interfere ; and, for two years following, I did no more than speak upon the subject to the mayor and the magistrates, and the gentlemen of the town, urging them to take some means to repress this systematic gambling ; but, in the year 1827, which was the third year, finding that the authorities would take no notice of it, I laid an information against one of the gambling houses, against Henry Oldfield, who is a very noted character in gambling. I brought the owner of the house, who is a very respectable tradesman in the town ; I brought the sister of the owner and his servants ; I brought the man who attended at the door, and invited people publicly, ' Roulette and Hazard going on upstairs '; I brought a gentleman, a respectable surgeon of the town, who had been in the room, and played there. Those parties I brought before the magistrates, they were examined upon oath. The owner of the house denied all knowledge of the object for which the room was let ; the gentleman, who had been present, owned that he had played, but denied his knowledge of the name of the game at which he played ; and, the result was, that the magistrates refused to convict. No further step was taken in that year ; but, in the following year, without again speaking to the authorities, I represented the matter to the neighbouring gentry, and the present Lord

Fitzwilliam, Mr Beckett Denison, one of the Members for the West Riding ; Mr Childers, the Member for Malton ; and, perhaps, 20 or 30 other gentlemen, in the neighbourhood, and in the town, joined in an association, professedly, to repress gambling in the town. The rules of the association were, that application should be made to the local authorities, and such legal means taken, as could be made available to induce the authorities to repress gambling. This was most respectably supported and published. The consequence was, that we had an *émeute* in the town : the inhabitants assembled at a public meeting, a gentleman, who is, now, one of the Borough Magistrates, was put into the chair, and a regular set of speeches made against the Anti-Gambling Association, and all parties concerned. I thought it my duty to go to the meeting ; and, of course, you may suppose, was very warmly received. I told them, very candidly and freely, my mind upon the subject. They heard me for a certain length of time ; but, finding the chairman refused to let me go on, I left the meeting, and had the honour of being pelted down the street on my way home, as a recompense for the advice I had taken the liberty of tendering them. The consequence of this *émeute* was, that our association fell to pieces. I am sorry to say, that the members who composed it did not choose, in the face of the unpopularity which it occasioned, to take any further step in it.

    .   .   .   .   .   .

" The extent of gambling in Doncaster for the last two or three years has been from six to twelve of the lower gambling houses and three of the higher gambling houses. The distinction between the one class and the other consists in this : that the lower gambling houses are kept by men who hire a little front shop, open to the street, for the purpose of taking mere passers-by ; the higher gambling houses, many of them houses of their own, which they have built in Doncaster, for the purpose of gaming ; a third class hire rooms of respectable tradesmen in the town, and occupy them ; and the popular opinion is, that there are clubs, and knots of gentlemen attached to each of those houses, who regularly go and play there. Oldfield, against whom the information was laid in 1827, was the keeper of one of the higher gambling houses, and I need scarcely state to the Committee that, popular as gambling is in the town, very strong remarks are made and a very strong feeling exists in the place, that, if the lower gambling houses are suppressed, it is unfair to the common people that the higher gambling houses should be permitted to continue ; and, when an information is laid against the low gambling houses, it is always matter of crimination ; ' Why did you not lay it against the gentlemen's houses? you are laying it against the houses of the poor people, but you will not lay it against the houses of the gentlemen.' Another circumstance connected with the races I may mention as a great public nuisance is, that the betting room, which is a building erected simply for the purpose of betting, is open on a Sunday, to the public, as on any other day, and during the time of Divine service in the evening more people, I am sorry to say, are assembled at the betting rooms than at church ; and there is a continual crowd filling half the street in front of the betting rooms the whole of the Sunday evening. A representation on the subject was made to the Chief Magistrate at the time, and the only answer we got to the representation to him was that he would communicate with the parties and endeavour to have it closed : it was closed during the morning and afternoon services, but it was open to the public, as before, during the evening service, and hundreds of those who are called gentlemen were assembled there betting, and all the affairs of the races going on quite as publicly as on any other evening of the week.

" 1024.—With regard to gambling on the race course, whether by thimble-riggers, or by roulette, or any other kind of gambling, whether in booths or not, are the Committee to understand that that has of late years entirely ceased to exist ?—That has been suppressed.

" 1025.—By the interference of the police ?—Yes."

A Mr John Rushbridger, who had charge of the ground at Goodwood, on which the races were held, was examined, and he deposed that there were only two gambling booths on the course, which paid £125 each for the privilege; whilst refreshment booths were only charged 10s. or 15s. They endeavoured, as far as possible, to keep thimble-riggers off the course.

The Clerk of the Course at Egham said there used to be eighteen gambling booths on the course, but now there were only fourteen, which produced a rental of £240 ; but a portion of the grand stand was let for gambling purposes, and that brought in a further sum. The thimble-rigmen were allowed on the course, as far as the distance-post, and formerly used to pay for the permission.

A Timothy Barnard was examined, and said he speculated in race courses. At Egham he paid the Lord of the Manor £300 for the race course, and cleared £240 by the gambling booths. He gave £600 for Epsom course, but could not give £300 if he were deprived of the privilege of letting gaming booths, because they were the mainstay of the other booths, such as the publicans' booths ; many having their liquors and wines of them, and therefore the publicans would not give near as much for the ground, except for those booths. They made the thimble-riggers pay 5s. or 10s. to be allowed on the course ; they were given a little ticket which they were obliged to wear in their hats, or their tables would be taken from them.

In *Bentley's Magazine* for 1846 we get a good account of the working of the betting rooms at Doncaster. The sub-scription was a guinea, and the number of subscribers was from 1000 to 1200. " The rent paid by the proprietary for the premises is said to be £500 per an. ; but this is reduced in its amount by the circumstance of the rooms being let off for trading, or warehouse purposes, during ten months of the year ; and taking this reduction at the reasonable sum of £150, it would leave £350 as the rent from the estimated subscriptions of £1050, which would give a clear surplus of

£700 per an., which alone would be a large return of profit. But other sources of income and annual return are open to the proprietary, by the sale of wine, spirits, soda water, and divers refreshments, which are in almost constant demand in the great room throughout each evening, and partially so in the day. The prices at which these articles are sold are by no means so moderate as they might be, even to secure a fair and liberal compensation for their outlay, and must, on the most moderate calculation, yield £100 clear at least in the week.

"But the *El Dorado* or grand source of income and wealth to the proprietors arises from the prolific revenue of the play or gaming tables, of which there are usually six in constant nightly operation during the racing week. The proprietors of the Subscription Betting Rooms are not ostensibly connected in the co-partnership of the banks, or in the business of the tables, but they are nevertheless largely interested in the successful issue of the week, as will be shown. In the first instance it should be stated that the sum of £350 or £400 is *paid down* to them by the party contracting for the tables and for the privilege of putting down the banks. This is all clear profit, paid in advance and without any contingency ; and in addition to this apparently large sum, so paid for the mere privilege of finding capital, there is a stipulation also on the part of the proprietors of the rooms that they shall receive a considerable part or share of the whole clear profits, or gains, of the week accruing from the tables, and this without the risk of a single shilling by them under any unlooked-for reverse of fortune.

.   .   .   .   .   .

"The play tables at the Betting Rooms, are, as before noted, six, or seven, in number, and of variety in the games played thereat. The roulette tables attract the crowd, as well as for the reason that the game opens to the player many modes of proportionate risk, as that it affords him opportunity to play smaller sums on any one event, than he can at hazard. At the former game, the lowest stake is half a crown ; at the latter, nothing less than the regal coin of a sovereign is permitted.   The pull, or percentage, of roulette against the player, being, however, nearly five times that of hazard, the small stakes played realise as large a result to the bankers.   It requires all the vigilance of a player to guard his interests at this game ; for, generally speaking, there is much confusion in the distribution of money staked by the many adventurers, on the numbers, and other points of speculation attaching to the game ; and dispute, not infrequently, arises between two or three different claimants for the produce of some fortunate, or winning result.   These contested claims often arise from inattention in the player to the exact position of his money on the board, but are, sometimes, occasioned by the attempt of some sharping knave to possess himself of something which does not belong to him.   The officials at the table, too, are most dexterous in their practical avocations,—more particularly so in the principle of drawing the money from the losing points of the game, immediately the winning number, &c., is called. The rapidity with which this operation is performed, is most remarkable, and gives immense additional advantage to the bank ; for, it very often happens that, in the general sweep, the adroit croupiers rake off much more than they are entitled to ; while, on the other hand, they can never, under any circumstances, be called upon to pay more than the loss attaching to the event."

Doncaster is now, I believe, very much purified, but Sir George Chetwynd describes the gambling that went on there in 1869.   " How changed is Doncaster now, from what it was in those days !   Then, after dinner, you would go to the subscription rooms and back horses for the Cesare-witch and Cambridgeshire at 100 to 1 to win large stakes, and even small bookmakers thought nothing of starting £20,000 books.   After making their bets, people used to go into an inner room where hazard was being played.   Hour after hour the game continued in full swing at a table crowded with punters, with green, black, red and white ivory counters before them denoting £10, £5, £25, and £1. There was an impressive stillness in the room, only broken by the voice of Mr F. Hall, one of the croupiers, who, rake in hand, gave vent to such utterances as, ' The Castor is backing in at seven, gentlemen. I'll take on the nick.' Then came the rattle of the dice, the bang on the table of the box, the quick announcement of the point, and the raking in of the counters on the losing columns, by the two croupiers, one of whom looked like a respectable tradesman, or a magistrate's clerk. Behind the players stood the proprietor, a tall, handsome man, with carefully trimmed white beard and moustache, more like a general than the keeper of a hell ; his countenance immovable, except when it relaxed, as he replied courteously to any one who addressed him.

" He is dead, so is one of the croupiers, so are half the players, old and young, whom I first saw at the table twenty years ago, when, for the first time, I was initiated into the mysteries of hazard, how to dash down a ten, or dribble a four, as if, really, there was skill about a game which consists in rattling two dice in a box, and winning, or losing by the points they declare when rolled out on the table."

We have seen how disreputable the Turf had become in 1844. If anything, it became worse. A class of men sprung up, called " tipsters," men who pretended to have exclusive and particular stable information which they were willing to impart to their dupes, say (to quote the advertisement of one of the fraternity), Single events, 3s. 6d. Derby or Oaks, 5s. each : yearly subscription, 21s.; half yearly, 10s. 6d. That these men made a profitable business of it, there can be no doubt, for the sporting papers were full of their advertisements, some of them of great length : and, then, also began that curse attending horse racing, the betting shop—which afforded a fatal facility to all classes, to gamble, and which led to crime, and its attendant punishment.

In 1852, these houses had become such a crying scandal, that a public meeting was held on 18th June, at the Literary and Scientific Institution in Aldersgate Street, over which Sir Peter Laurie presided, to adopt measures for the suppression of betting houses in the City of London, and a resolution was moved, and carried unanimously, that a petition be presented to Parliament for their suppression. In the same year, at a meeting of the Aldermen at the Guildhall, the foreman of the Inquest of Farringdon Ward Without, handed in a presentment, which he said related to a subject of great importance in the City of London ; the gambling and betting houses in the Ward, by which great mischief was done. Facilities were given at these houses, of which there were a great number in the Ward, for betting, from sums of threepence, or fourpence upwards ; and by these means, many servants and boys, who certainly had no money of their own to bet with, were induced to lay wagers that too often led them into a career of crime.

The Druid says: "The great list era, and all its attendant Ripe-for-a-jails, as *Punch* termed them, began with Messrs Drummond and Greville, who 'kept an account at the Westminster Bank' in 1847. Up to that time 'sweeps,' where every subscriber drew a horse for his ticket, had been amply sufficient to satisfy the popular thirst for speculation on a Derby, or St Leger eve ; and, although, in one instance, we ascertained that our ticket horse was a leader in a Shrewsbury coach, instead of being 'prepared,' it was satisfactory to know that there was, at least, fair play. Stimulated by the example of D. and G., the licensed victuallers took it up—and a nice mess they made of it—till the licensing magistrates stepped sternly in. From 1850 to the end of 1853, the listers were in their glory ; and, at one period, about four hundred betting houses were open in London alone, of which, perhaps, ten were solvent."

CHAPTER XVI

IN *Chambers' Edinburgh Journal* of 24th July 1852, is
an excellent article on "BETTING HOUSES." It says :
"'Betting Shop' is vulgar, and we dislike vulgarity.
'Commission Office,' 'Racing Bank,' 'Mr Hopposite Green's
Office,' 'Betting Office,' are the styles of announcement
adopted by speculators, who open, what low people call,
Betting Shops. The chosen designation is, usually, painted
in gold letters on a chocolate coloured wire gauze blind,
impervious to the view. A betting office may display on its
small show board, two bronzed plaster horses, rampant, held
by two Ethiopian figures, nude ; or it may prefer making a
show of cigars. Many offices have risen out of simple
cigar shops. When this is the case, the tobacco business
gives way, the slow trade and fast profession not running
well together. An official appearance is always considered
necessary. A partition, therefore, sufficiently high not to
be peered over, runs midway across the shop, surmounted
with a rail. By such means, visions are suggested to the
intelligent mind, of desks, and clerks. In the partition is
an enlarged *pigeon* hole—not far off, may be supposed to
lurk the hawk—through which are received shillings, half
crowns ; in fact, any kind of coin or notes, no sum appearing inadmissible. The office is papered with a warm crimson
paper to make it snug and comfortable, pleasant as a lounge,
and casting a genial glow upon the proceedings.

"But the betting lists are the attraction—these are the
dice of the betting men ; a section of one of the side walls

within the office is devoted to them. They consist of long slips of paper—each race having its own slip—on which are stated the odds against the horses. Hasty and anxious are the glances which the speculator casts upon betting lists ; there he sees which are the favourites, whether those he has backed are advancing, or retrograding, and he endeavours to discover, by signs and testimonies, by all kinds of movements and dodges, the knowing one's opinion. He will drop fishing words to other gazers, will try to overhear whispered remarks, will sidle towards any jockey-legged, or ecurial-costumed individual, and aim more especially at getting into the good graces of the betting office keeper, who, when his business is slack, comes forth from behind the partition, and from the duties of the pigeon hole, to stretch his legs, and hold turf converse. The betting office keeper is the speculator's divinity.

.   .   .   .   .   .

"There are various kinds of betting offices. Some are speculative, May-fly offices, open to-day, and shut to-morrow —offices that will bet any way, and against anything—that will accommodate themselves to any odds—receive any sum they can get, small or large ; and, should a misfortune occur, such as a wrong horse winning, forget to open next day. These are but second rate offices. The money making, prosperous betting office is quite a different thing. It is not advisable for concerns which intend making thousands in a few years, to pay the superintendents liberally, and to keep well clothed touters—to conduct themselves, in short, like speculative offices. They must not depend entirely upon chance. Chance is very well for betting men, but will not do for the respectable betting office keepers, who are the stake holders.

"The plan adopted is a very simple one, but ingenious in its simplicity. The betting office takes a great dislike in its own mind to a particular horse, the favourite of the betting men. It makes bets against that horse, which amounts, in the aggregate, to a fortune ; and then it *buys* the object of its frantic delight. This being effected, the horse, of course, loses, and the office wins. How could it be otherwise? Would you have a horse win against its owner's interest? The thing being settled, the office, in order to ascertain the amount of its winnings, has only to deduct the price of the horse from its aggregate bets, and arrange the remainder in a line of, perhaps, five figures. Whereupon the betting men grow seedier and more seedy: some of the more mercurial go off in a fit of apoplectic amazement; some betake themselves to Waterloo stairs on a moonless night; some proceed to the diggings, some to St Luke's, and some to the dogs; some become so unsteady, that they sign the wrong name to a draft, or enter the wrong house at night, or are detected in a crowd with their hand in the wrong man's pocket. But, by degrees, everything comes right again. The insane are shut up, the desperate transported, the dead buried, the deserted families carted to the workhouse; and the betting-office goes on as before."

The scandal, however, grew too grave to be ignored, and the Government took the matter up. On July 11, 1853, the Attorney-General rose in his place in the House of Commons, and said, he would now beg to move for leave to bring in a Bill for the suppression of betting houses, and, in doing so, he considered it was not necessary for him to make any lengthened statement on the subject, as the evils which had arisen from the introduction of these establishments were perfectly notorious, and acknowledged upon all hands. The difficulty, however, which arose in legislating upon this subject, was the disinclination which was felt against interfering with that description of betting which had so long existed at Tattersall's and elsewhere, in connection with the great national sport of horse racing. But these establishments assumed a totally different aspect—a new form of betting was introduced, which had been productive of the greatest evils. The course, now, is to open a house, and for the owner to hold himself forth as ready to bet with all comers, contrary to the usage which had prevailed at such places as Tattersall's, where individuals betted with each other, but no one there kept a gaming table, or, in other words, held a bag against all comers. The object, then, of this Bill, was to suppress these houses, without interfering with that legitimate species of betting, to which he had referred. It would prohibit the opening of houses, or shops or booths, for the purpose of betting ; and, inasmuch as it appeared that the mischief of the existing vicious system seemed to arise from the advancing of money, in the first instance, with the expectation of receiving a larger sum on the completion of a certain event, it was proposed to prohibit the practice, by distinct legislative enactment. The mischief arising from the existence of these betting shops was perfectly notorious. Servants, apprentices, and workmen, induced by the temptation of receiving a large sum for a small one, took their few shillings to these places, and the first effect of their losing, was to tempt them to go on spending their money in the hope of retrieving their losses ; and, for this purpose, it not unfrequently happened that they were driven into robbing their masters and employers. There was not a prison, nor a house of correction in London, which did not every day furnish abundant and conclusive testimony of the vast number of youths who were led into crime by the temptation of these establishments of which there were from 100 to 150 in the metropolis alone, while there were a considerable number in the large towns of the provinces. He believed this bill would have the effect of suppressing most of them ; or, at all events, of preventing the spread of an evil which was admitted on all hands. It had been suggested that the more effectual course would be the licensing of these houses ; but, for his own part, he believed that would be discreditable to the Government, and would only tend to increase the mischief instead of preventing it. He trusted and believed that the Bill which he now sought to introduce would have the desired effect, and he hoped the House would offer no objection to his bringing it in.

Leave was given, and the Bill was so in accord with the feeling of the House, that it went through all its stages without debate, and received the Royal Assent on 20th Aug. 1853, under the title of "An Act for the suppression of Betting Houses," 16 & 17 Victoria, cap. 119 : it became operative on 1st Dec. 1853. Its principal clause is Sec. iii., which deals with the penalty on owner or occupier of Betting House. "Any Person who, being the Owner, or Occupier of any House, Office, Room, or other Place, or a Person using the same, shall open, keep, or use the same for the Purposes hereinbefore mentioned, or either of them ; and any Person, who, being the Owner, or Occupier, of any House, Room, Office, or other Place, shall, knowingly, and wilfully, permit the same to be opened, kept, or used by any other Person for the purposes aforesaid, or either of them ; and any Person having the Care, or Management of, or in any Manner assisting in conducting the business of any House, Office, Room, or Place opened, kept, or used for the Purposes aforesaid, or either of them, shall, on summary Conviction thereof, before any Two Justices of the Peace, be liable to forfeit and pay such Penalty, not exceeding One Hundred Pounds, as shall be adjudged by such Justices, and may be further adjudged by such Justices, to pay such Costs attending such conviction, as to the said Justices shall seem reasonable ; and, on the Nonpayment of such Penalty and Costs ; or, in the first instance, if to the said Justices, it shall seem fit, may be committed to the Common Gaol, or House of Correction, with, or without, Hard Labour, for any Time not exceeding Six Calendar Months."

The effect of this Act was to shut up, for the time, the betting houses, but nobody can deny that there is as much of this ready money betting now as ever there was, and there is no difficulty in getting "a little bit on," if one wants to, without attending races and betting with the professional bookmakers there to be found. Children can lay their pennies and errand boys their sixpences, and, throughout the length and breadth of the country, the curse of betting permeates every rank, and, I am sorry to say, spares neither sex.

The police do something, in occasionally obtaining convictions, and magistrates have strained the interpretation of the word " Place " which occurs in the Act to its very limit —indeed it has only lately (July 1897) been settled that the betting ring at a race course is not a " Place " within the meaning of the Act. A bookmaker, named Dunn, was fined £1 for betting at Kempton Park race meeting. He appealed, and the magistrate's decision was reversed. The judges inquired into what was the real intention of the Legislature. This is sufficiently apparent from the preamble, which states that " a certain kind of gaming has, of late, sprung up, by the opening of places called betting houses," and we are justified in assuming that it was this " kind of gaming," and no other, which Parliament intended to suppress. Furthermore, when once this fact is appreciated, the use of the words " house, office, room, or other place " is no longer misleading, because " place " means something *ejusdem generis*, a " house, office, or room." It was impossible to maintain that an open race course, or an open enclosure upon a race course, is a " place " of the same kind as a " house, office, or room," or that the people who use it for betting claim to hold it against all the world, as they would in the case of their own offices.

As a rule, the higher class professional bookmakers are a very respectable lot of men, and are scrupulously honest in their dealings, which is more than can be said for some of their clients, even titled ones. Such men as Davis, Steel, and Fry dealt in vast sums, and no matter how hard hit, never once failed to meet their losses; and some of them have died rich. Gully is said to have left about a quarter of a million behind him, Davis's fortune at his death is variously stated at £50,000 or £150,000, and Swindells died worth £145,000.

As to these men's clients let Sir George Chetwynd tell a tale. " I should like Fry, Steel, Emerson, Baylis, and others, to publish their list of bad debts during the last few years. People would be astonished at the amount owed to these men, yet they rather condone the fact of being owed money, by hardly ever applying the remedy of making the loser a defaulter, and all sorts of people are going about to race courses, now owing the Ring money, the creditors hoping, some day, to recover a portion of it. The most disgraceful part of it is, that some of these defaulters are owners of race horses, gentlemen riders, and so forth. Personally, I have no pity for book makers who do not post a man for owing them money, after they have given him a reasonable time for payment. If this were done, a healthier tone would be given to betting; there would not be so much reckless plunging as there is, and it would be far better for backers and layers. I recollect once, on the day the Two Thousand was run for, some years ago, I was standing talking to Henry Steel, for whose judgment I have a great respect, and whom I have always found most straightforward in all his dealings. By his side was his trusty partner, Peech. All of a sudden, I saw the latter make hurriedly off in a bee line through the scattered crowd that thronged the bird cage, and, on asking Steel what was up, he laughed, and said, ' Oh, nothing, Sir George, it's only Bill after a bit of old '; meaning that he had seen a man who had owed him money for some years, and had gone to give him a gentle reminder of the fact."

My readers may not be aware of the awful punishment that awaits defaulters, and I cannot do better than give that knowledge in Mr Rice's words.

"What unfair play and loaded dice did at night, default-ing bettors—' welshers,' as they are now called—practised by day. The best legitimate Meetings, as well as the minor country side ventures, were infested with the rogues. They dressed well, wore frilled shirts and ' flash ' rings, and were, perhaps, better able to pay their way about than honest men. The Chichester ' extortioners,' with their guinea bed for a single night's lodging, were unable to keep these gentry away from the Ducal meeting; and the unmerciful dealings of mine hosts at Doncaster, Windsor, Warwick, and New-market, who enjoyed, in those days, an unenviable notoriety for the extravagance of their charges, were, likewise, power-less to clear their coffee rooms from the welshing community.

"Measures were taken to reduce the evil. To begin with, the Messrs Tattersall issued a code of new rules and regula-tions, to be observed, in future, by all subscribers to the betting room at the Corner. A subscription of two guineas per annum was fixed. Gentlemen desirous of subscribing were to give a week's notice, in writing, to Messrs Tattersall and Son, submitting references for their approval. Non-subscribers might be admitted on payment of a guinea; and, the room being under the sanction of the Jockey Club, all the members were to be obedient to any suggestions made by the Senate of the Turf, from time to time. Lastly, special attention was called to the forty-first rule of the Jockey Club, which enacted that any bettor adjudged to be a defaulter by the Stewards, should not be permitted to go on the Heath at Newmarket, and they should be excluded from the betting rooms there, and at Tattersall's.

"This step in a right direction was followed, a few months later, by the action of the Trustees of the Grand Stand at Ascot, who gave notice that all defaulters in respect to stakes, forfeits, or bets on horse racing, would be peremptorily excluded during any Meeting on the Heath at Ascot; and, if any one in default, did gain admission, on being pointed out to the Noble Master of Her Majesty's Buckhounds, or to the Clerk of the Course, he would, if necessary, be expelled by force, unless he were able to show that he had discharged all his obligations.

"At Goodwood, a similar active policy was pursued; no person, being notoriously a defaulter upon bets on horse racing, would be permitted to 'assist' at the Meeting. A contumelious defaulter having obtained admission to the Enclosure, he received peremptory orders to quit; and the example set by the Stewards of Ascot and Goodwood was promptly taken up by the better class of country Meetings;

and notices were posted, that if any person notoriously in
default, as to either forfeits, or bets, gained admittance, he
should be peremptorily expelled.   At Doncaster, it was
requested that all parties who had claims for bets, would
not fail to notify the same to Mr Butterfield, Land Steward
to the Corporation, prior to the races, at his office, or at the
Grand Stand.   Lord Eglinton, who had taken a prominent
part in the endeavour to stamp out this evil, wrote to the
Town Clerk : 'It gives me much pleasure to find that the
Corporation of Doncaster have passed the Resolutions.
Defaulters have become so numerous, and so audacious in
their proceedings, that it is absolutely necessary that the
strongest measures should be adopted against them.'   The
Corporation of Doncaster, at their meeting, when his Lord-
ship's letter was read, resolved, unanimously, that the Town
Clerk be requested, immediately, to confer with the pro-
prietors of the Betting Rooms, and that Lord Eglinton be
permitted to purify those rooms, as well as the Stand and
Enclosure.

"But to the influence and exertions of Lord George
Bentinck, the 'legitimates' owed the clearance of the Turf
from the hordes of welshers and other non-payers that
infested it.   This 'pleasing reform of the Turf' was
brought about by his active measures ; and it was admitted,
that had he not persevered to the utmost, even his powerful
influence would have been blighted, and the host of rotten
sheep left to infect the sound constitution of the remaining
flock.   But such was the effect of the sharp remedies employed, that, for some time after, it was safe to make a bet
with any man whom you might meet in the Betting Ring
at respectable Race Meetings, so effectually was the Turf
ridded of the pests that had infested it."

Probably, the greatest defaulter of modern times was a
man named Dwyer, who kept a cigar shop in St Martin's
Lane.   He, generally, gave a point or two more than the
current odds at Tattersall's, and, in 1851, he was doing, by
far, the largest business of any " list man " in London.

Owing to the promptitude and regularity of his payments, he gained a high reputation for solvency, and not only retained and increased his *clientèle* among the half-crown and shilling public, but had attracted the custom even of men of good standing in the ring. His humble patrons believed him to be every whit as safe as "Leviathan" Davis, and their confidence was largely shared by racing men of a higher calibre.

All went well till the Chester Meeting of 1851, the Cup being, then, the greatest betting handicap in the Calendar; so much so that, in that year it was calculated that upwards of *a million sterling* changed hands over that one race. Dwyer laid very heavily against the winner *Miss Nancy*. It had always been his custom to pay up on the day after a great race; and, consequently, at an early hour on Friday, the first of May, crowds of the lucky backers of Nancy made their way to the familiar cigar shop in St Martin's Lane, to receive their winnings in exchange for the tickets they held. Conceive their consternation when they found the shutters up, and the door closed, with other unmistakable signs that the bank had suspended payment. The news spread fast, and there was soon a mob of some thousands blocking up all the approaches to the cigar shop.

By and by it oozed out that a notice had been fastened to the shutters to the effect that Mr Dwyer would meet his friends and creditors that evening at the White Swan, Chandos Street, in order to make arrangements for discharging the claims against him. Of course, that hostelry was immediately besieged by a clamorous crowd, but the landlord assured them that he knew nothing of Dwyer or his whereabouts—all he could tell them was that, late on the previous evening, two gentlemen, who were perfect strangers to him, had called and engaged his "long-room" for a meeting of Mr Dwyer and his friends on the following day. Meanwhile, the cigar shop had been broken into, and the worst fears of the unfortunate victims were confirmed when they found that every scrap of furniture that was worth anything had been removed from the house during the night. The excitement in London that evening was tremendous—nothing else was talked of among sporting men but Dwyer's collapse, and it was afterwards found that he had bolted with £25,000 of the public's money. The rogue was never found.

The largest sum ever won by a horse was made by *Donovan*, who, in his lifetime, carried off stakes to the value of £55,354, 13s.; but the largest amount of "public money" ever won without betting by an owner in a single season is £73,858, 10s., won by the Duke of Portland in 1889 ; whilst Lord Falmouth, who did not bet, won nearly £212,000 in eleven years, from 1873 to 1883, and in 1884 he sold his whole stud for at least £150,000. Count Lagrange also won in stakes in five years, from 1876 to 1880, £73,000.

These sums, with the exception of the Duke of Portland's winnings, were made before the era of enormous stakes had begun ; and, according to a writer (*Rapier*) in the *Illustrated Sporting and Dramatic News* in 1892, 2559 horses ran flat races for £486,556, which sum was won by 947 competitors. These figures give us some insight into the enormous interests involved in horse racing, entirely leaving out the millions which must change hands in betting.

CHAPTER XVII

I HAVE written very fully on the Lottery in England,[1] but, in this History of Gambling in this country, it is necessary to go over the ground again, though, of course, at much less length. Some claim that the Romans introduced the lottery, in their *Apophoreta*, but these were simply presents given to guests at their departure after a banquet, and some-times they were so disposed as to create great merriment. The fourteenth book of Martial consists of an introductory epigram and 222 distiches, each describing and designed to accompany one of these presents which range from nuts to works of art and slaves.

So we may dismiss its Roman origin and examine into the generally accepted (because never questioned) theory of its Italian birth. That the Venetian and Genoese merchants did sometimes use the *Lotto* as a means of getting rid of their wares, is true—but the very name shows its northern derivation, for the Latin word for a lot is *Sors*. The Anglo-Saxon for " to cast lots " is Hleot-au. In Dutch it is Lot-en, Loot-en, and in Swedish, Lotta. Indeed, the first record I can find of any lottery is that of the widow of Jan van Eyck, which took place at Bruges on 24th February 1446, the town archives recording a payment to her for her lottery.

The first *public* English lottery was projected in 1566,

[1] " A History of English Lotteries," by John Ashton, London. 1893. 8vo.— *Leadenhall Press.*

but was not drawn until 1569. Only one authentic record of this lottery is believed to be in existence, and it is carefully preserved in the muniment room at Losely House, Artington, Surrey.[1] It is printed in black letter, and is five feet long by nineteen inches wide, so that I can only give the preamble to it.

" A verie rich Lotterie Generall, without any blancks, contayning a number of good prices, as wel of redy money as of plate, and certaine sorts of marchaundizes, having been valued and priced by the comaundement of the Queene's most excellent majestie, by men expert and skilfull; and the same Lotterie is erected by her majestie's order, to the intent that such commoditie as may chaunce to arise thereof, after the charges borne, may be converted towardes the reparation of the havens and strength of the Realme, and towardes such other publique good workes. The number of lots shall be foure hundreth thousand, and no more; and every lot shall be the summe of tenne shillings sterling onely, and no more."

And the bill, which was printed in 1567, winds up thus: " The shewe of the prices and rewardes above mencioned shall be set up to be seene in Cheapsyde in London, at the signe of the Queene's Majesties' Arms, in the house of M. Dericke, goldsmith, servant to the Queene's most excellent Majestie."

But people fought so shy of the scheme that the proclamation had to be backed by the recommendation of the Lord Mayor, and, this proving of no avail, the Queen issued another on 3rd January 1586, postponing the drawing on account of the slack subscription, and, this not succeeding, the Earl of Leicester and Sir William Cecil, as Lords of the Council, on July 12, 1558, sent a circular to all the authorities in the Counties of Kent, Sussex, Surrey, Southampton, and the Isle of Wight, begging them to do all in their power to get subscribers.

[1] A catalogue of the MSS. in this room has been published in the Seventh Report of the Historical MS. Commission.

By the terms of the lottery, the subscribers were to be anonymous, their subscriptions being accompanied by a "devise or poesie." Many of these remain in a little black letter book at Losely, and I give two or three from various shipping places.

> "Yermouth haven, God send thee spede,
> The Lord he knoweth thy great nede."

> "In good hope, poor East Greenwiche, God send us to remain,
> And of some good lotte to have the gaine."

> "Draw Brightemston[1] a good lot,
> Or else return them a turbot."

> "From Hastings we come,
> God send us good speed ;
> Never a poor fisher town in England,
> Of ye great lot hath more need."

At last, the Lottery was drawn, in 1569, as we learn from Holinshed. "A great lotterie being holden at London, in Poules Church Yard, at the west dore, was begun to be drawne the eleventh of Januarie, and continued daie and night till the sixt of Maie, wherein the said drawing was fullie ended."

Stow, in his *Annales*, tells us of the next Lottery, 1585 : "A lotterie for marvellous rich and beautifull armor was begunne to be drawne at London in *S. Paules* Churchyard, at the great West gate (an house of timber and boord being there erected for that purpose) on *S. Peter's*[2] day, in the morning, which lotterie continued in drawing day and night, for the space of two or three dayes."

As far as I can learn, the next public lottery was that of 1612, and I quote once more from the *Annales :* "The King's maiestie in speciall favor for the present plantation of English Colonies in *Virginia*, granted a liberall Lottery, in which was contained five thousand pound in prizes certayne, besides rewardes of casualtie, and began to be drawne in a new built house at the West end of *Paul's*,

----

[1] Brighton.   [2] June 29.

the 29th of June 1612. But, of which Lottery, for want of filling uppe the number of lots, there were then taken out and throwne away three score thousand blanckes, without abating of any one prize; and by the twentith of July all was drawne and finished. This Lottery was so plainely carryed, and honestly performed, that it gave full satisfaction to all persons. *Thomas Sharpliffe*, a Taylor, of London, had the chiefe prize, *viz.* foure thousand Crownes in fayre plate, which was sent to his house in very stately manner : during the whole tyme of the drawing of this lottery there were alwaies present diuers worshipfull Knights and Esquiers, accompanied by sundry graue discreet Cittizens."

There were three lotteries granted for the supply of water to the Metropolis, in 1627, 1631, and 1689, and a petition to hold a lottery for the same purpose in 1637, but this, I think, was not granted. There were many licences granted for various schemes, and there was one, called the Royal Oak lottery, for granting assistance to old Royalists, which seems to have been a swindle. Indeed, this may be said to have been the case with a good many of the Lotteries in Charles II.'s time, till, when Prince Rupert died, and his jewels were to be disposed of by lottery, the public would not subscribe unless the King consented to see that all was fair, as we see by the *London Gazette*, September 27— October 1, 1683 :

" These are to give Notice, that the Jewels of his late Highness Prince *Rupert*, have been particularly valued and appraised by Mr *Isaac Legouch*, Mr *Christopher Rosse*, and Mr *Richard Beauvoir*, Jewellers, the whole amounting to Twenty Thousand Pounds, and will be sold by way of Lottery, each Lot to be Five Pounds. The biggest Prize will be a great Pearl Necklace valued at £8000, and none less than £100. A printed Particular of the said Appraisement, with their Division into Lots, will be delivered *gratis* by Mr *Francis Child*, Goldsmith, at Temple Bar, *London*, into whose hands, such as are willing to be Adventurers, are desired to pay their Money, on, or about, the first day of

November next. As soon as the whole sum is paid in, a short day will be appointed (which 'tis hoped will be before *Christmas*) and notified in the *Gazette*, for the drawing thereof, which will be done in his Majesty's Presence, who is pleased to declare, that he, himself, will see all the Prizes put among the Blanks, and that the whole shall be managed with all Equity and Fairness ; nothing being intended but the Sale of the said Jewels at a moderate Value."

In another *London Gazette* of Nov. 22/26, 1683, we are told how this Lottery will be drawn, and, as it is rare to have an English sovereign mixed up in such a speculation, I transcribe it :

" As soon as the Money is all come in, a day will be prefixed, and published for the drawing thereof, as has been formerly notified.   In the morning of which day His Majesty will be pleased, publickly, in the Banquetting House, to see the Blanks told over, that they may not exceed their Number, and to read the Papers (which shall be exactly the same size as the Blanks) on which the Prizes are to be written ; which, being rolled up in his presence, His Majesty will mix amongst the Blanks, as may, also, any of the Adventurers there present that shall desire it.   This being done, a Child, appointed by His Majesty, or the Adventurers, shall, out of the Mass of Lots so mixed, take out the number that each Person adventures for, and put them into boxes (which shall be provided for the purpose) on the covers whereof, each Adventurer's Name shall be written with the number of Lots He or She adventures for ; the Boxes to be filled in succession as the Money was paid in.   As soon as all the lots are thus distributed, they shall be opened as fast as may be, and the prizes then and there delivered to those that win them ; all which, 'tis hoped, will be done and finished in one day."

There was a Lottery, in which the subscription was a penny, and the Capital prize was One Thousand Pounds, drawn on 19th Oct. 1698, at the Dorset Garden Theatre, near Salisbury Square, Fleet Street, but when William III.

came to the throne, it was seen that the Lottery was a very profitable thing, and the Government took it unto itself for its own purposes. In 1694, £1,000,000 was raised by Lottery, and in 1697, £1,400,000—but in 1699, by 10 and 11 Will. III., c. 17, lotteries were suppressed, the preamble to the Act stating, "That all such Lotteries, and all other Lotteries, are common and publick nuisances, and that all grants, patents, and licences for such Lotteries, or any other Lotteries, are void and against Law."

It must have been about this time (for in 1698-9 three expeditions sailed from Scotland to Darien) that Ward wrote in *The London Spy* a description of the Lottery fever in London :

"The *Gazette* and *Post-Papers* lay by Neglected, and nothing was Pur'd over in the *Coffee Houses*, but the *Ticket-Catalogues* ; No talking of the *Jubilee*, the want of Current Trade with *France*, or the *Scotch* Settlement at *Darien* ; Nothing Buz'd about by the Purblind *Trumpeters* of *State News*, but *Blank* and *Benefit*. *My Son had Five Pound in such a Lottery, but got nothing ; my Daughter*, says another, *had but Five Shillings, and got the Twenty Pound Prize.* People running up and down the Streets in Crowds and Numbers, as if one end of the Town was on Fire, and the other were running to help 'em off with their Goods. One Stream of *Coachmen, Footmen, Prentice Boys*, and *Servant Wenches* flowing one way, with wonderful hopes of getting an estate for three pence. *Knights, Esquires, Gentlemen* and *Traders, Marry'd Ladies, Virgin Madams, Jilts*, etc. ; moving on *Foot*, in *Sedans, Chariots*, and *Coaches*, another way ; with a pleasing Expectancy of getting Six Hundred a Year for a Crown.

"Thus were all the *Fools* in Town so busily employed in running up and down from one *Lottery*, or another, that it was as much as *London* could do to Conjure together such Numbers of *Knaves* as might Cheat 'em fast enough of their *Money*. The Unfortunate crying out, *A Cheat, a Cheat, a Confounded Cheat, nothing of Fairness in't.* The Fortunate, in opposition to the other, crying, *'Tis all Fair, all Fair; the Fairest Adventure that ever was drawn.* And thus, every Body, according to their Success, Expressing variously their Sentiments ; tho' the Losers, who may be said to be in the Wrong of it, to venture their Money, yet, were they most Right in their Conjectures of the Project, and the Gainers, who were in the Right of it, to hazard their Money, because they won, were most Wrong in their opinion of the matter. For I have much ado to forbear believing that *Luck in a Bag* is almost as Honest as *Fortune in a Wheel*, or any other of the like Projects.   Truly, says my Friend, I confess I cannot conceive any extraordinary Opinion of the Fairness of any *Lottery*, for I am apt to believe that whenever such a number of *Fools* fall into a *Knave's* hand, he will make the most of 'em ; and I think the *Parliament* could not have given the *Nation* greater Assurances of their especial Regard to the Welfare of the *Publick*, than by suppressing all *Lotteries*, which only serve to Buoy up the mistaken Multitude with Dreams of Golden Showers, to the Expence of that little Money, which, with hard Labour they have Earn'd ; and often to the Neglect of their Business, which doubles the Inconveniency.   The *Gentry*, indeed, might make it their Diversion, but the *Common People* make it a great part of their Care and Business, hoping thereby to relieve a Necessitous Life ; instead of which, they plunge themselves further into an Ocean of Difficulties.   What if one Man in Ten Thousand gets Five Hundred Pounds, what Benefit is that to the rest, who have struggled hard for *Fool's* Pence to make up that Sum, which, perhaps, falls to one who stood not in need of *Fortune's* Favours."

But the State Lotteries began again in Queen Anne's reign, for an Act (8 Anne, c. 4) was passed in 1710 authorising a loan of £1,500,000 by means of a lottery of 150,000 tickets at £10 each.   The money was to be sunk, and 9 per cent. was allowed on it for 32 years, and the prizes were annuities from one of £1000 to 14s. a year, which latter was given as a consolation to every holder of a blank.

Luttrell tells us how greedily they were taken up. "21st Jan. 1710. Yesterday, books were opened at Mercer's Chapel for receiving subscriptions for the Lottery, and 'tis said, above a Million is already subscribed; so that, 'tis believed, 'twill be full by Monday 7 night." And he also tells us that "Mr Barnaby, who lately belonged to the 6 Clerk's Office, has got the £1000 per ann. ticket in the lottery." This lottery was drawn by blue coat boys from Christ's Hospital, and from this time, until 1824 (except from 1814 to 1819), there was no year without a State Lottery.

There were Lotteries for everything, and to show how numerous they were take the advertisements in one paper, taken hap-hazard. *The Tatler*, Sep. 14/16, 1710: "Mr Stockton's Sale of Jewels, Plate, &c., will be drawn on Michaelmas Day.—The Lottery in Colson's Court will be drawn on the 21st inst.—The Sale of Goods to be seen at Mrs Butler's, &c., will certainly be drawn on Tuesday, the 19th inst.—Mrs Povy's Sale of Goods is put off to Saturday, 23rd inst.—Mrs Symond's Sale of Goods will begin on Wednesday, the 20th of this instant.—Mrs Guthridge's Sixpenny Sale of Goods, &c., continues to be drawn every Day."

The prizes did not always fall to those who needed the money, as Swift writes to Stella about a son of Lord Abercorn. Aug. 29, 1711: "His second son has t'other day got a prize in the Lottery of Four Thousand Pounds, besides two small ones of two hundred pounds each; nay, the family was so fortunate, that my Lord bestowing one ticket, which is a hundred pounds, to one of his servants, who had been his page, the young fellow got a prize, which has made it another hundred."

In 1721 private Lotteries were prescribed, by the 36th sec. of 8 Geo. I., c. 2, which imposed a penalty of £500 for carrying on such lotteries, in addition to any penalties inflicted by any former Acts; the offender being committed to prison for one year, and thenceforward until such times as the £500 should be fully paid and satisfied.

The first Westminster bridge was partially built through

the instrumentality of a lottery, the drawing of which began
on Dec. 8, 1740, at Stationers' Hall ; and by an Act of
Parliament (26 Geo. II., c. 22) passed in 1753, the nation
purchased for £20,000, the library and collection of Sir
Hans Sloane, and incorporated Sir Robert Cotton's library
with it.   Montague House was selected for their reception,
and a lottery to provide for its purchase was got up ; the
subscription to which was £300,000 in tickets of £3 each.
The Managers and Trustees of this Lottery were The Arch-
bishop of Canterbury, the Lord Chancellor, and the Speaker,
each of whom was to have £100 for his trouble.

In connection with this lottery was a gross fraud, and on
19th April 1755, Peter Leheup, one of the receivers of the
Lottery was tried at the King's bench and found guilty, 1st,
of receiving subscriptions before the day and hour advertised ;
2nd, of permitting subscribers to use different names to
cover the maximum of 20 tickets allowed to each holder ;
and 3rd, of disposing of the tickets which had been bespoke
and not claimed, or were double-charged, instead of returning
them to the managers.   For these *laches* he was, on the
following 9th of May, fined £1000, which he immediately
paid into Court.

In a lottery of 1767 a lady residing in Holborn was presented with a ticket by her husband, and so anxious was she
for its success, that on the Sunday previous to the drawing,
the clergyman gave out that " the prayers of the congrega-
tion are desired for the success of a person engaged in a
new undertaking."

CHAPTER XVIII

Blue coat boys tampered with — The two trials — Insuring tickets — Curious
Lotteries — Lever Museum and Pigot diamond lotteries — Little goes —
Stories of winning numbers — Decline of Lotteries — The last — Its epitaph
— Modern lotteries.

TWICE in the year 1775 were the blue coat boys, who drew
the tickets from the lottery wheels, tampered with ; and the
following accounts are taken from the *Annual Register* of
that year :

" 1 June. A man was carried before the Lord Mayor, for
attempting to bribe the two Blue Coat boys, who drew the
Museum [1] lottery, to conceal a ticket, and bring it to him,
promising he would, next day, let them have it again, when
one of them was, it seems, to convey it back privately to the
wheel, but without letting go his hold of it, and then produce it as if newly drawn ; the man's intention being to
insure it in all the offices against being drawn that day.
But the boys were honest, gave notice of the intended
fraud, and pointed out the delinquent, who, however, was
discharged, as there is no law in being, to punish the
offence."

" 5 Dec. By virtue of a warrant from Sir Charles Asgill,
was brought before the magistrate, at Guildhall, the clerk of
an eminent hop factor in Goodman's Fields, upon suspicion
of being concerned with a person, not yet apprehended, in
defrauding a lottery office keeper, near the 'Change, of a
large sum of money. This matter being undertaken by the
Commissioners of the Lottery, the Solicitor of the Treasury
appeared against the prisoner, and for him attended, as
Counsel, Mr Cox.

[1] Cox's Museum. A collection of Automata, &c.

" The first witness examined was the lottery office keeper he said, that about a fortnight ago, the prisoner insured No. 21.481 six times over for the subsequent day of drawing; that the conversation he had with the prisoner at that time, and the seeming positiveness there appeared in the latter, that the ticket would come up, caused him to enquire at other lottery offices, when he found the same number insured, in the prisoner's name, at all the principal offices about the 'Change; that the ticket was drawn the first hour of drawing the subsequent day.　This, with his former suspicion, alarmed him, and he immediately went to Christ's Hospital, and saw the boy who drew the ticket; that he interrogated him, whether he had clandestinely taken that number out of the wheel, or whether he had been solicited to do so, which the boy positively denied; that, observing that he answered rather faintly, he importuned him to divulge the truth, which, after some hesitation, produced an acknowledgment of the fact.

" The next witness was the Blue Coat boy.　He said that, about three weeks ago, the person who is not in custody, and whom he had known before he went to the Hospital, took him to a Coffee House, where they breakfasted together; that he wanted to know of the witness, whether it was possible to get a ticket out of the wheel; to which the latter answered, No.　That being, afterwards, solicited for the same purpose, by him, to secrete a ticket, he, at length, promised to do so; that, accordingly, he took two at one time out of the wheel, gave one to the person who called it over, and put the other in his pocket; that the person who induced him to do it was then in the gallery, and nodded his head to the witness to signify when was a proper time; that, after the witness came out of the hall, he gave the ticket to the person who sat in the gallery, and who was then waiting for the witness in the Guildhall Yard; that the next time the witness drew the lottery, the person before mentioned returned him the ticket, which the witness put in the wheel, and drew out the same day; that he did this three several times, and received from the person for whom he did it, several half guineas ; that he has heard the prisoner's name mentioned by him, but never heard the latter acknowledge any connection between them in insurance ; and, never before, saw the prisoner.

" The prisoner acknowledged he insured the ticket 79 times for one day. The mother of the person who was not apprehended, was next examined ; she proved an acquaintance between her son and the prisoner ; but denied any remembrance of ever hearing the latter mention anything relating to insurance. The prisoner was discharged.

" It is said that the person who absconded, got about £400 by the above fraud ; and would have got £3000, had he been paid in all the offices where he insured."

But, that such a fraud should not be perpetrated again, the Lords of the Treasury, on 12th Dec. 1775, issued an Order, of which the following is an extract :

" IT IS THEREFORE ORDERED, for preventing the like wicked practices in future, that every boy, before he is suffered to put his hand into either wheel, be brought by the proclaimer to the managers on duty, for them to see *that the bosoms and sleeves of his coat be closely buttoned, his pockets sewed up, and his hands examined ;* and that, during the time of his being on duty, *he shall keep his left hand in his girdle behind him, and his right hand open, with his fingers extended :* and the proclaimer is not to suffer him, at any time, to leave the wheel, without, first, being examined by the Manager nearest him."

They also " requested of the Treasurer of Christ's Hospital, not to make known who are the twelve boys nominated for drawing the lottery, till the morning before the drawing begins ; which said boys are all to attend every day, and the two who are to go on duty at the wheels, are to be taken promiscuously from amongst the whole number, by either of the secretaries, without observing any regular course, or order ; so that no boy shall know when it will be his turn to go to either wheel."

- *A propos* of insuring lottery tickets, Horace Walpole writes to the Countess of Ossory, 17th Dec. 1780 : " As folks in the country love to hear of *London fashions*, know, Madam, that the reigning one amongst the *quality*, is to go, after the opera, to the lottery offices, where their Ladyships bet with the keepers. You choose any number you please ; if it does not come up next day, you pay five guineas ; if it does, receive forty, or in proportion to the age of the *tirage*. The Duchess of Devonshire, in one day, won nine hundred pounds. General Smith, as the luckiest of all mites, is of the most select parties, and chooses the numeros."

On Jan. 6, 1777, two Jews were brought before the Lord Mayor, charged with counterfeiting a lottery ticket ; but, as they brought plenty of false witnesses, they were acquitted. But one, Daniel Denny, was not so lucky on Feb. 24, the same year, for he was convicted of the same crime. The *Annual Register* for this year says :

" The following is a true state of the different methods of getting money by lottery office keepers, and other ingenious persons, who have struck out different plans of getting money by the State Lottery of 1777.

" First, His Majesty's Royal Letters Patent for securing the Property of the purchasers.

" Secondly, A few office keepers who advertise ' By authority of Parliament ' to secure your property in shares and chances.

" Thirdly, Several schemes for shares and chances, only entitling the purchasers to all prizes above twenty pounds.

" Fourthly, A bait for those who can only afford to venture a shilling.

" Then come the ingenious sett of lottery merchants, viz. Lottery magazine proprietors—Lottery tailors—Lottery stay makers—Lottery glovers—Lottery hat makers—Lottery tea merchants—Lottery snuff and tobacco merchants—Lottery handkerchiefs—Lottery bakers—Lottery barbers (where a man, for being shaved, and paying threepence, may stand a chance of getting ten pounds)—Lottery shoe blacks—

Lottery eating houses; one in Wych Street, Temple-bar, where, if you call for six penny worth of roast, or boiled beef, you receive a note of hand, with a number, which, should it turn out fortunate, may entitle the eater of the beef to sixty guineas—Lottery oyster stalls, by which the fortunate may get five guineas for three penny worth of oysters. And, to complete this curious catalogue, an old woman, who keeps a sausage stall in one of the little alleys leading to Smithfield, wrote up, in chalk, *Lottery sausages*, or, five shillings to be gained for a farthing relish."

In 1782 an Act was passed, whereby lottery office keepers were to pay a licence of £50, under a penalty of £100 if they did not do so.

Sir Ashton Lever disposed of his Museum by lottery in 1758 by Act of Parliament, and another Act was procured to dispose of, by lottery, a large diamond, the property of the deceased Lord Pigot, valued at £30,000. This lottery was drawn on Jan. 2, 1801, and the winner of the prize was a young man, name unknown. It was, afterwards, sold at Christie's on May 10, 1802, for 9500 guineas. It was again sold, and is said to have passed into the possession of Messrs Rundell and Bridge, the Court jewellers, who are reported to have sold it to an Egyptian Pasha for £30,000.

But, in the latter part of the eighteenth century, a system of private lotteries, called "little goes" had sprung up, and they are thus described in the *Times* of 22nd July 1795 :

"Amongst the various species of Gaming that have ever been practised, we think none exceeds the mischiefs, and calamities that arise from the practice of private lotteries, which, at present, are carrying on, in various parts of the town, to very alarming extents, much to the discredit of those whose province it is to suppress such nefarious practices, as they cannot be ignorant of such transactions. 'The little go,' which is the technical term for a private lottery, is calculated only for the meridian of those understandings, who are unused to calculate and discriminate between right and wrong, and roguery and fair dealing; and, in this particular case, it is those who compose the lower order of society, whom it so seriously affects, and, on whom, it is chiefly designed to operate. No man of common sense can suppose that the lottery wheels are fair and honest, or that the proprietors act upon principles anything like honour, or honesty; for, by the art, and contrivance, of the wheels, they are so constructed, with secret springs, and the application of gum, glue, &c., in the internal part of them, that they can draw the numbers out, or keep them in, at pleasure, just as it suits their purposes; so that the ensurer, robbed and cajoled, by such unfair means, has not the most distant chance of ever winning; the whole being a gross fraud, and imposition, in the extreme. We understand the most notorious of these standards of imposition, are situated in Carnaby Market, Oxford Road, in the Borough, Islington, Clerkenwell, and various other places, most of which are under the very nose of Magistracy, in seeming security, bidding defiance to law, and preying upon the vitals of the poor and ignorant.

"We hope the Magistrates of each jurisdiction, and those who possess the same power, will perform their duty on behalf of the poor, over whom they preside, and put a stop to such a growing, and alarming evil, of such pernicious and dangerous tendency; particularly as the proprietors are well-known bad characters, consisting of needy beggars, desperate swindlers, gamblers, sharpers, notorious thieves, and common convicted felons; most of whose names stand recorded in the Newgate Calendar for various offences of different descriptions."

11*th Aug.* 1795. "On Friday night last, in consequence of searching warrants from the parochial magistrates of St James's Westminster, upwards of 30 persons were apprehended at the house of one M'Call, No. 2 Francis Street, near Golden Square, and in the house of J. Knight, King Street, where the most destructive practices *to the poor* were carrying on, that of *Private Lotteries* (called Little Goes). Two wheels, with the tickets, were seized on the premises.

Upon examination of those persons, who proved to be the poor deluded objects who had been there plundered, they were reprimanded, and discharged.

"The wives of many industrious mechanics, by attending these nefarious houses, have not only been duped out of their earnings (which ought to have been applied to the providing bread for their families), but have even pawned their beds, wedding rings, and almost every article they were possessed of, for that purpose."

Here are two anecdotes of the winners of the great prize, which was, usually, £20,000, from the *Times* :

27th Dec. 1797. "Dr B., a physician at *Lime* (Dorset), a few days since, being under pecuniary embarrassment, and his house surrounded by bailiffs, made his escape by a window, into a neighbour's house, from whence he fled to London. The furniture was seized, and the sale actually commenced, when it was stopped by a letter, stating that the Doctor, upon his arrival in London, found himself the proprietor of the £20,000 prize. We guarantee the truth of this fact."

19th Mar. 1798. "The £20,000 prize, drawn on Friday, is divided amongst a number of poor persons : a female servant in Brook Street, Holborn, had a sixteenth ; a woman who keeps a fruit stall in Gray's Inn Lane, another ; a third is possessed by a servant of the Duke of Roxburghe ; a fourth by a Chelsea carrier of vegetables to Covent Garden ; one-eighth belongs to a poor family in Rutlandshire, and the remainder is similarly divided."

In 1802, old Baron d'Aguilar, the Islington miser, was requested, by a relation, to purchase a particular ticket, No. 14,068 ; but it had been sold some few days previously. The baron died on the 16th of March following, and the number was the first drawn ticket on the 24th, and, as such, entitled to £20,000. The baron's representatives, under these circumstance, published an advertisement, offering a reward of £1000 to any person who might have found the said ticket, and would deliver it up. Payment was stopped.

A wholesale linen draper in Cornhill (who had ordered his broker to buy him ten tickets, which he deposited in a chest), on copying the numbers for the purpose of examining them, made a mistake in one figure, and called it 14,168 instead of 14,068, which was the £20,000 prize. The lottery being finished, he sent his tickets to be examined and marked. To his utter astonishment, he then found the error in the number copied on his paper. On his demanding payment at the lottery office, a *caveat* was entered by old d'Aguilar's executors ; but, an explanation taking place, the £20,000 was paid to the lucky linen draper.

Although these lotteries were a great source of revenue to Government, and, consequently, relieved the taxpayer to the amount of their profit, it began to dawn upon the public that this legalised gambling was somewhat immoral ; and, in 1808, a Committee of the House of Commons was appointed, to inquire how far the evil attending lotteries had been remedied by the laws passed respecting the same ; and, in their Report, they said that " the foundation of the lottery system is so radically vicious, that your Committee feel convinced that under no system of regulations, which can be devised, will it be possible for Parliament to adopt it as an efficacious source of revenue, and, at the same time, divest it of all the evils which it has, hitherto, proved so baneful a source."

Yet they continued to be held ; but, when the Lottery Act of 1818 was passing through the House of Commons, Mr Parnell protested against it, and, in the course of his speech, suggested that the following epitaph should be inscribed on the tomb of the Chancellor of the Exchequer : " Here lies the Right Hon. Nicholas Vansittart, once Chancellor of the Exchequer ; the patron of Bible Societies, the builder of Churches, a friend to the education of the poor, an encourager of Savings' banks, and—a supporter of Lotteries ! "

And, in 1819, when the lottery for that year was being discussed, Mr Lyttleton moved :

1. That by the establishment of State lotteries, a spirit of gambling, injurious, in the highest degree, to the morals of the people, is encouraged and provoked.

2. That such a habit, manifestly weakening the habits of industry, must diminish the permanent sources of the public revenue.

3. That the said lotteries have given rise to other systems of gambling, which have been but partially repressed by laws, whose provisions are extremely arbitrary, and their enforcement liable to the greatest abuse.

4. That this House, therefore, will no longer authorise the establishment of State lotteries under any system of regulations whatever.

Needless to say, these resolutions were not passed, but the Lottery was on its last legs, for, in the Lottery Act of 1823, provision was made for its discontinuance after the drawing of the lottery sanctioned in that Act. Yet this was not adhered to, and a "last lottery" was decreed to be drawn in 1826. Its date was originally fixed for the 18th of July, but the public did not subscribe readily, and it was postponed until the 18th of October, and, on that day it was drawn at Cooper's Hall, Basinghall Street. Here is an epitaph which was written on it :

In Memory of

THE STATE OF LOTTERY,

the last of a long line

whose origin in England commenced

in the year 1569,

which, after a series of tedious complaints,

Expired

on the

18th day of October 1826.

During a period of 257 years, the family

flourished under the powerful protection

of the

British Parliament ;

the Minister of the day continuing to

give them his support for the improvement

of the revenue.

As they increased, it was found that their
continuance corrupted the morals,
and encouraged a spirit
of Speculation and Gambling among the lower
classes of the people ;
thousands of whom fell victims to their
insinuating and tempting allurements.
Many philanthropic individuals
in the Senate,
at various times, for a series of years,
pointed out their baneful influence,
without effect ;
His Majesty's Ministers
still affording them their countenance
and protection.
The British Parliament
being, at length, convinced of their
mischievous tendency,
His Majesty GEORGE IV.
on the 9th of July 1823,
pronounced sentence of condemnation
on the whole race ;
from which time they were almost
NEGLECTED BY THE BRITISH PUBLIC.
Very great efforts were made by the
Partisans and friends of the family to
excite
the public feeling in favour of the last
of the race, in vain :
It continued to linger out the few
remaining
moments of its existence without attention,
or sympathy, and finally terminated
its career unregretted by any
virtuous mind.

In 1836 an Act was passed " to prevent the advertising of Foreign and illegal lotteries," but circulars still come from Hamburg and other places. In 1844 an Act was passed " to indemnify persons connected with Art Unions, and others, against certain penalties." Still there were minor lotteries and raffles, and the law was seldom set in force against them, any more than it is now when applied to charitable purposes ; yet in 1860 one Louis Dethier, was haled up at Bow Street for holding a lottery for £10,000 worth of Twelfth Cakes, and was only let off on consenting to stop it at once, and nowadays the lottery is practically dead, except when some petty rogue is taken up for deluding children with prize sweets.

CHAPTER XIX

WE are apt to think that company promoters and commercial speculation are things of modern growth, but *Projectors* and *Patentees* (company promoters and monopolists) were common in the early seventeenth century; and we find an excellent exposition of their ways and commodities in a poetical broadside by John Taylor, the Water poet, published in 1641. It is entitled *The complaint of M. Tenter-hooke the* Proiector, *and Sir Thomas Dodger, the* Patentee. Under the title is a woodcut, which represents a *Projector*, who has a pig's head and ass's ears, screws for legs, and fish hooks for fingers, bears a measure of coal, and a barrel of wine, on his legs respectively, tobacco, pipes, dice, roll tobacco, playing cards, and a bundle of hay slung to his body, papers of pins on his right arm, and a measure for spirits on his left arm, a barrel and a dredger on the skirts of his coat. With his fish hook fingers, he drags bags of money. This is Tenter-hooke, who is saying to his friend Sir Thomas Dodger, who is represented as a very well dressed gentleman of the period :

> " I have brought money to fill your chest,
> For which I am curst by most and least."

To which Sir Thomas replies :

> " Our many yeares scraping is lost at a clap,
> All thou hast gotten by others' mishap."

If any aske, what things these Monsters *be*
'*Tis a* Projector *and a* Patentee :
Such, as like Vermine o're this Lande did crawle,
And grew so rich, they gain'd the Devill and all.

Loe, I, that lately was a *Man* of Fashion,
The *Bug-beare* and the *Scarcrow* of this Nation,
Th' admired mighty *Mounte-banke* of *Fame*,
The Juggling *Hocus Pocus* of good name ;
The *Bull-begger* who did affright and feare,
And rake, and pull, teare, pill, pole, shave and sheare,
Now *Time* hath pluck'd the *Vizard* from my face,
I am the onely Image of disgrace.
My ugly shape I hid so cunningly,
(Close cover'd with the cloake of honesty),
That from the *East* to *West*, from *South* to *North*,
I was a man esteem'd of ex'lent worth.
And (Sweet Sir *Thomas Dodger*,) for your sake,
My studious time I spent, my sleepes I brake ;
My braines I tost with many a strange vagary.
And, (like a Spaniell) did both fetch and carry
To you, such *Projects*, as I could invent,
Not thinking there would come a Parliament.
I was the great *Projector*, and from me,
Your Worship learn'd to be a *Patentee* ;
I had the Art to cheat the Common-weale,
And you had tricks and slights to passe the Seale.
I took the paines, I travell'd, search'd and sought,
Which (by your power) were into Patents wrought.
What was I but your Journey man, I pray,
To bring youre worke to you, both night and day :
I found *Stuffe*, and you brought it so about,
You (like a skilfull *Taylor*) cut it out,
And fashion'd it, but now (to our displeasure)
You fail'd exceedingly in taking measure.
My legs were Screws, to raise thee high or low,
According as your power did *Ebbe* or *Flow* ;
And at your will I was Screw'd up too high,
That tott'ring, I have broke my necke thereby.
For you, I made my *Fingers fish-hookes* still
To catch at all *Trades*, either good, or ill,
I car'd not much who lost, so we might get,
For all was *Fish* that came into the Net.
For you, (as in my Picture plaine appeares)
I put a *Swine's face* on, an *Asses eares*,

The one to listen unto all I heard,
Wherein your Worship's profit was prefer'd,
The other to tast all things, good or bad,
(As Hogs will doe) where profit may be had.
Soape, Starch, Tobacco, Pipes, Pens, Butter, Haye
Wine, Coales, Cards, Dice, and all came in my way
I brought your Worship, every day and houre,
And hope to be defended by your power.

Sir *Thomas Dodgers'* Answer.

Alas good *Tenter-hooke,* I tell thee plaine,
To seeke for helpe of me 'tis but in vaine :
My *Patent,* which I stood upon of late,
Is like an *Almanacke* that's out of *Date.*
'T had force and vertue once, strange things to doe,
But, now, it wants both force and vertue too.
This was the turne of whirling *Fortune's* wheele,
When we least dream'd we should her changing feele.
Then *Time,* and fortune, both with joynt consent,
Brought us to ruine by a Parliament ;
I doe confesse thou broughtst me sweet conceits,
Which, now, I find, were but alluring baits,
And I, (too much an Asse) did lend mine eare,
To credit all thou saydst, as well as heare.
Thou in the *Project* of the *Soape* didst toyle,
But 'twas so slippery, and too full of oyle,
That people wondered how we held it fast
But now it is quite slipp'd from us at last.
The *Project* for the *Starch* thy wit found out,
Was stiffe a while, now, limber as a Clout,
The Pagan weed (*Tobacco*) was our hope,
In *Leafe, Pricke, Role, Ball, Pudding, Pipe,* or *Rope.*
Brasseele, Varina, Meavis, Trinidado,
Saint *Christophers, Virginia,* or *Barvaao;*
Bermudas, Providentia, Shallowcongo,
And the most part of all the rest (*Mundungo*[1])
That Patent, with a whiffe, is spent and broke,
And all our hopes (in fumo) turn'd to smoake,
Thou framdst the *Butter* Patent in thy braines,
(A Rope and Butter take thee for thy paines).
I had forgot *Tobacco Pipes,* which are
Now like to thou and I, but brittle ware.

[1] Trashy Tobacco—from the Spanish *Mondóngo,* paunch, tripes, black pudding.

> *Dice* run against us, we at *Cards* are crost,
> We both are turn'd up *Noddies*,[1] and all's lost.
> Thus from *Sice-sinke*, we'r sunke below *Dewce-ace*,
> And both of us are Impes of blacke disgrace.
> *Pins* pricke us, and *Wine* frets our very hearts,
> That we have rais'd the price of *Pints* and *Quarts.*
> Thou (in mine eares) thy lyes and tales didst foyst,
> And mad'st me up the price of *Sea-coales* hoyst.
> *Corne, Leather, Partrick, Pheasant, Rags, Gold-twist,*
> Thou brought'st all to my *Mill* ; what was't we mist ?
> *Weights, Bon*[2] *lace, Mowstraps,* new, new, *Corporation,*
> *Rattles, Seadans,*[3] of rare invented fashion.
> *Silke, Tallow, Hobby-horses, Wood, Red herring,*
> *Law, Conscience, Justice, Swearing,* and *For-swearing.*
> All these thou broughtst to me, and still I thought
> That every thing was good that profit brought,
> But now all's found to be ill gotten pelfe,
> I'le shift for one, doe thou shift for thyselfe.

The first loans to Government, in a regular form, took the form of Tontines, so called from their inventor Lorenzo Tonti. A Tontine is a loan raised on life annuities. A number of persons subscribe the loan, and, in return, the Government pay an annuity to every subscriber. At the death of any annuitant, his annuity was divided among the others, until the sole survivor enjoyed the whole income, and at his death, the annuity lapsed. As an example, a Mr Jennings, who died in 1798, aged 103—leaving behind him a fortune of over two millions—was an original subscriber for £100 in a Tontine : he was the last survivor, and his income derived for his £100 was £3000 per annum. Our National Debt began in 1689—by that, I mean that debt that has never been repaid, and dealings in which, virtually founded Stockbroking as a business. The Bank of England started business on 1st Jan. 1695, and, from that time, we may date the methodical dealing in Stocks and Shares. Of

---

[1] Fools : but there was also a game at Cards called Noddy, supposed to have been the same as Cribbage.

[2] Bone lace.

[3] Sedan Chairs ; said to have been introduced into England in 1581, and first used in London in 1623.

course there were intermediaries between buyer and seller, and these were termed " Stock brokers."   They first of all did business at the Exchange, but as they increased in number their presence there was not desirable, and they migrated to 'Change Alley, close by.   These gentry are described in a little book, published in 1703, called, *Mirth and Wisdom in a miscellany of different characters.*[1]

" A Stock Jobber

" Is a Rational Animal, with a sensitive Understanding. He rises and falls like the ebbing and flowing of the Sea ; and his paths are as unsearchable as hers are.   He is one of *Pharaoh's* lean kine in the midst of plenty ; and, to dream of him is, almost, an Indication of approaching Famine. He is ten times more changeable than the Weather ; and the living Insect from which the Grasshopper on the Royal Bourse was drawn, never leap'd from one Place to another, as he from one Number to another ; sometimes a Hundred and a half is too little for him ; sometimes Half a hundred is too much ; and he falls seven times a Day, but not like *David,* on his knees, to beg pardon for former Sins, but to be made capable of sinning again.   He came in with the *Dutch,* and he had freed us from as great a Plague as they were, had he been so kind as to have went out with them. He lives on the Exchange, but his Dwelling cannot be said to be the Place of his *Abode,* for he *abides* no where, he is so unconstant and uncertain.   Ask him what Religion he professes, he cries, *He'll sell you as cheap as any Body* ; and what Value such an Article of Faith is of, his Answer is, *I'll give you as much for a Debenture, as the best Chapman thereabout shall.*   He is fam'd for Injustice, yet he is a Master of *Equity* in one particular to perfection, for he cheats every Body alike, and is *Equal* in all his Undertakings.   The Den from which this Beast of Prey bolts out is *Jonathan's* Coffee House, or *Garraway's* ; and a Man that

---

[1] Also published in 1708 as *Hicklety Picklety.*

goes into either, ought to be as circumspect as if in an Enemy's country. A Dish of tea there, may be as dear to him as a good Purchase, and a Man that is over reach'd in either, tho' no Drunkard, may be said to have drank away his Estate. He may be call'd a true Unbeliever, and out of the Pale of the Church, for he has no Faith. Is a meer *Tolandist* in secular Concerns, at the very minute that he is ready to take up any Goods upon Trust that shall belong to his Neighbour. *St Paul's* Cathedral would be a Mansion-House fit for a Deity indeed, in his Opinion, did but the Merchants meet there ; and he can give you no subtantialler a Reason for liking *Salter's Hall* better than the Church, than because of its being a House of Traffick and Commerce, and the Sale being often held there. He is the Child of God in one Sense only, and that is by reason of his bearing His Image, but the Devil in many, for he fights under his Standard. To make an end of a Subject that is endless ; he has the Figure of a Man, but the Nature of a Beast ; and either triumphs over his Fellow Adventurers, as he eats the Bread of other People's Carefulness, and drinks the Tears of Orphans or Widows, or being made himself Food for others, grows, at last, constant to one place, which is the *Compter*, and the fittest House for such an unaccountable Fellow to make up his Accounts in."

Jonathan's was, especially, the Coffee House which stock jobbers frequented. Addison, in the first number of the *Spectator*, says, "I sometimes pass for a Jew in the assembly of Stock Jobbers at Jonathan's " ; and Mrs Centlivre has laid one of the scenes in her *Bold Stroke for a Wife*, at Jonathan's : where, also, was subscribed the first foreign loan, in 1706.

There was a Stock Exchange hoax in the reign of Queen Anne. A man appeared, galloping from Kensington to the City, ordering the turnpikes to be thrown open for him, and shouting loudly that he bore the news of the Queen's death. This sad message flew far and wide, and dire was its effects in the City. The funds fell at once, but Manasseh Lopez and the Jews bought all they could, and reaped the benefit when the fraud was discovered.   In 1715, too, a false report that the Pretender had been taken, sent the Funds bounding up, to the great profit of those who were in the secret of the hoax.

About this time the demon of gambling was rampant, every one wanted to find a short road to wealth ; naturally, there were plenty of rogues to ease them of their money, but the most colossal stroke of gambling was the South Sea Bubble, the only parallel to which, in modern times, is the Railway Mania, in 1846.

The South Sea Company was started in 1711, to have the monopoly of trade to the South Seas, or South Coast of America, a region which was, even then, believed to be an *El Dorado.*   As a trading company it was not successful, but, having a large capital, it dealt with finance.   On 22nd Jan. 1720, a proposal was laid before Parliament that the Company should take upon themselves the National Debt, of £30,981,712, 6s. 6½d. at 5 per cent. per annum, secured until 1727, when the whole was to be redeemable, if Parliament so chose, and the interest to be reduced to 4 per cent., and " That for the liberty of increasing their Capital Stock, as aforesaid, the Company will give, and pay into his Majesty's Exchequer, for the purpose of the Public, and to be applied for paying off the public debt provided for by Parliament, before Christmas, 1716, the sum of three millions and a half, by four equal quarterly payments, whereof the first payment to be at Lady Day 1721."   On April 7, the South Sea Company's Bill received the Royal Assent, the £100 shares being then about £300.

On April 12, the directors opened their books for a subscription of a Million, at the rate of £300 for every £100 Capital, which was immediately taken up, twice over. It was to be repaid in five instalments of £60.   Up went the shares with a bound ; yet, to raise them still higher, the Midsummer dividend was to be declared at 10 per cent., and all subscriptions were to be entitled to the same.   This plan answered so well, that another million was at once raised at 400 per cent.; and, in a few hours, a million and a half was subscribed at that rate. The Stock went up higher and higher, until, on the 2nd of June, it reached £890. Then, so many wanted to sell, that, on the same afternoon, it dropped to £640. The Company set their Agents to work, and, when evening came, the Stock had been driven up to £750, at about which price it continued until the bank closed on the 22nd June.

Very soon, a third Subscription was started, at the rate of £1000 for every £100, to be paid in ten equal payments, one in hand, the other nine, quarterly. The lists were so full that the directors enlarged it to four millions Stock, which, at that price amounted to £40,000,000. These last subscriptions were, before the end of June, sold at about £2000 premium ; and, after the closing of the transfer books, the original Stock rose to over £1000 per cent. At the same time, the first subscriptions were at 560, and the second at 610 per cent. advance.

This set every one crazy, and innumerable " bubble," or cheating, companies were floated, or attempts made thereat. Speculation became so rampant that, on June 11, the King published a Proclamation declaring that all these unlawful projects should be deemed as common nuisances, and prosecuted as such, with the penalty of £500 for any broker buying or selling any shares in them. Among these companies was one " for carrying on an undertaking of great advantage, but nobody to know what it is." Another was " for a wheel for perpetual motion, one million " ; and another " for the transmutation of quick silver into a malleable fine metal." Society was, for a brief time, uprooted.

The apogee of the Company had been reached : from this time its downfall was rapid. The Stock fell, and fell. The aid of the Bank of England was invoked, but it came too late ; goldsmiths and brokers began to abscond. On December 12, the House of Commons ordered that the

Directors of the South Sea Company should, forthwith, lay before the House an account of all their proceedings ; and, on Jan. 4, 1721, a Secret Committee of the House was ordered to report upon the Company. Then Knight, the cashier of the Company, absconded ; and a reward of £2000 was offered for his apprehension. On Feb. 15, the Parliamentary Committee made their first report—and a pretty one it was—bribery all over the place, and especially among the members of the Government. The bubble was pricked and thousands were ruined. Certainly, the fortunes of those directors, who had any, were seized for the benefit of the swindled, and only a small percentage of their wealth was allowed them for their subsistence. Finally, it was settled that the £7,000,000 which the Company stood pledged to pay over to the Government, should be remitted, and every Shareholder should receive £33, 6s. 8d. on £100 Stock : all else being irretrievably lost. Over the misery entailed on the avaricious public who were gulled, it is best to draw a veil, and use the episode as a warning.

Swift wrote a poem 60 verses long, on *The South Sea Project*, 1721, from which I extract the following :

> " There is a gulf, where thousands fell,
>   Here all the bold adventurers came,
>   A narrow sound, though deep as Hell,—
>   *'Change Alley* is the dreadful name.
>
>   Nine times a day it ebbs and flows,
>   Yet he that on the surface lies,
>   Without a pilot, seldom knows
>   The time it falls, or when 'twill rise.
>
>   Subscribers, here, by thousands float,
>   And jostle one another down ;
>   Each paddling in his leaky boat,
>   And here they fish for gold, and drown.
>   .   .   .   .   .   .
>   Meantime, secure on Garraway cliffs,
>   A savage race, by shipwrecks fed,
>   Lie waiting for the foundered skiffs,
>   And strip the bodies of the dead."

There were street ballads, of course, such as *The Hubble Bubbles*, A Ballad, by Mr D'Urfey, and one which I give *in extenso*.   A *South-Sea* Ballad : or, Merry Remarks upon *Exchange Alley* Bubbles.   To a new tune, call'd *The Grand Elixir : or The Philosopher's Stone discovered :*

> In *London* stands a famous Pile,
>   And near that Pile, an Alley,
> Where Merry Crowds for Riches toil,
>   And Wisdom stoops to Folly :
> Here, Sad and Joyful, High and Low,
>   Court Fortune for her Graces,
> And, as she Smiles, or Frowns, they show
>   Their Gestures and Grimaces.
>
> Here Stars and Garters do appear,
>   Among our Lords, the Rabble,
> To buy and sell, to see and hear,
>   The *Jews* and *Gentiles* squabble.
> Here crafty Courtiers are too wise
>   For those who trust to Fortune,
> They see the Cheat with clearer Eyes,
>   Who peep behind the Curtain.
>
> Our greatest Ladies hither come,
>   And ply in Chariots daily,
> Oft pawn their Jewels for a Sum,
>   To venture't in the Alley.
> Young Harlots, too, from *Drury Lane*,
>   Approach the *'Change* in coaches,
> To fool away the Gold they gain
>   By their obscene Debauches.
>
> Long Heads may thrive by sober Rules,
>   Because they think and drink not ;
> But Headlongs are our thriving Fools,
>   Who only drink and think not :
> The lucky Rogues, like Spaniel Dogs,
>   Leap into *South Sea* Water,
> And, there, they fish for golden Frogs,
>   Not caring what comes a'ter.

'Tis said that Alchimists of old,
　　Could turn a brazen kettle,
Or leaden Cistern into Gold,
　　That noble, tempting Mettle :
But, if it here may be allowed
　　To bring in great with small things
Our cunning *South Sea*, like a God,
　　Turns nothing into all things.

What need have we of *Indian* Wealth,
　　Or Commerce with our Neighbours,
Our Constitution is in Health,
　　And Riches crown our Labours :
Our *South Sea* Ships have golden Shrouds
　　They bring us Wealth, 'tis granted,
But lodge their Treasure in the clouds,
　　To hide it 'till it's wanted.

O, *Britain !* bless thy present State,
　　Thou only happy Nation,
So oddly rich, so madly Great,
　　Since Bubbles came in Fashion :
Successful Rakes exert their Pride,
　　And count their airy Millions ;
Whilst homely Drabs in Coaches ride,
　　Brought up to Town on Pillions.

Few Men, who follow Reason's Rules,
　　Grow Fat with *South Sea* Diet ;
Young Rattles, and unthinking Fools,
　　Are those that flourish by it.
Old musty Jades, and pushing Blades,
　　Who've least Consideration,
Grow rich apace, whilst wiser Heads
　　Are struck with Admiration.

A Race of Men, who, t'other Day
　　Lay crush'd beneath Disasters,
Are now, by Stock brought into Play,
　　And made our Lords and Masters :
But should our *South Sea Babel* fall,
　　What Numbers would be frowning,
The Losers, then, must ease their Gall
　　By Hanging, or by Drowning.

Five Hundred Millions, Notes and Bonds,
  Our Stocks are worth in Value,
But neither lye in Goods, or Lands,
  Or Money, let me tell ye.
Yet, tho' our Foreign Trade is lost,
  Of mighty Wealth we vapour,
When all the Riches that we boast,
  Consists in Scraps of Paper."

CHAPTER XX

First mention of the Stock Exchange—Attempt at hoax—Daniel's fraud—
Berenger's fraud—Bubbles of 1825—The Railway Mania—30th Nov. 1845
at the Board of Trade—The fever at its height—The Marquis of Clanricarde pricks the bubble.

IN 1734 an Act was passed (7 Geo. II., c. 8) entitled
"An Act to prevent the infamous practice of Stock
jobbing," which provided that no loss in bargains for
time should be recoverable in the Courts, and placed
such speculations outside the Law altogether. It was a
dead letter, but was in force till 1860, when it was repealed.

The first mention of the Stock Exchange as such, is in
the *Daily Advertiser* of Thursday, July 15, 1773. "On
Tuesday, the Brokers and others at New Jonathan's came
to a Resolution that, instead of its being called New
Jonathan's, it is to be named the Stock Exchange, which
is to be painted over the door." And here they abode
until, in 1801, the Stockbrokers laid the first stone of
a building of their own : having purchased Mendoza's
boxing room, the Debating Forum of Capel Court, and
buildings contiguous to that site.

On May 5, 1803, an attempt was made to hoax the
Stock Exchange, which was partially successful. On that
day, at half-past eight in the morning, a man, booted and
spurred, and having every appearance of having come off a
long journey, rushed up to the Mansion House, and inquired
for the Lord Mayor, saying he was a messenger from the
Foreign Office, and had a letter for his lordship. When he
was told he was not within, he said he would leave the letter,
and begged the servant to place it where the Lord Mayor

should get it the moment of his return ; which duly happened. The letter ran thus :

"Downing Street, 8 A.M.

"To the Right Hon. the Lord Mayor,—

"Lord Hawkesbury presents his compliments to the Lord Mayor, and is happy to inform him that the negotiations between this country and the French Republic have been amicably adjusted."

Thinking it genuine, the Lord Mayor published it, and wrote to Lord Hawkesbury, congratulating him ; but the forgery was soon exposed.

Meanwhile, Consols opened at 69, and, before noon, were over 70, only to fall, when the truth came out, to 63. Of course, all transactions, that day, were made null and void. Although £500 reward was offered, nothing was ever heard of the perpetrators of this swindle.

Under date of Aug. 20, 1806, the *Annual Register* says : "A most atrocious fraud was committed on a number of gentlemen at the Stock Exchange, it being the settling day, by a foreign Jew, of the name of Joseph Elkin Daniels, who has, for a long time, been a conspicuous character in the Alley. Finding that, in consequence of the great fluctuation of Omnium, he was not able to pay for all he had purchased at an advanced price, he hit upon a scheme to pocket an enormous sum of money, and with which he has decamped ; £31,000 Omnium was tendered to him in the course of Thursday ; in payment for which he gave drafts on his bankers, amounting to £16,816, 5s., which were paid into the respective bankers of those who had received them, to clear in the afternoon. Having gained possession of the Omnium, he sold it through the medium of a respectable broker, received drafts for it, which he cleared immediately, and set off with the produce. On his drafts being presented, payment was refused, he having no effects at his bankers."

A hue and cry was raised after him, and he was soon

discovered in the Isle of Man, whence he.could not be taken without the Governor's consent.   This was obtained, but there were so many similar rascals taking sanctuary in the Island, that it was not deemed prudent to execute the warrant in the daytime, and Daniels was arrested at night. Great was the uproar in the morning when the rogues found their companion had gone, and an indignation meeting was held to protest against the violation of their rights.   He was brought before the Lord Mayor on 16th Sept., but, owing to some technicalities, he was let go, although he had to make his appearance at a Commission of Bankruptcy.

In 1814 there was an attempted fraud on the Stock Exchange, which was the most daring ever perpetrated.   It was executed by one Charles Random de Berenger, a French refugee, and an officer in one of the foreign regiments.   It was alleged that, with him, were associated Lord Cochrane, the Hon. Andrew Cochrane Johnstone, and several others. It appears from the evidence on the trial, that, early in the morning of the 21st of February, a gentleman, dressed in a grey greatcoat over a scarlet uniform, on which was a star, knocked at the door of the Ship Inn at Dover, and said that he was the bearer of very important despatches from France. This gentleman, all the witnesses swore, was Berenger.

He sent a letter, signed R. Du Bourg, Lieut.-Colonel, and Aide-de-Camp to Lord Cathcart, to Admiral Foley, the Port Admiral at Dover, advising him that he had just arrived from Calais with the news of a great victory obtained by the Allies over Bonaparte, who was slain, in his flight, by the Cossacks, and that the Allied Sovereigns were in Paris. Berenger posted up to London, which he entered, having his horses decked with laurels, in order to make a stir.   It was felt on the Stock Exchange.   *Omnium*, which opened at 27½ rose to 33 ; but, as the day wore on, and no confirmation came of the news, they receded to 28½.   Business in that Stock was done, that day, to the tune of half a million of money.   Lord Cochrane and others had, previously, given instructions to sell Omniums for them, on the 21st of

February, to an enormous amount. One deposed that, on
that date, he sold—

<pre>
For Lord Cochrane .   . £139,000 Omnium
     „   Cochrane Johnstone . 120,000   do.
     „   do.   100,000 Consols
     „   Mr Butt   .   .   . 124,000 Omnium
     „   do.   .   .   . 168,000 Consols
</pre>

And he further deposed that he always considered that any
business he did for Mr Butt was to be placed to Lord
Cochrane's account.

Another stockbroker sold for the same three gentlemen
£565,000 Omnium. Another had sold £80,000 on their
account, and yet another had had instructions to sell a very
large sum for the same parties, but had refused.

In the end, Lord Cochrane and Mr Butt were condemned
to pay to the King a fine of a Thousand Pounds each, and
J. P. Holloway Five Hundred ; and these three, together
with De Berenger, Sandon, and Lyte, were sentenced to
imprisonment in the Marshalsea for twelve calendar months.
Further, Lord Cochrane, De Berenger, and Butt were to
stand in the pillory for one hour, before the Royal Exchange, once during their imprisonment. This latter part
of their punishment was, afterwards, remitted. Lord Cochrane's name was struck off the Navy List, he was expelled
from the House of Commons, his Arms were taken down
from his stall, as Knight of the Bath, his banner torn down,
and kicked ignominiously out of Henry VII.'s Chapel in
Westminster Abbey.

By very many he was believed innocent, and, on his seat
for Westminster being declared vacant, he was enthusiastic-
ally re-elected. He escaped from custody, was captured,
and had to serve his time. On June 20, 1815, he was told
his imprisonment was at an end, if he would pay the fine
imposed upon him ; and, on July 3rd, he reluctantly did so,
with a £1000 bank note, on the back of which he wrote :—
" My health having suffered by long and close confinement,

and my oppressors having resolved to deprive me of property, or life, I submit to robbery, to protect myself from murder, in the hope that I shall live to bring the delinquents to justice."

On the very day he was released, he took his seat again in the House of Commons; and, in 1832, he received a "free pardon," was restored to the Navy List, gazetted a rear-admiral, and presented at a Levée!

The year 1825 was remarkable for the number of bubble companies which were floated or not, and for the dreadful commercial panic which ensued, during which over seventy banks collapsed in London, or the country. Over £11,000,000 were subscribed to foreign loans, and £17,500,000 to different companies. In Parliament there were presented 439 private bills for companies, and Acts were passed for 288. Horace Smith sings of them thus:

> " Early and late, where'er I rove,
>   In park or square, suburb or grove,
>   In civic lanes, or alleys,
>   Riches are hawked, while rivals rush
>   To pour into mine ear a gush
>   Of money making sallies.
>
> ' Haste instantly and buy,' cries one,
> Real del Monte shares, for none
>   Will yield a richer profit;
> Another cries—' No mining plan
> Like ours, the Anglo-Mexican;
>   As for Del Monte, scoff it.'
>
> This, grasps my button, and declares
> There's nothing like Columbian shares,
>   The capital a million;
> That, cries, ' La Plata's sure to pay,'
> Or bids me buy, without delay,
>   Hibernian or Brazilian.
>
> 'Scaped from the torments of the mine,
> Rivals in gas, an endless line,
>   Arrest me as I travel;
> Each sure my suffrage to receive,
> If I will only give him leave
>   His project to unravel.

By fire and life insurers next,
I'm intercepted, pestered, vexed,
   Almost beyond endurance ;
And, though the schemes appear unsound,
Their advocates are seldom found
   Deficient in assurance.

Last, I am worried Shares to buy,
In the Canadian Company,
   The Milk Association ;
The laundry men who wash by steam,
Railways, pearl fishing, or the scheme
   For inland navigation."

In 1845 began the most wonderful era of gambling in modern times, the Railway Mania, which rose to such a height that it was noticed on Oct. 25. "During the past week there were announced, in three newspapers, eighty-nine new schemes, with a capital of £84,055,000 ; during the month, there were 357 new schemes announced, with an aggregate capital of £332,000,000."

On 17th Nov. *The Times* published a table of all the railway companies registered up to the 31st October, numbering 1428, and involving an outlay of £701,243,208. "Take away," it said, " £140,000,000 for railways completed, or in progress, exclude all the most extravagant schemes, and divide the remainder by ten, can we add from our present resources, even a tenth of the vast remainder? Can we add £50,000,000 to the railway speculations we are already irretrievably embarked in? We cannot, without the most ruinous, universal and desperate confusion."

The *Annual Register* for 1845 gives a graphic account of an incident in the Railway Mania. "An extraordinary scene occurred at the office of the Railway Department of the Board of Trade, on this day (Sunday, 30th Nov.), being the last day on which the plans of the new projects could be deposited with the Railway Board, in order to enable Bills to authorise them, to be brought before Parliament, in compliance with the Standing Orders.

" Last year, the number of projects in respect of which

plans were lodged with the Board of Trade, was 248 : the number, this year, is stated to be 815. The projectors of the Scotch lines were mostly in advance, and had their plans duly lodged on Saturday. The Irish projectors, too, and the old established Companies, seeking powers to construct branches, were among the more punctual. But, upwards of 600 plans remained to be deposited. Towards the last, the utmost exertions were made to forward them. The efforts of the lithographic draughtsmen and printers in London were excessive ; people remained at work night after night, snatching a hasty repose for a couple of hours on lockers, benches, or the floor. Some found it impossible to execute their contracts ; others did their work imperfectly. One of the most eminent was compelled to bring over four hundred lithographers from Belgium, and failed, nevertheless, with this reinforcement, in completing some of his plans. Post horses and express trains, to bring to town plans prepared in the country, were sought in all parts. Horses were engaged days before, and kept, by persons specially appointed, under lock and key. Some railway companies exercised their power of refusing express trains for rival projects, and clerks were obliged to make sudden and embarrassing changes of route, in order to travel by less hostile ways. A large establishment of clerks were in attendance to register the deposits ; and this arrangement went on very well until eleven o'clock, when the delivery grew so rapid, that the clerks were quite unable to keep pace with the arrivals. The entrance hall soon became inconveniently crowded, considerable anxiety being expressed lest twelve o'clock should arrive ere the requisite formalities should have been gone through. This anxiety was allayed by the assurance that admission into the hall before that hour would be sufficient to warrant the reception of the documents. As the clock struck twelve, the doors of the office were about to be closed, when a gentleman, with the plans of one of the Surrey railways, arrived, and, with the greatest difficulty, succeeded in obtaining admission. A lull of a few minutes here occurred ;

but, just before the expiration of the first quarter of an hour, a post chaise, with reeking horses, drove up to the entrance, in hot haste. In a moment, its occupants (three gentlemen) alighted, and rushed down the passage, towards the office door, each bearing a plan of Brobdingnagian dimensions. On reaching the door, and finding it closed, the countenances of all dropped; but one of them, more valorous than the rest, and prompted by the bystanders, gave a loud pull at the bell. It was answered by Inspector Otway, who informed the ringer it was now too late, and that his plans could not be received. The agents did not wait for the conclusion of the unpleasant communication, but took advantage of the doors being opened, and threw in their papers, which broke the passage lamp in their fall. They were thrown back into the street; and when the door was again opened, again went in the plans, only to meet a similar fate. In the whole, upwards of 600 plans were duly deposited."

Mr Francis, in his " History of the English Railway," says : " The daily press was thoroughly deluged with advertisements ; double sheets did not supply space enough for them ; double doubles were resorted to, and, then, frequently, insertions were delayed. It has been estimated that the receipts of the leading journals averaged, at one period, £12,000 and £14,000, a week, from this source. The railway papers, on some occasions, contained advertisements that must have netted from £700 to £800 on each publication. The printer, the lithographer, and the stationer, with the preparation of prospectuses, the execution of maps, and the supply of other requisites, also made a considerable harvest.

" The leading engineers were, necessarily, at a great premium. Mr Brunel was said to be connected with fourteen lines, Mr Robert Stephenson with thirty-four, Mr Locke with thirty-one, Mr Rastrick with seventeen, and other engineers with one hundred and thirteen.

" The novelist has appropriated this peculiar portion of

commercial history, and, describing it, says, gravely and graphically : ' A Colony of solicitors, engineers and seedy accountants, settled in the purlieus of Threadneedle Street. Every town and parish in the kingdom blazed out in zinc plates over the doorways. From the cellar to the roof, every fragment of a room held its committee. The darkest cupboard on the stairs contained a secretary or a clerk. Men who were never seen east of Temple Bar before, or since, were, now, as familiar to the pavement of Moorgate Street,[1] as the Stockbrokers : ladies of title, lords, members of Parliament, and fashionable loungers thronged the noisy passages, and were jostled by adventurers, by gamblers, rogues and impostors.'

" The advantages of competition were pointed out, with the choicest phraseology. Lines which passed by barren districts, and by waste heaths, the termini of which were in uninhabitable places, reached a high premium. The shares of one Company rose 2400 per cent. Everything was to pay a large dividend ; everything was to yield a large profit. One railway was to cross the entire Principality without a single curve.

" The shares of another were issued ; the company formed, and the directors appointed, with only the terminal points surveyed. In the Ely railway, not one person connected with the country through which it was to pass, subscribed the title-deed.

" The engineers, who were examined in favour of particular lines, promised all and everything, in their evidence. It was humorously said, ' they plunge through the bowels of mountains ; they undertake to drain lakes ; they bridge valleys with viaducts ; their steepest gradients are gentle undulations ; their curves are lines of beauty ; they interrupt no traffic ; they touch no prejudice.'

" Labour of all kinds increased in demand. The price of iron rose from sixty-eight shillings to one hundred and

---

[1] From Moorgate Street 83 prospectuses, demanding £90,175,000, were sent out. Gresham Street issued 20, requiring £17,580,000.

twenty per ton. Money remained abundant. Promoters received their tens and twenties of thousands. Rumours of sudden fortunes were very plentiful. Estates were purchased by those who were content with their gains ; and, to crown the whole, a grave report was circulated, that Northumberland House, with its princely remembrances, and palatial grandeur, was to be bought by the South Western. Many of the railways attained prices which staggered reasonable men. The more worthless the article, the greater seemed the struggle to obtain it. Premiums of £5 and £6 were matters of course, even where there were four or five competitors for the road. One Company, which contained a clause to lease it at three and a half per cent., for 999 years, rose to twenty premium, so mad were the many to speculate.

" Every branch of commerce participated in the advantages of an increased circulation. The chief articles of trade met with large returns ; profits were regular ; and all luxuries which suited an affluent community, procured an augmented sale. Banking credit remained facile ; interest still kept low ; money, speaking as they of the City speak, could be had for next to nothing. It was advanced on everything which bore a value, whether readily convertible, or not. Bill brokers would only allow one and a half per cent. for cash ; and what is one and a half per cent. to men who revelled in the thought of two hundred ? The exchanges remained remarkably steady. The employment of the labourer on the new lines, of the operative in the factory, of the skilled artisan in the workshop, of the clerk at the desk, tended to add to the delusive feeling, and was one of the forms in which, for a time, the population was benefited. But, when the strength of the kingdom is wasted in gambling, temporary, indeed, is the good compared with the cost. Many, whose money was safely invested, sold at any price, to enter the share market. Servants withdrew their hoards from the savings banks. The tradesman crippled his business. The legitimate love of money became a fierce lust. The peer came from his club to his brokers ; the clergyman came from his pulpit to the mart ; the country gentleman forsook the calmness of his rural domain for the feverish excitement of Threadneedle Street. Voluptuous tastes were indulged in by those who were previously starving. The new men vied with the old, in the luxurious adornments of their houses. Everyone smiled with contentment ; every face wore a pleased expression. Some, who, by virtue of their unabashed impudence, became provisional committee men, supported the dignity of their position, in a style which raised the mirth of many, and moved the envy of more. Trustees, who had no money of their own, or, who had lost it, used that which was confided to them ; brothers speculated with the money of sisters ; sons gambled with the money of their widowed mothers ; children risked their patrimony ; and, it is no exaggeration to say, that the funds of hundreds were surreptitiously endangered by those in whose control they were placed."

The Marquis of Clanricarde, in a speech, spoke very boldly as to the status, social and financial, of some of the subscribers to Railway Companies. Said he : " One of the names to the deed to which he was anxious to direct their attention, was that of a gentleman, said to reside in Finsbury Square, who had subscribed to the amount of £25,000 : he was informed no such person was known at that address. There was, also, in the Contract deed, the name of an individual who had figured in the Dublin and Galway Railway case, who was down for £5000, and who was understood to be a half-pay officer, in the receipt of £54 a-year, but, who appeared as a subscriber in different railway schemes, to the amount of £41,500. The address of another, whose name was down for £12,200, was stated to be in Watling Street, but it appeared he did not reside there. In the case of another individual down for £12,500 a false address was found to have been given. Another individual, whom he would not name, was a curate in a parish in Kent ; he might be worth all the money for which he appeared responsible in various railway schemes, but his name appeared for £25,000 in different projects, and stood for £10,000 in this line. Another individual, who was down for £25,000, was represented to be in poor circumstances. A clerk in a public company was down for upwards of £50,000. There were several more cases of the same kind, but he trusted that he had stated enough to establish the necessity of referring the matter to a committee. There were, also, two brothers, sons of a charwoman, living in a garret, one of whom had signed for £12,500, and the other for £25,000; these two brothers, excellent persons, no doubt, but who were receiving about a guinea and a half between them, were down for £37,000."

CHAPTER XXI

NOT particularly exaggerated is " Railroad Speculator " in *Punch* (Vol. viii., p. 244):

" The night was stormy and dark, the town was shut up in sleep : Only those were abroad who were out on the lark, Or those who'd no beds to keep.

I passed through the lonely street, The wind did sing and blow; I could hear the policeman's feet, Clapping to and fro.

There stood a potato man, in the midst of all the wet ; He stood with his 'tato can, in the lonely Haymarket.

Two gents of dismal mien, and dank and greasy rags ; came out of a shop for gin, swaggering over the flags :

Swaggering over the stones, these shabby bucks did walk ; and I went and followed those seedy ones, and listened to their talk.

Was I sober or awake? Could I believe my ears? Those dismal beggars spake of nothing but Railroad Shares.

I wondered more and more : Says one, ' Good friend of mine, how many shares did you write for? In the Diddlesex Junction line?'

' I wrote for twenty,' says Jim, ' but they wouldn't give me one'; His comrade straight rebuked him, for the folly he had done.

' Oh Jim, you are unawares of the ways of this bad town : I always write for five hundred shares, and *then* they put me down.'

' And yet you got no shares,' says Jim, ' for all your boast' : ' I *would* have wrote,' says Jack, ' but where was the penny to pay the post?'

' I lost, for I couldn't pay that first instalment up ; but here's 'taters smoking hot—I say, Let's stop, my boy, and sup.'

And, at this simple feast, the while they did regale, I drew each ragged capitalist, down on my left thumb nail.

Their talk did me perplex, All night I tumbled and tost ; and thought of railroad specs, and how money was won and lost.

' Bless railroads everywhere,' I said, ' and the world's advance ; Bless every railroad share in Italy, Ireland, France ; for never a beggar need now despair, and every rogue has a chance.' ''

But, should anyone wish to watch the progress of the Railway Mania, I would recommend a perusal of *Punch*, Vol. ix., in which appears, *inter alia, Jeames's Diary*, by Thackeray, afterwards published as *The Diary of C. Jeames De la Pluche, Esq.* The idea was started on p. 59, under the heading of—

"A LUCKY SPECULATOR.

Considerable sensation has been excited in the upper and lower circles in the West End, by a startling piece of good fortune which has befallen JAMES PLUSH, Esq., lately footman in a respected family in Berkeley Square.

One day, last week, Mr James waited upon his master, who is a banker in the city ; and, after a little blushing and hesitation, said he had saved a little money in service, and was anxious to retire, and to invest his savings to advantage.

His master (we believe we may mention, without offending delicacy, the well known name of Sir GEORGE FLIMSY of the firm of FLIMSY, DIDDLER, and FLASH,) smilingly asked Mr JAMES, what was the amount of his savings, wondering considerably how—out of an income of thirty guineas, the main part of which he spent in bouquets, silk stockings and perfumery—Mr PLUSH could have managed to lay by anything.

Mr PLUSH, with some hesitation, said he had been *speculating in railroads*, and stated his winnings to have been thirty thousand pounds. He had commenced his speculations with twenty, borrowed from a fellow servant. He had dated his letters from the house in Berkeley Square, and humbly begged pardon of his master, for not having instructed the railway secretaries, who answered the applications, to apply at the area bell.

Sir GEORGE, who was at breakfast, instantly rose, and shook Mr P. by the hand ; LADY FLIMSY begged him to be seated, and partake of the breakfast which he had laid on the table ; and has subsequently invited him to her grand *dejeuner* at Richmond, where it was observed that Miss EMILY FLIMSY, her beautiful and accomplished seventh daughter, paid the lucky gentleman *marked attention*.

We hear it stated that Mr P. is of very ancient family (HUGO DE LA PLUCHE came over with the Conqueror) ; and the new Brougham which he has started, bears the ancient coat of his race.

He has taken apartments at the Albany, and is a director of thirty-three railroads. He purposes to stand for Parliament at the next general

election, on decidedly conservative principles, which have always been
the politics of his family.

Report says, that, even in his humble capacity, Miss EMILY FLIMSY
had remarked his high demeanour.   Well, 'none but the brave,' say we,
'deserve the fair.'—*Morning Paper*.

This announcement will explain the following lines, which
have been put into our box, with a West End post mark.
If, as we believe, they are written by the young woman from
whom the Millionaire borrowed the sum on which he raised
his fortune, what heart would not melt with sympathy at
her tale, and pity the sorrows which she expresses in such
artless language ?

If it be not too late : if wealth have not rendered its
possessor callous : if poor MARYANNE *be still alive*, we
trust Mr PLUSH will do her justice.

JEAMES OF BUCKLEY SQUARE.

A HELIGY.

Come, all ye gents vot cleans the plate,
　　Come, all ye ladies maids so fair—
Vile I a story vil relate
　　Of cruel JEAMES of Buckley Square.
A tighter lad, it is confest,
　　Never valked vith powder in his air,
Or vore a nosegay in his breast,
　　Than andsum JEAMES of Buckley Square.

O Evns ! it vas the best of sights,
　　Behind his Master's coach and pair,
To see our JEAMES in red plush tights,
　　A driving hoff from Buckley Square.
He vel became his hagwiletts,
　　He cocked his at with *such* an hair ;
His calves and viskers *vas* siech pets,
　　That hall loved *Jeames* of Buckley Square.

He pleased the hup stairs folks as vell,
　　And o ! I vithered vith despair,
Misses *vould* ring the parler bell,
　　And call up JEAMES in Buckley Square.

Both beer and sperrits he abhord,
  (Sperrits and beer I can't a bear,)
You would have thought he vas a lord,
  Down in our All in Buckley Square.

Last year he visper'd, " Mary Hann,
  Ven I've an 'under'd pound to spare,
To take a public is my plan,
  And leave this hojous Buckley Square."
O how my gentle heart did bound,
  To think that I his name should bear.
" Dear JEAMES," says I, " I've twenty pound,"
  And gev him them in Buckley Square.

Our master vas a City Gent,
  His name's in railroads everywhere ;
And lord, vot lots of letters vent
  Betwigst his brokers, and Buckley Square.
My JEAMES it was the letters took,
  And read 'em all, (I think it's fair),
And took a leaf from Master's book,
  As *hothers* do in Buckley Square.

Encouraged with my twenty pound,
  Of which poor *I* was unaware,
He wrote the Companies all round,
  And signed hisself from Buckley Square.
And how JOHN PORTER used to grin,
  As day by day, share after share,
Came railway letters pouring in,
  J. PLUSH, Esquire, in Buckley Square.

Our servants' All was in a rage—
  Scrip, stock, curves, gradients, bull and bear,
With butler, coachman, groom and page,
  Vas all the talk in Buckley Square.
But O ! imagine vat I felt
  Last Vensdy veek as ever were ;
I gits a letter, which I spelt
  " Miss M. A. Hoggins, Buckley Square."

He sent me back my money true—
  He sent me back my lock of air,
And said, " My dear, I bid ajew
  To Mary Hann and Buckley Square.

> Think not to marry, foolish HANN,
>   With people who your betters are ;
> JAMES PLUSH is now a gentleman,
>   And you—a cook in Buckley Square.
>
> I've thirty thousand guineas won,
>   In six short months, by genus rare ;
> You little thought what JEAMES was on,
>   Poor MARY HANN, in Buckley Square.
> I've thirty thousand guineas net,
>   Powder and plush I scorn to vear ;
> And so, Miss MARY HANN, forget
>   For hever JEAMES, of Buckley Square."

But, joking apart, there is no exaggeration in Jeames. Look at a "Return to the Order of the Honourable the House of Commons, dated 8th April 1845, for an Alphabetical list of the Names, Description, and Place of Abode of all Persons subscribing to the Amount of £2000 and upwards to any Railway Subscription Contract deposited in the Private Bill Office during the present Session of Parliament," and amongst the names will be found many of the leading nobility, large manufacturing firms, names well known in commerce and literature, mingled together in a most heterogeneous manner. The same columns shew a combination of peers and printers, vicars and vice-admirals, spinsters and half-pay officers, M.P.'s and special pleaders, professors and cotton spinners, gentlemen's cooks and Q.C.'s, attorney's clerks and college scouts, waiters at Lloyd's, relieving officers and excisemen, barristers and butchers, Catholic priests and coachmen, editors and engineers, dairymen and dyers, braziers, bankers, beer sellers and butlers, domestic servants, footmen and mail guards, and almost every calling under the sun.

These, it must be remembered, were subscribers for £2000 and upwards ; those who subscribed for less, were supposed to be holders of £21,386,703, 6s. 4d. in Stock.

The first blow given to this frightful gambling was on Thursday, 16th Oct. 1845, when the Bank of England raised its Discount, which had such a disastrous effect, that by

Saturday, people began to be alarmed, and, as Mr Francis describes the situation, " Money was scarce, the price of stock and scrip lowered ; the confidence of the people was broken, and a vision of a dark future on every face. Advertisements were suddenly withdrawn from the papers ; names of note were seen no more as provisional committee men ; distrust followed the merchant to the mart, and the jobber to the Exchange. The new schemes ceased to be regarded ; applications ceased to be forwarded ; premiums were either lowered, or ceased to exist. Bankers looked anxiously to the accounts of their customers; bill brokers scrutinised their securities ; and every man was suspicious of his neighbour.

" But the distrust was not confined to projected lines. Established Railways felt the shock, and were reduced in value. Consols fell one and a half per cent.; Exchequer Bills declined in price, and other markets sympathised. The people had awoke from their dream, and trembled. It was a national alarm.

" Words are weak to express the fears and feelings which prevailed. There was no village too remote to escape the shock, and there was, probably, no house in town, some occupant of which did not shrink from the morrow. The Statesman started to find his new Bank Charter so sadly, and so suddenly tried : the peer, who had so thoughtlessly invested, saw ruin opening to his view. Men hurried with bated breath to their brokers ; the allottee was uneasy and suspicious : the provisional committee man grew pale at his fearful responsibility : directors ceased to boast their blushing honours, and promoters saw their expected profits evaporate. Shares, which, the previous week, were a fortune, were, the next, a fatality to their owners. The reputed shareholders were not found when they were wanted : provisional committee men were not more easy of access.

" One Railway advertised the names and addresses of thirty —none of whom were to be heard of at the residences ascribed to them.   Letters were returned to the Post Office, day after day.   Nor is this to be wondered at, when it is said that, on one projected line, only £60 was received for deposits which should have yielded £700,000.

" It was proved in the Committee of the House of Commons, that one subscription list was formed of ' lame ducks of the Alley '; and that, in another, several of the Directors, including the Chairman, had, also, altered their several subscriptions to the amount of £100,000, the very evening on which the list was deposited, and that five shillings a man was given to any one who would sign for a certain number of shares.

" Nothing more decidedly marked the crisis which had arrived, than the fact that every one hastened to disown railways.   Gentlemen who had been buried in prospectuses, whose names and descriptions had been published under every variation that could fascinate the public, who had figured as committee men, and received the precious guineas for their attendance, were eager to assure the world that they were ignorant of this great transgression.   Men, who, a month before, had boasted of the large sums they had made by scrip, sent advertisements to papers denying their responsibility, or appealed to the Lord Mayor to protect their characters.   Members of Parliament who had remained quiet under the infliction, while it was somewhat respectable, fell back upon their privileges when they saw their purses in danger.   There is no doubt that an unauthorised use of names was one feature of fraudulent Companies, and that, amid a list of common names, it was thought a distinguished one might pass unnoticed.   The complaints, therefore, of those who were thus unceremoniously treated were just ; but the great mass of denials emanated from persons who, knowingly, encountered the risk, and meanly shrunk from the danger.

" It is the conviction of those who are best informed that no other panic was ever so fatal to the middle class.   It reached every hearth, it saddened every heart in the metropolis. Entire families were ruined. There was scarcely an important town in England, but what beheld some wretched suicide. Daughters, delicately nurtured, went out to seek their bread ; sons were recalled from academies ; households were separated : homes were desecrated by the emissaries of the law. There was a disruption of every social tie. The debtor's jails were peopled with promoters ; Whitecross Street was filled with speculators ; and the Queen's bench was full to overflowing. Men who had lived comfortably and independently, found themselves suddenly responsible for sums they had no means of paying. In some cases they yielded their all, and began the world anew ; in others, they left the country for the continent, laughed at their creditors, and defied pursuit. One gentleman was served with four hundred writs : a peer, similarly pressed, when offered to be relieved from all liabilities for £15,000, betook himself to his yacht, and forgot, in the beauties of the Mediterranean, the difficulties which had surrounded him. Another gentleman, who, having nothing to lose, surrendered himself to his creditors, was a director of more than twenty lines. A third was Provisional Committee man to fifteen. A fourth, who commenced life as a printer, who became an insolvent in 1832, and a bankrupt in 1837, who had negotiated partnerships, who had arranged embarrassed affairs, who had collected debts, and turned his attention to anything, did not disdain, also, to be a railway promoter, a railway director, or to spell his name in a dozen different ways."

But a notice of the Railway Mania would be very incomplete without mention of George Hudson, the Railway King. He was born at Howsham, a village near York, in March 1800, was apprenticed to a draper in York, and subsequently became principal in the business ; thus, early in life, becoming well off, besides having £30,000 left him by a distant relative. In 1837 he was Lord Mayor of York, and the same year was made Chairman of the York and North Midland Railway, which was opened in 1839. In

1841 he was elected Chairman of the Great North of England Company, and, afterwards held the same position in the Midland Railway Company. He speculated largely in Railways; and in the Parliamentary return, already alluded to (p. 270) his subscriptions appear as £319,835.

He came to London, and inhabited the house at Albert Gate, Knightsbridge (now the French Embassy) where he entertained the Prince Consort, and the aristocracy generally. He was elected M.P. for Sunderland in Aug. 1845, and again served as Lord Mayor of York in 1846. The Railway smash came, and year by year things went worse with him, until, early in the year 1849 he had to resign his chairmanship of the Eastern Counties (now Great Eastern), Midland, York, Newcastle and Berwick, and the York and North Midland Railway Companies. He went abroad, where he lived for some time, and tried, unavailingly, to retrieve his fortune. In July 1865 he was committed to York Castle for Contempt of the Court of Exchequer, in not paying a large debt, and was there incarcerated till the following October.

He fell so low, that in 1868 some friends took pity on him and raised a subscription for him, thus obtaining £4800, with which an annuity was purchased. He died in London, 14th Dec. 1871.

In conclusion, as a place for gambling, the Stock Exchange is of far greater extent than the Turf. The time bargains and options, without which the business of the Exchange would be very little, are gambling pure and simple, whilst the numerous *bucket shops*, with their advertisements and circulars, disseminate the unwholesome vice of gambling throughout the length and breadth of the land, enabling people to speculate without anyone being the wiser. It is needless to say, that, as on the Turf, they are the losers.

CHAPTER XXII

BUT, paradoxical as it may appear, there is a class of gambling which is not only considered harmless, but beneficial, and even necessary—I mean Insurance. Theoretically, it is gambling proper. You bet 2s. 6d. to £100 with your Fire Insurance; you equally bet on a Marine Insurance for the safe arrival of your ships or merchandise; and it is also gambling when you insure your life. Yet a man would be considered culpable, or at the very least, negligent and indiscreet did he not insure.

Of the different kinds of Insurance or Assurance, as it is indifferently called, Marine Assurance is the oldest, so old, that no one knows when the custom began, as we see by the preamble of 43 Eliz., c. 12 (1601).

"AN ACTE CONCERNINGE MATTERS OF ASSURANCES, AMONGSTE MARCHANTES. WHEREAS it ever hathe bene the Policie of this Realme by all good meanes to comforte and encourage the Merchante, therebie to advance and increase the generall wealthe of the Realme, her Majesties Customes and the strengthe of Shippinge, which Consideration is now the more requisite, because Trade and Traffique is not, at this presente, soe open as at other tymes it hathe bene; and, *whereas it hathe bene tyme out of mynde* an usage amongste Merchantes, both of this Realme and of forraine Nacyons, when they make any greate adventure (speciallie into remote partes) to give some consideracion of Money to other persons (which commonlie are in noe small number

"

to have from them assurance made of their Goodes Merchandizes Ships and Things adventured, or some parte thereof, at such rates and in such sorte as the Parties assurers and the Parties assured can agree, whiche course of dealinge is commonly termed a Policie of Assurance; by meanes of whiche Policies of Assurance it comethe to passe, upon the losse or perishinge of any Shippe there followethe not the undoinge of any Man, but the losse lightethe rather easilie upon many, then heavilie upon fewe, and rather upon them that adventure not, then those that doe adventure, whereby all Merchantes, speciallie of the younger sorte, are allured to venture more willinglie and more freelie: And whereas heretofore suche Assurers have used to stand so justlie and preciselie upon their credites, as fewe or no Controversies have risen there upon, and if any have growen, the same have from tyme to tyme bene ended and ordered by certaine grave and discreete Merchantes appointed by the Lord Mayor of the Citie of London, as Men by reason of their experience fitteste to understande, and speedilie to decide those Causes; untill of late yeeres that divers persons have withdrawen themselves from that arbitrarie course, and have soughte to drawe the parties assured to seeke their moneys of everie severall Assurer, by Suites commenced in her Majesties Courtes, to their great charges and delayes: FOR REMEDIE *wher of be it enacted,*" &c.[1]

The Oldest Policy of Assurance I have been able to find is mentioned in the 6th Report of the Royal Commission on Historical MSS., where it is catalogued " 1604. A Charter partie, An Assurance of fish from Newfoundland."[2]

Mr F. Martin, who wrote an exhaustive book on the *History of Lloyd's and Marine Insurance*, says : " The earliest English policy of marine insurance, which we have been able to discover, bears date 1613, and though not a document issued actually by underwriters, but, to all appearances, a

---

[1] Commissioners were appointed to hear and determine such cases.

[2] In the collection of MSS. belonging to Lord Leconfield, at Petworth House, Sussex.

copy made for legal purposes, with some lawyer's notes attached, may be found historically interesting. The discovery was—with others subsequently to be referred to— the result of long and laborious researches among the, as yet, only partly known literary treasures of the Bodleian Library at Oxford. The original is among the Tanner manuscripts, numbered 74, fo. 32, and the manuscript is endorsed, 'Mr Morris Abbott's pollesye of Assurance dated the 15 of ffebruary 1613, 11 Jacobi.'"

A very old policy hangs, framed and glazed, on the wall of the Committee Room at Lloyds, dated 20th Jan. 1680, and it is for £1200—£200 on the ship and £1000 on the goods. The ship was the *Golden Fleece*, the voyage from Lisbon to Venice, and the premium was £4 per cent.!

Underwriting marine risks was in private hands, and although the underwriters had, some of them, offices of their own, most of the business seems to have been done at Coffee Houses, such as Hain's, Garraway's, or Good's; and there was also a central office at the Royal Exchange, as is shown by several early advertisements, one of which is the following, from the *City Mercury*, No. 255 (1680):

"Whereas Mr Daniel Parrot caused a Politie to be made Septemb. 28 last, on the *Charles of Plymouth*, from Newfoundland to Cadiz, which is subscribed by several Insurers, and the Politie lost, and a new Politie made: It is desired that all persons that have subscribed the Politie would come into the Insurance Office, and subscribe the new Politie, that it may be known who the Insurers are; and if any one has found the old Politie, they are desired to bring it to Mr Tho. Astley, at the Insurance Office on the Royal Exchange, and they shall be well rewarded."

The origin of the present Corporation of Lloyd's was in the Coffee House of Edward Lloyd, who, in 1688, lived in the very busy commercial thoroughfare of Tower Street, as appears from an advertisement in the *London Gazette* of 18/21 Feb. 1688, relating to a robbery. In 1691 or 1692 he moved to a more central situation, at the Corner of

Abchurch Lane and Lombard Street, where, in the summer of 1696, he started the famous *Lloyd's News*, of which the Bodleian Library has a complete set, with the exception of the first seven numbers.   It only reached seventy-six numbers, when it was discontinued for the reason given in No. 138 of the *Protestant Mercury*, Feb. 24/26, 1696 (1697). "Whereas, in *Lloyd's News* of the 23rd instant, it was inserted, That the House of Lords Received a Petition from the Quakers, that they may be freed from all Offices, which being groundless and a mistake, he was desired to rectifie it in his next : But return'd for Answer, it was added by the Printer, that he would Print no more at present."   And it remained in abeyance till 1726, when it was resuscitated under the title of *Lloyd's List*, a name which it now bears.

Lloyd's Coffee House served its purpose to the Underwriters for a time, but they found it inconvenient, and wanted a place of their own, so they took rooms in Pope's Head Alley, which they called New Lloyd's Coffee House, whilst they were looking out for suitable permanent premises.   Here, towards the end of 1771, seventy-nine Underwriters met, and each subscribed £100 towards building a " New Lloyd's."   After a considerable amount of house hunting, it was reported by the Committee, on Nov. 24, 1773, " that after many fruitless researches to obtain a Coffee House in Freeman's Court and other places, they had succeeded with the Mercer's Company for a very roomy and convenient place over the North West Side of the Royal Exchange, at the rent of £180 per annum " : and this selection being approved of, they moved into their new quarters on 5th March 1774.   There they have abode ever since, except for a brief period when the Exchange was re-building after its destruction by fire in 1838.

The underwriters did not always confine themselves to marine risks.   Malcolm, writing in 1808, says : " The practice of betting is tolerably prevalent at present, and by no means confined to any particular class of the community. In fact, I am afraid it might be traced very far back in the history of our Customs ; but it will be sufficient, for the information of the reader, that I present him with an article from the *London Chronicle* of 1768, which, I think, will remind him of some recent transactions in the City.

" ' The introduction and amazing progress of illicit gaming at Lloyd's Coffee House is, among others, a powerful and very melancholy proof of the degeneracy of the times. It is astonishing that this practice was begun, and has been, hitherto, carried on, by the matchless effrontery and impudence of one man. It is equally so, that he has met with so much encouragement from many of the principal underwriters, who are, in every other respect, useful members of society : and it is owing to the lenity of our laws, and want of spirit in the present administration, that this pernicious practice has not, hitherto, been suppressed. Though gaming in any degree (except what is warranted by law) is perverting the original and useful design of that Coffee House, it may, in some measure, be excuseable to speculate on the following subjects :

Mr Wilkes being elected Member for London, which was done from 5 to 50 guineas per cent.

Ditto for Middlesex, from 20 to 70 guineas per cent.

Alderman B——d's life for one year, now doing at 7 per cent.

On Sir J—— H—— being turned out in one year, now doing at 20 guineas per cent.

On John Wilkes's life for one year, now doing at 5 per cent. N.B.—Warranted to remain in prison during that period.

On a declaration of war with France or Spain, in one year, 8 guineas per cent.

And many other innocent things of that kind.

But, when policies come to be opened on two of the first Peers in Britain losing their heads, within a year, at 10s. 6d. per cent. ; and on the dissolution of the present Parliament, within one year, at 5 guineas per cent., which are now actually doing, and underwrote chiefly by Scotsmen, at the above Coffee House ; it is surely high time for administration to interfere ; and, by exerting the rigours of the laws against the authors and encouragers of such insurances (which must be done for some bad purpose), effectually put a stop to it.'"

In the secretary's room at Lloyd's hangs the following policy :—" In consideration of three guineas for one hundred pounds, and according to that rate for every greater or less sum received of William Dorrington ; we, who have hereunto subscribed our names, do for ourselves, and our respective heirs, executors, administrators, and assigns, and not one for the other or others of us ; or for the heirs, executors, administrators and assigns of the other or others of us, assume, engage and promise that we respectively, or our several and respective heirs, executors, administrators, and assigns, shall and will pay, or cause to be paid, unto the said William Dorrington the sum and sums of money which we have hereunto respectively subscribed without any abatement whatever.

"*In case* Napoleon Bonaparte shall cease to exist, or be taken prisoner on, or before, the 21st day of June 1813, commencing from this day.   London 21 May 1813."

Although originally intended for the Insurance of Marine risks only, other policies can be taken out at Lloyd's—such as Fire ; against Burglary—although this was also insured against during the South Sea Mania, under the title of " Insurance from housebreakers " ; against any lady having twins. *A propos* of this, there was an underwriter, some years ago, at Lloyd's, named Thornton—who was fond of writing speculative risks, especially overdue ships, and who died very wealthy.   He had a bet with a fellow underwriter —that he should pay him £1000 for every child the Queen bore ; but, if there should be twins, at any time, then Mr Thornton was to be paid £20,000.   Insuring that a race horse shall run in a particular race ; on interest under a will ; employer's liability to workmen ; accidents by tramcars ; solvency of commercial firms ; earthquakes ; and during the six months preceding the Queen's Jubilee of 20th

June 1897 a vast amount was underwritten, guaranteeing the Queen's life till that date—and also assuring that she should pass through certain streets. But these policies are not recognised by the Committee, and, should the underwriter fail, they do not rank for dividend out of the caution money held by the Corporation.

Besides Lloyd's Association, where each Member underwrites the amount he chooses, there are Marine Insurance Companies, which are of great utility for the large sums they underwrite. These are not all English, there are many foreign Marine Insurance Companies having Offices in London, as may be seen by the following list, which is very far from being complete :—Baden Marine, Bavarian Lloyd Marine, Boston Marine, Canton Marine, German Marine, Italia Marine of Genoa, Nippon Sea and Land, North China, Rhenish Westphalian Lloyds, Switzerland Insurance, Yangtze Insurance Association, &c., &c., &c. The first English Marine Insurance Companies were the Royal Exchange and the London, both established in 1720.

Insurance against Fire began the year following the Great Fire of London (1666), and the first Company for Assurance against Fire was the Phœnix, established about 1682, first at the Rainbow Coffee House, in Fleet Street, and, afterwards, near the Royal Exchange. Their system was to pay 30s. down, and insure £100 for seven years. The second was The Friendly Society, in Palsgrave Court, without Temple Bar, which was the first (in 1684) that insured by mutual contribution, where you could insure £100 for seven years by paying 6s. 8d. down and an annual subscription of 1s. 4d. And, thirdly, The Amicable Contributors, at Tom's Coffee House in St Martin's Lane (commenced about 1695), where a payment of 12s. would insure £100 for seven years, at the expiration of which time 10s. would be returned to the assured. This Society seems to have changed its name to the Hand in Hand Fire Office, who gave up their two establishments, at Tom's Coffee House, and the Crown Coffee House, behind the Exchange, to more suitable premises in Angel Court, Snow Hill, and notified the change in the *Gazette* of 1st Jan. 1714.

This Insurance Company (The Amicable) is generally considered to be the first institution for the Insurance of Lives, although Life Annuities had been in practice for a long time, but a writer in *Chambers' Encyclopædia* (Vol. vi., p. 175, ed. 1895) says that it did not begin life business until 1836.   The same writer continues : " The earliest known Life Assurance Company was established in 1699, and called the ' Society of Assurance for Widows and Orphans.'   This was what, now, would be called an *Assessment* Company.   It did not guarantee a definite sum assured, in consideration of a fixed periodical premium ; but, by its constitution it was to consist, when full, of 2000 members, who were to contribute 5s. each towards every death that occurred amongst the members.

" The earliest life assurance policy, of which particulars have been preserved, was made on 15th June 1583, at the ' Office of Insurance within the Royal Exchange,' in London. Full details of this Policy have been preserved, because it gave rise to the first authentic disputed claim.   The policy was for £383, 6s. 8d., to be paid to Richard Martin, in the event of William Gybbons dying within twelve months, and the policy was underwritten by thirteen different persons who guaranteed sums of from £25 to £50 each.   The premium was at the rate of 8 per cent.   William Gybbons died on the 28th May 1584, and the underwriters refused to pay because he had survived twelve months of twenty-eight days each.   The Commissioners appointed to determine such cases, held that the twelve months mentioned in the policy meant one full year, and they ordered the underwriters to pay.   These appealed to the Court of Admiralty, which had jurisdiction in such cases, and where, in 1587, two judges upheld the decision of the Commissioners, so that, eventually, the underwriters had to pay."

Mr Francis[1] tells us of the first known fraud in Life

[1] " Annals, Anecdotes, and Legends of Life Assurance." John Francis. 1853 : Lon.

Assurance. "About 1730, two persons resided in the then obscure suburbs of St Giles's, one of whom was a woman of about twenty, the other, a man, whose age would have allowed him to be the woman's father, and who was, generally understood to bear that relation. Their position hovered on the debatable ground between poverty and competence, or might even be characterised by the modern term of shabby genteel. They interfered with no one, and they encouraged no one to interfere with them. No specific personal description is recorded of them, beyond the fact that the man was tall and middle aged, bearing a semi-military aspect, and that the woman, though young and attractive in person, was, apparently, haughty and frigid in her manner. On a sudden, at night time, the latter was taken very ill. The man sought the wife of his nearest neighbour for assistance, informing her that his daughter had been seized with sudden and great pain at the heart. They returned together, and found her in the utmost apparent agony, shrinking from the approach of all, and dreading the slightest touch. The leech was sent for ; but, before he could arrive, she seemed insensible, and he only entered the room in time to see her die. The father appeared in great distress, the doctor felt her pulse, placed his hand on her heart, shook his head, as he intimated all was over, and went his way. The searchers came, for those birds of ill-omen were, then, the ordinary haunters of the death-bed, and the coffin, with its contents, was committed to the ground. Almost immediately after this, the bereaved father claimed from the underwriters some money which was insured on his daughter's life, left the locality, and the story was forgotten.

" Not very long after, the neighbourhood of Queen Square, then a fashionable place, shook its head at the somewhat unequivocal connection that existed between one of the inmates of a house in that locality, and a lady who resided with him. The gentleman wore moustaches, and though not young, affected what was then known as the Macaroni style. The Captain, for that was the almost indefinite title he assumed, was a visitor to Ranelagh, was an *habitué* of the Coffee Houses ; and, being an apparently wealthy person, riding good horses and keeping an attractive mistress, he attained a certain position among the *mauvais sujéts* of the day. Like many others at that period, he was, or seemed to be, a dabbler in the funds ; was frequently seen at Lloyd's and in the Alley ; lounged occasionally at Garraway's ; but appeared, more particularly, to affect the company of those who dealt in life assurances.

" His house soon became a resort for the young and thoughtless, being one of those pleasant places where the past and the future were alike lost in the present : where cards were introduced with the wine, and where, if the young bloods of the day lost their money, they were repaid by a glance of more than ordinary warmth from the goddess of the place ; and to which, if they won, they returned with renewed zest. One thing was noticed, they never won from the master of the house, and there is no doubt, a large portion of the current expenses were met by the money gambled away ; but, whether it were fairly, or unfairly gained, is, scarcely a doubtful question.

" A stop was soon put to these amusements. The place was too remote from the former locality, the appearance of both characters was too much changed to be identified ; or, in these two might have been traced the strangers of that obscure suburb, where, as daughter, the woman was supposed to die ; and, as father, the man had wept and raved over her remains. And a similar scene was, once more, to be acted. The lady was taken as suddenly ill as before ; the same spasms at the heart seemed to convulse her frame ; and, again, the man hung over her in apparent agony. Physicians were sent for in haste ; only one arrived in time to see her, once more, imitate the appearance of death ; whilst the others, satisfied that life had fled, took their fees, ' shook solemnly their powdered wigs,' and departed. This mystery, for it is evident there was some conspiracy, or collusion, is partially solved when it is said that many thousands were claimed and received, by the gallant captain from various underwriters, merchants and companies with whom he had assured the life of the lady.

" But the hero of this tradition was a consummate actor ; and, though his career is unknown for a long period after this, yet it is highly probable that he carried out his nefarious projects in schemes which are difficult to trace. There is little doubt, however, that the *soi-disant* captain of Queen Square was one and the same person who, as a merchant, a few years later, appeared daily on the commercial walks of Liverpool ; where, deep in the mysteries of corn and cotton, a constant attendant at church, a subscriber to local charities, and a giver of good dinners, he soon became much respected by those who dealt with him in business, or visited him in social life. The hospitalities of his house were gracefully dispensed by a lady who passed as his niece ; and, for a time, nothing seemed to disturb the tenour of his way. At length it became whispered in the world of commerce, that his speculations were not so successful as usual ; and a long series of misfortunes, as asserted by him, gave a sanction to the whisper. It soon became advisable for him to borrow money, and this he could only do on the security of property belonging to his niece. To do so, it was necessary to insure their lives for about £2000. This was easy enough, as Liverpool, no less than London, was ready to assure anything which promised profit, and, as the affair was regular, no one hesitated. A certain amount of secrecy was necessary for the sake of his credit ; and, availing himself of this, he assured on the life of the niece £2000, with, at least, ten different merchants and underwriters in London and elsewhere. The game was once more in his own hands, and the same play was once more acted. The lady was taken ill, the doctor was called in, and found her suffering from convulsions. He administered a specific, and retired. In the night he was again hastily summoned, but arrived too late. The patient was declared to be beyond his skill ; and the next morning it became known to all Liverpool that she had died suddenly. A decorous grief was evinced by the chief mourner. There was no haste made in forwarding the funeral ; the lady lay almost in state, so numerous were the friends who called to see the last of her they had visited ; the searchers did their hideous office gently, for they were, perhaps, largely bribed : the physician certified that she had died of a complaint he could scarcely name, and the grave received the Coffin. The merchant retained his position in Liverpool, and bore himself with a decent dignity ; made no immediate application for the money ; scarcely even alluded to the assurances which were due, and, when they were named, exhibited an appearance of almost indifference. He had, however, selected his victims with skill. They were safe men, and, from them, he duly received the money which was assured on the life of his niece.

"From this period he seemed to decline in health, expressed a loathing for the place where he had once been so happy ; change of air was prescribed, and he left the men whom he had deceived, chuckling at the success of his infamous scheme."

Nowadays, everything insurable can be insured ; you can be compensated for accidents ; if your plate glass windows are broken, if hail spoils your crops, or if your cattle die ; the fidelity of your servants can be guaranteed : in fact, this field of permissible gambling is fully covered—whilst betting on horse racing rears its head unchecked, stock jobbers thrive, bucket shops multiply, and so do their victims.

THE TATLER.

Edited with Introduction and Notes by George A. Aitken,
Author of "The Life of Richard Steele," etc. Four
volumes, small demy 8vo, with engraved frontispieces,
bound in buckram, dull gold top, 7s. 6d. per vol., not
sold separately.

(*See Special Prospectus.*)

EXTRACT FROM THE EDITOR'S PREFACE.

"The original numbers of *The Tatler* were re-issued in two forms in
1710-11; one edition, in octavo, being published by subscription, while
the other, in duodecimo, was for the general public. The present
edition has been printed from a copy of the latter issue, which, as
recorded on the title-page, was 'revised and corrected by the Author';
but I have had by my side, for constant reference, a complete set
of the folio sheets, containing the 'Lucubrations of Isaac Bickerstaff'
in the form in which they were first presented to the world. Scrupulous
accuracy in the text has been aimed at, but the eccentricities of spelling
—which were the printer's, not the author's—have not been preserved,
and the punctuation has occasionally been corrected.

"The first and the most valuable of the annotated editions of *The
Tatler* was published by John Nichols and others in 1786, with notes
by Bishop Percy, Dr John Calder, and Dr Pearce; and though these
notes are often irrelevant and out of date, they contain an immense
amount of information, and have been freely made use of by subsequent
editors. I have endeavoured to preserve what is of value in the older
editions, and to supplement it, as concisely as possible, by such further
information as appeared desirable. The eighteenth century diaries and
letters published of late years have in many cases enabled me to
throw light on passages which have hitherto been obscure, and sometimes useful illustrations have been found in the contemporary newspapers and periodicals."

HUTCHINSON, T.

LYRICAL BALLADS BY WILLIAM WORDSWORTH AND S. T. COLERIDGE, 1798.

Edited with certain poems of 1798 and an Introduction and Notes by Thomas Hutchinson, of Trinity College, Dublin, Editor of the Clarendon Press "Wordsworth," etc.   Fcap. 8vo, art vellum, gilt top.   3s. 6d. net.

This edition reproduces the text, spelling, punctuation, etc., of 1798, and gives in an Appendix Wordsworth's *Peter Bell* (original text, now reprinted for the first time), and Coleridge's *Lewti, The Three Graves,* and *The Wanderings of Cain.* It also contains reproductions in photogravure of the portraits of Wordsworth (by Hancock, 1798) and of Coleridge (by Peter Vandyke, 1795), now in the National Portrait Gallery.

The publishers have in preparation further carefully annotated editions of books in English literature, to be produced in the same style as their edition of the "Lyrical Ballads"—not too small for the shelf, and not too large to be carried about—further announcements concerning which will be made in due course. It is not intended to include in this series, as a rule, the oft-reprinted "classics," of which there are already sufficiently desirable issues.

Athenæum (4 col. review).—"Mr Hutchinson's centenary edition of the Lyrical Ballads is not a mere reprint, for it is enriched with a preface and notes which make it a new book. The preface contains much that is suggestive in explaining the history and elucidating the meaning of this famous little volume. Mr Hutchinson's notes are especially deserving of praise."

St James's Gazette.—"'Lyrical Ballads' was published September 1, 1798. By a happy thought this centenary is in anticipation very fitly celebrated—without fuss or futilities—by the publication of an admirable reprint of 'Lyrical Ballads,' with an adequate 'apparatus criticus' by Mr T. Hutchinson, the well-known Wordsworthian scholar, whose name makes recommendation superfluous. This is a book that no library should be without—not the 'gentleman's library' of Charles Lamb's sarcasm, but any library where literature is respected."

Notes and Queries.—"The book is indeed a precious boon. Mr Hutchinson is in his line one of the foremost of scholars, and his introduction is a commendable piece of work. No less excellent are his notes, which are both readable and helpful. One cannot do otherwise than rejoice in the possession of the original text, now faithfully reproduced. A volume which is sure of a place in the library of every lover of poetry."

Globe.—"It is delightful to have them in the charming form given to them in the present volume, for which Mr Hutchinson has written not only a very informing introduction, but also some very luminous and useful notes. The book is one which every lover and student of poetry must needs add to his collection."

STEPHEN, H. L.

STATE TRIALS: POLITICAL AND SOCIAL.

Selected and Edited by H. L. Stephen. 2 vols.
Uniform with "Lyrical Ballads."

ENGLISH PUBLIC SCHOOLS.

A new series of books upon the English Public Schools. No series of such School Histories exists, and the publishers believe that many boys, while at school and when leaving it, may like to possess an authentic account of their school issued at a moderate price. The series will, it is hoped, appeal also to old scholars, and to all interested in the history of English education.

(See Special Prospectus.)

CUST, LIONEL.

A HISTORY OF ETON COLLEGE, by Lionel
Cust, Director of the National Portrait Gallery.

LEACH, ARTHUR F.

A HISTORY OF WINCHESTER COLLEGE,
by Arthur F. Leach, formerly Fellow of All Souls', Oxford, Assistant Charity Commissioner.

ROUSE, W. H. D.

A HISTORY OF RUGBY SCHOOL, by W. H. D.
Rouse, of Rugby, and sometime Fellow of Christ's College, Cambridge. Illustrated from photographs, contemporary prints, etc. Pott 4to. 5s. net.

(To be followed by others.)

MODERN PLAYS.

Edited by R. Brimley Johnson and N. Erichsen.

It is the aim of this series to represent, as widely as possible, the activity of the modern drama—not confined to stage performance—in England and throughout the continent of Europe. It so happens that, though translations seem to be more in demand every day, the greater number of the Continental dramatists are at present little known in this country. Among them will be found predecessors and followers of Ibsen or Maeterlinck; as well as others who reflect more independently the genius of their own country.

Love's Comedy, which marks a transition from the early romantic to the later social plays, is the only important work of Ibsen's not yet translated into English. The name of Strindberg, whose position in Sweden may be compared to that of Ibsen in Norway, will be almost new to the English public. Villiers' *La Révolte* is a striking forecast of *The Doll's House*. Verhaeren is already known here as one of the foremost of Belgian writers, who, like Maeterlinck, uses the French tongue; and Brieux is among the most attractive of the younger native French dramatists. Ostrovsky's *The Storm*, painting "The Dark World," is generally recognised as *the* characteristic Russian drama. *The Convert*, by Stepniak, will be specially interesting as its author's only dramatic attempt.

The work of translation has been entrusted to English writers specially conversant with the literatures represented, who, in many cases, are already associated in the public mind with the authors they are here interpreting. Every play will be translated *in extenso*, and, if in verse, as nearly as possible in the original metres. The volumes will contain brief introductions, bibliographical and explanatory rather than critical, and such annotations as may be necessary.

The volumes will be printed in pott quarto, and they will cost, as a rule, 2s. 6d. net. or 3s. 6d. net. each.

EARLY VOLUMES.

HENRIK IBSEN

"Love's Comedy" (*Kjærlighedens Komedie*).

MAURICE MAETERLINCK

"Intérieur."—WILLIAM ARCHER.
"La Mort de Tintagiles."
"Alladine et Palomides." }—ALFRED SUTRO.

VILLIERS DE L'ISLE ADAM

"La Révolte."
"L'Evasion." }—THERESA BARCLAY.

SERGIUS STEPNIAK

"The Convert."—CONSTANCE GARNETT.

EMILE VERHAEREN

"Les Aubes."—ARTHUR SYMONS.

AUGUST STRINDBERG

"The Father" (*Fadren*).—N. ERICHSEN.

OSTROVSKY

"The Storm."—CONSTANCE GARNETT.

BRIEUX

"Les Bienfaiteurs."—LUCAS MALET.

HENRYK SIENKIEWICZ

"On a Single Card."—E. L. VOYNICH.

Arrangements are also in progress with representative dramatists of Germany, Spain, Italy, and other countries. Further translations have been promised by Dr GARNETT, Messrs WALTER LEAF, JUSTIN HUNTLY MACCARTHY, G. A. GREENE, &c.

KNAPP, ARTHUR MAY.

FEUDAL AND MODERN JAPAN, by Arthur May Knapp. 2 vols., with 24 photogravure illustrations of Japanese life, landscape and architecture. Small fcap. 8vo, ¼-bound, white cloth, blue sides, gilt top. 8s. net.

The work of one who has frequently visited, and for a long time resided in Japan, thus enjoying peculiar advantages for observation and comment.

The scope of the book includes a study of the history, religion, language, art, life, and habits of the Japanese.

Though written in a thoroughly appreciative spirit, it avoids the indiscriminating praise which has characterised so many works on Japan; and while covering ground which has become somewhat familiar, it presents many fresh points of view, and furnishes much information heretofore inaccessible to the ordinary reader.

ROSSETTI, DANTE GABRIEL.

THE BLESSED DAMOZEL, by Dante Gabriel Rossetti. With an Introduction by Wm. Michael Rossetti, a reproduction in Photogravure of D. G. Rossetti's crayon study for the head of the Blessed Damozel, and decorative designs and cover by W. B. Macdougall. Fcap. 4to, ¼-bound, art vellum, gilt top. 5s. net. (*See Special Prospectus.*)

The poem given here is as it originally appeared in *The Germ*, and consequently the version is one hitherto practically inaccessible. Mr W. M. Rossetti's Introduction deals fully with the history of its composition and the changes through which it subsequently went.

Illustrated London News.—"A fine bit of decorative art and an excellent sample of modern format. The frontispiece is very beautiful. Mr Macdougall's designs are rich."

The Sketch.—"It is really beautifully illustrated. The book is a veritable art treasure."

Speaker.—"This artistic and singularly interesting volume."

Birmingham Gazette.—"Every page contains a broad framework of beautiful design, in which the artist manifests his power in glorious sweeping lines and delicate tracery. A treasure to be appreciated. The noble poem is nobly decked out in every respect."

Manchester Courier.—"The decorative designs are at once original, harmonious and beautiful. A work which will be welcomed alike for its high literary value, and for the high artistic standard to which it attains."

HOUSMAN, CLEMENCE.

THE UNKNOWN SEA. A Romance by Clemence Housman, Author of "The Were Wolf." Crown 8vo, art vellum, gold top. 6s.

Literature.—"On the conception of Christian the author may be congratulated. He is ideal without sentimentality, and his sacrifice and death have the poignancy of reality, symbol though he is of the world's greatest idea."

Guardian.—"Decidedly powerful and effective. Its author has certainly a spell by which, like the ancient mariner, he can force people to listen to and accept his tale."

Pall Mall Gazette.—"The story is a powerful one, stirring the imagination with vague suggestions of mystery, and compelling interest throughout. For those who can appreciate fine writing, moreover, the style itself will prove an added attraction, and will not only sustain the reputation which Miss Housman has already made, but will also enhance the lustre of the talented family of which she is a member."

St James's Gazette.—"The qualities that commend this book are its fitting impression of the supernatural, its studied and generally successful use of words, and its appreciation of the beauty of visible things. It achieves an absolute effect of beauty. an effect of a kind extremely rare in English that is not verse. The book has beauty and sense—not, thank Heaven, common sense !—in it, and is quite remote from the common trash of the book market."

Nottingham Daily Guardian.—"'The Unknown Sea' is not a popular novel ; there is too much really fine work in it for that, but hardly a page fails to indicate the author's delicate methods and robust individuality."

SINJOHN, JOHN.

JOCELYN. A Monte Carlo Story by John Sinjohn, Author of "From the Four Winds." Crown 8vo, art canvas. 6s.

Daily Mail.—"The love, as love, is shown with such intensity that it sets the reader's heart athrob, and the Riviera setting is aglow with colour and life."

Outlook.—"He has set it against a charmingly painted background of warm Southern atmosphere and Mediterranean scenery, and he has drawn, in the persons of the delightfully commonplace Mrs Travis and Nielson—the polished cosmopolitan and professional gambler, with an unsuspected strain of tenderness beneath his impassive exterior—two of the best comedy characters that we have encountered in recent fiction."

Manchester Courier.—"A powerfully written story. The analysis of character is good, and the depiction of life in the Riviera is excellent."

BURROW, C. K.

THE FIRE OF LIFE. A Novel by C. K. Burrow, Author of "Asteck's Madonna," "The Way of the Wind," etc. Crown 8vo, cloth. 6s.

St James's Gazette.—"A clever story. The smoothly-written little tale with its rather ambitious title is a real pleasure to read, because it has a wholesome, manly tone about it, and the characters do not appear to be bookmade but of real flesh and blood."

Saturday Review.—"A good, careful, full-blooded novel of a kind that is not common nowadays."

Outlook.—"It has a point of view, a delicate sensitiveness, artistic restraint, subtlety of perception, and a true literary style. Mr Burrow proves himself an artist with many sides to his perception."

Literary World.—"Had we passed it by unread ours would have been the loss. A charming story based on somewhat conventional lines, but told with such verve and freshness as render it really welcome. Mr Burrow has admirably succeeded in writing a really interesting story, and, which is more uncommon, he has well individualised the different persons of his drama. 'The Fire of Life' should figure in the list of novels to be read of all those who like a good story, and like that good story well told."

Manchester Courier.—"The whole book is full of 'fire,' full of 'life,' and full of interest."

Nottingham Express.—"The author's style is clear and crisp, with a purity of diction it would be difficult to surpass."

PHILIPS, F. C.

MEN, WOMEN AND THINGS, by F. C. Philips. Author of "As in a Looking-Glass," etc. Crown 8vo, buckram cloth. 3s. 6d.

Daily Mail.—"There is hardly one of them which is not enjoyable. Mr Philips's manner is suggestive of the manner of Gyp. He is a capital chronicler of the surface things of life."

Manchester Courier.—"The author has deservedly secured favour as a writer of smart stories. In the present volume of short sketches we have the usual vivid delineation of character, clever dialogue, and at times good use of incident. The volume is decidedly entertaining."

Country Life.—"Everything that is written by the author of 'As in a Looking-Glass' is clever. There is ingenuity as well as pathos in these stories."